BENEATH THE SURFACE TENSION

BY

DIETRICH BIEMILLER

THE TOTALLY NOT
FAMOUS AUTHOR!

Printed in the United States of America

First Printing, 2016

ISBN 0-9975915-0-1

Biemiller LLC
PO Box 425
Lake Stevens, WA 98258

www.biemiller.net

Thanks to the late Frank Pajares, who planted the seed.

Thanks to the beta readers: Wendy Berry, Professor Tim Linnemann, Pastor Jami Fecher, and Woody Pidcock, who encouraged the seedling to grow.

Thanks to Theodora O'Brien, developmental copyeditor, and Jeff Karon, proofreader, who pruned the fruit.

–Prologue–

A small, unmarked jet aircraft labored through heavy rain, close enough to the sea for the pilot to worry about ground effect. The tide surged though volcanic rock outcroppings, buffeting the plane in spite of it hugging the east side of the cliff.

Inside, the single passenger swayed along the aisle, clutching the seat backs until he reached the cockpit. He was dressed in jeans and a gray shell, the hood thrown back to expose a bald head with a short goatee. He opened the door to the cockpit, bracing against the bulkhead for a particularly sharp roll.

"How long we got?" he called over the noise of the wind and engines.

The black pilot held up a finger, holding headphones against his graying temples. The man in gray waited for the message to finish. He entered the cockpit and closed the door behind him, reducing the noise considerably.

"The Mods say they struck again," the pilot said presently, with a grim look over his shoulder.

"Where?"

"Some place called Bodie, near the California-Nevada border. You want to change course?"

The gray man sat in the copilot seat, tapped the keys of a computer in the dash. The search engine, fed with the term "Bodie," immediately disgorged links to various news reports. "Damn," he muttered. The summaries were full of dire terms: victim, blood, knives, face paint. . . .

Farther down the screen, one of the hits with the same terms caught his eye. It was not from a news agency, and it was dated five years before the event. The gray man bypassed the news reports and clicked on it instead. His eyes narrowed. "What the *hell*?" he whispered.

"So we changing course for Cali?" the pilot asked.

"No. Seattle."

–|–

Human beings as a rule either remember their dreams, or they don't.

Ron Golden was one who didn't. Someone once told him that it was because they were probably too bizarre or horrible to remember, but that did not strike him as right. When he remembered them at all, they were bland and quickly forgotten anyway. Ron often realized he was dreaming, willed himself to remember, but still failed to do so.

But this day in early May, when the weather in Seattle was turning from months of overcast and drizzle to days of crisp sun, Ron woke with a dream he remembered, not because it was momentous or dreadful, but because he thought it was so stupid.

He dreamed of a short, squat man with long, gray hair and a wizard's beard. He wore square spectacles. He had a loop of plastic and a soapy-liquid-filled dish in his hand. Ron recognized it as one of those soap bubble toys. He dipped the loop into the liquid and blew through it with exaggerated skill. What emerged was a bubble, but not spherical. It was shaped in an intricate string pattern that Ron had not seen since grade school.

"Jacob's Ladder," the man announced portentously, then dipped the loop again.

With intense concentration, he huffed out another complex bubble in a string pattern. "Cat's cradle."

Another dip, and more furious puffing and blowing. A third string-pattern-shaped bubble emerged and floated by. "Witches' broom."

He dipped the plastic loop again, this time with a wink. Red-faced, the man blew hard, his expression a bug-eyed mask of concentration . . . and an actual coffee cup, filled with coffee, emerged. The old man caught it out of the air and sipped, pinky extended. "Coffee cup."

Ron chuckled in his sleep, then realized he could not chuckle in his sleep. He must still be dreaming. He then realized, as usual, that if he realized he was dreaming, he must be awake. There was more to the dream, though, he thought, trying to remember while coming more and more conscious. He knew he was forgetting the dream as he woke.

Wake up, Ron, the man in the dream urged.

His head was on a pillow. There was a warm, tickling sensation in his ear, and he realized it was Tracey, breathing. Tracey was still there?

It all came flooding back, with waking. Pop was dead. He still had to go through his things, clean up the room his dad had occupied for the last six months while withering away. Him losing his job, at the worst possible time, while the bills were piling up. Were they cutting off the electricity this week? Or should he pay the overdue rent, instead? Why didn't Pop leave money in his estate instead of papers with crazy scribbles? Remembering the doctor's visit to look into the mysterious weakness and aches and pains in his own joints, waiting for the test results, and wondering whether his insurance would cover it now that he was laid off. Wondering whether the company had laid him off to keep their health insurance rates low because they thought he might have the cancer that killed his dad. Wondering if the aches would continue to get even worse than they already were.

Ron let it sink back for a while, wishing he were back in the dream where it was all timeless and none of it mattered. Life was currently just as groundless as the dream. No use keeping his face in the pillow, though. Forward to the familiar waking state, like putting on clothes in need of a wash.

"What are you thinking?" Tracey whispered.

"It was just a dream."

"*You?* A dream? What was it?"

"Some old dude with a beard was blowing strings of bubbles. You want to interpret that?"

"Sure. Your brain assembling bits of random electro-chemical bits into chains that we try to make meaning of."

Ron snorted. "Balderdash. It was obviously a message from the beyond about . . . something. Something *important.*"

"Like . . . getting a job, for instance?"

"I'm working on it."

You could always try to find something other than software programming."

He rolled over, scratching his head. "I suppose. But you know the drill, I'm forty-eight years old and writing code is all I've ever done. I think they're discriminating against me because of my age. 'Designing video games isn't even real programming,' my ass. I should sue."

"Well, honey, if you want to sue somebody, sue your lame ex-employer for firing you because you had to take a lot of time off to care for Pop."

"They didn't fire me. I had to quit."

"You didn't *have* to."

He sighed. She was technically right, as usual, but the situation was more nuanced than that, also as usual. She had a knack for jumping to the answer without getting mired down in the pages of calculations. Yes, he could have clung to his job instead of trying to make it all the way over to Pop's place and make sure he was eating and taking his meds, then moving him into their house after that became too cumbersome. He could have been coding instead of listening to Pop's mind erode. Pop was a semi-famous musician, a cellist, just as adept with chamber music as plucking the instrument upright like a stand-up bass in a bluegrass band. He actually made a living at it. After the cancer got worse, though, he grew more obsessed and withdrawn, mumbling to himself about "the music of the spheres" and talking to invisible angels. Ron couldn't leave him alone, and Xed-Tech wouldn't allow him to work from home.

"I know, Ron, it was a hell of a spot you were in, and you made the best call you could at the time. But now you are screwed."

Her comment cut to the quick and there was nothing he could think of to say.

". . . Anyway," she continued, "I have to get to work. One of the momma sea otters may deliver her cub any time; she's way overdue."

"Now, see, *you* have a good job," Ron pointed out, pulling

on sweat pants, an egg yolk-stained t-shirt, and his old terrycloth bathrobe. He followed her into the kitchen to make some coffee. "Biologist at the Seattle Aquarium, how cool is that?"

She shrugged, tossed her shoulder-length silver hair. "You just have to know who to sleep with on the way to the top. Really, though, you just have to stay open to new things; keep your eyes open. Don't be afraid to fail now and again, either. Never say never. Winners never quit, and quitters never win. It's not how many times you get knocked down, but how many times you get up. . . . Am I missing any clichés? They seem to work on my kids."

Ron sipped coffee at the kitchen table while Tracey busied herself preparing for work. He leaned back in his chair and watched her put on makeup in front of the bathroom mirror he could see from his vantage point. He enjoyed watching her do this. She had a compact efficiency of motion that could be mistaken as jerky and uncoordinated, but Ron found it graceful. Tracey occasionally dropped comments about getting old, especially when applying makeup, but they both knew that she was still quite pretty. Fifty was hardly old.

"You should at least get out of the house today," she called. "Do *something*. It's been two weeks since the funeral, Ron. You can't live on what's in your checking account forever."

He sighed. "I can't live on what's in there for another week, much less the end of time. I'm not exactly broke, but I'm way, *way* bent."

She appeared in the doorway, ready for work in a white blouse and lab jacket and khaki pants, very smart and scientific. "Well, I'm off."

"You just wait. The Kid will make a comeback. Maybe I'll sign up for a season on a crab boat or something. Now is my big opportunity to reinvent myself. Maybe the bone-chilling cold of the Bering Sea will help my aching joints."

"When are you going to have that looked at?"

"I already know the cause," he said mysteriously.

"No, you don't."

"Yes, I do. It's *the devil*, of course."

"If by the devil, you mean deviled eggs, you may be right," she said, poking him in his slowly expanding midsection.

"No, *the* Devil. He's making me eat. And I'm not *that* overweight."

"I don't happen to join in your belief of the dark master of evil, Ron. He has a pretty cool job, though. I wonder if he has any openings for you." She opened the front door to leave, then paused, eyes unfocussed.

"Where would I put in an application, though?" He limped along, while Tracey closed her eyes, then scrunched her face in that way that indicated she was searching for the proper words.

Ron felt a rush of ice water in his gut. Time seemed to dilate. He looked past her into the grass in the front yard, noticed that there were dandelions that needed weeding. It also needed mowing, which would get rid of the weeds, at least temporarily.

"You're right. You do need to reinvent yourself," she said, looking at the floor. "You're too—what is the word I'm looking for?—not 'passive,' but . . . ." She paused, waving her hand. "Reactive. That's it. You just react to things, without starting anything for yourself. You don't have your own plan for the future. You don't really want *anything*. You are not worried about the crap car you drive, the house you rent instead of own, your lack of any retirement planning. It's a form of laziness. That's it, you have talent but you are lazy. Not *work* lazy, God knows you work hard, when you actually have work, but . . . it's more like lazy *thinking*. You are a bowling pin, and life just knocks you around like a bowling ball. She paused, stared at his reaction, which was to stand stupidly staring at her. "Feel free to insert your own metaphor."

He looked away. "You're right, of course. It would be easier, you know, if the bowling balls quit rolling down the lane so goddamn frequently."

"Well, here's your chance," she said far too cheerfully, with exaggerated eye blinks and a giant smile. "And Ron—no videogames today. You play that thing all day when you could be job-hunting."

"But honey, I'm researching. Playing *Dragon Throne* is my

job until I get a real job."

"Oh, *really,*" she said, overenthusiastically feigning belief. "You must be working very hard at your new job."

"Actually, I'm not bullshitting you," he said, pointing his finger at the ceiling. "They have a very sophisticated way of double-buffering the engine to achieve a remarkable level of granularity."

She nodded politely, and checked her watch with raised eyebrows.

"You see, when you design a world that a player can interact in, there are certain areas that need a lot of detail, like a machine you want them to operate, and other areas that don't need so much, like a line of trees or mountains in the distance, right?"

"I have no idea what you're talking about."

"So by using appropriate parallelization of the multiple interacting subsystems, like the physics, AI, geometric computation of the scene management graphics, you can load a lot into the game on the disc without resorting to too many cut scenes."

"Oh, I get it. You're trying to get me to leave."

"Then, when you add multiple script revisions on the fly from the MMORG angle, you have to re-write reality on the fly from as many viewpoints as you have players. Very challenging."

"Do I dare ask what a MOM . . . MORM . . . MORG is?" she asked with an expression of near-pain.

"Oh. Sorry. It stands for Massively Multiplayer Online Role-Playing Game. Many players all interacting in the persistent virtual world, simultaneously co-creating it, and with the original programmer overseeing it all. Sort of like a video-game version of the old Dungeons and Dragons paper game. Only instead of counting on everyone's imagination to approximate reality, they all have to see the same thing in that world."

"Uh-huh," she said, rooting for her keys in her purse. "Okay, you're starting to sound like Pop with his alien angels. I'm leaving now."

"Oh, and don't get me started on the quest programming.

You know why I originally quit playing *Dragon Throne*, before I got into the programming aspect?"

"Because you wanted to get a life?"

"Because it ran out of quests. The storyline just kind of stopped, the designers could only have so much happen before it just petered out into a random monster attack every now and then. I'm trying to design flexible storylines and quests based on what the players have done in the past, then let the program generate on its own. Back in the old *Dungeons and Dragons* game days, you had to have a 'Dungeon Master' to feed the narrative. I'm trying to get around the need for that."

She looked out the window from in front of the closet, gauging the weather in relation to the available coats. "So you're *working*, not just prancing through the mountains and forests, slaying dragons with your swords and spells?"

"Right. I mean, you see that monitor I have hooked up to the console? That lets me see real time what code is running. I'm taking notes and learning so when I get an interview I'll know what the players are doing. Not just what the players are playing. Like it looks like I'm doing. Besides, it's a Level 37 Axe of Smiting with Flame Enhancement, not a sword."

She shook her head with an eye roll and a half smile. "I see. Was it hard in the game to get that Level 37 Smiting thing?"

"You *bet* it was! I had to level up on my enchanting spells, then craft enchanted items to help forge it after multiplying the effects of smiting potions, then travel to the cave in UnderDreck Mountain and beat the boss demon to get the axe—"

"Well, maybe, *just maybe,* Ron, if you spent the same energy and ingenuity in *this* world, you could 'level up' your job prospects and finances."

Ron's mouth snapped shut. *Shit.*

Tracey arched one eyebrow, then opened the door, introducing a blast of outside air. It was early spring; the mornings still had a bite.

Ron watched her slim form walk down the driveway to her new VW Beetle, parked next to his old, faded blue Accord. He watched her drive away, went to the kitchen, poured some cereal, and thought about her observations. *Maybe I should think about this reality as more of a game.* In *Dragon Throne*, once the quests were done, one could amass millions of gold pieces, but to what end? One could build castles but could not really live in them; the character just sort of stood there inside. *And what would I do if I was living there? Eat some cereal and watch TV? Might as well do that in real life. And instead of waiting for quests to appear, I can always try to make some of my own.* Now was indeed a good chance to make a change, to really look at things and plan for the near future.

If only I could do it without feeling like a gun is pointed at my head.

Like this health problem. He really should call a doctor like Tracy insisted. He knew she was very worried about him, but trying not to show it in an effort to prevent him from worrying. In his younger days he had been athletic, wide-shouldered and lean, but age had crept into his midsection and joints, which raised things to a new level.

Ron had looked up his symptoms on the Internet, but it was less than helpful. It could be anything from arthritis to Lyme Disease to cancer. He had not been in contact with any ticks that he knew of, and arthritis would not account for the overall weakness and fatigue he felt, so there was a nagging worry. This was how it had started with Pop. . . He willed himself not to think about it.

Think about something else. Aha! The mystery dog poo!

Ron checked his watch. At exactly 8:17 every morning, the old woman from two houses down walked her dachshund past his house, sweeping deep into the front lawn. Before losing his job, the little piles of dog excrement had been waiting for him to clean up when he returned home every evening, but now he was able to prevent the stealthy attacks. Sure enough, the woman appeared on cue. He made sure she saw him through the big front window, sipping coffee, watching his turf. She grumpily moved off in search of another lawn.

Next on the new quest generator, Ron thought, *is a*

determined avoidance of exercise, and a shower. I can level-up strength tomorrow. No need to shave today. Maybe tomorrow it would get to the point of looking bad enough to shave. No need to change into actual clothes, either. The bathrobe and sweatpants are just fine. Let's increase health points with some food.

He checked the refrigerator, planning the meals for the day. There was ham for a sandwich, even though he didn't particularly like ham, and some ground beef to make something for dinner. No need to go to the grocery store, he thought, half relieved and half disappointed. He pulled out the milk and had a champion breakfast of corn flakes.

One of the worst parts of being out of work was daytime TV. Springer was always worth a quick look: It was good to see that some people in the world were worse off than he was.

For the time being, anyway, he thought.

Watching news and science channels didn't improve his sense of impending catastrophe. By 9:30 Ron learned that there was a secret underground government base under the Denver Airport, and terrorists were infiltrating American ports with suitcase atomic bombs. Alternate universes existed right alongside ours, with entirely different histories. Rips in the time-space continuum were allowing an infiltration of aliens from these alternate universes into local space, with goals of domination and conquest. Strange rod-like creatures fly all around us, only seen when accidentally caught by high-speed cameras. A mud-volcano was poised to erupt and take out the entire Pacific Basin with tsunamis. A species of giant shark still lived in the depths of the ocean, and zombies, time travel, and faster-than-light starships were a scientific possibility. Miscellaneous biblical prophesies showed angels and demons in our midst. Scientific studies had found that human activity in general had so severely damaged the global ecosystem that humanity's prospects for long-term survival were near zero.

Time to get to work, he thought, looking at the computer screen. The thought of going through his routine of scanning job websites and submitting online applications appalled him.

There probably aren't any new openings since yesterday, he justified. *And nobody posts new jobs on Fridays.*

He snatched up the game controller and switched it on, smiling about how Tracey had busted him. It was true that he was working to understand how the programmers had done what they did, but he wouldn't be doing it if he didn't enjoy the game immensely. He looked at the scene on the monitor, how it was almost photo-realistic. His character, a super high-level Paladin, was making his way through the Forest of Dark Sighs. The trees were gnarled with light-colored bark and golden leaves. The mountains in the distance looked as clear as a poster. He wondered if his character could climb a tree, and if so, whether the game engine would render the leaves in finer detail. Leaves were incredibly hard to pull off in the graphics, which were all rendered in polygons of finer and finer size the closer one's character could view them. Most games just left them as swaths of green without any fine detail except for some random black leaf outlines, but this one was remarkably detailed. He was working on a programming theory, "Attention-based Fluid Rendering," where the AI would render on the fly whatever background was necessary based on the viewpoint of the character, and wondered if this programmer had beat him to it.

The knock on the door came just as he was finishing the "Submerged Sword of Slumbering" side-quest and wondering if he should get out of the house before Tracey called. There were two men standing there. One was black with graying hair, wearing a nondescript suit and sunglasses; the other white, with a bald head, scraggly goatee, wearing jeans and a gray shell jacket. They flashed official-looking badges and ID cards.

"Good afternoon, I'm Special Agent Smithson, and this is Special Agent Johnson," the bald one said. "Can we talk to you for a few minutes?"

–2–

"Who are you guys?" He'd dubbed them Glasses Johnson and Baldy Smithson.

"We just told you," Glasses Johnson said.

"No, I mean, are you bill collectors or something?"

"Oh, no, nothing like that. We're from the government."

"Well, that narrows it down. Did I forget to pay my water bill?"

"Not exactly. We're from the federal government."

"Any particular branch?"

The agents looked at each other and shrugged.

"The executive branch, I think," Glasses Johnson said.

"No, I mean, what *agency*?"

"Hard to say," Baldy Smithson said, lips pursed. "It started out with the U.S. Space Command, but they needed some personnel with investigative experience, so they recruited us from the CIA and the FBI. But I guess we are still an offshoot of the Space Command."

"Can I see your badges?"

"We just showed you."

"No, you just waved them. Can I please *see* them?"

They showed them to Ron, who read "Space Command" on them. "Huh. You don't say. Come on in."

Ron showed them inside and they sat at the kitchen table. He tried to act nonchalant, but it wasn't every day that the U.S. Space Command showed up at his house. He wondered why he was bothering to act nonchalant, but it was hard to act otherwise in a bathrobe, stained t-shirt, and sweatpants. Maybe it was just how it was done, at least on TV.

"You want any coffee?"

"No, thanks," Smithson said, removing his gray jacket. "Hey, is that *Dragon Throne* you have running over there?"

Ron suffered a pang of guilt, but then realized that the agent was at least passingly familiar with the game. "Yeah. I'm not just playing the game, I'm a programmer and I'm working on game design."

The agents paused and gave each other a thinly veiled, meaningful glance.

"Really? What kind of game design?"

Ron wondered whether to give them the whole lengthy story, or the short version. "This is a sort of virtual world where players can interact with each other, and the game storyline. I'm just working on making it as real as possible."

Baldy Smithson nodded with pursed lips. "Huh. Interesting. We know the game. Does anyone else know you're working on this?"

Ron frowned. "Just my girlfriend. Fiancée. Significant other. Is that why you're here? Is my Attention-based Fluid Rendering theory a matter of national security?"

"No, it's probably just a coincidence. But we are wary of coincidences lately. Hey, if you're getting into the line-by-line code there, are you programming in any cheat codes?"

"No, I'm not a big fan of cheat codes."

"Why not? What's wrong with having unlimited lives, ammo, super-strength, and other powers?"

Ron shook his head. "What is the fun in that? Especially in an online game where other players are involved, that really pisses them off. Any time there are no common ground rules, it takes all the fun out of things."

It occurred to Ron that an hour ago, he'd told Tracey that he'd quit playing the game originally because of running out of quests. He remembered now that it was only partially that; the main reason was that he'd beefed up his character with cheat-coded super-weapons and armor, and had lost interest because there was no more challenge to the quests that were left. *Or maybe that the quests weren't designed with that level of powerful tools in mind. . . . I wonder if I can design multiple layers of storylines based on the capabilities of the player. . . .*

Ron shook himself out of his reverie when he felt the agents staring at him. "Hey, wait a minute, are you guys from the FBI anti-piracy division? I'm not changing any of the code here, and even if I was I wouldn't be selling it."

"Oh, no, nothing like that," Glasses Johnson said. "We do have a few questions about a web page you programmed a few years ago."

It was Ron's turn to stare blankly. "What web page?"

Smithson produced some screen shots from his jacket pocket. They showed a website titled "100 Year Mystery Murders."

It took Ron a second to recognize what he was looking at. "Oh, yeah, I remember that; it's from a website I made for school. I went back to college to study web design, maybe five years ago, and this was for a class project. Sorry, I've probably designed dozens of websites on the side since then, up until about a month ago."

"What happened a month ago?" Johnson asked, interest suddenly piquing.

"I lost my job. Got laid off. Or quit, to take care of my dying father. They hired a younger guy instead of taking me back. They said he had a newer skill set. Games on cell phones, and I didn't have enough cell phone game programming training. And is this fair, to a guy who has been around since Pong?" He looked back and forth between the agents, still wondering if they were FBI Anti-Piracy agents. "What does this have with you guys being here?"

The agents exchanged glances. "Let's talk about the web page for a minute. What gave you the idea in the first place?"

Ron thought back to the computer class, the project, desperately sitting up late the night before it was due and just letting the ideas come. "Well, we had to design a website as a project for this class. Most of the other students were making them up for fake businesses—you know: retail stores, doctors' offices, and such. I wanted mine to be more informal, more personal, but still get a reader's interest. I decided to do a fictitious personal website. Most people's personal sites and blogs are *really* boring, just droning on and on about minutiae of their days, or rambling on about their idiotic views of politics and current events and such. I wanted mine to have a story."

"So nobody helped you? Gave you the idea?"

"Nope."

"And you made up this whole thing about a gang of guys in war paint that kill people every hundred years, out of the blue?"

"Yeah." Ron smiled sheepishly, then continued. "I thought about using clowns, but I've always hated clowns. Mimes, too. But I needed something that would stand out across lots of eras. I found an old picture of a murder scene that looked like it could be from nineteen-fifteen, then scanned it, and faked a newspaper clipping from the *Seattle Times* and photoshopped the whole thing into a PDF. I made up a story about how the two people in the picture had been tracked down by a gang of guys in war paint and murdered. Then I faked eighteen-fifteen, where another group of war-painted guys had murdered a family. In that story, I said that a similar murder had occurred in Prague in seventeen-fifteen where guys dressed like harlequins had done in a whole manor. I made the whole site look like it was made by a guy who had connected these dots, and then researched archives the world over and found that, sure enough, a bunch of Kabuki actors had murdered a Japanese family in sixteen-fifteen, and found even older records in Florence, Italy where stripe-painted-faced devil worshippers had killed some monks in an abbey in fifteen-fifteen. So, the whole thing was wrapped up by the guy saying: 'Watch out for guys wearing war paint ten years from now, in twenty-fifteen.' Anyway, the project was due, I sat down the night before with a pot of coffee, switched at some point to Wild Turkey, and voilà, the web site was turned in."

The two agents sat silently, staring at Ron.

"I got a B."

More staring.

"So here it is, twenty-fifteen," he said.

The agents sat, blinking, waiting for him to catch up.

"Oh, shit. You're kidding."

"What, you don't watch the news?" Smithson asked.

"You don't think that I . . .? Wait! Oh, shit—"

"No, nothing like that," Smithson said. "We don't think you killed him."

"Oh, my, God."

The agents let him sit, watched him process the information.

"So . . . somebody saw the website somewhere and thought it was real, and decided to dress up in war paint and kill someone to keep the streak going or something?"

"Well, that is one possible explanation."

"Where did this happen?"

"At a historic state park in California. A ghost town, where they mined gold in the old days. We checked the flight records; no record that you went anywhere, and you could not have driven back that fast even if you did do it."

The questions crowded into Ron's mind rapidly, and he sank into his chair, exhaling, hand across his brow and eyes. "Okay, so, I'm very confused. First of all, why are you here? And why are you here so fast if you know I didn't have anything to do with this? And is that website even still up? Why would anyone do this? And what exactly did they do? And what do you mean 'one possible explanation'?"

"One thing at a time, Mr. Golden. We are dealing with some very cunning, very evil people. Stopping them is proving to be very difficult," Glasses Johnson said.

"See, here's the *really* weird thing," Smithson said, pausing for dramatic effect, and scooting his chair closer to the table. "You know the other historical killings you made up on the web page? The ones in nineteen-fifteen, eighteen-fifteen, and before? Those *actually happened. Exactly like you wrote about.* We had to research them like crazy, but found that you were entirely accurate. And we know for a fact that you *didn't* know about them when you wrote the web page."

Ron blinked. Chills ran up his spine. His mind reeled.

"They may not have even happened *until* you wrote about them."

–3–

Ron's mind stopped reeling and froze, like sand thrown into gears. He shook his head dumbly, examined the soggy texture of the corn flakes he'd poured earlier and forgotten about.

Johnson produced a photograph and slid it across the table to Ron, deftly avoiding a small puddle of milk. "This was taken yesterday at that ghost town, Bodie."

Ron examined the picture. The sky was blue, with wispy white clouds. A body was lying in a crumpled heap near some antique-looking iron machinery. There was blood, blood on the body, and in stained patches in the dusty, tan-colored rocks.

"It was a tourist from France. They let the mother and her two children go. They had no interest in them. This time the murderers were dressed in normal, modern-looking clothes, but had white face paint with red-and-black painted stripes and patterns on their faces. They also had huge spiders and snakes on their shoulders. The mother and kids are still out of their minds. Four of these painted bastards ran after them with knives and screaming like banshees. All the other tourists in the area fled, too. The family was visiting the old gold-mining town, kind of a hobby for a lot of Europeans. They like to visit the Old West sites, ghost towns and the like," Johnson said, recovering the photo.

"What does all this possibly have to do with me?" Ron asked.

"Well, you did the website that either predicted this attack or caused these guys to choose this place at this time. We've run up against these face-painted guys before, so we wondered why they struck there. Your site came up when we ran a search on the attack. We researched any connection you might have with the place, and found you might have had an ancestor named Bobby Golden, who immigrated there from back east. While he was there he was known as 'Cornish Bob' Golden. We think he is involved with these killings."

Ron slowly shook his head, mystified. "Involved?"

"Well, we're not sure if there's a connection either, except that here you are, having made a website that accurately yet 'accidentally' described a pattern of murders by men with painted faces that took place every hundred years, and predicted another murder ten years later which happened to actually take place, *again by guys in face paint*, in a place where one of your ancestors lived."

Johnson added, "Well, there is more to the story than that. The murdered French guy had a rare gene that these people are . . . well, interested in . . . *eradicating*. Your website made us suspect that you might have this gene."

"Gene?" Ron muttered. "And what do you mean, '*eradicating*'?"

Slowly, his field of view began to darken. Something drew his attention outside. His gaze drifted out his kitchen window, across his front lawn, and into the street, where a dark car was slowly cruising by. He looked into the driver's seat, saw a man in a leather jacket clutching the wheel. With visceral disgust, Ron saw that there was something hairy, with long spindly legs, perched on the man's shoulder. It was far too big to be a spider, but that was what it appeared to be. The legs jerked, and the spider scuttled around to the other side of the man's head. Suddenly the man turned his head, and Ron knew something else was wrong. It took a moment for it to dawn on him. It was the face. It was painted white, with complex red-and-black lines over the white, staring back at him. The eyes were like two black pools in the midst of the pattern, moving in slow motion, staring at him. His breath caught.

The two agents, following his line of sight at his reaction, saw the car and its driver and exploded into motion. Smithson dove across Ron, knocked him to the floor and began barking into a radio microphone. Johnson whipped a long-barreled pistol from under his suit jacket, crossed to the front door, flung it open and assumed an isosceles shooter's stance behind and around the doorframe. His pistol followed the car while it suddenly accelerated and sped away.

Ron's heart was beating madly in his chest, and he vainly struggled to get out from under the bald agent. He then thought better of it and stopped, sweat springing out all over his body.

"Move him!" Johnson called over his shoulder, eyes never leaving the street, gun barrel as steady as a rock as it panned the area. Smithson grabbed Ron by the shirt collar, and dragged him deeper into the house while producing his own pistol from his waistband. He propped Ron's back against the brick fireplace in the living room and placed himself between Ron and the window, gun trained at the street. Johnson left the front door and dashed from cover to cover, past Ron's car, behind a bush, and then took a position behind the brick mailbox. Tense seconds passed, until the sound of another car screaming past the house reached them, and they heard the low throbbing of a helicopter.

Smithson holstered his weapon. "He's gone," he said, helping Ron to his feet.

"Holy *crap*," Ron said, voice wavering, his whole body shaking. He was gratified to notice that he had not soiled himself.

Glasses Johnson reappeared, speaking into a hand-held radio. "The yard is big enough for the helo to land in." He turned to Ron. "It'll be here in ninety seconds, and I think it would be best, Mr. Golden, if you were on it."

Ron nodded, then held up his hand. "Wait. My girlfriend?"

"We will have to protect her, and her kids too, so they won't use them to get at you," Johnson said. "Is her daughter, Chris, still in school at the University of Washington?"

Ron nodded.

"We'll get a team on the way to secure her. Her son, Jeremy, is in boot camp at San Diego, and we think it is best that he stay there for now. We have a call in to his commanding officer, and we'll decide what to do about him."

Smithson produced a small spiral notebook, consulted it. "No other family? Brothers, sisters, mom, dad?"

Ron shook his head. "Mom died when I was a kid, and Pop just passed away. Nobody else."

Smithson nodded, snapped the notebook shut. "I'm sorry, Mr. Golden, they got moving on this a lot faster than we thought they would. We would have contacted you sooner if we had been sure."

The sound of the helicopter got louder, then deafening. Dirt and debris started swirling around the front of the house. It landed in the yard. *Which still needed mowing*, Ron noted with embarrassment.

The agents crouched, flanking each elbow, and escorted him toward the sliding door at the side of the helicopter. Ron wasn't sure whether he needed to crouch or not, or why people did that when the rotors were so high over their heads, but crouched anyway. The door slid open to reveal a bench with a large, muscular man in a white polo shirt with the Space Command logo on it. He had a crew cut, square jaw, sunglasses, and a headset. He looked like a linebacker from the 1960s. The man extended his hand. Ron was unable to tell if he was trying to help him into the helicopter or shake his hand.

"My name is Special Agent Clay," he shouted over the rotor wash and engine roar.

"Ron Golden," he said, and shook his hand while trying to keep his bathrobe from flapping.

"I'm glad that you were fired last month, Mr. Golden," yelled Clay, "because we may like to hire you if you're a carrier of the gene like we think."

Ron barely registered the last comment. "Hire me? Cool. Where are we going?"

"We have a facility near the Denver International Airport."

"Really? Like the secret underground base?"

"How the hell did you know about that?"

"It was on TV a while ago," he said stupidly, and allowed himself to be pulled into the helicopter, still in his bathrobe. He vaguely pictured flying bowling pins, and a sailboat in a gale.

-4-

Most Ultra-Secret Government Bases that Tracey had ever seen on the movies had been very sleek, high tech, modern, and opulent. They had automatic swishing doors like on Star Trek, fancy futuristic furniture, complicated control panels with huge TV screens and lots of dials and computers, million-dollar windows far under the sea showing marine life, young beautiful people in jumpsuits, and expensive booze in martini glasses with big olives and great food.

The secret base under the Denver International Airport was nothing like that, she found to her chagrin. Most of the walls were concrete, the food was reminiscent of a school cafeteria, and even the computer equipment looked secondhand and dated. While filling out paperwork on the way in, she had even noticed a memo taped to the office wall extolling the frumpy employees to conserve copier paper and office supplies.

The day before, nondescript "government agents" had briskly entered her office at the Seattle Aquarium, handcuffed her, and hustled her into an unmarked van over the shocked protestations of the other aquarium staff. They had whisked her off at high speed to Boeing Field, where an unmarked Gulfstream Airplane immediately took off eastward over the Cascades. Ron and her daughter, Chris, were already on board. Ron had tried his best to explain his afternoon, but made little sense. Chris had also been practically abducted on campus.

They had landed at the Denver airport, taxied into a little-used part of the tarmac, and were escorted down long, deserted-looking hallways, into a key-activated elevator that went down, down, down.

They were taken to separate rooms, which looked like generic motel rooms, except the doors locked from the outside. Dinner, in the form of a plastic tray with Salisbury steak, rubbery frozen beans, and mashed potatoes and gravy, had been brought in by a woman in a Space Command uniform. The TVs only showed local network programming. She watched the inane shows anyway to pass the time and stave off the anxiety of imprisonment. She took a shower and dried off with the paper-thin towels after searching the room for hidden cameras. Eventually, she fell asleep.

It was now 8:00 AM. Tracey was dreaming again.

This time, she was in a desert with tan sand and a yellowish sky. The sun was very intense, and there was a faint smell in the air of . . . something . . . what, incense? She was walking across the sand, looking for Ron. She saw him struggling across the dunes, miles away, and called out to him. He heard her voice, but could not tell from which direction, so he continued to wander. He carried a hammer in one hand and a small golden ball in the other, like an orb and scepter.

She noticed movement, like flecks moving across her eyes, then saw that the flecks were small, flying things. They were everywhere! One of them came closer, and she stared at it, dumbfounded. It was greenish-brown, lumpy, and semi-transparent, an eight-inch rounded tubular jellyfish—it looked very much, upon closer inspection, like a pickle, covered with tiny hairs that undulated as it flew. It floated along, waist-high, across the sands. She followed it up the face of a sand dune.

As Tracey crested the top of the dune, the flying creature was already far away. She could see down into a small valley a mile away where there was a tent. Inside the tent, she somehow knew, was a woman. The woman called out to Ron in a seductive voice, but he couldn't tell from where she called. Tracey was suddenly on the crest of the dune overlooking the tent (had she flown?). She could still see Ron struggling across the sands, showing no interest in the tent. A shadow started falling across the entire expanse of the desert, sharp and black. She looked up, and saw an enormous metal shape, blotting out the sun, falling toward them.

A voice, deep and mellifluous, spoke: "He hath loosed the

fateful lightning of his terrible swift sword. . . ."

Tracey looked down, saw a large knife in her hands, coated with a black, tarry substance. Her hand moved without volition. She slashed herself across her stomach and screamed. Just before the massive metal structure crashed into the ground on top of them all, she woke to the woman agent standing in the doorway, still dressed in a Space Command uniform.

"Good morning, Miss Springs," the businesslike agent greeted her.

"Good morning, Officer Whoever You Are," Tracey answered, still panting with barely repressed fear from the dream. "Have you transmitted my request to whoever is running this prison to allow me to call my lawyer, who will promptly get me the hell out of here and sue you all for false arrest, false imprisonment, assault, and whatever else she can think of?"

The sergeant's mouth did not move, but her eyes conveyed a smile. "Yes, ma'am, I did, and Special Agent-in-Charge Clay has asked me to again convey his sincerest apologies for the manner in which you were removed from the public for your safety. It was decided that your life and the lives of others could have been in jeopardy had we taken the time to attempt to explain the reasons for wanting your . . ." she paused, searching for the right word, "'presence,' and it was best just to 'arrest' you and take you here. Ma'am."

"Well, so far, I have seen nothing to indicate to *me*, at least, that this was at all in any way necessary, proper, just, or even *legal*," Tracey said curtly. "So far, I have had *no explanation* as to why I am here. Not to mention that things are made even worse because of bad food and a room that looks like cast off nineteen-seventies furniture from a discount hotel chain. *Ma'am.*"

The sergeant smiled, and escorted Tracey down the hallway. She shook off the effects of her dream. She dreamed almost every night and almost always remembered them. More accurately, she was unable to forget them. Often, they predicted what would happen the following day, but she was convinced that this was because whatever thought fragments were already in her brain were assembled into patterns that made sense in retrospect. She was a Researcher at the Seattle Aquarium, had gotten there by rising through the ranks in the Giant Pacific Octopus project, and was firmly grounded in a scientific worldview wherein dreams were highly subjective and unimportant except as curiosities.

Tracey was led into a large, windowless room with a few folding tables, but the only seating available were antique-looking school desks. Ron had squeezed himself into one and folded his hands on the attached desktop. Chris had reluctantly sat herself in one of them, too. Ron, despite his attempt to look like an attentive student, looked like hell. Chris, usually a stylishly dressed twenty-year-old college student, didn't look much better. Her brown hair was unkempt.

"They didn't remember a comb or brush in my room," she explained with a mock cheerful smile.

Across the room, a set of double doors swung open and a lab-coated man pushing a large-wheeled metal cart entered.

"He looks like a middle-aged Pee Wee Herman," Chris whispered.

Ron and Tracey repressed laughter.

"Good morning," the man said, stopping the cart near them.

They examined the top of the cart, and saw a collection of needles, vials, gauze, and other medical supplies.

"Oh, crap, I thought that was going to be breakfast," Ron said.

"Breakfast after blood samples," the man said.

Another technician entered, fit a surgical mask across Tracey's face, and started putting on latex gloves.

"Why the hell do you think you can take our blood?" Tracey asked angrily.

The lab-coated man recoiled in surprise. "Has nobody explained this to you?"

"No, not really," Ron said.

The man motioned to the phlebotomist to pause, removed a cell phone from his lab coat pocket and made a quick call in a low voice. He deftly replaced the phone in his lab coat pocket. "My name is Professor Langston LaGrue. I am the Chief Science Officer here. The Managing Special Agent-in-Charge, John Clay, is on his way and will be here shortly, and will explain everything. While he is doing that, however, we need to examine your blood samples to determine whether you are carriers of the Pangborn Gene."

"Why not?" Ron said, rolling up his sleeve. "They mentioned giving me a job if I had whatever that is."

The technician drew a vial of blood; Tracey and Chris relented as well. As the technician left with the samples, the tall, broad-shouldered man from the helicopter entered the room.

"Ah," Professor LaGrue said, "may I introduce the Managing Special Agent-in-Charge of this facility, Special Agent John Clay."

Clay hesitated in the doorway for a moment, eyeballed one of the little desks dubiously, then perched on top of it. He was graying, but still had a full head of hair. Clay had an affable yet electric air about him, and steely blue eyes. He wore a white polo shirt with a U.S. Space Command seal, and jeans. His angular form and defined muscles made it obvious that he was a former military man of a less scientific bent. He was tall and had large bones, even in his head.

"Good morning, Mr. Golden. Glad to see you again, and meet your friends. You are probably curious about why you are here, what this place is, who we are, what we want with you, and so on," he began.

Tracey raised her hand, like a student in class. He motioned to her.

"Yes, Agent Clay? What *exactly* are we doing here, and just what the *hell* is going on?"

"I'm glad you asked that," Agent Clay said, with the merest ghost of a smile crossing his lips. "Welcome to White Mountain, built concurrently with the Denver International Airport in nineteen ninety five. The airport topside is fifty-three square miles total. Our part, the underground, is approximately ninety square miles, in nine successively deeper sub-levels." Agent Clay paused, mulling over how to proceed. "Any discussion of the genetics involved here?"

"Not as of yet," the professor stated primly, rocking from heels to toes. "Not until just now have the DNA tests been started."

"Very well," Clay continued. "Okay, let's see, where to begin. I suppose with who we are. The U.S. Space Command is not to be confused with the Air Force Space Command, or the Naval or Army Space Commands, either. Those are three of our component commands, along with NORAD. Our main mission is conducting all integrated attack warning and space operations, including control of space, direction of space support activities, and use of space assets to enhance the force effectiveness of other combatant commands."

"What the hell does that mean?" Chris asked.

"We protect what's over our heads. Not only from terrestrial threats, but any other."

"Aliens?" Tracey asked.

"Well, mostly cyber security. But aliens, too. Somebody has to deal with that. Anyway, that aspect was the forgotten stepchild of the command. It was all missile defense this, cyber-attack-from-China that. But things changed when the rift opened up."

"Rift?" Ron asked.

"Let's get to that later. If your genetic makeup checks out, it may turn out that we will have to push our departure date up and send Professor LaGrue with you to act as the scientist on the team."

LaGrue's eyes grew round, and he sat down in one of the desks. "Oh, my. Thank you, sir."

"Mission? Team? Professor Pee Wee is going to be on what 'team'? And send us in where?" Tracey asked.

"Professor 'Pee Wee'?" Clay asked, and stifled a laugh. "I guess that sort of fits. Well, as far as where we're going, it isn't necessarily 'out' into space at all. It is more like 'in' to space. As predicted by hyperspacial and quantum field theories and recently confirmed here, there are, of course, um . . . other universes."

"Did he just say 'recently confirmed here'?" Tracey whispered to Ron.

"The alternate universes are not within our space-time,

but kind of lie alongside it, kind of like playing cards in a deck, or pages in a book. Or you can think of it like a clump of soap bubbles, with membranes separating them. Some of these universes are very much like our own, and differ from it in only very subtle ways. Some are very, very different. The irony is, it is easier to get to those other universes through gaps in the expanding space-time than to travel beyond the horizon in our own."

He paused, trying to let that sink in.

"So, let me make a leap here," Ron said. "If we can get to other universes from ours, this secret underground base was made to get to those other universes."

"Not exactly, but close. Something punched a hole from one of those universes, right here, back in '93. We had to build all this, including the whole airport, as cover to contain it."

"I read something about that," Ron said. "People wondered why they built the airport way out here in the plains so far away from town."

"At first, they thought the suddenly appearing hole was an attack. But it turned out to be something else."

Tracey raised her hand again. "Look, all this stuff has stupefied me beyond the capacity for coherent thought. You people are all just *fucking nuts*. I just want to go home, and forget all this ever happened. Can we at least get some water in here? Or if not breakfast a cup of goddamn *coffee?*"

"So, Professor," Ron wondered out loud, "what could punch through one universe to another?"

LaGrue spoke up. "Well, sometimes they happen naturally, but those are usually unstable and last only a short time. And are subatomic. But this one was as big as a Buick, and didn't disappear, so we knew it was artificial. It takes something with immense energy, but with that energy contained or at least carefully directed, because otherwise it would have blown the whole planet to bits. The only thing we know of that could have accomplished this kind of effect on the fabric of space-time is a singularity, otherwise known as a black hole. And if a big enough black hole was freely exposed right at the crust of our planet, it would have sucked the entire Earth into it in a microsecond. So, it must have been contained, and the only way we can think of doing that is through a stasis field, where time itself is suspended. And the only reason for having a black hole trapped in a stasis field is either as a doomsday weapon or as a faster-than-light drive that works by stretching or contracting space-time into wormholes."

They all blinked at him.

"It wasn't a doomsday weapon, or we wouldn't be here now. The singularity was still contained when it punched through. We sent probes in, expecting the rift to collapse at any moment, but it never did. The probes discovered the skeleton of a big, interstellar ship. It looked battle-damaged, and the rift was probably caused by the drive unit leaking, or partially rupturing before some fail-safe kicked in."

"So, there's a rip, a hole, a tunnel, pick the description you like, to another universe right here below this airport, with a spaceship on the other side of it?" Ron asked.

"Affirmative," Special Agent-in-Charge Clay said. "We have a rift here, with a spaceship on the other side. An *inoperable* spaceship. What we want, though, is to try to salvage the propulsion system. Not to mention any other technology we can salvage from over there."

They all sat in silence for a while, mulling this.

"So, okay, the Space Command takes over the dealings with the ship, because they are not sure if there is a threat, right?" Ron said.

"Right. But they needed skills that they were not used to dealing with, of course. Xenobiology, Materials Science, you name it. And when the genetic component of things started making itself more urgent, they started recruiting talent from investigative agencies like the FBI and CIA. That is where Smithson and Johnson came from, not the military side."

"Okay, what is this 'genetic component' you guys keep talking about?" Ron asked.

"Let's wait and see what the results are," Clay grunted. "No sense worrying you about all that if it doesn't pan out."

"What is it like?" Chris asked.

"The other universe? Very similar to this one, from what

we can tell so far. In fact, it could *be* this universe, *our* universe, either on another planet at some unknown distance from Earth or even Earth at a different time. Or both. Any of those things are possible, and we just don't know at this point," Clay answered, then narrowed his eyes conspiratorially. "Would you like to see it?"

Ron and Tracey answered at the same time.

"Sure," he said.

"No way," she said, shaking her finger at Clay and LaGrue. "You think you can just abduct us all and dazzle us with all this bullshit and off we'll go across the sand dunes, just like that?" Tracey noticed that all the eyes in the room were now centered on her.

"We never said anything about sand dunes," Agent Clay said.

"Uh-oh," she said.

–5–

The dark car, once clear of the area of Ron Golden's house, slowed. They blended into the flow of Seattle traffic heading north on Aurora Avenue.

"Well, that waren't no proper job." A man in the back seat chuckled. He was dressed in denim jeans and jacket, with cowboy boots and a black Stetson hat with silver coins around the band. His face was painted white with red-and-black patterns, even the large mustache, which looked oversized on his short frame. A long, black snake was coiled around his neck, with the tip of its tail inserted into his left ear.

The man in the front seat, face also painted, glanced over his leather-jacketed shoulder nervously, trying to gauge whether his boss was angry or not. The large, black spider on his shoulder placed one of its long, black legs in the man's ear and adjusted its position as he moved.

"Don't worry, me bey, you colony rats are not used to field work. How could you be, fresh from a stinky, crowded tin can orbiting a lifeless rock?"

"I passed Early Twenty-first Century training," the man in the front seat grunted, with furrowed brows.

The man in the back seat snorted. "Look, me 'ansum . . . Ginon, is it? That your name? Ginon 22, or someth'n? We definitely need to come up with a nickname. The Jack you're replacing was one of me best; he'd been on me team the longest. You have big shoes to fill. But yer teasy basic training is going to amount to two things fossick'n out here in the field, ol' son: diddly, and shyte. You stick with ol' Cornish Bob, though, and he'll pull 'ee through."

The man in the front seat said something under his breath into the end of another of the long black spider legs that was hovering in front of his mouth, then just drove with hunched shoulders. Finally, he glanced back over his shoulder into the back seat, eyebrow raised. "What did you say?"

Cornish Bob laughed. "Yeh, I s'pose they don't have much use for accents or slang up there in your space colony, and I doubt your familiar could look it up anywhere. I was born and raised in Cornwall, me bey, and made it over to your universe way back in eighteen seventy nine or so. But some things scat down hard."

The new trainee, still unsure of what to say, continued driving past a rolling green graveyard. He thought it strange that the graveyard was on both sides of the road. *Did they build the road through the middle of it? Typical early twenty-first century.*

"Well, I better call this in. Yeh did manage to get the bug planted, and we heard the website me great-grandson made."

"Call it in?" Ginon said nervously, glancing at Cornish Bob in the rearview mirror. "You mean to her? To Eiffelia?"

"Who else, yeh chucklehead?"

The man in the front seat stiffened.

Cornish Bob smiled wryly as he adjusted the head of his black snake to point to an area a few feet in front of him. "What, she makes you nervous, does she?"

"She's the Goddess!" Ginon 22 stammered from the front seat. "The Ruler of the Universe, come to dwell in our midst to lead her chosen people to victory against the demon foes!"

Cornish Bob hesitated, unsure whether to enlighten his new recruit sooner rather than later. He chose later. There was a risk of mental instability if too much of the truth was revealed too soon, especially so soon after they were re-animated. Pangborn carriers like them were spared from the mind-numbing drugs that the rest of the population was injected with daily, but they had still been spoon-fed from birth on Eiffelia's mythology. Eventually, he would learn the truth about the war, and about Eiffelia herself, but not now, not in the midst of a field assignment. He pinched the head of the snake, activating its transmitter.

A shimmering, glowing, six-inch-tall figure of a woman

appeared, floating in the air in the back seat. Even at this size and from a parallel universe she was serene, radiating a calm, but terrible, power.

"What is your report, Bob?" she asked, her voice at once melodious but pregnant with an ancient, immense gravity.

"Your new hand-picked recruit for my team did well," Bob answered, his voice shedding much of its accent. "He managed to plant the listening device on my grandson's front windowpane, while they were sitting at the table talking, no less! We retrieved the address for the website that he made that revealed some of those full gene carriers."

"Well done, Ginon 22. Bob, you will take your team back in time in that world-branch and kill them all, in exactly the same manner as he described. I am about to proceed with my plan to collapse that universe into our own, but I must keep it intact before collapsing it, to prevent any further new branches."

Cornish Bob watched with amusement as his new recruit stared around him at the world they were in, knowing that it would all soon cease to exist. He wondered if the new recruit was the type to try to wreak as much mayhem and wrest as much pleasure as he could before that occurred.

"But first, Bob, I have another task for you. This will be an excellent opportunity for your new recruit to get his feet wet. I have intelligence that the Sea Tribes will try to pirate one of my cargo tankers in the southwestern Pacific in the next day or so. It is called *The Acolyte*. I want you to take your team there and ambush them. Make an example. They are causing me woe, and I want them to think twice before daring to steal from me again."

"As you command, Goddess," Cornish Bob said with exaggerated flourish.

Her image flickered, then vanished.

"God is great," intoned the recruit, trembling.

"Yeh. She's great, all right. So let's get rid of this piece o' shyte car and stank back over to our universe. We have some Sea Tribesmen to scat down."

Ginon began looking for a parking lot to abandon the car. They pulled into a strip mall with a K-mart, and stopped.

"I don't understand," Ginon began, hesitantly. "The Tribes. She said that they were stealing from her. How can this be? She is the Goddess, the Queen of the Universe. How can she not reign supreme on her planet of origin, the original Earth? I thought the Sea Tribes were just a few vermin outlaws."

Cornish Bob pulled a long, thin wire from the abdomen of the snake wrapped around his neck, then removed a small electronic device the size of a pack of cigarettes from his jacket pocket. Ginon 22 recognized it as the rift generator, which enabled their travel between universes. Cornish Bob plugged the thin wire into a tiny socket and fiddled again with the head of his snake. A graphic representation of the interconnected branchings of the universe they were in and the nearby stable parallel universes appeared as a three dimensional holographic projection in the back seat between them.

How much like a tree it looks, with branches stretching into infinity like a fractal, Bob thought. He watched the infinitesimally quick flashes of new alternate universes springing into existence, then being absorbed back as the lines of potentiality failed to establish enough differences to create a stable new branch. Each branch, representing an entire parallel universe, was surrounded by eleven thin layers of quantum potentiality, like bark on the tree.

Ginon 22 looked over the front seat at the projection. He had never seen it represented in this way, only on the small screen on the rift generator itself.

"Eleven dimensional layers, around each universe branch," Bob said knowingly, narrowing his eyes. "You know how you can line up two mirrors facing each other and stand between them, so your reflection bounces back and forth?"

Ginon 22 nodded, a puzzled expression on his face.

"You know how many reflections of yourself you can see in each mirror before they get too small or sharply angled to see any more? No matter how large the mirrors are, or how perfectly they are lined up?" Bob continued.

Ginon shrugged.

"*Eleven,*" Cornish Bob said, voice laden with mystery,

then leaned toward the front seat. "Coincidence?"

"Really?" Ginon asked, fascinated.

"Nah, I'm just making that up," Cornish Bob said, then laughed uproariously.

"Is there anything else we need to accomplish in this universe before we jump back and ambush the Sea Tribe pirates?" Ginon asked.

"Not unless you need something at K-Mart," Bob said. "Let me dial in the jump and we'll be off."

"Right here? In the car?"

"Hmm . . . you're right, that won't work. Too many things would come with us in the jump. Like this car. Let's go into the store. Stow that damned spider. They only have primitive familiars here, called 'smart phones.'"

They walked into the K-Mart after stowing their spider and snake familiars. Cornish Bob strolled over-casually through the men's wear department, whistling, grabbing armloads of jeans.

"This should attract the attention of the store cop." He winked at Ginon.

They made their way to the dressing rooms. Cornish Bob parted the cheesy curtain with a flourish, motioned Ginon 22 into the changing room, then followed him in, closing the curtain with a last, suspicious-looking glance around.

"That should get the store cop salivating." He chuckled. He entered data into the rift generator that would land them on the bridge of the ship, *The Acolyte*.

"Why do you want to attract the attention of the security person?"

"So I can be amused at the thought of the guy waiting for us to come out of the dressing room, then when they get tired of waiting and check on us they will go nuts trying to figure out how we just vanished," Bob said matter-of-factly. "You ready for this? How many jumps from one universe to another have you made?"

"This will be my second," Ginon 22 confessed uncomfortably. "Just the one from our universe to here to meet up with you. I didn't like it much."

"Well, yeh prob'ly won't like this one, neither," Cornish

Bob stage-whispered.

He activated the rift generator. There was a yellowish flash, and they felt their insides lurch, contort, invert, flatten out, compress. And they were standing on the bridge of a cargo ship. It was nighttime, but the moon revealed the massive mid-ocean waves mounting and disappearing into deep troughs.

Ginon 22's stomach lurched, this time from the queasy rolling of the ship's deck. They could not see the horizon in the darkness, which compounded the effect. It was cold.

The captain of *The Acolyte* was bearded and wore waterproofed coveralls with an insignia of rank on the shoulder, but his eyes were drugged, sheep-like, nestled in deep sockets in his pattern-painted face. His demeanor lacked the in-command air of a seasoned skipper. His snake familiar was fat and copper-colored.

"Welcome to *The Acolyte*," the captain beamed, oozing friendliness. "I'm Captain Patrick 14."

Cornish Bob took in the surroundings with a glance, and tossed the armload of pants in a corner of the cabin. "To answer your previous question, and continue your training so that you will eventually be useful to the team," Cornish Bob said to Ginon 22, pointedly ignoring the captain's greeting, "the Sea Tribes, who formally named themselves 'The Confederated Sea Tribes of Pacifica,' or 'Atlantica,' or whatever feck'n waters they choose to live in, are indeed vermin outlaws. They are nothing more than a loose group of societal castoffs and misfits that Eiffelia has no use for. They have chosen to refuse the authority of the rightful Queen of the Universe and live beyond her control and authority in the oceans. They artificially adopt the unstructured anarchical government of whatever historical tribal societies they choose to admire and emulate. They adorn their suits with tribal markings, like ridiculous poseurs.

"They are able to live underwater by use of artificial gill equipment. When found, they are exterminated. I am right shocked that there are any left at all. Those that exist do so at their peril, and only because Eiffelia the Queen of the Universe has not seen fit to expend the manpower and resources to eradicate them completely. They are like cockroaches, or rats, or other vermin. Hard to get them all. They hide underwater, where infrared cannot track them, and our projectile weapons are neutralized. The only way to get them, therefore, is at close quarters. Guns, if on a ship; knives and propelled spears if underwater.

"Ironically, it is their lack of cohesive organization that makes them difficult to eradicate. No central authority. This makes them vulnerable, though, when it comes to production of food, equipment, and raw materials. That is why they turn to pirating Eiffelia's ships. They need to know the routes and cargo carried, so are forced to bribe this information from the Un-numbered living in Eiffelia's floating cities. That is how we control them. That is how we know such a pirating party is headed here, and that is why we will kill them, me bey."

There, Cornish Bob thought, *as much for Captain Patrick, who will undoubtedly report directly to Eiffelia, as it was for the new recruit.*

Ginon 22 blinked. The captain glanced back and forth between them, a placid, happy expression on his face, like a puppy straining to please.

"Where is the rest uh me team, Cap'n Patrick?"

"I . . . ah, they are in the Captain's Mess," he answered as helpfully as he could convey.

"Take me there, yeh feck'n bus driver," Cornish Bob drawled.

The captain oozed out of the cabin before them, and led them across the slowly tilting decks to a door on the other side of the superstructure. On the way, Cornish Bob took stock of the vessel: midsized container ship, not overloaded, narrow spaces between the containers that might provide cover for advancing Tribe pirates. He quickly formulated his strategy.

Captain Patrick 14 opened the door to the Captain's Mess, and motioned them inside. Cornish Bob scanned the room, took a mental roll call. They were all present: Dog Face George; Dechambeau; Black Taylor; and Skunky, the former caveman.

"Ere, wos on there, me beys?" Cornish Bob nodded.

The team grunted and mumbled their greetings, awaiting orders, spider legs in their ears piping music or TV shows. They were dressed as crewmen in the shapeless, papery coveralls, but were armed with MP-5 submachine guns and stun grenades. They tossed Ginon 22 a shotgun.

"Set your familiar to channel seventeen," Black Taylor said.

Ginon 22 stuck one of his spider's legs in his ear. Cornish Bob seated the tip of his snake's tail in his, then produced a 1911 Colt from a shoulder holster under his denim jacket. He chambered a round, then returned the pistol to its place. "Here's 'ow we do this, me 'ansums."

–6–

It was mid-morning, and the seas had calmed. The captain and crew were safely barricaded in the forward hold, when Cornish Bob heard the shock wave reverberate through the ship. *The Acolyte* lost headway and coasted to a stop, powerless. One of the pirates had activated explosive charges under the ship that disabled the propellers.

Now it was just a matter of waiting in tense expectation for them to come over the sides and attack. They didn't have long to wait. A rapid double-burst of static in his snake tail earpiece signaled one of his men keying his spider-leg mic that he had had seen the enemy, but that they were too close to verbally report. He adjusted his black Stetson hat and peered out of the windows on the bridge at the containers below. He saw no signs of Sea Tribesmen, but knew that the reports would soon come.

"Three of them, from aft, coming to the superstructure between the red containers," Black Taylor whispered in his earpiece. "I can barely see 'em; it looks like they have active camouflage on their suits."

Cornish Bob's brow furrowed in surprised concern.

"Two more, from fore deck," Dechambeau said from his position on the bowsprit. "They appear to be just holding their location for cover. Good thing it's broad daylight or I would have missed them."

"You do the same, lad, stay out of sight and cover them," Cornish Bob instructed quietly into the mouth of his snake.

"Six more, from the port beam," Dog Face George reported.

"The three will probably go below, while the six will climb the superstructure and head here for the bridge," Cornish Bob said.

"I've got the three going below," Black Taylor said.

"I'll follow the six up, and Skunky 'n the new guy and I will catch them in a crossfire just before the bridge," George confirmed.

"That should do 'er," Bob said. "But keep a sharp eye, me beys, they have something we didn't expect with that active camouflage." He peered again out of the window, and this time could barely make out the two pirates between two containers near the bow. There were only faint, bleary shimmers against the background to betray their presence.

The Sea Tribe pirates must have been moving quickly. Skunky and Ginon 22 launched their ambush, with the staccato pops of the MP-5 interspersed with the roar of the twelve gauge. There were screams, shouts, and noises of metal striking metal. The hatch opened, and one of the Sea Tribe pirates stumbled through, just as Dog Face George opened fire on the pirates who'd retreated for cover.

The pirate slammed the hatch closed, and spun around with a drawn spear gun, only to stare into the barrel of Cornish Bob's .45. Bob blinked. It was a *woman.*

They froze, each with the other in their gun sights. In the long seconds that followed, they heard a stun grenade go off far below deck, probably Black Taylor disabling the three pirates who'd gone below. Bob dared not turn to see if Dechambeau had taken out the two pirates from the bowsprit, but was forced to assume that he had during the firefight at the bridge. Time seemed to have turned gelid. He smiled at her, since her spear was pointed unwaveringly at his center mass. He noted her eyes widen for the briefest of seconds, then she abruptly shifted her spear's aim to the middle of his neck.

Shit, he thought. A spear even through his heart would not have killed him, but a shot severing his brain from his spinal cord would. He broke out in a cold sweat, his stomach a knot of pain.

Cornish Bob studied his foe. She was tall, slender, and very pretty, with brown hair just below her shoulders, still slicked back and wet. She wore a skin-fitting suit of gray rubbery fabric, adorned with blue rings and spirals and a large skull and crossbones. A streamlined bundle on her back with a scooped opening must have been the artificial gills. The weapon she held appeared to be a spear gun, but with multiple spears that fed into the barrel. The handle of a long knife protruded from her calf, too.

"Well, what have we here, pirate or mermaid?" he finally asked. He watched her mind race.

"I have your captain under my control, stay in the stairwell," she called through the closed door.

Cornish Bob nodded, noticed the black tarry substance on the point of her spear. "Stay out there for a tick, lads," he called. *If that feck'n new bird blunders in here with his shotgun . . . .*

She regarded him with narrowed eyes, circling the perimeter of the room to keep from being attacked from both front and rear.

"You did not shoot me," she said, cocking her head.

Her observation conveyed more meaning than the obvious, Bob realized. He was no drugged sheep like the captain and crew, nor was he a military man, doped for aggression, or he would have fired the moment she came through the door. *Here is no simple-minded pirate. . . I wonder if she guesses who we really are? She did change her aim point from my chest to my neck—* "You obviously have more Tribals around in the water to recover cargo and watch for aircraft, but here you are, cut off from their help. My men have the ship. Why not just surrender?"

"And have your master execute me as an example? Burned at the stake, like we have seen you do to heretics like me on your television transmissions? Or would you drug me like her slack-jawed lackeys, an even worse fate?" She broke into a wolfish grin.

Yeh, she knows who we really are and yet she hasn't fired, either.

"You have no choice here, lass," Cornish Bob said soothingly.

"You are right," she said, still circling. "But *you* do. You don't have to serve her."

Cornish Bob raised an eyebrow, still keeping her in the

sights of his pistol. "You think I should hand in resignation papers? And then what, she just lets me go and I go jump in the water and live with the fishes?"

"Maybe not that simple," she said, lowering her spear gun by the slightest of margins. "But I am friends with . . . her enemies. Her *real* enemies, the *real* war she is fighting, not the sham war she is fighting with the demons or aliens or whoever she says."

Cornish Bob revealed his shock only by a slight widening of his eyes. *Holy shyte! She's one of them! I've got to take her alive!* "Well, well," he said, *his* mind racing. "At last I meet one of you. The Trident, the Swords of the Spirit, vanguard of the New Kingdom."

"So you know who I am, too," she said. "And the offer still stands. You don't have to keep doing this for her. All this killing, for a lie. This could be your opportunity, your bolt of light on the road to Damascus."

He paused, and actually considered it. He wondered what to say.

There was a slight noise from the hallway, and she glanced away for the barest second.

He fired.

The bullet ripped through the bicep of her left arm, shattering the bone, sending the spear gun spinning across the room. She sank to her knees, hissing, gripping the wound. As he circled, gun still leveled, she collapsed lower, eyes locking with his. As he cautiously approached, her brown eyes glazed over and she collapsed face down to the floor. He turned her over with the toe of his boot and jerked back a step as her knife clattered out of her hand. A long cut had appeared on her abdomen, through the suit.

He kicked the knife away, noting that there was more of the tarry substance on the blade. *Poison? That took some kind of guts. These people live up to their reputations.* He grabbed the head of his snake. "Get in here, Taylor, and check this fish."

The door burst open. Black Taylor and Skunky slunk stealthily in, MP-5s at the ready. Ginon 22 appeared more cautiously, shotgun at his shoulder.

Black Taylor placed his fingers at her throat, feeling for a carotid pulse. "She's gone," he announced.

Cornish Bob took stock of his men. Two of them had spears protruding from their chests. The wounds oozed thick black liquid. He winked at Ginon 22, the new recruit.

"Now you see why it is worth it to undergo the death and reanimation process. Short of a shot to the top of the spinal cord that severs the brain's connection to the central nervous system, we don't go down. Even the poison has no effect, since we have very little circulation or need for oxygen."

Dechambeau and Dog Face George yanked the spears out of their chests unceremoniously and tossed them aside.

"Get on the military frequency," Cornish Bob ordered, "and tell them to send in the air cover. But be careful, they probably have rockets. Tell 'em to come in low and hot, and set the fuses on the bombs to go off ten feet below the surface."

We're not out o' the woods yet, he thought. *And after this, we fossick on back to the past in the other universe to kill those other poor bastards my great-grandson wrote about on that web page, then try to recruit or kill him, too.* He sighed. "A Cousin Jack's work is never done."

–7–

What a day, Langston LaGrue thought. *I'm going through the rift!*

Because they were going through the rift, their knowledge was going to be expanded by vast leaps after the years of waiting, viewing that damned alien landscape through high-powered optics and finicky, unreliable robotic probes, scanning every wavelength of radiant energy through that damned hole for any shred of data about what was going on over there. In days past, every shred of mysterious data would have infuriated him, he would have been sure they were secret messages from the cosmos. Until that morning, he was considered unqualified to actually make the crossing because of his reliance on his Paxil, without which he would resort back to his Obsessive Compulsive Disorder-induced hell. He shuddered to remember those days.

He glanced at Tracey. They were walking along sublevel three from the classrooms and living quarters, toward the more secure areas and the trip down. The woman, Tracey Springs, had been confirmed as a recessive carrier of the Pangborn Gene, as were her daughter Chris, and son, Jeremy.

Ron himself, wonderful luck, had been confirmed as a rare full gene carrier through the DNA testing. Full carriers were absolutely necessary to venture through the rift; they were the only ones who could distinguish between the old space-time reality and any changes in the new universe that were undetectable to normal people.

Those with the single Pangborn recessive genes, however, were also valuable for their ability to experience prescient dreams. Their experience of alternate universes was beyond time, but limited to the subconscious. Tracey had been able to make a direct hit with her dream of the rift, and could prove more valuable by going with the team than by staying behind, like the daughter. The study of the interplay between consciousness and reality through collapsing the wave function through observation was proving difficult, but the payoff could eventually prove even bigger than a working interstellar drive.

If only I could convince them to fund that research more. Well, I can do what I can in the meantime.

"So tell me more about the dream you had this morning, Ms. Springs," he asked. "First of all, do you often remember dreams?"

"Often," she answered distractedly.

"And what else did you see in your dream about the sand dunes?"

They stopped in front of large, steel security doors. Clay placed his hand on a glass plate on a pedestal and spoke his name clearly into a camera. The doors swung open to reveal a long hallway and a bank of elevators with larger than normal doors. The woman agent accompanying the party pressed the call button.

"I saw . . . well, the sky was yellowish, and there was a smell of perfume or incense around."

"I never heard any reports from Jack Strong or his party about any smells," Clay said in an aside to Professor LaGrue.

"Who's Jack Strong?" Ron asked.

The elevator arrived, and the group, consisting of Ron, Tracey, Chris, Clay, the professor, and the woman agent, got on board the cavernous car. They started to descend after a low-pitched groan.

"Abandon hope, all ye who enter here," Chris muttered.

"I don't believe in the Devil," Tracey whispered.

"The embodiment of evil exists," Ron whispered in retort. "Just look at our Professor Pee Wee."

Tracey fought back laughter.

"Jack Strong was the last double recessive we had who could enter the rift and at least have a good chance at getting a party back here," Professor LaGrue answered. "I say a good chance, because after five or six trips in a few years ago, he and the whole party wandered off into the desert and never came back. That is one of the mission objectives we have for your team, Ron, to find out what happened to them."

"Okay," Ron said, "there you go again, mentioning a team and a mission. Please tell me what you have in mind here, and why me. Us. Whoever."

LaGrue glanced at Clay, not sure how much he could divulge.

Clay shrugged, nodded, and held his hand toward Ron, giving permission.

"Well, this is not the first rift between our space-time and some other . . . space, time, or universe. They happen all the time, not all of them artificially like the one here caused by the ship. They often just happen naturally. Maybe through the interaction between consciousness and the wave function. We're not sure how many there are, if any at all. Maybe with some more funding . . . ." he said pointedly at Clay. "They come, they go, some are large, most are tiny, smaller than quantum particles. Some last a long time, most pop in and out of existence in fractions of a second on the Planck time scale right out of the quantum foam. If they get big enough, they get more stable. They have weird effects.

"Most people have a certain physical revulsion to the rift border, but we noticed that one of our recruits didn't. That was Jack Strong. We did some testing. We had to do a good deal of it, much to Strong's misery and discomfort. What we found was that he, and only he, had a gene that countered this effect, discovered by one of our researchers named Pangborn. We had no idea at the time why it was there, why it evolved."

"Or *if* it evolved," Clay added.

"You see," LaGrue said, "if someone without that gene crosses through a rift, they are eventually unable to distinguish whether what they encounter on the other side is unique to that universe, or existed all along in this one. There are some very, very weird effects that take place near the border of the rift, and things only tend to solidify once you get far enough from it."

LaGrue noted that Ron, Tracey, and Chris were baffled. "Perhaps an example would clarify things. The last team we sent in with Strong became convinced that the communications specialist on that team had died and did not exist. She was there, obvious to Jack Strong, but all the other team members had no conception who she was at all. Thought she was someone else they had just met. And even weirder, *she* started to think she was a new person, too. And the other team members were sort of a combination of themselves and whoever their counterparts were in that world. They knew some things about here, and somehow knew things about that world, too.

"They described it as being two people at once, with the one from that universe getting stronger and stronger as time went by, to the point that the person from here felt like a fly trapped in a web, powerless to act, but observing everything. Without Strong being there, the results could have been disastrous. The interplay between consciousness and the material world likely takes place beyond time and space, using the brain as a hardware receiver. But without more research . . . ."

"Enough, Doctor," Clay grunted. "Mr. Golden wants hard science, not woo-woo."

LaGrue was about to retort that this *was* hard science, but it occurred to him that perhaps he *should* shut up about it, lest they construe his interest in the matter a manifestation of his former illness.

The elevator doors opened, and LaGrue noted the intake of breath from the visitors as they took in the size of the cavern that now made up sublevel four.

"Here we do material testing of parts of the ship," LaGrue explained.

They walked between rows and rows of worktables, technicians in lab jackets working on unidentifiable machinery and electronics. LaGrue was glad that Ron, Tracey, and Chris were not looking too closely or asking too many questions. The next series of sub-levels, where the biological testing and more interesting technological research was taking place, more or less lined up so they could take the elevator past them without stopping. Even this work, mused LaGrue, glancing around, was endlessly fascinating. The hull of the ship, for instance, was made of some kind of organic calcium-based substance, not an exotic metallic alloy as originally thought.

What would his colleagues in the academic world think if they had the opportunity to be doing this work? He used to envy them, their ability to work openly, to publish, be recognized. Long ago, he had lost his job at a major research facility at a leading university due to his former condition, but was then approached by a shadowy figure named Mr. Barman, who represented a multinational partnership called The Mods. He was offered the chance of doing real, cutting-edge work for them under the guise of the Space Command. For many years, he regretted losing his chance to work in public, always laboring in secret, always a few months or years behind his colleagues, unable to take advantage of the collaborative cooperation that academics enjoyed. In the early '90s, he had ventured out to the campuses, posing as a corporate think tank researcher, to try to establish such ties with other scientific minds. He found, instead, that there was as much an atmosphere of competition and secrecy there as there was between governments. And now, since the rift opened up in '93, there was nowhere else on Earth he would rather be. Except actually going into the rift. *Which is happening*, he reveled. *They must have realized I can take enough medications with me that I won't run out.*

His condition had started in his early twenties, while riding a bus to a college Mechanical Engineering class. It was a stressful time. On one foggy day, the bus startled a bird from a metal railing on the side of the road, and it flew alongside with the bus just feet from his window. It was flying flat out, but kept pace with the bus for several seconds. Their eyes locked, his wide and blue and the bird's small and black. With a flash of white under-wing, the bird veered away, and LaGrue turned his head to follow it. The bird plunged earthward, wings held tightly to its body, then at the last moment flared its wings and expertly glided between two trees.

LaGrue was profoundly affected. The beauty, grace, and technical flight ability that the bird exhibited was exquisite. He thought about it all the way to class, marveling at what the bird had done. Once at the Mechanical Engineering class, he decided to make a model of the bird as his class project. Surely building an ornithopter would not be too difficult. It proved more difficult than he thought. Making a small, bird-sized flying model was possible for self-powered flight for a short time, but it could not be directed. Making it remote-controlled was possible, but not one that could self-direct like the bird. And even the radio-controlled flight models LaGrue found could only be directed in clunky, ugly movements, nowhere near the nimble grace and elegance that an actual bird achieved effortlessly. He tried to simulate the calculations it would take to control the flight: The angle and articulation of the wings and tail, morphing the body shape, sensing the air speed and changes in wind direction, angular momentum, actuating the feathers, and a host of other variables, and was baffled. The number of calculations required was staggering. *How can so much computing power be contained in a brain the size of a lima bean?* It would take a quantum computer, he realized.

He failed to build the bird, and thus failed the class, his only bad grade ever. LaGrue could have shrugged, moved on, giving the mystery of nature its due, but could not. He worked, worked, and obsessed about the matter, sure that he could eventually solve it.

Months later, he was again on the bus, heading toward his first job, another stressful time. He rode with his eyes closed, hoping that he would avoid seeing another bird. The sunlight, as the bus moved along, was interrupted by trees, bridge pylons, and buildings. The flashes seen through his closed eyelids, it seemed to him, were a pattern. At first he ignored it, but over time, he became convinced that they were signals, a secret communication from the universe, meant to help him understand the mysteries of bird flight. He learned Morse code, and daily recorded the letters that the light flashes imparted. They made no sense, but he realized it must be a deeper code. He spent more and more time trying to decode the signals, and had to keep his obsession secret. The more he decoded, the deeper the levels of complexity emerged, until he could no longer keep up his work at his job. If only he had a guide, a universal conscious being who could help him decipher the mysterious messages! But that was impossible superstition. But perhaps it wasn't. He began praying to universal spirits for guidance. After months of nothing, he willed himself to stay awake, night after night for over a week, sifting meaning from every occurrence as though it were an omen from the beyond. The nebulous webs of interconnected meaning always drifted two thoughts away from his grasp.

After the inevitable crash and the diagnosis of Obsessive Compulsive Disorder, he took time to recover through Behavior Therapy and his medication. Over the years, he rose in seeming normalcy to his current position. The medication dulled him, however, and he worried both that his former brilliance was no longer there, and that if it returned it would be at the cost of his sanity.

They reached the security checkpoint for the lower levels. Uniformed guards oversaw the fingerprint, retina-print, and voice-print checks for Agent Clay and Professor LaGrue. The woman agent, apparently with insufficient clearance, waited behind while they passed through what looked like a bank vault door. Once on the other side, men and women assistants divided them, and led them into men's and women's locker rooms prior to entering the first of the clean rooms. Each of them was required to remove their clothes, shower with chemicals, submit to an electrostatic field bath, then dress in coveralls.

"It's a lot more thorough on the way back out," LaGrue told Ron.

Two decontamination procedures in two successive clean rooms later, the men and women reunited and loaded into another cavernous elevator car. LaGrue felt the eyes on him while he pressed the button for Sublevel Nine, bypassing the other four levels.

"This will take a while to get down," he informed them. "The rift is pretty deep, and moving deeper at the rate of about two feet a year."

"It moves?" Ron asked.

"Yes, our universe and whatever space-time it is

connected to through the rift are pretty stable in relation to each other, but there is some relative momentum. Or it may be just amplified jitters at the quantum level."

"So what happens when it gets deep enough to go right through the crust and hits molten rock?" Chris asked.

"We don't know," Professor LaGrue answered with a sideways glance. "It may ooze into the other side and cool, making a plug, or it may deplete the entire inside of the Earth's molten core and destabilize the planet and knock us off orbit or cause catastrophic seismic events. We hope to close it by then, just to be safe."

"Gee, I hope so, too," Chris said.

"So which level do you do the experiments on the alien life?" Tracey asked out of the blue.

"What makes you think that there are any alien life forms to do experiments on?" LaGrue asked, shocked.

"I saw what looked like flying pickles in my dream, and figured maybe those were real, too."

There was a long pause. Ron and Chris glanced at her, eyebrows raised.

"That is exactly what we call them," Professor LaGrue said. "Flying pickles. It sounded better than flying turds, anyway. We have no idea how they fly, they have no wings or any internal organs filled with lighter-than-air gas. We don't know whether they have any awareness or intelligence, how they eat, how they reproduce, or anything else about them. They just fly around, seemingly randomly. They are most . . . mysterious. We still can't figure out how birds fly, much less them," he said, and broke into a sweat. "As you can imagine," he continued, wiping his brow, "we are taking some rather stringent precautions to keep them from getting out topside."

LaGrue remembered back to when they first discovered the nature of the rift, and tunneled down to it, and one of the flying pickles had almost escaped into Colorado. He mopped sweat anew.

"They got aliens in there?" Chris whispered to her mother.

"Pickles. Hairy ones. That fly," Tracey whispered back.

"I *knew* it. Government cover up."

The elevator ground to a halt. LaGrue always loved this

part, when the doors opened and revealed the rift, especially the effect it had on those seeing it for the first time.

The rift looked like shimmering yellow film on the floor of the rock-hewn chamber, about twenty feet across. The surface undulated slightly, as though it were a pool of water. Warmth radiated out of it, and there were many cameras, parabolic dishes, antennae, and other detection equipment bristling from the ceiling over it. Several lab-coated technicians were hunched over panels and screens nearby, monitoring the detectors.

They walked to the edge, feeling gritty sand underfoot that had blown through the rift and looked . . . down? In? The level of the horizon didn't match up. They were looking *down* into the bottom of the floor, but once looking through the rift they were looking *across* the surface of the dunes. The horizon was at a 90 degree angle to what seemed up and down inside the chamber.

Professor LaGrue felt the familiar throbbing, buzz-like sensation in his head and felt his intestines grip in the familiar, visceral, nauseous feeling.

"I'm gonna be sick," Chris moaned, then retreated to a corner.

"I don't feel anything. Are you guys feeling something?" Ron asked.

"Yes, we get some symptoms of nausea and disorientation, but you full Pangborn gene carriers don't get that. I hear it goes away for us once you cross the barrier and move into the other terrain a bit."

"You've never been in there?" Ron asked.

"No; without a full carrier like you we can't go in there; we have not been able to locate another Full, until you, since Jack Strong went missing. We have thrown several probes and roving robots in, though."

"Are my genes that rare?"

"We think it is about twice as rare as Albinism. That mutation is carried by about one person in a thousand. The chances of two people both carrying that gene is probably one in a million. If they produce a baby, then the chances of that baby being a double recessive is about one in four million.

So, in probably the whole Northwestern U.S., there may be one or two people with the full gene. Add to that the fact that there is no way to tell short of a DNA test whether you have it, and it makes finding one of you pretty tough. It's tough enough to find albinos, and they are pretty obvious. The odds of you meeting and starting a relationship with Tracey, who is a single recessive, are pretty long, too. I'm starting to think there is some kind of mechanism at work here."

"We're not making any babies, for the record," Tracey observed.

They all stared down into the rift, past the undulating, shimmering surface, and across the dunes. The yellowish sun was beginning to sink behind the dunes.

Ron pointed to a rounded, massive metallic wall nearby. "Is that the ship?"

"Yes," LaGrue answered. "Did you see anything about that in your dream?" he asked Tracey.

She stood looking at it a moment, then answered quietly, "Yes, I saw it begin to fall from the sky, then I saw a knife in my hand, and felt something in my stomach ripping. And a voice said a line from the 'Battle Hymn of the Republic.' And whoever that woman in the tent was, she better keep her hands off Ron."

LaGrue mulled that over. She must have been talking about Valentina Pavlov, the communications specialist. She had been chosen not just for her knowledge of communications equipment, but for her sex appeal. She might have to use her looks to gain an advantage over any local humans who might live in the alternate universe. That was the excuse, anyway, of having her along. She had been very persuasive on that front. Hearing that there may be a connection to Ron, even in a dream, filled him with a pang of dread, for LaGrue lusted after her from afar himself. But such a woman would never have interest in him, despite his superior intelligence. Because that was how it worked. *In this universe, anyway.*

A translucent green animal with undulating cilia floated out of the rift and into the room.

"Oh, look, is that one of the flying pickles?" Chris asked.

"Yes. They drift in and out of the rift, occasionally. We make sure they don't get any farther than this room."

They watched in fascination as it drifted around, then their attention was drawn back to the surface of the rift, impossible to ignore. LaGrue noted just how quickly people could get used to seeing an alien creature for the first time when all it does is float around without interaction, like an airborne aquarium fish.

"So how do you get in there?" Ron asked. "Do you just sort of jump in and end up lying on your back on the other side?"

"That's pretty much it. It looks kind of weird when you see it done. And to get back, you have to lay down on your stomach then kind of slide your way through the surface, and someone on this side has to grab you and pull you up."

He noticed Ron staring intently at the flying pickle. The animal hovered in front of Ron for a moment, then flew back through the rift. Ron slowly moved closer to the edge, peering in. It dawned on him that Ron intended to jump in. Before he could say anything, Ron gathered himself and leaped over the edge.

–8–

Adrian Smithson exercised his God-given talent of blending into the surroundings when Professor LaGrue, Ron, and two strangers, who he guessed were Tracey and her daughter, Chris, entered the rift room. The lab coat was all the three strangers needed to glance at to assume he was just another technician, in spite of his bald head. He busied himself staring at a monitoring screen near the rift.

The flying pickle floated lazily around the room, and he pointedly ignored it, even though it was talking in his head.

<Are these the three new people you told me about?> the flying pickle thought to him.

<Yes. The man is the carrier, and the woman and her daughter are partial carriers. The Horribles are trying to kill them,>" Smithson thought back. He sensed the flying pickle reach out along the universe lines, probing.

<The woman has managed to put herself in position to protect him, but unlike her counterpart in the Sea Tribes, has not managed to undergo the training. She has a long path before her before she is ready to assume the mantle in the Trident here. You will have to pair with him until she is ready.>

Smithson nodded.

<Watch her, too,> the flying pickle continued, *<and try to get her to start down the path of her training. She's one of those 'science should replace religion' people now.>*

Smithson nodded. This would be a challenge.

Flying pickles were helpful to his work; they were unseen observers, life forms that could serve as sensory platforms for consciousnesses far away in space or time.

<Oh, interesting. There is another mind channeling this body. It is Tracey, with Andrew Morrow, from Otherwhen! I'll

have to meet you later.>

Smithson felt the presence in his mind leave, as the flying pickle was occupied by another consciousness. He saw Ron look directly at the flying pickle, then follow it toward the rift.

*****

"You," Tracey informed Ron, eyes narrowed and each syllable punctuated by a point of her finger, "are a *moron.*"

They sat in Tracey's room, three hours after Ron had attempted his jump. While at the apex of his leap, a hand had gripped Ron's upper arm like a vice-grip and returned him to the floor. It had been one of the technicians sitting at a console, who had moved quicker than any human being had a right to. The strength required to do that did not match up with his size, which was only average.

He was not a technician.

LaGrue had introduced him as Adrian Smithson, Security Specialist for the team, after Tracey's heart had stopped trying to bash its way out of her rib cage. It was only then that Ron had recognized him as the gray-jacketed bald man who'd visited him at his home.

"I'm sorry," Ron said, rubbing his face in his hands while Tracey paced the room in front of him.

"Why did you do that?"

Ron smiled sheepishly. "You wouldn't believe me if I told you."

"After all we've seen lately? Really? Why don't you try me."

"It talked to me."

"What talked to you?"

"The flying green pickle thing."

She stared at him amazed. "Oh. Okay. What did it say?"

"You didn't hear it?"

"No, Ron. I didn't hear it."

He rubbed his chin. "It said, 'Jump in the rift, Ron.'"

"Jump in the rift, Ron? Really?"

"And there's more. It was a voice in my head, and it sounded like *you.*"

"So the flying pickle said 'Jump in the rift, Ron,' to you in my voice, and you just had to try to jump though some kind of wormhole? Into another universe? It doesn't make sense."

"None of this does," he muttered.

"Ah ha! We come to the essence of the matter. A few days ago, our biggest concerns were your job, and getting on after Pop. Then, we had to worry about what the results of your medical tests were. Now they want you to be on some team to go into another universe and find spaceship engines and missing agents, or something. And keep the war paint dudes from killing people, however that fits in. If this were the movies, or one of your damn video games, we'd just by God go along with all this and off we'd go into some kind of fool adventure without a second thought. But *God-freaking-damn it,* Ron!"

He sat, rubbing his face, regarding her through his fingers. She looked angry.

"This isn't how you behave, Ron."

"That's just it. I'm tired of how I behave. I have done nothing exciting in my whole life. Just drift around in the wind, like your sailboat metaphor. This is the kind of thing I used to sit around daydreaming about, or use as the plot of a video game. I mean, why not? What would you rather do, just go back and . . . and . . . read the paper while fixing dinner, and watch TV? Maybe rent a movie, and then fill up the tank and go to the office the next morning? Repeat again the next day? What is the point of that?"

"The point of that? That is *life,* mister. Life isn't a video game, or some kind of fantasy. You take out the trash, you shower and you brush your teeth, and do your laundry. You work your job, buy stuff, and save for retirement. Once you find a job again, that is. Once you decide what you want to look for."

"You had to bring that up."

"I like my life. Or what it used to be, anyway. We were doing great things at the aquarium. The Giant Octopus project was just getting off the ground with the Japanese. One child was in school, the other in boot camp, ex-husband no longer sniffing around. Without people in make-up or wormholes or flying alien pickles."

"We can't do that now, not until the Clowns of Death are dealt with."

"Says who? These government types? They have yet to tell us what is really going on here, Ron. We are *definitely* getting the watered-down version of the story here. They may be the war-paint guys themselves. Maybe *they* are the ones who want to figure out a way to go back in time and kill those double recessives. And you too, for all we know. And you know what? I don't think they are with the government anyway. Too many people with too much money and the government sucks at keeping secrets."

"That may be, but what are we supposed to do?"

"And what if you *are* really sick? You think you are in any condition to go gallivanting around in another universe? Do you think they would take you if they knew you had . . . some kind of disease?"

It occurred to Ron that she was thinking the worst, too. *Not arthritis. The C word.*

Tracey resumed pacing. "I can ask to go home, but they probably won't let us. I can just go on strike and refuse to go along with all this, but that will hardly accomplish anything. They will probably just keep me here for my own 'safety,' and I'll never be heard from again, except on a milk carton, until someone else resolves things."

"We can just go along for the ride and get to the bottom of all this and fix it as best we can," he suggested. "I'm not sure we have as much of a choice here, though."

"That is just it. What choice is there?" She slowed her pacing, then stopped. Her face started contorting, and she burst into quiet sobs.

Ron leaped to his feet and embraced her, felt her shoulders convulsing as she buried her face in his shoulder. "It will be all right," he tried to reassure her.

She cried and cried, and Ron wondered whether to sit her down, and what to say.

There was a knock at the door. Ron wondered briefly whether he should ignore it or sit Tracey on the bed and answer it, but she gathered herself immediately, wiped her eyes with her arm and opened the door. It was Clay.

"Good timing, Agent Clay," she said. "I see you are watching your monitors and picked the exactly correct moment to make an appearance."

Clay was taken aback. "We have no cameras in your rooms, I assure you."

She turned stiffly into the room, and Clay followed in her wake.

"We were just discussing . . . all this," Ron said.

"I'm sure you are still quite confused about this whole situation, and that is why I'm here. I want to answer all your questions. Fully, honestly, no bull. You need to make some informed decisions."

Tracey narrowed her eyes, nodded. "Okay, first of all, who are you guys *really*? And don't give me that Space Command crap."

Clay grinned sheepishly. "No, we really are Space Command. Or were, anyway. We have evolved. The operation is jointly directed by a group called The Mods. Don't bother looking for them on the New York Stock Exchange, they are private. The partner I deal with is named Mr. Barman."

"Mods? You mean like they are groovy? Or do you mean 'Moderators'? Or maybe they make 'Modifications' to the program? " Ron asked.

Clay shrugged. "Maybe all three. Just a name we came up with for them."

"They aren't from around here, are they?" Tracey asked.
"No."

Ron looked back and forth between them. "You mean from some other planet?"

"Perhaps some other universe. They showed up right after the rift happened. They approached us in the Space Command after determining it was our area of concern, and told us that it wasn't an attack directed at us. They told us to just ignore it, but how could we do that? I pulled strings to tap into the ocean of military black-ops funding, and built this base. There were some reports made up to send through the Congressional oversight chains through the Joint Chiefs, but nothing very specific and after some of the Congressmen went home for good, the oversight lapsed. And with no whiz-bang military tech coming, and no requests for additional funding like they are used to, the Pentagon lost track, too.

We didn't tell them it was a rift into another universe, just another UFO crash. So this whole operation is just my little kingdom.

"*Another* UFO crash? Roswell. I knew it," Ron said.

"So why keep it secret?" Tracey asked.

"For all the obvious reasons."

"No, they aren't obvious. Enlighten me."

Clay shrugged. "Well, we have this rift in the middle of our continent. Whether the public is ready for this kind of sea change is debatable. I'm not usually one to play patriarch, but if I ask higher-ups for guidance, the decision is already made. If our government knew about it, and made it known, what would the Chinese, Russians, and for that matter the British, Japanese, and hell, even the Canadians do? They would all demand access, a cut of the materials, and we would have another arms race and cold war. Maybe even a hot one."

Tracey nodded sideways. "So what's the deal with the guys in face paint with spiders and snakes? We heard all about the wormhole into another universe—are they from there? And why are they trying to kill us, and why the makeup?"

Clay nodded. "Yes, they come from the other universe and we know they are tracking down Pangborn carriers like you. They have the ability to travel back and forth between their space-time and ours at will, instead of relying on a fixed rift like we have to. They may have the benefit of going to the future to find news reports of murders of Pangborn carriers, *by men in war paint*, then go back in time and actually carry out those murders. Mr. Barman has only told us so much, but his people seem to be at war with the war-paint people in some fashion, and our Pangborn carriers have the ability somehow to change things for both sides. I do know that our guys don't want them dead, but theirs do; so once we find them we try to protect them."

"But if we wanted to take our chances and go back to our lives, you would let us?" Tracey asked.

Clay hung his head, lips pursed, mulling that over. "I can't keep any of you against your will. If you really want to go, knowing all the risks, knowing that you would be choosing to do humanity a big disservice, knowing the warpaint guys could kill you at any time and we would be hard-pressed to do anything about it, you could still of course go."

"I want to go home," Tracey said simply.

Clay let out a long sigh, nodding slightly. "You can leave whenever you like. I only ask that you keep this facility a secret."

"Of course. Who would believe me anyway? You will probably be staying, right, Ron?"

"Of course not," he said, surprising both Tracey and Clay.

"I'm not going to leave you alone to fight off face-painted murderers by yourself. And you better not let Chris go on any missions without me, either."

"We weren't planning on sending Chris into the rift anyway. We want to take her and Jeremy to a safe house we have on an island in the Caribbean, where the only access is by air and boat, all controlled by us."

"If they'll be safe there for a while, let's do that," Ron said. "And if a few months go by and I'm sure that Tracey is not in any danger, we'll talk again about me coming on this mission-thing by myself."

Clay held out his hand, and they shook it in turn.

"Just out of curiosity," Ron asked, "who *would* have been going on this mission?"

"Well, there was me, you, and Tracey; she would have been along for her dreams. Then Langston LaGrue, and one person you didn't meet, our communications specialist, Valentina Pavlov. Oh, and one you met at your house and again when he grabbed you by the arm—our security specialist, Adrian Smithson."

"It's probably a good thing I won't be going anyway; I think I am sick. Maybe even very sick. Did you find anything when you did all those medical tests?"

"No, but we weren't looking for that. What's going on?"

Ron told him about the tests, and the results that were probably waiting for them back in Seattle.

Clay looked at the floor thoughtfully, nodding slightly.

"So when can we leave and go home and find out about

his tests?" Tracey asked, seizing the opportunity of bridging the subject.

"I can have you both on a plane to Seattle within an hour," Clay said quietly. "I just want to make sure you have the best chance of survival as possible. Whether you are sick or not, you may not last long at all if the Paints are after you. I need to tell you both some more about your genes."

They sat down, Tracey barely containing her satisfaction, Ron his disappointment.

"They already identified you, so they may not come with striped faces this time. But they may. They may not even come after you. But they probably will."

"I don't want a bunch of disguised agents hanging around trying to protect us," Tracey said.

Clay rolled his eyes. "Fine. Your decision. But please listen. Tracey, you are a single recessive, so you have lots of dreams. LaGrue is convinced that there is some connection between your gene and how consciousness collapses the wave function beyond time. Us folk with normal genes have to do it inside time. Or something like that. He's trying to get funding to research all that but the Mods have no interest in doing that because they already know how it works.

"I'm not sure I can explain this right, but apparently the gene isn't like regular DNA coding that is inheritable through genetics; it rides along on RNA and is, how to put this? Sort of implanted when one universe calves off from another. It is either a 'hard implant' like Ron's, or a 'soft implant' like yours, and they both work differently. Full carriers like Ron act like the shared boundaries between universes. Think of two soap bubbles that stick together. We are all like little molecules on the surface of one of the bubbles, but have counterparts on the other bubble. Ron is part of the membrane that is shared by both bubbles, so there is only one of him. The single recessives are close, and because the membranes are made of consciousness, they can dream into both spheres."

Ron and Tracey observed him mutely, struggling to keep up.

"So my dreams actually do have some kind of connection

to reality beyond chance neuronal firings," Tracey concluded.

"Told you so," Ron whispered.

"Not only a connection, but to hear the Mods talk, they use the same process to do more than just observe."

"Like what?" Tracey asked.

Clay exhaled sharply and furrowed his brows. "I'm not sure, it was just overhearing them talk to each other. They can be squirrelly when you ask them this stuff directly. I get the impression they can actively dream stuff into and out of existence. Like having the cheat codes for reality."

"There it is again, cheat codes!" Ron exploded.

"Well, don't worry, my dreaming isn't *quite* there yet," Tracey joked.

"Hey, don't sell yourself short," Clay said. "That one dream you had was really accurate, and will likely help us for some time to come. We have researchers looking up the 'Battle Hymn of the Republic' for any clues there. And you will probably have more dreams, and you should do your best to remember and listen to them. Feel free to call me with anything if it remotely deals with us. But remember, like Freud said, sometimes when you dream of a cigar, it means just that: a cigar."

"And a flying pickle is just a flying pickle."

Clay blew out a long breath, then slapped his thighs and stood up. "Okay, then. I'll walk you up and see that you get on the plane, and please remember that you can call for help at any time. Don't hesitate to use this," he said, handing them a card. Tracey glanced at it, saw it simply had a telephone number on it.

—9—

Thirty minutes later, they stood in the Space Command hallway, dressed in the same clothes they'd been wearing when they arrived: Ron feeling silly in his bathrobe and Tracey in her suit with the aquarium name tag. They carried nothing but the card that Clay had given them.

They said their goodbyes to Chris, who looked forward to traveling to the Caribbean island resort. Ten minutes later, Ron and Tracey were winging their way back to Seattle in the unmarked white plane. Tracey wondered what the catch was. It was all too easy.

They started their descent toward a vast, level expanse of cloud punctuated by a few tall peaks that were Mount Rainier, Mount Adams to the north, and Mount St. Helens and Mount Hood to the south. Ron reminded himself that once they were below the clouds and in the seemingly perpetual gloom of the northwest, only a few thousand feet up the sun was always dazzling above the clouds.

They flew closer and closer to the cloud layer.

"It always looks like a landscape," Ron said.

"Not the real world, that is a layer underneath," Tracey answered.

They passed through the opaque clouds, punched through the bottom, and found themselves in the familiar drizzly overcast. They landed at SeaTac, left the runway, and entered a nondescript hanger near the cargo carriers. A taxicab was waiting for them, driven, Tracey had no doubt, by an agent.

Ron started to give the driver his address, but the driver apparently already knew it. Then he recognized him as Agent Johnson. "Hey, Johnson!" Ron greeted.

Johnson smiled back from behind his sunglasses.

"You are *not* hanging around to protect us," Tracey demanded.

"No, ma'am. Strict orders for hands off."

He drove them north on Interstate 5, through North Seattle, to Ron's little house, and coasted to a stop out front. Ron and Tracey looked around the neighborhood nervously.

"*Damn* it!" Ron cried.

The agent crouched in his seat, pulled his pistol halfway out of the holster.

"Look at all the little piles of poop from that damn dachshund!"

Tracey groaned.

"You want me to at least go in with you and check out the house?" Johnson asked.

Tracey relented, and they walked to the front door, trying to peer through the blinds. The door was unlocked.

"It may have been that I forgot to lock it, with all the helicopter flying," Ron reasoned after they glanced at each other.

"Stay here for a minute, and be very quiet," Johnson ordered, and produced his pistol. He went catlike through the door, closing it behind him. Tracey and Ron waited. Ron nonchalantly looked around the neighborhood, and noticed at least one house where someone was peeking through the blinds to see what was going on.

"Come on in," Johnson called. He was just putting away his weapon. "Did a quick sweep, nobody at home. Do you notice anything missing or out of place?"

Ron did a cursory walk through. It didn't *exactly* look as though anything had been touched, and nothing was immediately noticeable as missing.

"It looks . . . just not right somehow. I can't put my finger on it."

"Well, maybe someone has been through here. They are gone now, though. Do you want me to hang around for a while?" Johnson asked.

"We'll be fine," Tracey answered quickly.

"It could have been the landlord, looking to see if I was dead from choking on a sandwich since I didn't pay the rent," Ron postulated.

"We took care of that," Agent Johnson said.

"Oh! Uh, thanks."

Agent Johnson left with a long glance over his shoulder and a reminder to call if they needed anything.

Tracey and Ron were left standing alone in his living room.

"Been a long four days, hasn't it?" he asked.

They fought off a feeling of impending threat for the next hour. When Ron checked the answering machine, the sense of dread deepened: The little LED light was blinking madly. There were several messages from the doctor who had administered the tests.

"He didn't say what the results were," Ron worried.

"Probably nothing. He could have been calling to tell you they were negative," Tracey reassured him.

"No, if they were negative, he would have said so on the message. It is probably positive for something. And we can't call him back to ask today. It's Sunday."

Tracey mulled this over silently. They went to the grocery store to re-stock what had spoiled in the refrigerator. They ate roasted chicken for dinner, waiting for men with painted faces and dinner-plate-sized spiders on their shoulders. None came.

That night Chris called, and told them that she and her brother Jeremy had been flown to the island in the Caribbean. "It is kind of like a resort. The food is much better, and they said I can hang out on the beach. There are some other people staying here, too. They say that they are also single Pangborn recessives. I wonder if there is some other reason they want to keep us here. Is this a big Government Breeding Program?"

"They are just keeping you safe," Ron said. "They said the gene doesn't work that way."

"Yeah, tell that to Jeremy before he gets someone pregnant. I think he's using that as a line to get laid."

*****

The next morning, Ron and Tracey stared at each other over the telephone. He picked up the handset and dialed the doctor's office.

"Dr. Chiang is not in at the moment. May I take a

message for him?" the pleasant receptionist asked.

"Yes, this is Ron Golden returning his call. I believe he has some test results."

There was a barely noticeable pause. "Yes, Mr. Golden. The doctor wanted to speak with you personally. I'll have him call you as soon as he returns."

"Thank you," Ron said. A void appeared in the pit of his stomach.

Ron and Tracey continued staring at each other.

"You don't know anything yet," she said, again trying to calm him.

Ron was convinced that he did.

A short time later the phone rang, with Dr. Chiang on the line. "Yes, Ron, your test results came in. I would like you to come in and talk about them."

"So what is it?" Ron asked flatly.

"I really think you need to come here and discuss it. Right away."

Ron agreed to come in that afternoon. He placed the receiver on the cradle gently. Tracy wrapped her arms around him.

That afternoon, Dr. Chiang breezed into the examination room with what could be mistaken for a cheerful mood. "The test came back positive for Chondrosarcoma, a kind of bone cancer that arises in the cartilage, Ron," he said carefully, "but it isn't a sure thing that you have it. The blood test we did measures an enzyme called alkaline phosphatase, but elevated levels of this can occur for other reasons. It is a very rare kind of cancer, too, so it may well be nothing serious. I want to send you to a specialist to confirm the diagnosis."

"That isn't what Pop had," Ron puzzled.

The rest of the meeting was a dark haze of treatment options, symptoms, disease progression, time remaining. Ron hoped that Tracey was keeping up with it all.

On the drive home, she put a brave face on it. "He said it wasn't a sure thing that you even have it," she said stoically. "That test he gave you is known for a high percentage of false positives. There is a good chance that you just have the beginning of rheumatoid arthritis."

He nodded, stared wide-eyed at the road. "Look on the bright side. No more worries about reinventing myself."

Tracey shook her head. There was much more to say that would eventually be said. Ron stared out the window at the green trees. He tried to think about something else. Scary guys with war-painted faces and pet snakes, for instance. Anything but the appointment with the specialist in two weeks.

Nobody with painted faces that night. Or the next day. Worrying about them took his mind off of his aches and pains, but he worried more and more about them anyway. He was surprised that Tracey wasn't. He remembered back to the leather-jacketed man driving the car in front of his house, how he had not even noticed the striped face until it turned toward him. The black eyes haunted him.

On the third day, Ron could not help himself and went to a gun store. He paid for a Colt Python .357 magnum revolver, the scariest-looking and sounding gun he could find, and hoped that nothing would happen in the three days he would have to wait for it. He decided not to tell Tracey about it, on the chance that she would think that he was buying the gun for some other reason than protection.

Nothing happened by the end of the waiting period. When he picked up the gun at the gun shop, and a box of ammunition to go with it, he was almost embarrassed to think that there was any need for it. All the same, he took it home, and opened the boxes on his bed. He hefted the thing in his hand, looked uncomfortably down the barrel. It seemed heavier than guns looked on TV. He opened the box of shells and tried to remember how the store clerk had showed him how to load it. He managed to get the cylinder to swing aside from the frame, and carefully slid the six bullets into it. He resisted the temptation to spin the cylinder and spin the pistol around on his finger like a cowboy, sure that he would manage to kill himself with such antics. He slid the weapon and the ammunition under some shirts in his closet and threw the boxes away before Tracey came home from work.

Tracey had explained to her staff that there had been a mix-up and that the agents were from the FBI, who had mistaken her for a smuggler who had been storing drugs in bins of seafood used to feed their fish. Her staff seemed to buy the story, but there was gossiping, of course.

Defiantly optimistic, Ron started combing through the want ads and on-line job sites again. He scheduled an interview with a computer game company over in Kirkland. Three days later, he told Tracey over dinner that it went well, but that they had to wait two days for the president of the company to return from a trip to Germany for a second interview.

The appointment with the cancer specialist arrived. Scans were done, blood was taken. Results would be forthcoming in a few days.

Ron resumed his 8:17 lawn defense against dachshund attack, and the old woman from two houses down barely even paused to see if he was in the window. Apparently she still had not figured out that she could vary her routine by five minutes and miss him. He mowed the lawn, took the trash out, washed dishes, did the laundry. His Level 42 Paladin advanced to Level 64, and started the Troll Bane Dagger quest, all while trying to improve his own programming theory. The detail would have to increase in granularity depending on what the character was interacting with. He was almost there.

He switched brands of coffee. Tracey liked the old kind better.

Ron had three days to kill before the second interview, so he decided to tackle the job of going through Pop's room. The formerly spare bedroom had stood with the door closed since the paramedics had arrived for that last trip to the ER. He was grateful that Tracey offered to help. The door creaked open, revealing the unkempt bed, the brown recliner, a shaft of sunlight with dust motes floating in it, illuminating the paramedics' discarded tubes and medical supplies on the floor, cast there in haste on the last day. There was still the Pop smell on the air.

Pop had kept playing his bass in the clubs with his band until the pain became too much, then moved in with Ron. Ron's mother had died years ago, and there was nobody else for Pop to turn to.

At first, Pop had puttered about the house, attended periodically by the visiting nurse, but after a month or so he took to sitting in the brown recliner all day, watching the TV. After a while, Ron could tell that even though the TV was on, Pop wasn't actually watching it. His head was turned to the side, eyes either glassy or closed. Later, he took to conversing with nobody, and would stop when Ron or the nurse would enter the room.

"Who are you talking to, Pop?" Ron had asked.

"Angels. And your mother," Pop had said.

"What are they talking to you about?"

Pop smiled and looked away. "Music of the spheres, my boy."

As things progressed, he asked for paper and a pencil, and would scribble notes and pictures in his spidery hand. Pop refused to show them to anyone, and Ron hadn't thought to look for them until now. It took him a while to find the notes, mixed up with junk mail sales fliers and old newspaper, but he assembled a pile of sheets. They were covered with penciled-in notes with intricate diagrams of interconnected wavy lines and points with geometric shapes. The handwriting was nearly illegible. Ron decided to put the notes aside and tackle them after the second job interview at the software company.

The second interview went well, and Ron was told to expect a call within a few days, probably with a start date. They were working on a game called "Space Golf," where the courses were set on other planets with different gravity. Ron had never played regular golf, and had only come close to visiting another planet once, but convinced them that he could put some realism into the characters' motions.

They celebrated that night with a bottle of wine.

Secret underground bases in Denver, rips into another universe, strange genetic mutations, and war-paint-faced murderers became fuzzier and fuzzier in their minds.

Of course, that was when they struck.

−10−

Tracey should have suspected that something was looming that day, she had dreamed again, just before waking, still a little hung over.

At first, she thought that she had returned to the desert of the other world in her previous dream, but noticed differences. The sky, instead of yellowish, was a deep, clear blue. There was only one small, puffy cloud in all of that vast sky. The sand was similar, but had more small rocks mixed in. There were low, dusty bushes around. The air felt crisp, electric, but thin, as though she was at altitude. She was on a hill overlooking what looked like a small town. There were no paved streets, just tracks in the dusty soil. The buildings, what were left of them, were mostly weathered wood. Many of them were in ruins. Some were small ramshackle houses, but here were other, mysterious-looking structures.

She looked around: What she at first had thought was the crest of the hill, rose to even greater heights. Nearby there was an opening in the ground: a hole surrounded by squared stone blocks. She crept to the edge, looked in. There was no bottom. It disappeared into an inky blackness. She searched the nearby ground and found a stone to drop in.

As it left her hand, a voice behind her spoke: "The one you want is at the bottom of the hill. It's a tunnel instead of a shaft."

She turned and saw a man in a uniform of green pants and tan shirt. He was old, with round glasses and an expansive gray beard. For some reason, inexplicable save for the particular logic of dreams, the old man wore a pair of diving fins. The details of his uniform and appearance were otherwise fuzzy, indistinct. He was kindly, eyes twinkled, but were deep, and he had a note of— sadness?—about him.

The sound of the rock hitting the wall or bottom of the shaft made her spin around. It had fallen for a long, long time. When she looked back, the man had vanished, but far below, in the town, shaggy shapes were moving toward her from different locations. They were low to the ground, and, one by one, started joining together into a pack of black-and-white-striped wolves, patterned almost like zebras, slinking up the hill toward her. There was nowhere to hide. She turned back to the shaft and looked for a ledge to jump to. There was none.

She had just decided to run for it up the hill when she heard a snuffling, animal sound behind her. She turned and saw the striped wolves circling, teeth bared. She saw that instead of their fur itself being colored, it was slathered with what looked like a black-and-white mucous-like substance, making the fur spiky and wet. It nauseated her. The wolves surrounded her, snarling and slavering with white-rimmed black-eyed madness, and there was nowhere to run. She was near panic.

But they did not attack. She looked for an opening in the ring, and saw one near the higher peak of the hill. She started to run, but then froze, sinking nerveless to her knees. Coming down the hill was something invisible, but massive. She heard it rolling, slowly and inexorably dragging through the sand, displacing the low bushes, and heard small rocks cracking as they were crushed under its weight. Waves of terror washed over her from the invisible, unstoppable force. Even the wolves gave way, whimpering as they backed. She screamed, then turned on her hands and knees, crawled to the edge of the pit and threw herself in.

She'd woken with a start, panting. Ron had not been awakened. She debated telling him about the dream, decided against it. He would only take it as an excuse to call the Space Command people. Nonetheless, she was shaken. She decided to go to work late that morning.

*****

Ron woke, made the coffee.

"I'm not feeling particularly well," Tracey told him. "I want you to take me in around ten."

He nodded, munching on a donut. "Hangover?"

"That, and another dream. Just need a shower and a few

minutes. And you shouldn't eat donuts, they are bad for you."

He raised an eyebrow.

"You have years to come, I'm sure of it."

The dachshund lady came and went. He decided to shave and dress reasonably nicely, in case the game company called and wanted him to come in and fill out any paperwork, or the doctor's office called and wanted to tell him whether he was going to die or not.

"Don't wear that shirt," Tracey told him with an immediate glance. He paused, halfway through buttoning it.

"Why not?"

"It's the lint shirt," she said. "You know, the one that attracts cat hair, dog hair, fibers, who knows what else and from where else. And it is impossible for some reason to brush it or tape-roller it off."

She was right. It was a pain in the ass, but it was his lucky shirt. The last time he wore it, he'd gone through six squares of sticky tape from the rolling lint remover, then had a whole new crop of fibers to remove before he reached the door. But later that day, he had narrowly avoided being run over by a car in a crosswalk. Tracey had tried to convince him to just toss the damned shirt, but he argued that he could always wear it for working in the yard. Of course, he always forgot to wear it for yard work. He made a mental note to remember next time and went looking for the lint roller. He needed luck that day: medical test results *and* job offers were pending.

They drove Tracey's Beetle south on Aurora Avenue, through the Battery Street tunnel and along the Viaduct.

"Damn it, Ron, you are covered in lint already."

He cursed himself. He should have changed the shirt, or maybe put another layer over it.

Ron glanced down from the elevated roadway at the Waterfront, where the Seattle Aquarium straddled a pier jutting into the Puget Sound. He noticed a crowd of people in front, and thought that there were an unusual number of tourists there that morning. They crept north along Alaskan Way after getting off the Viaduct, along the waterfront piers.

Traffic was heavy. Tourists were just beginning to arrive for the day's visits to the shops and attractions.

They noticed a knot of men with duffle bags lounging a little too casually near the entrance. They were dressed normally, two in jeans and flannel shirt, one in khaki pants and a golf shirt, one in a gray suit, another, Ron saw with a stab of fear, in a denim jacket and black hat. He looked closer, and saw what looked like a thick black necklace around his shoulders. It could well have been a snake. Ron strained to see their faces, but they were turned away from them.

"Keep driving," Tracey said tensely. "Don't stop here."

As they drove slowly by, hindered by the northbound traffic, one of the men turned and made eye contact with Ron. His face was painted in white, with red-and-black lines and circles. In unison, the others turned, staring at Ron and his car. Their faces were striped, too. A thin, segmented limb reached out from under one of the men's jackets and nestled into his ear.

"What the *hell*!" Ron said.

The men started shouldering their way through the crowd toward them.

"Go. Go faster!" Tracey yelled, as they watched the painted men run at full tilt after them along the waterfront sidewalk.

"I can't! There are cars in front of me," Ron protested.

"Go around!" Tracey ordered.

Ron glanced into the left lane for oncoming traffic, waited for the single car to pass, then accelerated across the center line and sped north. He checked the rearview mirror, saw the stalkers still pelting along furiously but futilely after them.

Ron grabbed Tracey's hand. It was shaking. "Where are the cops when you need them?"

"We don't want to get stopped right now. What are we supposed to tell them, that people in war paint are chasing us and trying to kill us? Hell, while we were stopped telling them that, they could come up and kill us all."

Ron realized she was right. His mind raced. "So what do we do? Are you ready to call Clay?"

Tracey hesitated, then sighed. "Give me your damn cell phone." She fished around her purse for the card that Clay had given her, and dialed the number. "Crap. A recording is saying that your service has been disconnected. Did you pay your bill?"

"I should still have a month or so before they cut it off," he said. "Try yours."

She did. Her service had been disconnected, too. They glanced at each other, suspecting the worst. She always paid her bills.

"We gotta get home," Ron said, jaw set.

"Why? That's the first place they'll look for us after missing us at work. I knew I shouldn't be on time this morning. I bet they got to the aquarium right when we would have gotten in on any other morning, and just decided to wait for us out front."

"It will only take a second," Ron insisted. They drove back north to his neighborhood.

He parked a block away and snuck through his backyard into the back door of his house. He stood for a tense minute, listening for sounds inside, heard nothing. He cursed the pain in his hips and legs. He ran straight for the bedroom, and grabbed the pistol from its hiding place, then walked through the house with it held before him like he had seen in countless cop movies. There were no stalkers.

He grabbed the land-line phone, intending to call Clay, but sure enough, the line was dead. He briefly considered asking next door if he could use their phone, but didn't want to be caught wandering around the neighborhood when the painted stalkers showed up.

It occurred to him that he could make a stand there at his house. *Who are they to run me from my home?* He then realized how silly it was to throw his life away just because of a concept of a home. It could just as easily be a cave as made of lumber. He set to work quickly, wracking his brain for what else he could possibly need within the scant minutes he had before he imagined the stalkers arriving. He couldn't think of anything.

Aha! I could change my shirt! He paused, though. *Which*

shirt to put on, instead? He decided to leave the lint shirt on. It was lucky, after all. He opened the refrigerator, saw that he had a half a gallon of milk. He considered pouring it down the sink, so that it wouldn't spoil and ruin the rest of the contents. He realized that he knew, on some level, that he was not coming back any time soon. He started making a mental list: take out the trash, after getting rid of not just the milk but the rest of the perishable food, too. He wondered about the food in the freezer, and how to get his plants watered. He wondered how much dog crap would accumulate on his front lawn. He broke out in cold sweat, after realizing he had just wasted over a minute with these inanities. He grabbed a kitchen knife, some canned chili, a flashlight, some matches, and the box containing the rest of his .357 magnum cartridges. Hurriedly, he crossed to the back door. He peered around, saw nothing. As nonchalantly as he could, he walked through the back yard.

Halfway across, he heard tires squeal from the front of the house and heard a car door slam. He ran without looking back. "Too close, too close," he repeated to himself.

Tracey took his place in the driver's seat when she saw him coming. She started the engine. He slid into the front seat, white as a sheet.

"Go," he said.

She went. They got on Interstate 5, heading south toward downtown.

"Where to?" she asked. "Seatac Airport? Boeing Field? That's where the Space Command guys had that plane."

"Go for Boeing Field," he said.

"And what was so important that you just *had* to go back there?"

"This," he said coolly, and pulled the canned chili out of the backpack. "Whoops, not that, *this.*" He slid the pistol partway out.

"Oh, crap."

"So, they know where you work, and where I live. What else do they know?"

"LaGrue and Clay said these guys can travel through time, or from other dimensions," she answered. "We have to assume they know *everything.* Your license plates, where you hang out, our friends . . . you *know* they were the ones who cancelled the cell phones. They may even be able to tell if we use our ATM cards, for all we know. Heck, they may know where we are going before *we* do."

That sobered them.

"So we can't get on an airplane if we can't hook up with Clay and his boys here. Can't risk a bus or train, either."

"We just need to get to a pay phone. Duh," he said.

She glared at him, then his eyes strayed to the car in the next lane to their right. The first thing he noticed was that seated in the front seat was a man wearing a black hat, red plaid flannel shirt, and a denim jacket with face paint, like it had been carelessly caked on. A black snake was writhing around his neck. He was looking straight ahead. He almost failed to tear his eyes from him and look in the back seat, where the window was down. The cavernous barrel of a shotgun was inching from it.

He tried to speak, but failed. Sound would not come. He grabbed Tracey's arm and pointed, and Tracey followed his finger. She slammed the brakes just as the gun fired. The 00 buckshot traveled through the space they had vacated a microsecond before, slamming into the window and door of the SUV to their left in the next lane. The stalkers braked a second later, but the SUV that had just been shot veered across their lane and crashed into the stalkers' door, spraying glass. Ron and Tracey skidded to a stop, raising a cloud of smoking rubber. They braced for impact, expecting to be rear-ended by a car behind them, but that car swerved to their right, missing them by a hand's width. With a sickening crash, it also slammed into the stalkers' still-spinning car.

Tracey's fingers were curled in a white-knuckled death grip on the steering wheel, still bracing for an impact from behind. All the cars behind him, however, managed to stop. They looked ahead to the smoking wreck of the stalkers' car, and with a visceral shock, saw several of them emerging from the still functional driver's side back door. They started staggering toward them, one of them still clutching the shotgun.

"Off the interstate!" Ron yelled.

Tracey put the car in reverse, weaving through the cars that had managed to stop behind them. When she reached a big enough gap, she turned the car north against the traffic, and accelerated the last few hundred yards toward the 50th Street off-ramp.

"We have to get out of here and ditch this car," Ron growled, while the sounds of sirens wafted toward them. "There are probably fifty cell phone calls going to the Seattle PD right now. What is close by with lots of people, pay phones, and somewhere to hide the car while we wait for the Johnsons?"

"I'll head for the University of Washington," she decided.

–11–

They found a parking garage near campus at a grocery store, and found a spot as deep in the covered structure as possible. Ron grabbed his backpack, and they made their way to the campus as fast as they dared that wouldn't attract attention. A blue Seattle Police cruiser flew by, heading for the accident scene. It didn't stop, and Ron was relieved to notice that the officer showed no sign of recognizing them.

They race-walked toward the campus for a few minutes. Ron was sickened to hear gunfire start in the distance back around the accident scene.

"Who is shooting at who?" Tracey wondered.

They were passing by one of the many bars that lined 45th Street. Helicopters arrived, hovering over the area they'd left.

"We should pop in here and see what's on the news," Ron said. "And call Clay."

"Hell, we could use a drink while we wait, too," Tracey agreed. She was still shaking.

The bar was empty of customers at that hour, and wasn't the kind of place to get a lunch crowd. They sat at the bar and asked the barkeep, probably a student and who looked barely old enough to sell alcohol, for two beers and the remote to the TV.

They flipped channels until they found a local news station that was airing a live feed from a helicopter.

The screen showed the accident scene. The stalkers' car was disabled, and there were several other wrecked and smoking vehicles littering the area amid a carpet of broken safety glass, oil, and radiator fluid. They counted at least twenty police cruisers, fire engines, ambulances, and the SWAT team van. The police had surrounded the area, and were firing at the stalkers' car. Other officers were leading motorists from other cars to safety, crouching.

Their beers arrived. "Turn up the volume," Tracey urged. Ron fumbled with the remote.

". . . the gunfire is continuing, we have just been instructed to pull back out of the airspace," the reporter narrated excitedly. "We'll continue to report as long as we can. It appears as though at least two officers are down. The assailants are heavily armed, and we are hearing the police speculate on their radios that they have some kind of body armor under their clothing, because their shots seem to be having no effect."

They watched as the camera jerkily zoomed in and out, first at a man with his face painted, spraying bullets from some kind of submachine gun, seemingly unruffled, then at a tight group of officers retreating, firing, while they dragged away the lifeless form of what looked like a SWAT team member.

"Is that happening right now?" the bartender asked, drying a beer mug. "That's right over there, a few blocks away on I-5," she muttered, staring fascinated at the screen.

The stalkers regrouped, staying in a close knot, and hopped across the concrete barrier separating the southbound lanes from the express lanes. They started trotting east through now-abandoned cars. The helicopter camera zoomed in, showing them crossing the barrier into the northbound lanes, then start climbing the grass embankment leading to the 45th Street on-ramp. Police followed them, still firing, perhaps angling for head shots to avoid the armor. The stalkers, unconcerned at the firepower being directed against them, inexorably topped the embankment and started trotting along 45th Street toward the bar where Ron and Tracey were watching them on the television. They took turns to spin around and return suppressing fire.

"You might want to close shop *right now*," Ron advised.

"I think you're right," the bartender said. She scuttled around the bar and locked the solid wood front door.

"They know we are here," Tracey croaked.

"How? They're probably just escaping and will run right by here on the way to wherever they're going," Ron said, not believing it himself.

"I don't know, they must have some kind of homing device or something."

Ron rolled his eyes.

"Oh shut up, it sounds corny but how else could they have been onto us so quickly on the highway?"

They watched the television screen as the stalkers moved toward them, heard the gunshots grow louder, then deafening. They were right outside.

"I'm out of here," the bartender cried, racing for the back door.

–12–

Ron and Tracey had just a second to consider joining her, when the front door erupted into splinters with a deafening burst of gunfire. Five war-painted men strode through the door, smoke still pouring from the lead stalker's barrel. They were all soaked with a tarry, black, viscous liquid that oozed from holes in their bodies.

"Lordy, I am feckn' *thirsty!*" one man announced, in an overly loud voice with a strange accent.

It sounded half rural English and half cowboy. He was short, slightly built, and had an oversized mustache that could have been fake stuck under his grease-painted nose. He was the one dressed in jeans and a denim jacket with a snake for a necklace. He held himself like a little rooster. The submachine gun he carried seemed to dwarf him.

"Get the door," he said over his shoulder to one of the other men, dressed in khaki pants and a red golf shirt, now soaked black.

That man closed what was left of the door and started dragging benches across it as a barricade.

Ron and Tracey sat wide-eyed and still as church mice, expecting to be shot.

"Lousy service in here." The head stalker laughed, then jumped the bar and helped himself to the beer tap.

The barkeeper and a sixth stalker, dressed in a black leather jacket, emerged from the rear of the bar. The bartender had apparently been intercepted trying to escape through a back door. With her was another employee, apparently a dishwasher or cook, judging by the apron, hands up.

"Go on, do what you came to do—" Ron started.

The lead stalker waved him silent, looking carefully at Tracey. "Have we met, me bird? You have a familiar face." He scrutinized her from behind the beer mug. "I think. . . ." he began, then scratched his head under his black hat, ". . . you were on a ship, with a spear gun? You were one of the Trident? This not ringing any bells? You were trying to get me to join the other side, instead of us trying with you. I think I have already killed you once. But it wasn't you, after all."

Ron and Tracey glanced at each other. *This guy is NUTS.*

He removed his denim jacket, wrung some of the tarry substance from it, and hung it on the back of a bar stool. He was wearing a nylon webbing pistol belt and tactical suspenders under the jacket, on which were hung a large pistol in a holster and various ammunition pouches.

"Oh, proper job, we made the news at noon!" He laughed, glancing at the television over the bar. The other stalkers joined him. "Looks like they are setting up a perimeter and calling for the big guns." He pointed to one of the crew. "Turn down the sound, we have some talking to do." He pointed to another stalker. "You, go wave that bartender girl around and yell that we have hostages. That should slow them down for a while, and keep 'em from lobbing in a gas bomb."

The men complied. The barkeeper screamed as one of the stalkers, dressed in a gray business suit, dragged her to the door, pressed the barrel of a pistol into her head, and yelled at the police outside, threatening to kill her if their demands weren't met.

"Nice touch." The lead stalker laughed, downing his beer. "I figure we have about a half hour at least before they storm the place."

"I want a beer, too, Bob," one of the other painted men pleaded.

"Of course, where are my manners?" He waved his rifle at the barkeeper, who had been returned to her place under guard. The dishwasher was there, too. "Hey, pour us all one, will you, love?"

She fainted. The stalkers laughed uproariously. Bob, the lead man, started filling mugs.

Ron and Tracey stared numbly at their captors.

"What's the matter, cat got your tongues?" Bob chided, raising his eyebrows. "Oh, you're probably worried about us killing you or something."

"The thought c-crossed our minds," Ron stuttered.

The stalkers laughed.

"Well, that all depends," Bob said, placing his submachine gun on the bar after snapping a new magazine into place and chambering a round. "You could join us, instead."

Ron and Tracey regarded him dumbly.

"Oh, we don't kill everybody. We give them an option, and only—and I'm just guessing here—maybe one in twenty decides they would rather die than join up."

Ron, with glacial slowness, started reaching into his backpack for the pistol.

"I mean," Bob continued, "we're the *good* guys."

"You're crazy," Tracey stated simply.

"Oh, please. What a tired cliché," Bob snapped, taking a long pull on his beer. "I'm not crazy just because I'm wearing war paint and shoot people for a living. There is a war on, and we really *are* the good guys. There is a lot at stake, you know. So much so, in fact, that I am willing to shoot my great-great-great—how many 'greats' is that?—great-grandson, if he won't join us." He raised his eyebrows at Ron.

Ron closed his hand around the grip of the gun in his backpack.

"Yeah, you heard right, Ron," the leader continued. "I'm Bob Golden. I was born in eighteen and forty six, in Cornwall, then emigrated with my family to the good ol' U.S. a few years before the Civil War heated up. I met a girl. She married another man, in spite of his being a brute. I challenged him to a duel, but she convinced me to leave town before going through with it. Ah, sweet Julia. . . . Anyway, my pa was a miner, so I followed in his footsteps, like a proper Cousin Jack."

"Yeah, I heard about this somewhere," Ron replied, cocking the hammer of his pistol. "You went to California."

"Ah, proper job, me 'ansum! You know about Bodie, then. That's where I earned the nickname Cornish Bob. That is also where I finally got out of this universe and into the real one. It was an accident, really. I was moonlighting as a night watchman down at the Syndicate works, and there was a tremendous explosion. It was in the summer of eighteen seventy nine. It was the underground powder magazine owned by the Giant Powder Company that had just blown, but there was more to the story than that. What caused the explosion, you may ask, me bey? It was a little rift, a tiny quantum level wormhole, kind of thing that happens all the time. Just, that when it happens in the middle of a powder magazine full of two tons of black powder, it can spark an explosion. And this was a *big* one: It vaporized the two guys that had just left the room, and the boarding house next to it was all scat to pieces, and the hoist works, and it killed half a dozen other people and destroyed everything for a good ways around."

The painted-faced stalker pulled out a handkerchief from his shirt pocket and mopped his forehead, smearing some of the black stains. He fished through another pocket and produced a bottle of antacid tablets. He shook out four of them into his palm, popped them in his mouth and crunched away.

"Just a touch of indigestion," he said with a lopsided smile. "Brought about by stress. Anyway, what started out as a wee little temporary rift turned into one big enough to crawl through, using the concentrated force of the blast as a catalyst. I was fossickin' around the results of the explosion and found it. I hid it, of course, thinking that I could use it to some advantage. And me ol' son, *did I!* I was able to wriggle through and found that the *real* universe, the one that this universe is a derivative of, was on the other side. And things are different there, let me tell you—"

Ron whipped out the pistol, and leveled it at Cornish Bob's heart, a scant ten feet away across the bar. "Thanks for the life story, it was *really* fascinating, but we'll just be leaving now."

Cornish Bob's eyes widened and a smile spread across his grease-painted face under the mustache. His eyebrows arched in mock surprise. "Oh, *no!*" he groaned dramatically. "You wouldn't shoot your ol' grandpa, would you?"

"Not if I don't have to," he said, taking Tracey by the arm and backing away toward the recovered bartender, and dishwasher, still under close guard.

"Oh, but you *do* have to, me bird," Cornish Bob said. "You are not leaving here without shooting me. Not alive, anyway," he added.

Ron fired. The shot was deafening in the enclosed space of the bar. A new hole opened in Cornish Bob's chest, and a spatter of the black liquid sprayed the bar and liquor bottles behind him. Cornish Bob did not even flinch.

"Oops," Bob said. "I should kill you right now, but since you are my *kin*, however teasy that was, I'll give you just one more chance. We're already dead, me bey, re-animated corpses. Like your zombies, but without rotting. So you can't kill us. You didn't notice that we were already riddled with leaking holes?"

Ron jammed the pistol back into his backpack. "Sorry, had to try."

Cornish Bob laughed. "No harm, no foul," he said, splaying his hands. "So anyway, as I was saying before your *very rude* attempt to extricate my non-working aorta from the back of me rib cage—"

"Let them go," Ron tilted his head at the bartender and dishwasher. "Her, too," Ron added, touching Tracey.

"Eh?" Cornish Bob answered, distracted. "No, I don't think so. Tracey carries the gene, and those two are the only hostages the cops outside know about. If they leave, the cops start coming in for us before we have a chance to conclude our business. And if I can't convince you to join us, you *all* die and we slip right out of here back to the real world."

"You can come and go at will?" Tracey asked.

"Of course. It is very expensive, so only I have one, but yes, my rift generator allows for a temporary rift. You know . . . rift . . . generator. . . . Get it?"

"Then why do you need us? What possible use are we to you, if you are so technologically advanced?"

"A fair question, me lad," Cornish Bob responded, lacing his hands behind his head and leaning back on his barstool. "Like I said, there is a war on. Over in the real universe. That universe is in danger of being absorbed into an even older, bigger universe. Think of it like two little soap bubbles clinging to a big one. If there is enough permeability between the boundaries, poof! Only one universe remains, the older, dominant one. The bad guys over there are trying to make that happen, to get our universe to merge with that older one. My boss, the ruler of the universe, is fighting to keep that from happening. She is willing to do anything, even try to get other derivative universes, like yours, to merge with hers. Full carriers, like you and me, are uniquely situated to either help or hinder that process."

"How?"

"Too complicated to get into at this point," Cornish Bob dismissed with a wave. "But trust me, your universe is expendable for this. It is *eventually* going to be merged into ours, when she is done with it, and only one will remain. Hers. That is why I don't really care about killing anyone other than you. The cops, or anyone else over here are nothing. You are all illusions, your whole universe. Unreal. Just like shooting characters in a video game."

The inter-universal stalkers smiled and exchanged glances.

It occurred to Tracey that they considered all the gunfire into their zombified bodies to be just that: teenagers playing a first-person-shooter video game, who couldn't be hurt. Tracey had seen kids playing those video games that Ron designed, and how they shot video characters for the hell of it, just because "it wasn't real." "How do you know that your universe will be the one to survive if they . . . whatever . . . come together like two soap bubbles?" Tracey asked.

"Oh, please," Bob sneered at her again. "You have *no idea* what you are talking about. You can trace the history, and look at the places where this universe branched off. You can see it in who was born, who died, who didn't invent something that changed the universe, who did. Small changes breed universes with only minor differences, which are almost immediately subsumed back into the original, with nothing more than a touch of déjà vu feeling to those in it. Big enough differences make enough of an original membrane to float away entirely. This universe is like a tick, just barely big enough to count at all. It is just a tiny bump on our universe's arse."

"So why don't you just merge it with yours and be done with it?" Ron asked.

"Another excellent, insightful question! I marvel at your speed in grasping your insignificance," Cornish Bob said, pouring himself another beer. "It is because *she is not done with it*. There are certain . . . *needs*, shall we say, that she has for it. There is a certain raw material that has been effectively expended in our universe. If we had all the time in the world to cruise all over space looking for it, we could find it . . . but like I said, there is a war on. We need it now, and the easiest place to get it is: *Ta daaaa*! Right here. The second your universe is absorbed, it becomes ours, with no more raw materials available. So we're waiting until the easily found material is gone before absorbing you."

"What is it?" Tracey asked.

He regarded her with immense gravity, then glanced around conspiratorially. He leaned forward, whispering. "Herring fish."

She looked at him blankly.

"Just kidding." Cornish Bob burst into forced laughter, shaking his finger. "Sorry, poppet, I just can't tell you that right now. Join us, and you could eventually prove useful and learn all. Or you can die, and be removed from the possibility of harming her."

"Who the hell is this 'she' you keep referring to as the ruler of your universe?" Ron asked.

"Correction, me 'ansum. Ruler of *our* universes, as in plural. *All* universes, for that matter. And once again, you are going to have to make this decision with the information you have before you. Just like you will just have to wonder how someone born over a century ago can be standing before you looking *so* good in makeup. Or why we're wearing this makeup at all in the first place."

"Yeah, what is with the clown paint, anyway?" Tracey asked.

"Clown paint! Well, I guess I can see why you would think that. No, me bird, we ain't bozos. The Queen Goddess rules many worlds, and this is just how she keeps up a uniform culture between them. Different stripes and colors and shapes mean different things. So her children, from different times and places can tell at a glance whether anyone else is also one of hers, and how they serve her. Sort of her mark. How else could someone on a far-off world tell that we were chosen to be her Holy Horribles Parade? She recruits all over. For instance, Dechambeau there got his start in the Court of Louis XIV," he said, indicating the man in the golf shirt, "and he has similar markings to me. And Skunky there was born a feckn' *cave man.*" He pointed to another. "Ginon 22 here was born on an orbiting colony circling a star over a hundred fifty light years from Earth, two universes over," indicating the stalker guarding the bartender and dishwasher. "Shytehole of a place, Ginon's colony. And you will have to decide soon, because it will not be long before the SWAT team or the National Guard or the FBI or somebody comes in here looking to heroically kick arse."

The phone rang.

"Ah ha!" Cornish Bob laughed, holding up his index finger. "Speak of the devil." He picked up the receiver with a flourish, and spoke in a clipped, guttural voice. "We have twelve hostages. You know our capabilities. We will provide a list of our demands in five minutes, then you will have an hour to comply or we will begin killing them." He hung up. "I hope that was the cops."

The stalkers laughed.

Cornish Bob picked up his submachine gun and smoothly leveled it at Ron and Tracey. "So what will it be, kids? Our way or the dead way?"

Ron stared at the metallic, pitted barrel of the gun and the black, deadly opening at its end. He willed himself to think, but his mind was numb. He almost found the situation comical.

"Speaking of the Devil, I'm not interested in that job anymore," he muttered.

Cornish Bob narrowed his eyes in puzzlement.

"I dreamed of this," Tracey whispered.

"What happened?" Ron asked.

"I'm kind of curious about that myself," Cornish Bob said.

*****

It was at that moment that Adrian Smithson, Security Specialist, struck.

Ever since keeping Ron from jumping into the rift, and he had been assigned by the flying pickle to watch Ron and Tracey, he'd convinced Clay to allow him to keep them under observation and protect them. He had accompanied them back to Seattle on the airplane, posing as a crewman, and wearing a brown-haired wig. Neither Ron nor Tracey had recognized him as the "technician" who'd grabbed Ron's arm at the rift. His ability to blend in, not draw attention to himself, had proved itself again.

Smithson and a small flock of unseen flying pickles followed them home in another, unmarked Space Command car. He and his green escorts had hovered around their neighborhood, Smithson posing as a garden worker, mailman, and poll-taker. It was amazing just what people overlooked, even with the most rudimentary of disguises. Wear shorts and carry a shoulder bag, and the brain immediately labels a person and fills in the rest: Mailman. Walk around the neighborhood wearing a blond wig and a clipboard: Political signature-seeker. Kneel down in a flower bed: landscaper.

That morning, he had followed them to Tracey's work, three car-lengths back, dressed in jeans and a flannel shirt, the perfect pan-Seattle uniform. He had waited behind while Ron and Tracey sped off from the front of the Aquarium. It was then that the flying pickles had informed him that Eiffelia's Horribles were present. When he saw them pile into a car, he drove off quickly toward Ron's house, reporting to Clay on the radio embedded in a tiny chip in the bone behind his left ear, that the Horribles were making their move.

He had gotten to Ron's house seconds too late, tires squealing to a stop out front. Immediately he sought to follow them, but was unable to catch up. He guessed that Ron and Tracey were going to make a run for Boeing Field, and made his way onto Interstate 5 southbound. He had almost caught them when the stalkers opened fire, and had to follow them as best he could off the highway through the maelstrom of cars, fleeing drivers, and emergency vehicles.

The flying pickles caught sight of Ron and Tracey ducking into the tavern, and passed this on to his thoughts. He had parked as soon as he could, and worked his way in through the locked back door by deftly and efficiently picking the lock. He had just enough time to grab an apron to pose as a kitchen worker before the bartender ran by him on the way to the door, only to be cut off by the painted-faced man in the denim jacket. She had the good sense to keep her mouth shut about not knowing him, thankfully. Perhaps she thought he was one of her captors.

It had just been a waiting game at that point, once it became apparent that he would not have to immediately protect Ron from being shot. Once he confirmed that all the members of the Horribles were zombies, he had to revise his plan of producing his own pistol and shooting as many stalkers as he could.

Smithson acted as though his arms, raised over his head, had become tired, and the stalker guarding him had allowed him to lower them to hang them by his side, instead. He worked the folding blade out of the sheath strapped to his left forearm under the flannel sleeve and slipped it into the palm of his hand. He knew his first move would be against the zombie nearest him. He would have to do this by hand, and it would have to be a massive attack to the connection between the body and its means of control, the brain. The only choice was the timing.

The decision was made for him when Cornish Bob aimed at Ron with his assault rifle. He looked for his opening, his target the Horrible nearest at hand. With one fluid motion, he snapped open the folding knife, and moved in behind the man. He quickly closed in behind his still-unwary adversary, breaking his balance by pushing his knee into the hollow in the back of the Horrible's knee, twisting and dropping his weight slightly. Smithson tilted the man's head up with his left hand and plunged the tanto-tipped blade into the side of the Horrible's neck, severing the spinal cord from the brain stem between the first cervical vertebrae and the base of the skull.

The man stayed alive, gurgling and clutching at his

throat, just long enough to support his weight while Smithson moved him between Cornish Bob and Ron and Tracey. Cornish Bob aimed his automatic rifle, but hesitated to fire, perhaps unsure whether firing would hasten the SWAT team's entry or not. Ron and Tracey made the instinctive response to duck behind the dying man, too.

Smithson began backing out of the room, into the hall between the bar and the back door. The stalker's body was beginning to get heavy, and the black substance replacing his blood made holding on to him slippery, but they were all able to crouch behind the shield as they retreated.

*****

Cornish Bob decided to shoot them anyway, but noticed one of the flying pickles drifting nearby. With a curse, he shot at it instead.

The SWAT team outside, hearing the gunfire, chose that moment to begin their assault on the bar through the front and back doors. A flash/bang rolled through a gap in the door, and detonated with a thunderclap. The remains of the door began shuddering under the impact of a compact battering ram.

Cornish Bob raised his hand. "That's all right, me beys, let them go," he said cheerfully, unaffected by the deafening explosion. He snatched up his denim jacket. "But remember, we have unfinished business. Especially you," he said, pointing at Smithson.

The remaining four Horribles gathered into a tight group, and Cornish Bob manipulated something on his black nylon-web pistol belt. With a bright yellowish flash and a lingering smell of ozone, they were gone.

–13–

Five days after the striped-faced men had shot the town up, Clay strode to the head of the conference table in the Seattle safe house suites, hidden in an unmarked floor in a well-known twelve-story software company in South Lake Union. The elevators had no button for that floor; it could only be accessed by a nondescript card access reader.

There was a blackboard on one wall, and a floor-to-ceiling monitor on one of the others. Ron, Tracey, Professor LaGrue, Adrian Smithson, and Agent Johnson were already seated. Valentina Pavlov was on the way.

The repercussions of that day had been significant. Six police officers had been shot, one fatally, when the bullet had entered under his armpit through a gap in his body armor. Twelve drivers on the highway had been severely injured, either in the initial accidents or the following gunfire. Twenty cars and eight storefronts had been struck by bullets. Police and insurance investigators, in spite of interviewing hundreds of witnesses from both the scene of the incident and the waterfront, had been unable to identify or find the assailants. Both daily papers and all the local television news organizations had had a field day, especially when the bartender came forward with her story.

Clay had listened to and recorded the entire exchange between Ron, Tracey, and the stalkers through the radio embedded in Adrian Smithson's skull. He had decided to fly out with the whole team to try to defuse the situation, and to spy on the official forensic investigation into the one stalker casualty. Smithson had moved quickly to secure the scene before the police arrived, preventing them from discovering the mechanical spider the stalker carried, by flashing his Space Command identification which generated even more media frenzy and conspiracy theory blog fodder when that became public.

Ron remembered back to that moment, crouching defensively in the walk-in cooler with Tracey, watching Smithson standing over the dead man, his gray eyes unblinking, prepared to keep the police from taking them into custody. He had killed without glee or pleasure, but without hesitation or remorse. The stalker's leg trembled, and Ron was overcome with a wave of revulsion, and was sick. He had seen hundreds of killings over the years on television and movies, but witnessing it in reality, smelling the artificial black blood, hearing the foamy rattle as the man died, affected him viscerally.

Since that time, like when passing Smithson in the hallways of the safe house, he was struck with what an odd thing Smithson was: How he did not stand out in any particular way unless you took the time to look, then one would notice the bald head, the effortless glide of his walk, and the laser-like focus on whatever he was attending to. It occurred to Ron that he was almost robotic, sitting at the conference table, eyes focused on nothing yet everything.

Ron looked around the table at the others. LaGrue was inspecting his fingernails with apparent dissatisfaction. Clay checked his watch. Johnson waited passively. Tracey was staring at his shirt. *Oh crap, it's the lint shirt. He* could almost see fibers from across the room magnetizing to it.

"Does anyone have a lint roller?" Ron asked in a wee voice, breaking the silence. Tracey buried her face in her hands.

"Good morning," Clay greeted, placing his splayed fingertips on the glass table top. "Welcome to Seattle, Professor LaGrue. Ron, Tracey. The only member of your team you have not yet met, Valentina Pavlov, is on her way down, and should be here presently. I have also just been informed that one of the Mods, Mr. Barman, will make a short appearance a bit later to give us some guidance.

"Meanwhile, by way of update, the police have finished the autopsy and DNA testing of the dead man, and we have managed to intercept what was left on the way to disposal and do our own tests at White Mountain. Very odd results. His mitochondrial DNA is consistent with what Cornish Bob described, as someone who could have come from some other planet, and an analysis of his teeth minerals showed no match with any local community on Earth, so we know he didn't grow up anywhere around here. He appeared to have been dead for some time, but was in a state of arrested decay; his tissues had been treated with some kind of chemical process. How his metabolism ran, what fueled him, and how his circulatory, nervous, and other systems worked is still a mystery. I'm glad Smithson had the good instinct to go for the nervous system. Maybe the guy calling himself a zombie was a giveaway."

Smithson shrugged. *Hardly an instinct,* he thought. *I've run into the Horribles before.*

"The electronic spider he was carrying has also been sent back to White Mountain for analysis. So far, we have identified it as a very advanced small computer, joined with some kind of communication device, and a power pack to run the legs. One or two of the legs go into the ears and act as headphones. The others are coated with tiny sticky hooks so it can cling to fabrics or even smooth surfaces like walls. It plays videos by way of a small holographic projector visible only from the angle of the owner. It has a GPS tracker, it can use the cellular networks, the Internet, and who knows what else. If Apple or Samsung or Microsoft or someone gets their hands on this thing, they'd make a mint. We are also looking at his shotgun, which appears to be manufactured by no gunsmith I've ever heard of."

Valentina Pavlov chose that moment to enter the room. Tracey noticed all the men in the room sit up a little straighter and pull in their stomachs. LaGrue was especially comical, his studied air of aloofness with obvious agitation was palpable. Valentina *was* stunning: She could have been a blond-haired blue-eyed model, or a movie starlet, but still had a girl-next-door look to her. She radiated a sensuality, in spite of being dressed in a skirted business suit and carrying a laptop bag.

"Ms. Pavlov, this is Ron Golden and Tracey Springs. Ms. Pavlov is going to be our communications specialist, in charge of keeping the lines open between White Mountain and wherever we happen to go. She's also, incidentally, a medical doctor, which could prove useful."

"Pleased to meet you. I have heard so much," she said warmly.

"We might have met once before," Tracey said, shaking her hand after Ron.

Valentina raised an eyebrow. Tracey leveled a steely gaze at her, with a firm smile.

"I would love to talk to you some more later," Valentina said.

"Good idea," Clay said. "What I would like to do at this point is discuss some of the new information that Cornish Bob let slip during his try at recruiting Ron and Tracey."

Clay passed out sheets of paper with topics printed on them. "A war, derivative universes, Female Ruler of that Universe, painted men from other times, Bodie, some raw material they desperately need, and . . . . Am I missing anything? And how this all relates to us, I suppose."

They all sat silently for a moment, perusing the topics.

"So I'm going to want ideas from each department: Science, Security, Communications, Dreams, and . . . whatever you want to contribute, Ron."

Ron frowned. *My DNA, maybe?*

Clay crossed to a blackboard, wrote "WAR" on one side.

"Allow me," Valentina said, removing a tablet from her bag. She tapped the screen, and the wall-sized monitor lit up. "WAR" appeared in foot-tall letters.

"Very nice." Clay continued, "Okay. Cornish Bob mentioned that there was a war on, and that he was on the good guy side. What do we know about this war so far?"

Professor LaGrue raised his hand. "Universal scale. If the ship on the other side of the rift is any indication, faster-than-light drives on big ships. Weaponry and defenses beyond our technology."

Those terms were typed into the tablet, and appeared on the wall.

"We have not heard any guidance from the Mods yet," Adrian Smithson said, "but from what I know from past interactions, those are the two sides. And we can confirm

Cornish Bob is *not* on the good guy side, in spite of what he says."

Clay cocked his head and regarded Smithson with narrowed eyes. *Past interactions?* He knew that Smithson had some kind of more complicated relationship with the Mods than he had himself, despite being the nominal commander. He made a mental note to question Smithson further, should the briefing from Mr. Barman prove less informative. "Langston, what is your understanding of the physics that Cornish Bob was talking about?" he asked, changing the subject.

"He was describing how one universe can pop another new one into existence based on decisions made or changes that occur as different statistical probabilities," LaGrue answered. "That theory has been around for a long time, and would solve some of the paradoxes that would occur as a result of time travel."

"What kind of paradoxes?" Ron asked.

"You know, the old saw about how if you had a time machine and went back in time to the night your father met your mother, and prevented them from meeting. Would you cease to exist? If so, how would you have traveled back to prevent them from meeting and making you?"

"Like that movie *Back to the Future*," Clay put in.

"Um, right. Or here is another one: What if your dad gave you a fancy pen that had been passed on to him by his grandfather. You get in a time machine, go back in time with the pen, and give it to your grandpa when he was a kid so you can be sure he has it to pass on to his son, and from him to you. So . . . where did the pen really come from? Who manufactured it? That paradox works with ideas, even. Let's say Colonel Sanders' chicken recipe comes into your hands by breaking into the KFC vault, and you go back in time to when Colonel Sanders was—what, a colonel?—and give him the recipe of those eleven secret herbs and spices. So who thought up that recipe?"

"My head hurts again," Tracey said, in monotone.

"Anyway, one way to get around that kind of paradox is to have a new universe pop into existence every time something happens that would otherwise be a paradox. In one universe, you do manage to keep your parents from meeting, and you cease to exist in the future *of that one universe.* But in the other universe, you fail and are born to try again. It is called the 'Many Worlds Interpretation' of quantum physics, but less than twenty percent of physicists ascribe to it. There are problems with it, like the conservation of energy theorem: Where does the energy to make all those new universes come from?

"The part I have not heard before is when he described the magnitude of the changes affecting whether that newly 'calved' or popped-out universe goes on existing or eventually gets absorbed back into the original one, when the effect of the change no longer matters. Like soap bubbles re-forming into one. *That* is fascinating. And it may solve that conservation of energy problem." LaGrue reflexively grasped at his yellow pad and began distractedly writing equations.

"If we are to assume that Cornish Bob is right, and we have no reason not to, then we are in danger of being absorbed back into his universe," Smithson pointed out. "If that happens, what happens to us?"

"We cease to exist. If there is another Adrian Smithson in that other universe, he remains. With whatever experiences and realities that are his," LaGrue answered.

"Well, that sucks," Tracey said.

"To say the least," Clay said. "And apparently there is a powerful being in that universe who is involved in a war with someone else, who wants to have that universe absorbed into yet another universe, and 'she' is trying to stop it. But we don't know who 'she' is, or whether we want to help her or not. Or what would happen to us if that happened. What we *do* know is that she is using people from other times to help her, and they are wearing face makeup to designate their jobs or rank. One is supposedly from Renaissance France and another from the Stone Age, at least. Any ideas about that?"

"What we don't know," Professor LaGrue started, "is whether they are from our universe at those times or from the other one at those times."

"Would that matter?" Ron asked.

LaGrue shrugged. "Don't know, don't know."

"If she is recruiting here, then Pangborn carriers must be rare there, too," Valentina Pavlov pointed out.

"We know Cornish Bob is from this universe, at least, and the one that got killed from two universes over was from another, obviously."

"Wait a minute. . . ." LaGrue said, holding up his finger. "No, lost it. No . . . I got it. A partial point, anyway. Look, if this 'ruler of the universe' is sending operatives into our universe, killing people in the past, there must be a reason. A reason *to* do it and a reason *why those people*. They must be worthy of being killed for some reason. Why was she trying to either recruit or kill Ron? Full carrier. Those people in history must be full gene carriers, too. So she was trying to recruit or kill them."

"So the genes might be the raw material she is looking for," Tracey mused. "And has it occurred to any of you supra-geniuses that maybe the rift you have all been exploring might have been a trap specifically left by that queen to attract full gene carriers? You have already lost one through there, you know."

The mortified silence made it obvious that indeed it had not occurred to them.

"Makes sense," Clay said. "Which brings up Bodie that Cornish Bob mentioned Bodie, which is that old ghost town in California. That is not the first time Bodie has come up on our radar; we have the French tourist getting killed there not too long ago, as we talked about. What do we have on that, Valentina?"

She tapped the screen of her tablet, and a website appeared on the wall-sized screen. "A good bit. Bodie is now a Historic State Park in California. It used to be the second biggest city in the state, during its heyday. Gold was discovered there back in the late eighteen hundreds, and there was the typical rush. It got a reputation as being the roughest town in the West, with a murder or gunfight every night. Lots of saloons and brothels, only one church that was built only after the town started to decline. Now it is a ghost town, maintained by the California Park System in a state of 'arrested decay.'"

"What about the French tourist? Did we test him for Pangborn?" LaGrue asked.

"That would be a good idea," Clay muttered, making a note.

Tracey was staring intently at the screen, showing ancient wooden buildings, high desert sage brush, and cobalt blue skies. "Oh my God," she said. "I've seen that place."

"A dream?" Clay asked.

Tracey nodded, and described the dream in detail. Afterward, they all pondered it silently.

"Well, the black-and-white wolves are pretty obvious: They must be the guys with the painted faces," Ron said. "What about the guy with the beard wearing flippers, and the tunnel? And could that invisible thing be the ruler of the other universe?"

Tracey placed her face in her hands, and sighed. "I don't know. It was all very upsetting. Even more than the last one."

"So why dream of Bodie right before you meet a guy who was there in the eighteen-eighties?" Clay pondered. "And then have a man tell you that what you are looking for is not on top of the hill, but in a tunnel? What are we looking for? Why are we looking?"

"My guess," Ron said, "is that what we are looking for is the rift that he was talking about. It may still be there."

Clay pursed his lips and nodded. "That makes three references to Bodie in the past week. Sounds pretty clear to me: We should go there and see. We also need to figure out what the raw material is, and protect it from the Horribles at all costs. Cornish Bob said that once they get what they need, they'll try to collapse this universe into theirs. We need to stop that from happening."

"Bodie is remote," Valentina said. "It's about three hours south of Reno, the closest large airport. If we are planning a field trip, may I suggest the RV?"

"Excellent idea," Clay agreed. "I want all of you to provide Valentina a list of what equipment you will need within an hour, and I'll have the RV loaded and flown to Reno within the next twenty-four hours."

"What is the RV?" Ron asked.

"The recreational vehicle," Clay answered with a wry smile. "You'll get a chance to ride on it when we leave Reno. It is my baby; I designed it myself."

"One last thing," Valentina said. "This may be something, maybe not, but I want to bring it up nonetheless. Back at White Mountain, you asked me to research the 'Battle Hymn of the Republic,' because Tracey heard a line from it in her dream. Well, two things came up from that that may be applicable. One: The author of the words to the song came up with them in a dream. Julia Ward Howe dreamed the words to the entire song, woke up, and had to scramble around for a stub of pencil to get them all down before she forgot them. Could she have been a Pangborn recessive carrier? Two: The version we have now is not the original version; she changed them for publication." She tapped the tablet, and words appeared on the wall screen. "In the later version, the one that got published, the last verse reads like this:"

He is coming like the glory of the morning on the wave,
He is wisdom to the mighty, He is honor to the brave;
So the world shall be His footstool, and the soul of wrong
His slave,
Our God is marching on.

"But in the *original* version, the one that came to her in a dream, it is worded like this:"

He is coming like the glory of the morning on the wave,
He is wisdom to the mighty, he is succor to the brave,
So the world shall be his footstool, and the soul of Time his
slave,
Our God is marching on."

They pondered this.

"So," Clay said, "the change went from 'the soul of time' to 'the soul of wrong.' It makes more sense as soul of wrong. What was she talking about, making the 'soul of Time' into God's slave?"

Valentina shrugged. "Don't know. Just thought I would point it out, given the fact that the words first appeared in a dream in eighteen sixty one, without making particular sense then, and now the words came up in another dream a few weeks ago, and reference harnessing Time while we are dealing with potential time-traveling Horribles guys."

"Thank you, Valentina, we will have to mull that over and see," Clay said. "Let's all get to work on gear and logistics of getting to Bodie."

A receptionist appeared and whispered into Clay' ear. His eyes widened. "Ah ha, ladies and gentlemen, it appears that our esteemed benefactor, Mr. Barman, has arrived. And he has brought another of the Mods, a Ms. Duma. We've never had two of them at once before."

Mr. Barman and Ms. Duma entered the room with an air of repressed electricity. Barman was balding, somewhere in his late seventies, with round glasses, and a dark gray suit and tie. Ms. Duma was plump, matronly, in her fifties; had a large halo of black hair that spilled out of what looked like several attempts at tying it up, and wore too much make-up and a too-form-fitting blue dress for her size. They took station at the head of the table while Clay took a seat at the other end. They both made a cursory review of the foot-tall letters printed on the wall screen.

Barman cleared his throat. "Good afternoon." He coughed. "We thought it best to make an appearance, given the gravity of the recent events and the delicacy of your handling."

Nobody said anything.

Ms. Duma shifted her weight back and forth from one ample hip to the other. "It seems they either have no questions or too many to know where to start," Ms. Duma said with a sideways glance at her partner.

"That is our fault," he answered. "We have not exactly been generous with facts about what is going on beyond their immediate surroundings."

"That could not be helped," she argued.

Mr. Barman shrugged. "Our discussions on this have been extensive, but when all was said and done we agreed that flexibility would be required. Now is the time to be somewhat transparent, in spite of the risks."

"What risks?" Clay asked.

"This seed may either fall on rock, and be ignored, or be eaten by the birds of existential nihilism, and lead at best to the dark night of the soul or outright suicide at the worst. Or, as is hoped, it will grow into something useful."

Ron looked around at the others seated around the table, and noted that none of them were in a big hurry to open their mouths, but all seemed willing to hear what the partners would divulge.

"You new people, Ron and Tracey, the others only know a bit more than you do. We came and recruited them, had the underground base built near Denver under the ruse of being the U.S. Space Command. Of course, this was without the oversight of your actual government."

Tracey had had enough. "Okay, I'm lost here. Who are you people? Where are you from? Are you from another country, or another planet?"

Mr. Barman barked a dry laugh, face remaining deadpan. "Ms. Springs, we are from neither. Has Professor LaGrue explained the multiverse theory to you?"

It was Ron's turn for a flinty laugh. "He tried. We didn't exactly get it."

"It wasn't through any lack of wanting to," Tracey answered.

"Well, we are not from this universe. Nor are we from another universe exactly. You have all been discussing dreams. Do you know where these take place?"

Ron noted Professor LaGrue fumbling for a pen and paper. This appeared new to him as well, and might help him to ask for funding his research.

"Inside our brains, I think," Tracey answered.

Ms. Duma smiled. "Not exactly. Not entirely, at least. There is a place beyond time and space where they occur. That place is created by human consciousness. We come from a place like that, while at the same time no place or time at all, while not created by humans. We can call it the *Otherwhen*, for lack of a better term. It is not the same as a separate universe, which have their own stable spacetimes. It is a bit more . . . ." She paused and seemed to be searching for words. "*Fluid.* The floor of this building is such a 'place.'" She looked specifically at Ron. "Ron, I believe you are working on a computer game design where players co-create a world through what they focus on, using a common programming architecture? 'Attention Based Fluid Rendering,' I think you call it?"

Ron sat shocked, he was pretty sure that he hadn't mentioned that to anyone present. "Yes, that is my theory," Ron muttered.

LaGrue scribbled furiously.

"It's sort of like that," Ms. Duma agreed. "But the 'game designer' for our world has made certain ground rules that you might find surprising. For instance, Ron, does your world design include 'cheat codes?'"

Ron suddenly remembered Johnson and Smithson asking him about that, and realized that was where the Mods had heard of this. "No, no cheat codes. Like I told Smithson and Johnson, that makes the game no fun for the players, in the long run."

"What about the short run?"

"Well, that depends on the player," Ron said, warming. "We took all kinds of classes on game design, and it boiled down to how the game engine interacted with the story. You gotta use the proper proportions of skill on the one hand and challenge on the other could lead to maximum enjoyment, or good gaming, in our case. Too much challenge, too hard a game, and people got frustrated. Too little challenge, too much skill, and people got bored. When it is mixed in the right balance . . . ah, there it is. The full immersion, losing the self, timeless magic. Using cheat codes throws that all out of whack."

"Right. Exactly. Then you get the enjoyment, the learning, the purpose. But how about the code-creator? Can he get into the program and make edits? Or can a hacker get hold of the cheat codes and try to mess things up?"

There was silence. Then: "That would depend on the game engine. And what the Moderators were willing to do about it," Ron said, scrutinizing them for their reactions.

"Uh, just a moment," LaGrue said. "Are you claiming that there is, in fact, a Creator? That would either be a claim for the existence of God or an admission that this universe is an artificial construct, like a video game."

"Yes," Ms. Duma said.

There was a pause.

"Well which is it?" Tracey said impatiently.

"There is . . ." Ms. Duma paused, looking for words, ". . . a GROUND. A base, a framework on which patterns of reality are hung. Energetic patterns make up matter, but patterns on top of what? Vibrations, but in what medium? The ground and the patterns are the same thing, both are animated by the breath of conscious beings in a great shared dance, music of the spheres, a resonance of the shared 'I am.'"

"Music of the spheres?" Ron asked. "My father used to talk about that before he died. What does that mean?"

"Perhaps he will tell you someday," Ms. Duma said. "He did leave notes. And who knows, maybe he will tell you in person."

LaGrue snorted. "Gobbledygook woo," he said. "Dead is dead. Are you saying that we continue to exist beyond time, space, and any universe as part of some 'Ground'? And this 'ground' is God, I suppose? Or is he one of the conscious beings in your dance to the celestial harp music? If you are claiming the existence of God, do you have any *evidence* of this?"

"None that you would accept."

LaGrue nodded, vindicated.

"You see, it depends on what you mean by evidence," Barman said. "Evidence for a claim can only be in the same nature as the claim made. Historical claims can only be proven with historical evidence. Mathematical claims require mathematical proof, not scientific. Evidence can be a dial on a meter, if you mean scientific quantifiable reproducible evidence, or it can mean testimony or circumstantial evidence if you think of it like evidence admissible in court."

LaGrue scowled. "Well, I require the former. Extraordinary claims require extraordinary proof. And now I suppose you can just relegate my refusal to buy this theory, which has occurred to every half-brained college freshman on weed, to me being one of those hard grounds that the seeds fell on."

Ms. Duma shrugged. "Look, if Ron took on a character in Dungeon Throne and had the programming to speak to the other characters in there and tell them it was all a construct, the characters would either be annoyed that he was ruining the illusion or deny it utterly based on the evidence that surrounded them."

"Depending on whether they were player characters or not?" Ron asked.

"Oh, no," Mr. Barman said. "You are all player characters, all right. It just depends on how finely tuned you are to the game."

"Please explain," Tracey said.

"Mystics, madmen, and dreamers are only half playing at 'reality,'" Ms. Duma explained. "They know there is more to things than they appear, they just don't know exactly what. They are like cracked eggs. They pay the price for their 'poor play' by being marginalized. Materialists and athletes and the rich and powerful are dialed right into the game. They are playing hard. They are solid eggs. But they are deluding themselves into thinking this is reality, and not the big game."

"So you are saying," Ron mulled, "that you are from where we are from when we are not here playing this video game of our lives in this universe. And that when we die we are done playing the game and go back to whatever you are like wherever you are?"

Duma and Barman answered only with elusive smiles.

"And what are you two while you are here, then?"

"We are projections. Not fully injected into this Ground and invested for a lifespan like you are," Ms. Duma said.

"So you really are Mods. Moderators *and* Modifications of the programming," Ron said.

"Yet you are here, interacting with the material world," LaGrue pointed out. "So what is the difference?"

"Well, duration for one thing. Once we are done projecting here we cease to exist on this Ground until we need to reappear. And it takes a little work to pull this off. Interacting with material objects is optional, and takes more energy. Just standing here talking, appearing to be solid is hard enough."

"So you are only solid when you want to be?" Ron puzzled out. "And do you look like your real selves? Can you be in our world like you really are?"

"Oh no, we would shatter the Ground if we were to do that. We only project. Projecting from the outside, we have to account for the angle and motion of your building on the land, the land's curvature on the rotating planet, the planet's movement around your sun, the sun's movement around the galactic core. . . . If we were to start losing a little concentration . . . ."

With a subtle shift, the visual edges of Mr. Barman and Ms. Duma began to blur, flicker, and tilt in relation to the floor. With a sickening lurch, they appeared to be standing at a 60 degree angle to the floor. The humans were astonished, dizzied, and fought the urge to re-orient themselves in relation to the Mods. With a slight flash, the Mods were suddenly standing before them as though it had not happened.

"Don't do that again," Valentina moaned.

"Sorry." Ms. Duma laughed.

"So your 'screen' and ours are not lined up," Ron said. "And this is all some kind of Virtual Reality Massive Multiplayer Online Role Playing Game? So who is the Big Dungeon Master?"

"That you will have to decide for yourselves," Mr. Barman said.

"So what possible difference does this make, even assuming it is true?" LaGrue asked, tenting his hands.

"It makes all the difference, in one sense," Ms. Duma said. "And on the other hand, it doesn't make any difference whatsoever."

"Then why tell us? Why go through all the trouble to expose your secrets, deal with us, and appear in this world at all?" Clay asked.

Mr. Barman flashed a ghost of a smile. "Well, you cannot help but notice when we first approached you. Right after the rift opened up. We wanted to warn you. And we want to get our rift generator back."

"The rift generator? Like the one Cornish Bob had?"

"That's the one."

"There is only one?" LaGrue asked. "You don't have any others?"

"And, as to why we are here with you right now instead of just dealing with your higher-ups in government, is to do some recruiting," Ms. Duma said.

They stared at her with narrowed eyes.

"We need to have Ron and Tracey," she continued. "Ron, once you were outed as a gene carrier, we had to make sure you with us instead of the other side. And Tracey, you will have to start your formal training soon."

"Formal training for what?"

"Part of what we do is train those who possess certain attributes to protect those who have other certain attributes to protect them from certain dangers," Ms. Duma answered.

The Space Command personnel stared expectantly for further explanation.

"Ah, sorry," Ms. Duma said with a slight smile. "We have the irritating tendency to be overly vague because we cannot be satisfyingly clear. What I mean is that what you call the 'Pangborn gene' is manifested fully in Ron here and partially in you, Tracey. But it is not exactly a gene like hair color, race, or any such inheritable trait. Those genes are imprinted directly into the DNA. Normal genes can replicate on cell division and be passed on through procreation with other beings. The Pangborn gene, while it manifests in the genetic code, is not inherited nor can it be transmitted through cell replication or division. It appears directly from the Ground, and disappears into it upon death."

"Through what mechanism?" LaGrue asked, pen poised over his notes.

"Through the deliberate choice of conscious agents from the Ground altering the code," Mr. Barman answered. "You can analogize it to little spirits possessing or hijacking the genetic code of the gene carriers, which meld back into the Ground and disappear when cells die. They do not manifest when DNA replicates, or when sperm and ova join, like other reproductive cell processes. That is why our enemy has had no luck in breeding gene carriers. The full expression of this genetic pattern, when it chooses to manifest, has the effect of preventing the collapse of alternative universes into each other, which would otherwise be absorbed by surface tension."

"So if I understand you correctly," LaGrue said, "if someone has this gene, they can keep an entire universe from disappearing that otherwise would."

"That is correct," Ms. Duma said. "And now you see the value of possessing and controlling one who has that gene."

"An entire universe full of . . . everything," LaGrue said. "Material, energy . . . people."

They all pondered the magnitude of this.

"And those who partially manifest the gene, like Tracey, have their roles, too. There are many levels of consciousness, and only some are connected to the material world. Dreaming is such an alternative one, and you humans are just beginning to discover the purposes and capabilities of it. Tracey, your training will center on that, and one of the benefits of it will be to provide protection to a paired full gene carrier. It is no accident that you ended up mated to Ron. Your genes conspired to bring that about."

Tracey blushed, frowning.

"Don't worry, you won't be able to fully take on that mantle until your training is complete. In the meantime, Smithson will have to substitute. He has temporarily lost his charge."

Clay glanced at Smithson. *Knew he had some connection I didn't see. Was he supposed to be guarding Jack Strong? Will have to interrogate him about this later.*

"For now," Barman said, "you need to focus on the matter at hand, the mission before you."

Tracey shook her head. "I'm sorry, but this is really pissing me off. You say you are aliens from another universe, or cheat-coders, or something. And most of the Space Command people here just take this at face value. Either you are clever computer projections or liars or crazy or—"

The Space Command people sat in silence, their

incredulity tempered with curiosity. They were embarrassed both because Tracey had asked about this and that they had never done so.

Mr. Barman nodded with a lopsided smile. "Or we are what we say we are. That is okay; it is good that you are annoyed with this. It shows you have a solid root into the Ground's rules of how things should be. You are a solid egg, and yet a dreamer, too. That is quite rare and may help you later."

Tracey resumed her scowl. *Rules of how things should be? Help me do what later? TRAINING?*

"By all means, go down to Bodie and look for that rift," Mr. Barman said, again looking at the discussion topics on the wall screen. "Recover our rift generator. And of course your friend Jack Strong. God knows we are running out of gene carriers here. That little Cornish Bob fellow mentioned a rift being made there, and there it might still be. If not, go back to Denver and use that rift; but it might still be manned by enemies as a trap. That is how this whole thing started, you know."

"What started?" Clay asked. "Your war? Sounds like it was going pretty strong for them to grab your rift generator."

"That is a tale for another time," Barman stated. "But that is indeed another reason that prompted our intrusions into this world's affairs. She stole the rift generator from us because she cannot manufacture one on her own, and without it our options are severely limited."

"Who exactly is our enemy?" Clay asked.

Ron thought it odd that Clay did not know, either, in spite of a longer term contact with the Mods. He also noted that Smithson was not the least bit curious. *Did he know about them already?*

"The ones you have seen," Ms. Duma said, "call themselves 'the Horribles.' They work, like they told you, for an entity that calls herself 'the Queen of the Universe.' She is not, of course, but she is quite powerful and dangerous. We have been waging a guerilla resistance against her from both sides for some time. It is possible that you may run into some of our agents."

"So will you be giving us any cool equipment to help us over there?" Ron asked.

"Equipment? Like what?" Mr. Barman asked.

"You know . . . ray guns, x-ray-vision glasses, super-strength flying suits? Alien goodies? . . . . Cheat codes?"

Mr. Barman blinked. "No, nothing like that."

"We don't work that way," Ms. Duma said. "All you need to take as far as we are concerned are your brains, hearts, and hands."

Nobody said anything to that, although Ron was pretty sure that the Space Command people intended to take considerably more than those.

"Well, we must be off now. God's speed to you all," Mr. Barman said abruptly, and they scurried off.

Tracey shook her head in their wake. "Well, there they go, off to the Netherwhen. A lot of help they were."

"Otherwhen. They said 'Otherwhen,'" Ron corrected.

"Whatever," Tracey rejoined. "Who cares what they call it if they don't explain what it is or how it can help us? And how is it you guys, who have had contact with this guy before, still don't know anything about them? How do you know they aren't the bad guys?"

Clay spread his hands. "We don't. They have been very tight-lipped and vague. You see how they are. All codes and hidden meanings. It's like they are trying to cram more into the English language than it can carry."

"Do you buy all that about this being a big video game?" Tracey asked.

LaGrue slammed his hand on the desk. "Garbage," he hissed. "They are obviously energy projections, but entirely from within our universe, or from a different universe in the multiverse, at most. There is nothing outside of that. What interests me is why they are trying to pawn that off on us."

"Like they said, I can't see that it makes a bit of difference at this point, even if it is true," Clay said with raised eyebrows. "The only thing to do is get on with the game, if that is what it is."

He adjourned the meeting to allow LaGrue, Smithson, and Pavlov time to compile their lists of needed equipment.

−14−

Ron and Tracey wandered back to the safe house apartments down the hall.

"Well, that was weird. And useless."

"Well, weird at least," Ron said. "Kind of monumental if it is true that all of reality is a big version of Dungeon Throne."

"Really? And how is that monumental? If we are locked into this virtual reality until we die, what difference does that make?"

"I don't know. I just feel that it does. I'll have to mull that over. Maybe . . . like, what happens after we stop playing the game? What kind of 'real life' elsewhere do we have?"

Tracey considered this.

"And," Ron continued, "they said that our whole universe was like my game design theory. Are they programmers? Mods as in moderators? Other Player Characters just more leveled-up? Do they have the cheat codes? *That* would make a difference."

"What the hell are these 'cheat codes' you're talking about?"

Ron rubbed his chin. "Well, it is a game thing. Some games have codes that the players can find out about that let them have advantages in the game. It started with programmers using them to test what they were designing, but later they were exploited by players, to get unlimited money, lives, ammunition, invisibility, invulnerability, that sort of thing."

"Well, if those Mod types have the ability to give us advantages like that, then why the hell don't they?"

"Maybe they don't. Maybe the bad guys got the cheat codes by taking the rift generator."

There was a knock on their door. It was Adrian Smithson and Valentina Pavlov.

"Sorry to interrupt," she said, "but we have to put these

equipment requisitions together and need to get some measurements and preferences from you."

"Oh, you mean we are taking more than our hands and our hearts?" Tracey rolled her eyes. "Come in." She was still suspicious of hidden cameras.

"We'll take our hands all right, but we need something in them. Weapons," Smithson said. "We are going into what may be a war zone, so we need to have you both squared away."

"And I need to implant the sub-voca chips so we can all stay in touch," Valentina said.

"No, thanks," Tracey said. "No electronics will be implanted in my head."

"I'll pass on that one as well," Ron said.

Valentina fidgeted a moment. "Well, I suppose we could scare up some of the old belt radios with earphones."

"What did you have in mind for weapons and stuff?" Ron asked Smithson.

"Lightweight Kevlar vests, at the minimum. Concealed sidearms, backup knives, maybe."

"I still have my .357," Ron told him.

Smithson asked to inspect it, then gave it his stamp of approval. "If you would like to practice, we have a range on site. What about you, Tracey?"

"I don't want a gun, either. I have never shot in my life, and frankly the thought of shooting someone after the other day makes me ill."

"And being shot yourself doesn't?" Ron asked. "Look, I get that you wish none of this was happening, and you want everything to be like it was, but you can't stick your head in the sand and act like it isn't."

"I think a little .38 Special revolver would be suitable," Smithson said. "We could load it up with the right ammunition. No need to chamber rounds, fish for safeties. I could show you how to use it in a flash down at the range."

"All right," Tracey reluctantly agreed.

Valentina touched Tracey on the arm. "Why don't you two boys get a head start down there, and I'll bring Tracey along in a minute."

Ron and Tracey exchanged glances.

"Sure," she said. "You guys go ahead."

Smithson and Ron left.

"Tracy, I just wanted to take a minute to put your mind at ease. I sensed a bit of . . . tension back there at the meeting."

Tracey nodded. "I am not normally a jealous type. I hate it when women view men like they are hot commodities, as if we are seagulls fighting over a dead fish. I don't think most men are worthy of all the work some women put into catching one. Not that Ron isn't worth fighting for, he's a good man and those are rare. And *because* he is a good man, I trust him. That said, I am worth fighting over myself, and he realizes it. Normally, I wouldn't pay too much attention to this, or feel as competitive, but I had a dream." She told Valentina about her first dream.

"I can see why you are concerned," Valentina said, touching Tracey's arm consolingly. "And you do seem like someone he should be willing to fight for. Women like you are rare, too. Maybe even more rare than good men, in my experience. But you know, are you sure it was even me inside that tent?"

Tracey shrugged.

"Besides, I have my eyes on someone else," Valentina confessed.

"Really?" Tracey asked, feeling better about her. "Do tell. And please tell me it isn't LaGrue, even though he is panting after you like a puppy."

"Ugh." She grimaced. "No, definitely not him. There is something off about LaGrue. But it is someone on the team. I feel like a schoolgirl," Valentina said, face reddening, "but I have a thing for Adrian Smithson. He's so, I don't know, dedicated, focused. He is capable of tremendous violence, yet he's so courteous. You know, he is religious, too. And strong! He can do one-armed pull-ups! It just drives me nuts thinking of what else he is capable of . . . ."

Tracey laughed. "Well, I hope you find out someday. He kind of creeps me out, though, after the other day, speaking of being creeped-out by team members."

"I know what you mean, but he's really not like that, a cold-blooded killer or anything. I've never seen him kill anybody in front of me, though. Not sure how I would react to that, either. I don't blame you for being put off with him. Anyway, I did hint around with him a while ago, but he was having none of it. He's probably one of those guys who thinks he couldn't afford to get emotionally attached, it wouldn't be fair on the woman. . . ." She trailed off, then abruptly changed the topic. "Let's catch up with the guys. I need to switch gears down at the range."

She led them down the hall. They reached the firing range. Tracey noticed the acrid smell of expended cordite.

Ron and Smithson were examining an assault rifle, which looked like something out of a science fiction movie.

"Check this out, Tracey," Ron ogled. "This is a . . . ." He glanced at Smithson for a prompt.

"Heckler and Koch XM8 battle rifle," Smithson recited, placing a magazine into the rifle and smoothly chambering a round. "The Army was thinking about replacing their M-16s and M-4s with it."

"Yeah," Ron continued. "It's the latest thing . . . and has . . . oh, you tell her," he surrendered.

"The XM8 has a replaceable fiber reinforced polycarbonate shell, which can be switched out depending on terrain, and four replaceable barrels which can convert it from a compact to a carbine to a sniper rifle to a heavy rate-of-fire tripod-mounted automatic within two minutes in the field," Smithson recited, pointing out the features.

"Oh, brother," Valentina mocked, "boys and their toys."

"It fires standard 5.56mm NATO ball rounds, but is lighter and more reliable than an M-16. It has a state-of-the-art integrated optics package, with an infrared laser target designator, IR target illuminator, and close-combat red-dot sight. It has two attachable weapons systems mounted on the stock under the barrel. Standard is a 40mm grenade launcher or a shotgun, but I modified the second hard-point rail to remove the shotgun and accommodate two pressurized canisters, one of acid and the other of a propellant and oxidizer. When activated, it shoots a plasma of flaming acid."

"Holy crap," Ron said.

"And do you know whether *any* of this will kill one of

those Horribles guys?" Tracey asked.

"No, it will not," Smithson answered forthrightly. "But we do know that a direct shot that destroys the connection between the brain and the body will kill them, or at least render them powerless. They are zombies, after all. And who knows, the flaming acid could incapacitate them without such a precise shot. So, better to have these weapons than not. Besides, there may be any number of other bad guys to shoot at."

"What else will you be stocking?" Ron asked.

"I'm thinking that we may have a limited amount of ordinance to carry, so maybe just the XM8 and a sidearm, and the standard supplemental tools. I think I will carry the Springfield XDM this time instead of the Sig Sauer P229. It carries just as many rounds of .45 caliber rounds as the 9mm on the Sig, and that may be helpful scrambling spinal cords. We'll also need some explosives, like a couple of claymores, some M2 SLAMs, maybe a couple of blocks of C4 and some Primacord."

"Well, you seem to be ready to take on just about anything," Tracey said, raising an eyebrow. "You think you could squeeze a fighter jet into the car, too? Or maybe a light-saber?"

"If only we knew what we were going to be taking on, I could narrow the focus a bit," he answered. "Meanwhile, let me show you two how to shoot."

They donned sound-suppressing headphones and safety glasses, and Smithson gave them a short round of instruction. Ron found that he enjoyed it, to his surprise. He sighted down the barrel of his pistol, lining up the two white dots at the back end of the barrel with the single dot at the end, placing the whole construction on the target . . . he felt his awareness travel across the air, onto the paper, onto the circular marking of the paper, seemed to meld the target, his pistol, and himself into one construct, one thing, as he squeezed the trigger. . . . His .357 roared, much louder than Smithson's .45, with a large muzzle flash. Ron saw the neat hole an inch away from the bull's-eye.

"Nice shot," Smithson said. "You seem to have a knack for

this. Have you ever shot before, or studied Kyudo?"

"Kyudo?"

"Zen archery. Active meditation; effortlessly hitting the target, literally and as a metaphor for life. Never mind."

"No, really," Ron said, "this is interesting."

Smithson sighed. "Maybe another time. I have to sweep up this brass."

"I'll help," Valentina said, looking for another broom.

Ron and Tracey left the range area with a knowing glance at each other, careful not to trip on any of the brass shell casings on the way out.

*****

Smithson and Pavlov swept in silence for a little while, shoving the shell casings down the firing lanes for later retrieval.

Both felt the tension between them building, and both looked for something to say.

Say something! Valentina thought. At no point in her life had she ever had to be the aggressor in any romantic interaction. Even as a young girl, her lanky beauty had been like an intoxicant for pedophiles, several of which had forced themselves on her. When she reported these attacks to her English immigrant mother, she refused to believe her, perhaps due to her own fear of deportation should she "rock the boat" with criminal reports. For a time, Valentina purposely dressed shabbily and made efforts to appear unkempt and dirty, but found that this only attracted another species of verminous abuser. As she grew into a young woman, her beauty blossomed. Her anger and shame was redirected into a feeling of power over men, and she was able to parlay her looks into money, apartments, and even eventually medical school. She became the spider instead of the fly. Eventually, though, this galled her, and she turned away from physical desire and concentrated on her work. Until Smithson, that is. Perhaps what attracted her was that he did not seem attracted to her. This had never happened, and it intrigued her.

"So, are you hungry?" he finally blurted out awkwardly.

"Of course," she said. "It's been a long day."

"Ah . . . so, I know a good Pakistani curry place?"

She smiled lopsidedly. *Maybe instead of avoiding women out of altruism he is just clueless with them!*

"Sure. That would be great."

He made a pathetic attempt at concealing a sigh of relief. "Great. Okay, well, maybe we should see if Ron and Tracey want to go."

"Let's do that," she said. *Yup. Clueless it is.*

*****

The four of them met at the elevator bank, and piled into one of them. Smithson activated the card reader, then pressed the button for the ground floor.

They hustled into the drizzly city streets. Tracey looked back at the building they had just exited. Something struck her as odd about it.

"Twelve floors," Ron whispered.

"Huh?" Tracey whispered back.

"The elevator had buttons for twelve floors, and I just counted the building from the outside. Twelve floors."

"So?"

"So if there was a floor hidden in there somewhere that we were just on, where is it?"

"Oh, you know, it must be like those buildings where there isn't a thirteenth floor, or at least there is, but it's labeled as the fourteenth. Or something."

"That doesn't make any sense. Besides, look at the size of the building. You think it's wide enough to have all those apartments, meeting rooms, and a freaking gun range in there? And why were there no windows? You can see windows on every floor from here."

Smithson, who overheard them, wheeled around with a grin. "Your first taste of Otherwhen," he said, walking backward. "These things happen when dealing with the Mods. That floor is there, but it isn't."

"How many places do they have like that?" Tracey asked.

"As many as they want," Smithson answered mysteriously.

He turned up his jacket hood to the drizzle, then led them many blocks to a nondescript hole-in-the-wall curry place.

They all ordered the lamb and spinach curry on Smithson's recommendation, and were not disappointed.

-15-

Ron watched the others eat, and was struck at how nonchalant they were in spite of just being told that everything around them was as unreal as playing a game of Dungeon Throne, just more granular. *Did they not understand this? Not believe it? Maybe Clay was right when he said it made no difference.* He remembered back to what Cornish Bob had said, that everyone in this universe was unreal, that the real universe was another one. Was that true? Isn't that what the Mods said? The Horribles already considered people in this world as no more than characters in a video game, and had fun shooting them like game players do. Wasn't that what Mr. Barman and Ms. Duma were saying, too?

He thought back to his five years of work on a first-person shooter computer game. His boss had constantly stressed realism in programming the characters and the enemies they would shoot. "I want the gamers to think those bad guys are real!" he had exhorted. "After gunning them down, I want them to wonder if those guys had pictures of their families in their *wallets*!" Was God just the Big Game Programmer, just on levels of detail far beyond what we can produce? Are we just characters in his "game"? Did God just solve the Attention Based Fluid Rending problem quicker than he did, and was this world just his own MMORPG on an infinite scale, like they said? Is that why the Mods won't give us the cheat codes, because that would ruin the flow of this game?

And who is playing this game, and what is beyond it, where the programmers and game designers are? Are we souls, playing this game? What are we when the game is through? What about counterparts in other universes? If there was another Ron Golden in that universe, who had the soul? He shuddered, then remembered that Ms. Duma had said that because of his full Pangborn gene, there was only one of him. But what about Tracey? Are we all player characters, like she said, or are some of us NPCs?

"You're awful quiet. What are you thinking about?" Tracey asked, dabbing curry from the corner of her mouth with a napkin.

"Religion, and what the Mods said," he answered.

Smithson chuckled. "Just play, man."

They thanked the proprietor, and started back to the software building.

"How long have you studied your martial arts thing?" Ron asked, filling the silence that was growing more pregnant between Smithson and Valentina.

Smithson pursed his lips while he walked in the dark drizzle, thinking. "Since before I went into the military. Like a lot of smaller-framed kids, I got picked on in school. Fear is the wrong reason to get started, but the most common, I guess. If you don't find something else in it, like something spiritual, I mean, you tend to drop out. I didn't." He looked as though he was searching for the right words. "I knew a guy, a senior student in one of my Aikido classes, who had this theory about life. He said that each and every one of us was here for *a purpose*. When most people hear that, he told me, they think that it is some *big* life mission, like curing a disease, or founding a new sandwich chain or something. Some people tone it down a little, and feel that their life mission is to do a good job, or even just to have kids that grow up to do some big thing. This guy, he had it different. He knew he had something to do, but thought 'What if the thing I'm supposed to do is really, really small, like pick up a nail out of the road, which prevents an accident, that prevents the death of a guy who would go on to have the kid who discovered the cure to the common cold?' He thought, 'What the hell, what if most of us have some miniscule, seemingly unimportant yet crucially important thing to do as their goal in life?' This guy was convinced that there was some little thing, and that *he had already done it*. He just knew that his goal on this Earth had been accomplished. He was done. The rest was gravy."

They reached the door to the software building, but

lingered outside in the cold mist, wanting to hear more before retiring.

"It gave the guy," Smithson continued, "a very laid back attitude. Nothing really bothered him, he was able to relax and enjoy things. He was taking Aikido just to enjoy the learning, and the feeling of effortless movement and being attuned to the energy of it. He didn't worry about his job, or usual day-to-day stuff. He rubbed off on me, too. I started to be convinced that I had done what I had been destined to do, too. Maybe it was saying something nice to someone in a park, and then that person decided not to kill himself. I didn't know, but I felt that there was some good deed, rippling out like a wave in a pond, that I had already done it and that it was enough. It didn't have to be recognized, and in fact, it would have made it better if nobody even knew I did it. So shines a good deed in a weary world." He paused, thinking back.

"What happened?" Valentina asked.

"I moved on, got sent to Afghanistan. That attitude didn't survive there long. There was a lot of senseless death there, and that kind of thinking cheapened it. It was kind of crappy, in the face of all that misery. It occurred to me also that we may, just maybe, have *more than one* purpose in life, and mine was not necessarily over. It began to grow on me that I did have something else to do, some purpose yet undone. I knew that I had to keep sharp and trained so that I would be around to do it, whatever 'it' was, when the time came. I couldn't selfishly relax, like my Aikido friend. It also occurred to me that the whole idea of having to *do* something, rather than *be someone*, was wrong. And then it occurred to me that maybe the point was not doing something, or being someone, but having the experience of living and learning and loving without the overlay of either of them."

And that was when I was approached to do the real training, he thought, but was unable to tell them. *When the student is ready, the master appears.*

Nobody showed any inclination to open the door, so they continued to stand outside the building in the drizzle, brought out as white streaks in the streetlights.

"How about you all? You finished your missions in life yet?"

"Not me," Valentina said. "I feel the need to settle down and raise a family. But I'm afraid I'll never meet the right man." She sent a sidelong glance at Smithson, who showed no indication he understood the hint.

"Not me, either," Ron said, also oblivious. "I'm a bowling pin. A sailboat with no tiller. I don't even know what my mission is, other than program a world."

"Well, that isn't necessarily bad," Smithson said. "A lot of Eastern philosophies stress *not* having any ego-driven plans and goals. How about you, Tracey?"

Tracey considered for a moment. "I think that we have two. Well, I can only speak for myself, anyway, but these could just as easily apply to anyone if they wanted to accept them. First, I want to . . . how to say this . . . increase a sense of sacredness, of holiness—no, *wholeness*, in my life— not just for myself, but for everyone around me. Like we were just talking about."

"Touch and be the mind and eye of God," Smithson said.

"Right. Well, but without the need for a god. And second, learn what I'm supposed to learn in this lifetime."

"Interesting you say both of those things, Tracey," Smithson said. "I'm part of that . . . *group*, you could say, that Barman mentioned, who have goals like those as part of their basic mission. Barman mentioned your training starting soon. Perhaps you would be interested in starting at some point?"

"I think I can accomplish my goals by raising sea otters and octopi, and working in the garden at home."

Just what the best ones say, Smithson thought. "How about you, Ron? You said your mission in life was to build a world?"

"My mission in life," he said, with an inscrutable gaze into space, "is to create a video game with as much reality as reality, just on a smaller scale, not just use my genes to keep one in existence. And of course, since in video games you can't really eat, to eat as much good fried chicken in the real world as I can."

Tracey shook her head. "You're a genius."

"Good plan." Smithson nodded, one eye narrowed. "But too bad you didn't mention that before we had curry."

"There is always hope for tomorrow," Ron joked to move along.

For me, too, Smithson thought, but not about chicken.

*****

Later, Tracey lay in the dark, eyes opened, staring at the black ceiling in their room at the twelfth-floor living quarters. The accommodations were significantly better than those at White Mountain.

"Are you awake?" she whispered.

"Mmm-hmph," Ron mumbled.

"Are we ever going to get out of this? I mean, how is this going to end and we get back to regular life, like it was?"

She heard Ron sit up on his elbow, thinking. "I don't know. The Horribles zombie guys *are* trying to *kill* us. Me, at least, and probably you if you are roped into trying to protect me or something. Do we have to kill them all, or can we convince them to stop? It seems we can't just hide from them. Will I have to look over my shoulder for the rest of my life, however long that might be? Can we just seal off the rifts between the worlds? What good would that do, if they can make their own? I mean, what exactly are we trying to do? What is a win here? And even if we manage somehow to do that, what if it turns out the cancer test wasn't wrong, and I have to start popping pills and getting irradiated?"

"Exactly."

He lay back down, joined her in staring at the ceiling in the dark. The lack of answers lay like a beast in the dark. Eventually, they slept.

*****

By mid-morning, Clay had assembled them, ready to travel, at the building loading dock. Johnson pulled a dark sedan to the doors, and they loaded in for the trip to Boeing Field. Ron and Tracey exchanged glances.

"Uh, we were wondering," Ron said, scratching his arm, recalling the night before. "How is all this going to resolve? I mean, when will it be okay for us to go back and live in

Seattle as a Game Programmer and Aquarium Biologist?"

Clay sighed. "Wish I knew. It may come down to ending the threat to our security by eliminating the threat on the other side. We have to find out just what we are up against first, since the Mods were less than clear about it. That means either using one of those rift generators like Cornish Bob used or going through a rift ourselves. I hope we find the one in Bodie that Cornish Bob used; we should only use the one at White Mountain as a last resort and watch for the trappers."

"I just feel like this is some kind of bad dream," Tracey said. "We have no choice but to stumble along, powerless."

"I understand," Clay reassured her. "I have no easy answers, though. We're all stumbling along at this point."

"Welcome to my world," Ron muttered.

Clay stared out the window. People often looked to him for answers, and it was rare for a clear answer to come. It was just expected of him, being the one in charge, to know more of what was going on. They all assumed he had some kind of pipeline to the Mods. Perhaps it was just a hope that he knew more. He had learned over time to keep up the veneer of knowledge and control. His career had steadily advanced because of the skill, but it wore on him more the higher and faster he had advanced. *I wonder if the team will start looking more to Smithson for that, now that they outed him. Still have to have a chat with him about that.*

–16–

They traveled the rest of the way in silence, and boarded the unmarked white Gulfstream. Johnson stayed behind with the sedan after bidding them farewell and good luck.

The team flew south. After three hours, they circled the Reno International Airport, watching the treeless desert hills while waiting for a gap in the civilian air traffic. They landed, and taxied not into the terminal, but into a series of large hangers on the side of the field.

"Air National Guard," Clay explained. "One Hundred Fifty-Second Airlift Wing, the 'High Rollers.' They were courteous enough to fly the RV out of Denver for us, after our people stocked and equipped it for us."

They disembarked the plane, the Air Force support crew saluted, and led them to the RV.

"Okay, Ron and Tracey, look this thing over and tell me if you see anything out of the ordinary about it," Clay asked, with poorly suppressed enthusiasm.

Ron and Tracey politely walked around the RV, while Professor LaGrue, Valentina, and Smithson stood by, rolling their eyes at Clay' boyish enthusiasm.

The RV appeared to be a normal Winnebago, all the way down to the Nevada plates, the stickers showing which states it had traveled to. There was even a bumper sticker that read "We're spending our grandkids' inheritance."

Once inside, Clay pointed out the advanced weapons, communications, armor, fabrication, and support systems. "The roof folds back into the sides and exposes a retractable turret with a 105mm tank gun. It sleeps six, and the kitchenette is fully stocked. We can live on this thing as a self-sustained base for a month."

Ron oohed and aahed appreciatively as they pulled onto State Highway 395 and headed south. Tracey politely withheld comments about how the Mods probably could have made an even more impressive vehicle, but for some reason would not do so.

Smithson approached Ron and Tracey, bearing body armor and holsters. "Now would be a good time to put these on. The vests are the latest lightweight models, made of several layers of Kevlar. Most body armor is useless against knife attacks, so we had to use a special material to protect against that."

They donned the vests, which were surprisingly lightweight and did not restrict movement much. Ron also put on a shoulder holster for his Colt Python, and covered it all with a lightweight flannel jacket. Tracey mounted her small revolver inside her waistline in the small of her back, also concealing the vest and gun with a light jacket. It struck her as stressful to have the gun so close to her, and wondered if she would forget it was there. The lump in the small of her back while she sat proved impossible to ignore. She eventually put the pistol into her jacket pocket. They mounted the little radios that Valentina Pavlov gave them on their holsters, and put the Bluetooth ear bud speakers in their pockets.

They passed the capital building in Carson City, and continued on through Minden and Gardnerville. The strip malls and gas stations were gradually replaced with longer and longer stretches of wide open, treeless, stark terrain. They passed a sterile-looking lake, and crossed the California Border. The agricultural check station was closed. The road meandered through steep-walled canyons, where magpies flitted from the roadside onto fences. It looked like something out of a car commercial, without the ubiquitous "professional driver on closed course" disclaimer.

After another hour of driving thorough mountains, they passed a wide, grassy field dotted with cattle. The Sierras loomed purplish in the west. They approached the town of Bridgeport, California, and stopped for gas. Bridgeport was a small town, but was the biggest group of buildings they had seen for hours. The smell of sage and cows was in the air, which was remarkably clean and crisp in the late afternoon sky.

"Please stay in the cab," Smithson said to Ron and Tracey. "I don't know how the Horribles could possibly know we are here, but you never know."

Clay swung up the stairs into the cab, and called over to Valentina to activate the communications bank. She opened a wood panel, disguised to look like a pantry, revealing a large computer screen and panels of dials and readouts.

"Cellular is weak here, but the Comsat uplink is crystal," she reported. After a few moments of tapping, an Asian woman in a lab coat appeared on the screen.

"Good afternoon, Lieutenant Park," Clay greeted her. "Any update on the mechanical spider we sent you from the dead zombie?"

"Not much," she answered, from the jerky video image. "Just an animated communicator/computer/GPS/cellphone/holographic projector, that I plan to steal the design for, then enter the public sector and retire in fabulous riches."

"What about a rift generator?"

"No luck. It appears that only the head Horrible had one of those."

"How are they powered?"

"It isn't giving off any radiant energy of any kind we can measure. The power supply looks like a little silver marble in the abdomen, but it doesn't have any wires or leads attached to it. We have no idea how it works."

"Well, keep on it."

"We'll keep you posted," she answered.

They headed south again out of Bridgeport. The turnoff to Bodie was seven miles away. They pulled onto the Bodie Road, and read the signs warning them that there was no gas or other services there, and that the last three miles of the road was rough and unpaved. The road twisted for ten miles, through rocky outcroppings, until the hills became even higher and the vistas opened out. Not a single tree could be seen in the high desert scrub, only rocks, sage, and the occasional bird or small mammal scurrying across the road. The pavement ended, and they had to slow to a crawl on the dusty washboard. Tracey peered worriedly out the right side window at the sheer drops onto rocky steep slopes.

The sun was dropping as they rounded the crest of a ridge and saw Bodie laid out in a valley below them. Most of the buildings were made of ancient, weathered wood; some leaned crazily, supported by poles; some were mere piles of lumber. One big, metal-sided building stood on the hillside, looking like some kind of factory. A cemetery behind a fence rested on a hill on the left side of the road, approaching town. The hill beyond the town was sprinkled with lighter-colored tailings piles. The high desert sage was reclaiming the town.

They came to a small kiosk in the middle of the road, placed to sell tickets. Smithson slowed, but the kiosk was closed. A leaning sign next to a rusting ore cart welcomed them to the Bodie State Historic Park, and informed them that the altitude was 8,375 feet. They pulled the RV slowly to the parking lot. By the time they reached it, a white pickup truck with a California State Parks logo was heading toward them, raising a cloud of dust.

Clay exited the cab down the retractable metal stairs as the truck rolled to a stop. A ranger stepped unhurriedly out of the truck. He wore green pants, a tan shirt with state park patches, a badge, and a Smokey-the-Bear-like hat. He was armed with a pistol and a radio. His eyes were striking blue, with crow's feet. He sported a gray, cowboy-like mustache.

"Sorry, folks, the park closes at six," he said in a relaxed, friendly but authoritative drawl.

He appeared to have had to chase tourists off countless times after closing, and was merely waiting for one of two responses: begging to be allowed to stay past closing, "We drove many miles and won't stay long"; or an inquiry into the nearest camping areas. He got neither.

Clay introduced himself, and the two of them slowly walked off a few paces. Clay showed him his identification. They conversed in an unhurried manner.

Here are two men accustomed to being listened to, Ron thought.

The Ranger pointed some things out on the ridge, Clay nodded.

"Can we get out?" Ron asked.

Valentina held up her hand. "Not yet. This could be an important and delicate beginning. We need to pay our respect."

Presently the ranger drove away, and Clay re-entered the cab.

"I told Ranger Tanner that we are here to investigate the murder of the French tourist. And look for a rift into another universe. He has allowed us to camp up at the old boy-scout encampment, and has further invited us to attend a bonfire over the top of the bluff this evening. Apparently, there are scientists who show up every spring to study the pikas, and they throw a party of sorts when they arrive and leave at the end of the season."

"The pikas?" Ron asked. "What are the pikas?"

"Small, rabbit-like rodents that live in mountains in rock piles," Professor LaGrue answered. "They don't hibernate, and spend all winter under feet and feet of snow, doing who knows what."

Smithson drove out of the parking lot, along the edge of town, and onto a road that paralleled the bluff. A few hundred yards past the stone shell of a building was an area with greener grass. It appeared to be nothing more than a turn-around for campers and RV's.

"This is it," Clay announced.

They pulled in. The only structures were a small housing for a pump and a Port-O-Let.

"Lovely," Tracey announced as she exited the RV with the others.

"I'm starving," Valentina said. "What did the guys in Colorado stock for us?"

They looked in the galley, and found ground meat. Smithson and Valentina retracted a grill from the side of the RV, and soon they all smelled the aroma of grilling burgers.

"Nothing like eating outside," Ron said, munching a burger. "Everything tastes different, and better."

"It may taste different because this is buffalo," Valentina informed him.

The stars came out by the bright millions. They were awed.

"We don't get this much in Seattle," Ron admitted. "Too much overcast and when it isn't rainy we have city lights."

"We are in the middle of nowhere and at altitude," LaGrue said. "This is why they put observatories in places like this. Or even higher up, like Hubble."

A short while later, they saw a flashlight bobbing its way along the road through the blackness. It was Ranger Tanner, coming to escort them to the bonfire party with the pika scientists.

"Good evening," he announced, and was introduced around. Ron and Tracey immediately liked him.

"So you live here year round?" Valentina asked.

Again, Tanner smiled. It was one of those questions that he was probably asked a thousand times, like how many saloons were in town, and how many murders there were per day back then, being as Bodie was "The Baddest Town in the West."

"Yes, the Rangers, Park Aides, and maintenance crew mostly live here, inside the historic structures. And yes, it is hard in the winters, it sometimes gets a long way below zero and we have to park out close to the highway and snowmobile in and out with supplies."

They began walking toward the town, along the well-worn paths. They had each recovered an LED flashlight from the RV equipment storage bins.

"Your boss has tried to tell me a little about what you folks are doing here," he continued, playing his flashlight around at some of the old buildings they trooped through. "We thought the guys with war paint were gang members out of LA. We had no idea they were from another universe, and the hole might be right here somewhere. Sounds kind of nuts to me." He chuckled. "But I will do whatever I can to help out. I've lived here for years and never seen what he was talking about, though."

They started up the hill, past the massive, metal-covered building.

"That is the Standard Mill," Tanner explained. "That is where they used to crush the ore and extract the gold. Be glad to take you all on a tour of the building tomorrow, if you like, but don't expect me to get in period costume like our other park aides do."

"One thing I may have forgotten to mention, speaking of costumes, or make up, at least," Clay said. "Those stripe-faced killers might be trying to kill Ron and Tracey, too."

The ranger stopped, and looked back at Clay with one narrowed eye. "That may have been important to mention. We don't exactly have a lot of weapons up here, just a couple of pistols. What kind of threat is this?"

"Just the four or five men. They have normal clothes, but wear war-paint-like make up. And they carry guns. Oh, and they are zombies. But not the slow, shambling stupid kind, they act normal. But if you want to kill them you have to hit them in the neck and sever the spinal cord."

Tanner shook his head slowly. "Zombies. I'll be damned. Well, the tale grows weirder. If you weren't who you are, I'd think you were bullshitting me." He showed the briefest ghost of a smile. He pulled his radio from his belt. "Two oh three to Base."

"Base here," came a voice from the radio.

"Keep your eyes open for tonight and the next few days, Mike."

"For anything in particular?"

Tanner rolled his eyes, pursed his lips. "Those guys with the war paint. They may have guns this time, not just knives. And if you have to use something more violent than harsh language, go for the spinal cord in the neck."

There was a long pause, with a burst of static. "Uh, okay. Roger on the war paint and neck shots."

Ranger Tanner looked for a moment as though he was going to speak, but then shook his head and continued walking up the trail.

Valentina thought it best to attempt to defuse the tension by putting the Ranger back into familiar territory. "So what used to go on up here on this hill?" she asked, knowing full well they were entering the mining district.

"This is where the majority of the mines were situated, along the Bodie Bluff," he answered. "The geological formation where the gold is lies underneath us, shaped kind of like a fan, but layered, more like the pages of an open book. They never did find the mother lode—the spine of the book—though. Also over here is the old terminal building of the railroad, where they used to crawl up a grade with loads of lumber from across Mono Lake. Now nothing lives over that side of the bluff other than pikas and some scientists from time to time."

They walked on in silence for a while, after Tanner unlocked a padlocked gate in a barbed wire fence. "This area is normally off limits. It's dangerous if you don't know where the mine shafts are. Especially at night. Funny thing about those guys in makeup," he eventually said to Clay. "I was just looking at one of the books we have in our library yesterday, and saw a picture from the eighteen-eighties during one of the July Fourth parades. There were several townsfolk with Indian-like face makeup, but normal-looking clothes of the time. We always assumed they were just dressing up like Indians."

Clay eyed him sharply. "You mind if I take a look at that book tomorrow?"

"Not at all."

Tracey slowed, then stopped. The others noticed her and also slowed down. "This was where I was in my dream. There is a hole right over there, isn't there?" she asked Tanner, playing her light toward a raised concrete square structure, about two feet high.

"Yes, in fact, there is," Tanner said. "That's the opening to the Lent shaft, the deepest hole around here. You don't want to fall in there; it's twelve hundred feet straight down. That's close to a quarter of a mile."

She passed it, shuddering and looking around. It may have been her imagination, but she felt a tendril of cold air rising from the black hole.

–17–

They crested the hill, passed the old railroad building, and followed an almost invisible path down the other side of the bluff. They spied a bonfire a few hundred yards away.

When they reached it, they noticed several other uniformed park employees and a few others who they guessed must have been the pika scientists, seated around on rocks and a few coolers. The bonfire was roaring, and Ron wondered how far they had to lug the wood. They were introduced around to various park aides and staff. Professor LaGrue nodded professionally at the other scientists.

"Like dogs sniffing each other," Tracey whispered to Ron.

They were offered beers by the scientists, and all but Smithson accepted.

"Did we think to bring . . .?" Clay whispered to Valentina.

"Way ahead of you," she said, producing a bottle of whiskey from her backpack. "We have all sorts of trade goods for when we meet the natives on the other side of the rift, and I figured why not break them out now for the local natives."

The Jack Daniels was greeted enthusiastically and shared around.

They were all warm and toasty in an hour, despite the high-altitude cold air. Professor LaGrue had engaged in a scientific discussion with the pika naturalists, while Valentina held court with a number of the unattached male park employees.

Ron looked around for Smithson, but he was nowhere to be seen. *Probably lurking in the shadows like a ninja.*

"So I don't get it," one of the scientists said to LaGrue, "what mechanism spins off a new universe, and what decides whether it collapses back into ours like a soap bubble or not?"

"That is *exactly* the most interesting thing," LaGrue responded, pointing his beer bottle for emphasis. "First, I think that any chance event has the effect of springing a new universe into existence. I think it happens all the time. Some things, however, have a big effect on what happens while some things do not. Let's say I decide to drink this whole beer in a minute instead of over twenty minutes. Probably will have no effect on the grand scheme of things, so any universe that I spin out because of that choice or chance will not make a big difference, so that universe will not make changes important enough to keep the universes from snapping back into synch like soap bubbles joining back together. But let's say, on the other hand, I decide to chug six beers, then drive drunk down the highway. If I get into a head-on collision and kill someone who would have gone on to give birth to the kid who would have grown up to invent artificial intelligence or a faster-than-light star drive would be a big change. Probably enough to spin off a universe that stays in existence."

"I still don't get it," Ron said. "How can a 'chance event' spin off another universe? Is it a matter of chance, or choice? I mean, didn't you choose to drink six beers? Choose to drive, anyway? So do our brains have the ability to split off a new universe? And is it a new branch, or, if the Mods are right, isn't this just a 'save point?'"

"Maybe," LaGrue said, stroking his chin. "I guess it could be thought of as a save point, if you buy their bull. As far as brains doing the branching, biocentrists theorize that consciousness affects the quantum realm, like the collapse of the quantum mechanical wave function. Not just affect it, but create the whole thing. Like, if nobody is looking at the moon, *it isn't there.* Just a cloud of probability until some consciousness collapses the wave function by observing it. Others argue that this is simply human-centric pseudo-science." *And maybe,* he thought, *consciousness is what gives the necessary energy bump for spinning off a new world to begin with . . .? Is it really choice instead of chance?*

"Here's an example," one of the pika scientists nodded and said. "Late in the Civil War, a sniper took a shot at President Lincoln while he was alone riding a horse. The bullet went through his hat. What if that sniper had hit Lincoln? He would not have been re-elected; Sherman may not have taken Atlanta. It may have changed the course of the war. But the sniper hadn't *chosen* to miss, that was just the result in the physical world."

"There you go," LaGrue agreed. "That is an example of what I'm talking about. Right there, another universe was probably spun off, one where Lincoln was killed. If the South had gone on to win the war because of that, somewhere, out there in the M dimension, is a universe very different from ours where the South won. Same thing can be said about World War II if Hitler had discovered the bomb."

"I got one on that same track," one of the Bodie employees said, a short man with a bushy gray beard and square glasses. "My father told me that he was working for the Navy back in the later days of World War II in the Pacific. They were trying to invent an artificial gill, so our frogmen could infiltrate Japanese harbors undetected. What if he had succeeded *and* the Axis had won with the help of evil extra-terrestrial forces? What if the last remaining free people had been forced to retreat to the oceans, using those artificial gills? What if they were forced to live in hiding, doing occasional raids on shipping, living in artificial reefs, farming fish? What if they adopted a semi-tribal society, merging elements of various cultures, trying to stay alive against the totalitarian state?"

The scientists fell silent, looking at the bearded park aide with round eyes.

"Well, that was a pretty damn elaborate 'what if' scenario," Ron stated.

The bearded man shrugged. "I used to wonder about it all the time. This just seemed to be a good time to bring it up."

"Well, there is no telling what kind of parallel universes exist right next to ours, like joined soap bubbles," LaGrue said, taking a pull on his beer. "I wonder if our mythology is based on some kind of passages between the universes. We may have dragons, unicorns, elves, and monsters living right next to us and how would we know it? If parallel universes are able to be affected by consciousness and not just physical effects, this could happen."

Ron's ears perked up at the mention of dragons and elves.

"Hey, any of you guys play 'Dragon Throne'? Speaking of making worlds and all, someone did a good job with that one."

Several of the pika scientists nodded.

"Yeah, I play that all the time," one of them said. "Very photo-realistic environments, and you can move around in them almost anywhere you want and manipulate a lot of the objects. But nowhere near all of them. I still want to be able to tip a bookcase over or move a table against a wall so I can jump on something higher than otherwise. I guess the detail is there unless you look too closely."

"That's the granularity problem I've been working on in my game design," Ron said. "I'm trying to get the AI to see what the player is doing, then add code on the fly that wasn't there originally to 'fill in the blanks' and make it a more seamless experience, like real life. But the amount of RAM and hard drive space is making that difficult."

"Funny you should mention that," LaGrue said. "The real universe is pixelated like that, too, the closer you look. Matter, energy, space-time . . . they are all pixelated. They exist in fundamental units that can't be broken down any smaller. Which in turn means there are a finite number of these in any given universe, which means further that they are hypothetically computable, with a big enough computer. So at the rate we are advancing computers, we should be able to simulate a universe in the not-too-distant future."

"Heck, we might be in a simulation right now," another pika scientist said.

"Woooo!" another said, waving his hands in the air, and they all laughed.

"So you're saying what the Mods were saying about the Big Dungeon Master programming this universe is not so big a deal."

"Correct," LaGrue pointed. "We will be able to do it ourselves, too."

"Then why do you think what they're saying about this being a simulation is bullshit?"

The pika scientists who thought they were joking looked puzzled.

"Well, obviously, I can't disprove it." LaGrue scowled, taking a pull from his beer. "But when they started talking about how there was a war going on with some other alien, I knew they were making it up. If they were the all-powerful code-writers, why not just write that code out of existence?"

Ron nodded. *Good point.* "But what about consciousnesses? How will you simulate those if it will be so easy to program this in the future? How will you get your players to think it's real and not know it's a game, like we've got going on here? I mean, I can stick a Virtual Reality helmet on my head and it can simulate a world, and maybe someday we can even make a Holodeck. But we would still know it is us, playing a game. I don't feel that about real life."

"Well," LaGrue pondered, "I guess it boils down to whether you think our brains make consciousness or not. I happen to think they do, that they are made of atoms and run on twenty-five watts of electricity. They are just like any machine, so they can be replicated like anything else. Nothing magical about it. So, yes, I think we can make consciousness in a computer. So, Ron, in the future when you're making Dragon Throne 9, you'll be able to put the entire universe on the console and program conscious beings to 'live' in there, and see only what they need to see when they need to see it. Just like the universe works, where particles only have a definite state when they are observed."

"No way could I put in an entire universe," Ron argued. "No way a single human could have time to program it. And what would be the point of it? Not and make it an interesting life."

"Ah, but what is best in life?" one of the scientists asked.

"To crush the enemy. . . ." said another scientist.

"To See Them Driven Before You!" joined in more, louder.

"AND HEAR THE LAMENTATION OF THEIR WOMEN!" they roared as a group, and laughed.

"I don't think you can generate consciousness, even with a supercomputer," Ron argued. "You can't do more than simulate the appearance of thought with silicon and steel."

"The RIDDLE OF STEEL!" interrupted one of the tipsy pika scientists, unwilling to give up the Conan references. "I never understood why Thulsa Doom just gave him the answer like that."

"Did he?" came a new voice from the shadows. Heads snapped toward the source. It was Smithson, who had apparently been listening.

"Sure," answered the scientist. "He said steel isn't strong. Flesh is stronger. What is steel without the hand to wield it? Then he ordered the girl to jump off the cliff, and sent Conan to ponder this on the tree of woe."

"Ah, but did Thulsa tell the whole story? What, after all, is flesh without the spirit to wield it?"

There was a general pause to ruminate on this.

"Remember this, Ron," Smithson continued, "dark masters of evil will tell you just enough of the truth to serve their own ends. Then they send you off to be crucified."

"*No mas*," Ron said. "I'm getting tired and drunk and muddled."

Tanner and Clay lost the thread of the conversation when it turned from physics to movie nerdery. They passed the bottle between them, exchanging law-enforcement tales. More time passed, the fire grew lower, as did the level in the bottle. Ron was enjoying staring into the fire, which he remembered being fascinated with when camping as a child. The drink had him pleasantly buzzed, to the point that he could almost ignore his aching joints. It occurred to him that he could start drinking more. *Starting right now!* The thoughtful gaps in conversation widened.

"So, where do you want to look for this wormhole or rift thing?" Tanner asked.

Clay rubbed his jaw, then told Tanner all the clues he had: about Cornish Bob, how he had worked for the Syndicate Mill, about the explosion in the powder warehouse in July, 1879, how that explosion formed the rift, and what the Horribles had been up to since. He told him about the other universe, and how it was poised to swallow theirs. Tracey told him about her dream.

"Now *that* rings a bell," Tanner said, when told about the old, bearded man. "Silas Bell, that is. He was one of the park aides here for many years. Just works part-time now. He's a walking history museum. Si lives over in the hills north of Mono Lake, at least during the summer. He vanishes for the winters around here—they get powerful cold. He's a great guy. That's him, right over there."

They glanced over at the man who had talked about the artificial gill suits. He smiled and hoisted his beer bottle in salute.

"He's the guy in my dream, I think," Tracey said, squinting through the flickering firelight. "The one with the flippers."

"Heck, I think he's the guy from *my* dream," Ron said, suddenly remembering back to the bearded guy with square spectacles blowing the string bubbles he had dreamed about the morning the same morning the Space Command came knocking. *Wake up, Ron.*

He told Tracey about the dream, and Clay and LaGrue leaned in to listen as well.

"You never told me you dreamed about that," Tracey said. "You don't remember dreams. Now you dream something about the same guy that I dreamed about, who is sitting right over there, with strings and blowing breath into something that becomes reality, on the very morning all this stuff started, right before we sit through a lecture from aliens on string theory and multiverses, and get told that your genes keep universes like that from popping like soap bubbles, and you only think to mention that now?"

Ron's face reddened and he shrugged helplessly. "But I did tell you. You said it was only brain fragments that didn't mean anything."

"Well, that was *then*," Tracey argued.

"It may mean something," Clay stated. "Maybe we'll talk to Bell tomorrow. Anything else sound familiar?" he asked Ranger Tanner.

"Well, all of it and none of it. There were lots of miners here, some from Cornwall, some from all over. I read about that explosion a long time ago, it made the papers then. It was a terrific blast. Two tons of dynamite and black powder can pack a wallop. Several fatalities, and several miraculous survivals. I will get some of my people researching tomorrow for any references to Cornish Bob in any of the old papers or books."

"What about tunnels?" Tracey asked, remembering back to her dream. *It's a tunnel, not a shaft.* "Any of those left?"

"Well," Tanner drawled, rubbing his chin, "you can still get into the Bulwer Tunnel. It goes into the bluff not far from where your rig is parked, in fact. And it may be close to the site of the explosion."

"Can we go in there tomorrow?" Clay asked.

"Sure," Tanner agreed.

Unspoken, they knew it was time to call it a night.

They said their goodnights to the pika scientists, wished them good luck in the upcoming pika study season.

More than slightly tipsy, they made their way back over the bluff, where Ranger Tanner bid them a good evening and diverged to his historic home.

–18–

They spent a cramped, claustrophobic night in the RV. The camper was designed to sleep a maximum of six. Two of the beds were doubles, and Tracey and Ron preferred to sleep together. Valentina, the only other woman, was too shy to offer to share the other double with Smithson, so she and Clay took single bunks while Smithson shared with Professor LaGrue. Clay was a snorer.

In the morning, they took turns in the cramped shower while others nosed in the small refrigerator for eggs and bacon for breakfast.

Ron stood outside, watching the sun rise over the hills in the east, and Tracey joined him. She noticed a trace of moisture in the corner of his eyes.

"Are you crying?" she asked.

He sniffed. "Of course not. It's just a pretty sunrise, that's all. That and a bit of a hangover." A lone cloud floated near the horizon, changing shape as they watched. Tracey watched him closely. *Is this an episode of sacred connection, or is he was worried that he has only a limited number of sunrises left?*

Ranger Tanner drove his white pickup into the camp, and produced a book. He declined an invitation to join them for breakfast, then thumbed through the book for Clay.

"Hey, Ron, Tracey," Clay called, "come here and look at this."

It was a picture of Fourth of July revelers from 1880. Several were in antique-looking clothes, with face paint.

"Recognize any of these guys?"

Ron and Tracey both stabbed a finger at the same person on the end, with a slight build and striped grease paint.

"That's him. That's Cornish Bob," Tracey said definitively. "The short, skinny little spud crossing his arms on the left, with the big, fake-looking mustache. Cocky little bastard."

"Wait," Tanner said. "You've seen this guy?"

"Yeah, he tried to shoot us last week." Ron nodded.

Tanner shook his head. "This whole thing is very weird and unbelievable, and getting worse."

"Are you sure this is a Fourth of July picture?" Tracey asked. "Any chance it could be just a picture taken on the street of guys in face paint?"

"I suppose it could be, even though these Horribles, as they called them, were common for that holiday," Tanner agreed. "I think the author just assumed it was a July Fourth holiday, because most people don't walk around with war paint on their faces. Book says it was from July ninth, too. So who knows, given the current situation?"

"Did you call them Horribles?" Ron asked.

"Right there in the caption of the picture," Tanner said, pointing it out.

"I will be damned," Clay muttered.

"Anyway, if you're ready to go down into the Bulwer Tunnel, let's go," Tanner urged them. "But bring your flashlights and wear mud shoes. And old clothes, it's kind of muddy at the opening."

"We don't have old clothes," LaGrue said.

"Speak for yourself," Ron announced, and produced the lint shirt with a flourish from where he had hidden it rolled up under his other shirt.

Tracey groaned.

"Hey, don't complain. You said I should keep it for mowing the lawn, and this is just as dirty as that. Besides, it's lucky." Ron pulled the shirt on over his other one.

The rest of them didn't have old clothes or mud shoes to change into, but Ron, Tracey, Clay, Smithson, and LaGrue nonetheless followed Tanner out of the camp. Valentina remained behind to monitor the communications with White

Mountain.

"If you go very far into the underground, you'll be cut off from contact," she warned them.

They wove their way through the scrub, crossed a dry creek bed, and walked to the base of the bluff. Ron didn't see any mine entrance, and grew curious when Tanner started scanning the ground, walking westward out of town.

"Ah, there it is," Tanner finally said, and led them to a small hole in the ground.

They stood around the hole, which was no more than three feet across and two feet wide.

"That's *it*?" Tracey asked. "How is that big enough to be a mine?"

"Well, time has piled up some dirt, and we have had to constantly keep it open. But we don't want tourists crawling all through there, either, so we don't open it up very much. You just have to lie down next to it and wriggle in on your belly. It opens up after a few feet."

Smithson doffed his backpack, lay down on the ground in front of the hole, and slithered in. In a few seconds, his arm reappeared to grab his pack, then both it and he were gone. A short while later, his voice echoed out of the hole.

"He's right, it opens up almost immediately. The tunnel is wide-open rock."

Ron went next. He wriggled into the dark hole on his stomach, and slid down a short incline of dirt to the floor of a stone tunnel. It was large enough for three of them to walk abreast, and stretched straight back into the mountain. The floor was muddy, and there was a musty, closed-in feel to the cool, moist air.

They were soon joined by Clay, LaGrue, and finally Tracey.

"It goes back about three thousand feet," Tanner called from the opening, "Then stops. There are a few crosscut tunnels that lead to winzes for ventilation. Those are still open, so don't worry about getting enough air. Should be safe enough as far as cave-ins go, just don't go hammering on the walls or anything."

"You're not coming?" Tracey called up.

"No, thanks, I don't want to have to change uniforms this early in the morning," he called back. "You should be able to find your way back with no problem; there is no other way out or in. At least as far as I know. Come into town later and tell me if you find one."

Clay thanked him, then looked around the group, brushing dirt off his clothes. "Okay, let's get looking."

"What exactly are we looking for?" Ron asked.

"You saw the rift at White Mountain," LaGrue answered. "Just look for one of those. It may not be as big, though, since Cornish Bob mentioned 'crawling through.'"

Then moved off down the tunnel, splashing in the puddles in the cold mud, their flashlights playing around the rock walls and curved ceiling. Tracey was struck with just how much work it would have been to blast their way through the solid rock in search of gold.

After what seemed like a long way, another tunnel opened off at right angles to their left. Clay assigned Smithson and Tracey to go down that tunnel, then to meet back up at the main shaft. They continued. Another tunnel opened on their right. Clay sent Ron and LaGrue down the right tunnel, then continued on alone.

Ron wondered if the side tunnel would narrow, but it held its width for a long way. He started to feel the air moving.

"You feel that?" he asked Professor LaGrue.

"Yes, but it could be the ventilation shaft that the Ranger was talking about."

They continued on to the end, found a narrow shaft rising through the rock of the roof. There was faint daylight visible far up the shaft, and they felt a slight draft.

"Is that the surface?" Ron asked.

They stood looking up into it for a minute.

"I don't know," LaGrue said. "The angle works; it could pop out on the ridge somewhere. What is that smell?"

Ron smelled it, too; it was salt. "Smells like salt air, like the ocean."

"Could be a breeze from Mono Lake," LaGrue pondered. "That is an alkali lake, many times higher in salt content than the ocean. Seagulls even fly over the Sierras to nest there, and eat brine shrimp by the millions."

"Brine shrimp? You mean like Sea Monkeys?"

LaGrue laughed. "You had those, too, when you were a kid?"

"Yeah, I thought they would have little crowns and tridents like on the package, though. I felt cheated."

"It's miraculous enough to get a packet of dead, dried up stuff and then have it come to life in a bowl of water."

They looked up the shaft. "Looks like a hard climb," Ron said. "You any good at climbing?"

"We could try to find the opening from the outside."

"Yeah, but what if we can't find it? What if there is *no* opening on the top? What if this is the rift?"

LaGrue sighed, nodded. "Okay, you go. I have that nauseous feeling of a rift nearby, too. It may just be breakfast, or the altitude, or claustrophobia from these tunnels, though. I'll give you a hand up."

Ron placed his muddy foot in Professor LaGrue's interlaced fingers, and scrambled to hold on to the sides of the shaft as he was lifted up. He managed to find a ledge with his fingertips, and hauled himself up while LaGrue pushed on his rapidly disappearing foot. It was a tight fit. He scrambled up as quickly as he could, trying not to hurry himself into a fall. It took him only a minute to realize that the shaft did not get all the way to the surface, and that the daylight came from a rift.

He pulled himself up to it, gasping. Looking in, he saw that he was several hundred feet in the air, looking straight down at a vast expanse of ocean. Five feet below him was an opening to a large metal bin with a grate on the bottom. The bin sat on a tower, jammed with machinery, which sat on a building, which sat on a floating barge. Ron could see no land in any direction. The machinery was quiet, and the whole place looked abandoned.

"Holy shit," he called down the shaft breathlessly.

"You found it?" LaGrue exclaimed, excited. "What luck! Get back down here!"

Ron slid back down, eyes glowing, and described what he had seen, then: "Let's catch up with Clay and the others."

–19–

Clay, along with Tracey and Smithson, were waiting for them where the tunnels joined. None of them had found anything but the ends of their tunnels.

Clay wanted to see the rift immediately.

One at a time, Clay and Smithson scrambled up and then back down the shaft, which could accommodate only one person at a time. Tracey and LaGrue laboriously clambered up as well, not to be left out.

When Tracey dropped back to the floor of the tunnel after her viewing, they were already discussing the next move. None of them had thought to bring a digital camera. Clay decided to return to the RV to plan the next step.

On the way back to the tunnel entrance, Clay, LaGrue, and Smithson suddenly looked at each other.

"What is it?" Tracey asked.

"A burst of static from our sub-voca chips," Clay explained. "It sounded like Valentina, trying to reach us. She sounded worried, stressed out. We had better get out soon."

They picked up the pace. Clay scrambled out of the tiny hole first, followed by Smithson. Ron went out next, and noticed that Clay and Smithson were listening intently through the chip in their skulls. He remembered the tiny radio, and fumbled the ear bud into place.

" . . . just started emitting some kind of radiant energy, maybe in response to an outside signal," a female voice was saying. Ron recognized it as the woman technician he had seen on the feed from White Mountain the day before.

"What kind of energy?" Clay asked.

"Not sure, but it has a very strange property. Most radiant energy goes out in waves until something either bounces it or absorbs it. This energy radiates out for about a foot, then it just . . . disappears. Like it's going right out of this space-time. That is why we didn't notice it before. It could have been transmitting for some time."

"And you say it's coming from that dead Horribles's spider device?" Smithson asked.

"Yes, that one," she said from Colorado, with a hint of worry.

"So we have no idea what's being communicated," commented Professor LaGrue, who had joined them.

"No, sir," she answered.

There was a brief burst of static, and Clay narrowed his lips, considering the repercussions.

Ron motioned to Tracey to put in her radio earphone.

"Valentina, disable our sub-vocas, make it so we can only communicate with White Mountain through the Comsat uplink, but keep our local connectivity," Clay ordered quietly.

"Done," Valentina said.

"I want to make sure nobody mentions this rift, even accidentally," Clay explained. "We don't know who else could be listening."

They went back to the RV, where Valentina was speaking with Lt. Park in Denver over the computer.

"Lieutenant Park," Clay said, "if you have not already done so, I want that communications device put in a box. Isolate it. Make it a LEAD box, if you have one."

"Already done," she said. "We can still measure that pulse for about a foot around it, though."

"Damn," Clay muttered. "Here we brought that thing right into our headquarters, and it may be transmitting. That was *stupid*." He rubbed his face in his hands. "How long has it been doing this? How long were we down in that hole?"

"About two hours," Valentina answered nervously. "But the thing could have been transmitting the whole time it's been there."

"Well, *shit*." He leaned into the camera, so Lt. Park could see and hear him clearly. "Park, I want you to evacuate the base. Get everyone out of there, and leave the spider there. Do it *now*."

"Yes, sir," she said, a slight tremor in her voice. They heard an intercom come to life in her room, and Lt. Park listened intently for a few seconds. "Sir, I think I should patch you in on this. It's from the monitoring station on level nine, near the rift. Please repeat."

She manipulated switches, and they heard another voice.

"We are picking up multiple signal sources from the probes in the desert on the other side of the rift," the voice said. "Looks like another ship has come into orbit."

"Get everyone out, Park. *Move*," Clay ordered.

"Sir, the communication device is . . . well, it's *talking*," she said.

"Put a mike up to it." They all crowded around the screen. Agent Park disappeared, then they heard the sound of an intercom being set up, presumably near the device. They heard the sound of an alarm start droning in the background.

"Hullo?" a familiar voice asked.

Ron's blood turned icy.

"Cornish Bob calling Ron Golden, Cornish Bob to Ron. Are you all standing around geeking at the familiar? There in your *secret base*? In Colorado?"

Clay put a finger to his lips, shook his head.

"Something has just left the ship in orbit," the technician's voice said. "It appears to be entering the atmosphere—"

"So, Ron," Cornish Bob's voice continued, "you had your chance to join up, and I guess you passed. I tried my best. I really did."

"It didn't burn up on reentry. It appears to be an aircraft or missile," the technician chattered on. "Accelerating past Mach 2—"

"But she isn't one to give second chances," Bob said.

"We're computing the trajectory. It looks like it's headed right for us, through the Rift—"

"So, I guess this is goodbye, Ron and Tracey, and I can only hope that the little bald guy is standing next to you. And a lot of other gubmint agents, to boot. But we can't let you have that toy from my buddy's body, now can we?"

"Impact in five seconds—"

"'Bye, Ron. Have a nuclear day."

The screen flashed white, then went dead.

-20-

They all sat dumbstruck. There was nothing to say. Clay stood up stiffly, then walked out of the RV and off into the sage scrub. Tracey left the cab, too, and Ron joined her. They realized that Clay, LaGrue, Smithson, and Valentina knew those employees, had friends there.

They stood, blinking in the bright sun, listening to the sound of crickets and the wind through the sagebrush. Clay stood in the scrub, arms akimbo, staring off to the east. They watched him gather himself, then return to the RV. Ron and Tracey joined him.

"Flash traffic from the Mods," Valentina informed Clay.

"I'll take it privately," he said quietly, and they all piled out of the RV.

Tracey and Ron did not know what to say. They watched the white pickup truck slowly drive toward them, again raising a cloud of dust. It pulled to a stop nearby and Tanner emerged.

"I just heard on the news that there was an earthquake near the Denver Airport," he informed them.

"We know," Smithson said simply.

Tanner nodded. It dawned on him that they may have had a more personal connection to the event.

"Did you know people there? They are saying it was a six point five on the Richter scale."

"It wasn't an earthquake," Smithson said, turning away.

Clay appeared at the top of the RV stairs, and motioned them all over. Tanner pointed toward his truck, asking if he should leave, but Clay motioned him over, too.

"Mr. Barman has informed me," he said, "that there is a *world of shit* hitting the proverbial fan. It is only a matter of time before it gets public that this was more than an earthquake. We have been ordered to head through this rift with flank speed and get as far away from it on the other side as possible before the bad guys have a chance of lobbing another nuke through it. Ranger Tanner, it is high time you and all your people hightail it out of here until we figure out if it's safe. You'll need to close the park down and keep the public out for a ten mile radius of here. You can use the RV. Park it on the side of the road on that back road in here from Lee Vining, and if you see anything even vaguely resembling a painted face, shoot it. If you can, anyway. They are sending in a battalion of Marines that are getting trained at the Mountain Warfare Training Center north of Bridgeport to back you up."

Tanner raised an eyebrow but took this news in stride.

Ron sheepishly raised his hand. "Uh, that bunch of Marines. Are they coming to help or to arrest us?"

Clay paused only for the briefest moment. "They said it was to help us. But it wouldn't be too bad an idea not to be around when they get here and find out. Our orders," he continued in a louder voice, "are to infiltrate that other universe, locate the threat to us, and neutralize it if possible. This is an intelligence gathering mission at this point, but if we see an opportunity to strike from cover, we'll take it. Ron, Tracey, this is optional for you. Maybe, *just maybe*, Cornish Bob thinks you are dead. He was talking like he thought you were there in White Mountain. What made him think that, I don't know. They have been at least one step ahead of us for a long time, though, and he may be barreling down here right now to make sure we don't find the rift he told us about. I think he may be regretting that, and he probably isn't thinking we found it already. We have Tracey's dream to thank for that. So, you can either come with us, or . . . not."

Ron looked at Tracey.

"We still don't have much of a choice. I don't think Cornish Bob is stupid enough to just assume we're dead," Tracey said.

"So you go?"

Ron and Tracey glanced at each other.

"We go," Ron said.

"Good," Clay said. "We should go *soon*. Within the hour," he ordered.

Before the Marines get here, Ron thought.

They bustled into their preparations.

Tanner drove off to give his orders, then returned to help.

"That barge on the other side of the rift looked like it was a long way from land," Clay commented to Smithson. "Do we have any boats?"

"No. We do have one diving rig in the RV, a military quality rebreather."

It took them two hours instead of the one, but they were able to pack six backpacks and two large nylon duffels with what they might need. Weapons, explosives, food, survival equipment, whiskey, and other trade goods. They decided to take as much gold as they could pack in among the rest. LaGrue was secretly glad that he had thought to bring a full bottle of his psych meds. They started out to the mine.

Clay tossed Tanner the keys to the RV. "Take care of her," he instructed, with a wink. "And get your people out of here."

"On the way. And good luck."

They filed through the sage to the opening of the mine, then wriggled in one at a time.

"One last thing," Clay told them as they made their way to the side tunnel. "Smithson and Valentina were already trained in this, but Langston, Ron, Tracey, listen up. Once we go through, we need to *pay attention to Ron.* He's the one who will be able to remember this universe, and notice the changes between them. If he tells you that your name is Fred and you are a hairdresser, or whatever, we need to listen to him. If he tells us that we don't have . . . uh, flying pickles in our universe, or flying cars for that matter, we need to listen to him. We don't want to end up like Jack Strong's team. And Ron, if you hear any of *us* talking crazy, please don't hesitate to speak up about it. You're the double recessive."

"I feel sorry for you all." Tracey laughed. "Now I'm not the only one that has to listen to him. Or try to get him to talk, for that matter."

They reached the base of the shaft leading to the rift. Smithson unzipped one of the duffels, rifled around in it for a moment. He produced a length of braided rope, several pitons and carabiner, and a rock hammer. Without even a hand up, he nimbly scrambled up the shaft.

They heard him hammering the pitons into the wall, and clipping the carabiners and rope to them. One end of the rope descended from the shaft opening.

"Okay," Adrian called out.

"How weird is this?" Ron asked. "The other end of that rope is in another universe." Ron looked at the rope like it was charged with electricity.

"You want me to go through first, or do you want Ron to?" Smithson called down.

"Let's have Ron go first," he called back. "Just in case we suffer from the rift effect disorientation. Ron, just lay low, don't go anywhere but on top of the platform, and wait for the cavalry."

Smithson slid down the rope, and held it out for Ron. Ron started climbing, but was embarrassingly grateful for a hand up from Smithson and Clay. He saw that Smithson had knotted the rope around several pitons and carabiners at the top of the shaft, letting the rope pay out into the other world, where it coiled on the bottom of the rusting, metal bin. He looked out/down, at the vast expanse of ocean under the barge, which was starting to look smaller and smaller.

"Okay," he called out. "I'm about to go through." He fought off a momentary hesitation, then reached along the rope through the rift. Nobody was going to stop him this time. Or the lucky lint shirt.

-21-

The barrier between the two universes was barely noticeable, just a faint tingle like his arm was asleep. Once through, his arm felt the gravity of the other world, and started pulling him the rest of the way through. He let it pull him: His head went through, experiencing a momentary blackout, like he had fainted. Then his shoulder, torso, and . . . he was falling! The gravity of the new world worked at right angles, and he grabbed the rope and slung around to keep from falling. Ron caught himself, and lowered himself the rest of the way to the bin. He started to call up through the rift, but thought better of it: If there were occupants of the barge he didn't want to alert them to his presence. He tugged the rope instead.

It struck him: He was in another universe! Nothing felt different, though, except for the new heat and humidity. He scanned his surroundings.

The bin he was in was just tall enough so he could look over the edge. It was rusted metal, with a grate on the bottom, below which were what looked like metallic crushers. He looked over the edge. The bin with the grate in the floor was around four stories above the surface of the sea. Ron scanned the horizon in every direction. It was all ocean. The water was tropical and bright blue, like it glowed. There was a dark smudge that might have been an island far off where the sun was starting to sink into the horizon. It was warm, with a slight salt breeze. He heard the gentle slap of the ocean swell against the lowest deck of the barge.

Ron looked up at the rift, just in time to see Smithson flip through it and nimbly descend down the rope with one of the duffels. Ron started to speak, but Smithson held a finger to his lips and whispered, "Let me check the structure over first."

Ron watched as Smithson pulled the XM8 out of the duffel, and assembled it. He slung the weapon over his shoulder, then jammed his pistol into a thigh holster. He walked the perimeter of the bin, scanning the outside edge. Smithson found what he was looking for, apparently a ladder, and swung himself over the edge of the bin. He vanished with a final point at the ground at Ron's feet, indicating that he was to stay put. Ron crossed to where Smithson had gone down, and peered over the edge. Smithson had reached the first level of the machinery below, and crept into it, quiet as a cat.

Behind him, Clay dropped to the bin floor with the other duffel. Ron put a finger to his lips, and indicated to him with gestures that Smithson had gone over the edge. Clay joined him, and watched as Smithson climbed down to the next level of machinery.

They all heard the voices at the same time. Smithson froze, then melded back into the machinery. Ron and Clay strained to hear, but could not make out any words. It sounded as though the voices came from the lowest level, near the sea.

Smithson reappeared, looked up at Clay and Ron. He pointed to his eyes, then down the ladder, nonverbally communicating: "I'll go check it out." He vanished down the ladder. The voices continued, but they still couldn't make out what they said.

Tracey and Valentina made it down the rope into the bin without incident, but Professor LaGrue fell with a crash and a yell. Ron looked over his shoulder, and saw that he was all right, dusting himself off. There was noise from below, though. The voices shouted, and there was the sound of an engine starting up.

"Damn," Clay hissed.

A motor boat revved, then shot away from the platform. Ron saw that there was one man aboard. He was black, dressed in a papery-looking two-piece jump suit, with long, black, braided hair.

Smithson's head reappeared over the top of the bin. "They were so scared the one guy took off and left his friend. He's still down there."

"Let's go," Clay said. "Valentina, you come too, this is a

communications thing. The rest of you stay here. Smithson, did either of them see you?"

"No."

"Then you find someplace to cover us from above and stay out of sight."

Clay, Valentina, and Smithson climbed down the ladder to the lowest level. They passed several levels of rusting machinery, pipes, and tanks, with rooms with salted-over windows that they didn't have time to peer through. The lowest level was more pontoons, grates, and docks for boats to moor, a scant foot above the surface of the gently undulating electric-blue tropical sea. They saw that the man the pilot of the boat had left behind was agitatedly looking for another boat, but could find nothing. Valentina and Clay climbed down to the lowest level, knowing that somewhere in the machinery above, Smithson was training his weapon on the man should he prove to be a threat.

He was also black, with long, braided hair. He wore rubber sandals, and a black and white version of the papery jump suit. He had, Ron noted with concern, one of the large mechanical spiders on his shoulder. He was afraid, and seemed almost ready to fling himself into the sea.

"Don't come any closer!" he yelled, then brandished the spider in front of him at arm's length. "I'll call out the Navy!"

"He speaks English; that will make this much easier," she whispered to Clay. "Don't worry," she called out, flashing a smile and holding her arms out, showing her hands were empty. "We don't want to hurt you. We need your help."

Clay nodded.

The man paused. "Who are you?"

Valentina took a risk, said, "We're here for the same reason you are."

"For gold? There isn't any left. Where's your boat?"

"It sank," Clay called out.

"Those damn Sea Tribes!" the man spat. "They still around?"

"Who?" Valentina asked.

"The Tribes. Hell, we thought *you* were Tribe!" He laughed.

"No, we're not . . . Tribals. Tribesman. Sea Tribals,"

Valentina said. "We're not even sure they sank our boat."

"Well, let me call Maurice back. He left me, that bastard."

The man spoke into his spider, apparently trying to convince his friend to return. Valentina and Clay walked over to him.

"Leonard Ring," he introduced himself, holding out his hand.

"Good to meet you, Leonard," Clay said, shaking his hand. "I'm John, and this is Valentina. We have a few more friends topside; they went up to explore around."

"They find anything up there? Any flakes of gold?"

"What do you think?" Valentina asked.

Leonard laughed. "Well, you know how stories spread."

"So what stories did you hear?" Clay asked.

"Oh, you know, that they used this place to mine the sea floor for gold, extracting the gold from the muck. I wasn't really expecting to find any leftovers, but just wanted to look the place over while the city passes by, you know. Just curious."

"So, where are you from, Leonard?" Valentina asked.

He looked at them like they were insane. "New Sydney. Same as you, I hope. We're not near any other cities, are we?"

Valentina sensed that he was not being sarcastic. "No, no other cities nearby. Just didn't recognize you, that's all."

"Well, New Sydney is a big city," he defended.

"Not so big as New Tokyo," Clay added, wondering just how he knew that.

"Is your friend coming back?" Valentina asked. "I don't want us to get caught out here if there are any more of the Tribes around."

Leonard spoke into his spider again, then placed the end of one of its legs to his ear.

Ron thought it didn't look nearly as creepy as when the Horribles did it.

"He said he was on the way back," Leonard said with obvious relief. "So, what happened to your boat?"

"Oh . . . it, uh, it sank," Clay said.

"*Not* from the Tribes, though," Valentina added, attempting to cover for Clay' stumbling.

Leonard looked around as though he wished a boat, any boat, would materialize.

"We are not near any tuna migrations here, so don't worry," Clay said. He again wondered how he knew that, and why it was important. He reasoned it must have been the effect of going through the rift. "Look, Leonard, don't worry. We're not Stripes." He wondered where that term had popped into his head from. "Just get us back to the city and you will never hear from us again."

Leonard's eyes narrowed. "Are you on the run from the Stripes? I mean, I may be able to help. You don't look like you're on the Milk."

"What did you have in mind?" Clay asked.

"I know some people, who may be able to help you, uh, you know, who live under the numbers. They may be able to set you up under the numbers, too."

"We would appreciate that," Clay said.

Leonard looked more relieved. They heard the sound of a boat approaching. "That's Maurice Drew," he said. A minute later, the boat reappeared. Maurice piloted it back into the slip. Suddenly, Leonard jumped on board after catching the rope Maurice threw, leaving Clay and Valentina standing surprised on the dock. "Gun it, man!" Leonard yelled, "They're Stripe spies!"

Maurice jammed the engine into reverse, but Smithson opened fire from the level above. The gunfire was deafening in the enclosed bay, the bullets tracing a neat arc into the water just off the bow of the boat. Maurice powered down the engine, and held his hands in the air. Clay motioned to Leonard to throw him the bow line, and Leonard reluctantly complied.

"I *told* you, we are not Stripes," Clay growled, securing the line to a cleat. "Tell the rest of them to come down," he ordered Smithson.

Smithson called to the three on top of the structure to join them. They did, bearing the duffels between them.

"So, what were you really doing here?" Clay asked Leonard and Maurice.

They exchanged glances, hands still in the air.

"I told you," Leonard explained, "We were—"

Clay halted him mid-sentence with his hand. "I'm asking Maurice. Maurice, what were you two doing here?"

"We were salvaging, you know, checking the tanks for gas and stuff," Maurice lied. Leonard rolled his eyes.

"You *idiot*," he said, smacking Maurice on the head.

"So what was it really? Selling dry goods to the Sea Tribes? A little fresh produce? Some smokes? Or was it a little more . . . shall we say, lucrative trade? Information? Shipping schedules? Bills of Lading?"

"*No*, it wasn't like that," Maurice stammered.

"It was drugs," Leonard confessed.

"Drugs?" Clay asked, swinging into interrogation mode. "If you were dealing, where are they? Show me your product."

Leonard and Maurice went tongue-tied.

"I thought so. You're passing on routes and cargo information to the Tribes, aren't you?"

"What the hell is going on?" Ron whispered to Tracey.

"These guys were selling cargo ship route information to the Tribes," Tracey whispered back.

"Oh," Ron said. He then realized that he had no idea what Tracey was talking about. He then wondered how Tracy and Clay and the rest of them knew what they were talking about.

"Clay, can I talk to you a minute?" Ron asked. Clay joined him. "So, what is the plan here, sir?" he whispered.

"We get these guys to give us a ride back to New Sydney, and trade our promise not to talk for their contacts with the Un-numbered. Once we are established, we make our next plans."

"Got it," Ron whispered again. Clay started to turn, but Ron grabbed his arm. "Actually, I don't get it. Who are the Tribes, what is New Sydney, and what is the Un-numbered? And who are the Stripes?"

Clay' eyes widened. "This is fascinating! All those things must be different from our universe—"

Ron began to be alarmed. This was going to be more confusing than he thought.

"New Sydney," Clay explained, "is a floating city. It rides the currents around the South Pacific, like New Tokyo and

New Los Angeles circulate the north Pacific. New London and New Boston circulate the North Atlantic, and New Bombay goes around in the Indian Ocean. Everyone has an identification number, which is the only way they allow anyone to carry a familiar. Like one of the mechanical spiders, or snakes. They have all sorts of other animals for familiars, but those are the most popular and useful. Mostly useful to the Stripes, because they track your location and record everything around you. You have to have a familiar or you get arrested. If you don't get arrested, you have to live underground, without a number. That is, if you live in the cities, you do so running the risk of getting arrested. You can also live outside of the land and cities, in the ocean, but the Confederated Sea Tribes of Pacifica are throwbacks: criminals, pirates, savages. They declared war on the government and society in general, and the government has fought back by hunting them to the verge of extinction. You are better off taking your chances with the Milk."

"So, the Sea Tribes are not, uh, they don't have numbers, either?"

Clay looked at him quizzically. "Uh, no. They are just the tribes that live in the sea, outlaws. A lot like pirates, or Indian tribes, I guess. Lots of the native islanders went underwater, but they incorporate bits and pieces of lots of cultures. Japanese dress, that kind of thing. The last of the real human race. Stripes hunt them down, because Stripes run things, like the government and the military. Not only locally, but off planet, too."

"It sounds just like what that pika scientist was talking about," Ron mused.

"What pika scientist? What's a pika?"

"Um, okay, never mind," Ron said, trying to keep up. "So, how do you carry something familiar around with you?"

"Something familiar?"

"You said they carry something familiar."

"Oh, that is a familiar, like . . . I guess like they used to think witches hung around with. Like the spider we found on that dead Stripe. Dead Horrible, I mean. Looks like a living animal, but has wireless uplink, GPS tracking both ways, video phone, TV, carries all your finance and medical records. It also delivers Milk. A way for the Stripes to track everyone and keep tabs on movements and convey propaganda. And medicates them, did I mention? "

"You mentioned meds a couple of times now. You mean most of the populace is doped up?"

"That's why the Un-numbered are outlaws, too; they just avoid their Milk while living in the cities."

"Oh." Ron nodded. "So what were these guys selling to the Sea Tribes?"

"The Tribes don't produce many goods themselves, and surely can't grow food other than fish and seaweed. So they turn to pirating cargo ships. These guys were selling information about a ship, its route, and what cargo it carries."

Ron thought about this for a moment. "So, if they were here talking to the people who live underwater—the Sea Tribes, was it? Then where are the Tribals now? Did they come and go, or are these guys still waiting for them to show up?"

Clay blinked and stiffened. "That's a good question." He turned to Leonard and Maurice with a sudden pang of concern. "Hey, where is the Sea Tribe you were dealing with?"

-22-

"All around you," said a deep voice from the water at their feet under the docking bay.

Ron gasped, as what looked like a piece of the water detached itself from the surface of the ocean and heaved itself up onto the platform next to them. It had the outline of a man, and Ron saw that he was dressed in a suit that made it appear that the man wearing it was camouflaged with whatever was in the background behind him. He stared hard to see that it was a man, with some kind of apparatus on his back. The man then touched an area near his belt, and the suit turned a solid gray color, decorated with white swirl patterns worked in with the design of octopus tentacles.

Ron could tell now that he was bearded and had pushed some streamlined bubble-shaped goggles onto his head. There was some kind of facial gear, which had been swung to the side, probably breathing equipment. He was wearing fins on his feet and webbed gloves, also made out of the transparent material. The man quickly removed them and attached them to the belt at his side as he stood up. Ron noticed that there was not a sound as he exited the water, not so much as one drop had clung to his suit.

Ron looked quickly around, and saw that there were at least a dozen of these people, and realized that they could have been standing around the edges of the landing platform unnoticed for some time. They deactivated the camouflage of their suits, and Ron noted that they had similar white-patterned spiral markings, with octopus tentacle designs worked in. They carried weapons, showing the end of what looked like sharp, barb-tipped metal spears protruding from the ends.

"Let's make them crab food and get on, Braun," said one of the Tribe from the edge.

The one that had stood in their midst raised his hand.

"Not yet, Maloko. You are always in a rush. You enjoy this stuff too much. Killing is nothing to rush into, even killing Stripes."

Maloko sniffed loudly in protest.

"Nobody move," Clay instructed coolly, loud enough for Smithson to hear. "You are all being covered by one of our people from an elevated position with an automatic weapon. If you make any sudden hostile actions, he will fire."

Smithson surveyed the situation from above, moving the red dot in the sighting reticule of his battle rifle between the Tribesmen identified as Braun and Maloko. He felt something cold, something hard tickling him behind his left ear, and froze. With exaggerated slowness, he looked back over his shoulder at the point of a barbed spear protruding from the end of a gun-like weapon. There was a tarry substance on the end of the spear . . . poison? He slowly lowered his battle rifle to the metal grate he was crouching on, and spread his hands away from his body.

"I have lost my position," he called down to Clay, hoping that the spear would not be loosed into his head. He heard muffled laughter behind him from the person holding the spear and realized with shock that it was a young girl.

"I have him covered," the girl called mirthfully down to the group below. "I could have made the noise of a wounded elephant seal and you wouldn't have heard me," she taunted Smithson quietly.

"Bring him down with the others," Braun ordered.

Smithson slowly rose to his feet, looking for an opening. The girl was maddeningly casual with the spear gun, but seemed to give him no easy avenues of disarming her. He started walking down the catwalk to the ladder, the girl following behind. As he turned a corner approaching the ladder, he saw that there was another gray-suited Tribesman poised with a spear gun waiting there.

Without hesitating in his motion, Smithson altered his course, and in one smooth action had placed the Tribesman between him and the girl, preventing her from firing without hitting him. He pulled on the barrel of the spear gun, waiting for the man to pull back in an effort to regain possession of the weapon. He did, hard. Smithson offered no resistance to the pull, merely redirected it with a twisting motion over the Tribesman's head. This was the last thing he expected. He lost his balance, falling backward, and released the spear gun in an effort to keep from falling off the catwalk. Smithson continued the motion, leveling the spear gun at the girl and backing toward the ladder. She froze, uncertain whether to fire or not. Smithson kept his spear centered on the middle of her chest. He considered diving into the sea, but thought the Sea Tribes would have the advantage there. Instead, he ascended the ladder to the upper decks.

"I lost him," she called out to her troop below. "He's climbing up, and he took Johl's spear gun."

"Let him go, Andrea," Braun called back.

Clay and Braun eyed each other warily.

"Where can he go?" Braun asked rhetorically.

"He can go up and recover his bag of weapons and take out the lot of you," Clay said.

"Not before we cut every one of you down," Braun answered evenly, with a half-smile, rubbing the bridge of his nose where the close fitting mask had marked it.

Ron surveyed the scene with a growing sense of . . . what? Was it humor? It all seemed so ridiculous. "Why does anybody have to kill anybody here?" he asked, incredulous.

They all looked at him, puzzled.

"Get on with it, Braun," called Maloko, the impatient voice. "Let's get this over with and head back before the one that got away gets high enough to use his familiar to call in an air strike."

"You understand this is how it has to be," Braun explained helplessly. "Maybe we can spare the women. They are a spoil of battle, and maybe even adapt and marry into the Reef. But the rest of you . . . ." He splayed his hands and shook his head.

Ron saw Tracey and Valentina draw closer together, both fighting off the urge to grope for their pistols. He saw the cold looks in the eyes of the Tribe, Clay's calculating glances, and Professor LaGrue's near panic. Ron knew he should be afraid, and his breath caught in is throat, but it was not with fear. He felt at ease, and understood that things would happen as they should, without knowing why. Looking at the Tribe, he felt an overwhelming sense of compassion for them. Tears of—relief? Joy?—welled up in his eyes, and he laughed. It was an easy laugh, from the belly, with no hint of hysteria, and they all looked at him, amazed.

"Wow," he said. "So here we are, all about to start killing each other. And to think only a few days ago the biggest worry I had was whether a dachshund was shitting on my lawn. Then I get cancer, we have inter-universal war and murderous painted zombies and nuclear explosions and now it is . . . and I can't believe I'm saying this . . . *tribesmen* with *spears*. And to top it all off, I'm wearing my lucky lint shirt. There is no way I'm going to die wearing this shirt."

The Sea Tribesmen paused, shifting uncomfortably.

"Did he say he had a *lawn*?" one of the Tribe whispered loudly.

"And a shirt made of lint?" asked another.

Braun warily approached Ron, heedless of the other Tribe or of Ron's team. "You say you have a lawn," he said sharply. "Do you mean a lawn, like with grass?"

Ron shrugged. "Sure, it has grass. The parts of it that aren't clogged with dandelions, anyway. It needs mowing, though. But it has a great little path made out of stepping stones that goes to the driveway."

"I do the gardening," Tracey added, seizing any topic other than killing them.

The Sea Tribesmen buzzed with apparent amazement.

"I know your voice," Braun said, amazed. "Tracey Dory! I thought I recognized your face, but knew it could not be. But here you are! We all thought you were killed while trying to take that cargo ship that turned out to be a Stripe ambush."

Tracey felt an odd stirring at the mention of the name Dory. "I-I'm not sure I'm the same person you're thinking of. Who is your Tracey?"

"Tracey Dory, wife of Officer Jon Dory, and head of the pirates of our Reef, the BlueRings. I can see you are not her, but are as like unto her as a twin." He scrutinized her closely. "You do not live on New Sydney," Braun said matter-of-factly. "Tracey Dory would never be taken alive, nor would her twin. And you obviously are not on the Milk. Besides, nobody there has a lawn. Nobody even on the continent has a lawn. So either you lie, or you are not of this Earth."

Ron looked to Clay for guidance, but Clay only looked back blankly.

"Well, you called it. We are not of this Earth. We are from another universe, with an Earth somewhat like this, but not much, from what I can tell so far. Over on our side, we don't have anyone living in the ocean, and no familiars. And no Stripes, or Un-numbered. But we do have zombies with faces painted with stripes trying to kill us."

There was a long, awkward silence. Tracey waited for the spears or bullets to start flying. Clay and LaGrue were trying to reconcile the fact that their own world did not have the Sea Tribes, familiars, the Stripes or the Un-numbered, which was now difficult to conceive.

Braun slung his spear gun across his shoulder. "It is a good thing you spoke," he said. "We were about to make a mistake," he added, over his shoulder at Maloko. The other Tribe relaxed and stowed their weapons, and cautiously approached them.

"Strong asked all the Reefs to be on the lookout for visitors from another world. And here you are. We should have thought sooner; we knew that Maurice and Leonard were here without you, and there are no other boats here and no aircraft have come. I knew something did not add up, but could not figure out what it was. Now we know, you are those visitors from another universe."

"Strong asked you?" Clay asked. "You don't mean Jack Strong, do you?"

The Tribesmen murmured in astonishment.

"Yes," Braun said. "He came from your world, apparently, but has become one of us. The fact that you know his name is further proof that we would have been overly hasty to kill you."

Clay mulled that over. . . . Strong had become one of them?

"We have to leave, and soon," Maloko suggested.

Braun nodded. "It is never a good idea for us to be above the surface so long."

"Where are we going?" Tracey asked.

Ron looked back and forth between Maurice's boat and Braun's troops.

"With them," Clay decided quickly. If Jack Strong had chosen to join these people . . . .

"There is a problem. We don't have underwater equipment, except for one rebreather unit," LaGrue said.

Braun's eyes widened. "You have a rebreather unit with you? Jack Strong mentioned that technology; we should look at it to see if it can improve our gillsuits. But for now, we may have to field-share the oxygen tubes for those without suits." He spoke to his troops. "How many spare masks do we have? Who is willing to share an ox-line?"

There was a rustle among the Tribes as they passed up several masks, and several hands went up to volunteer to help.

"Not enough," Braun said. He pondered the situation. "Without gillsuits, you would slow us down and endanger us all. We could share oxygen, but the problem here is masks. Without them, you would be pretty helpless. There are patrols around lately, and if we have to stay near the surface we could be spotted on infrared. Perhaps you should go back to New Sydney with Leonard and Maurice," he said, "then when we are able to secure enough gillsuits we can come back and get you."

Braun turned to Leonard and Maurice. "Do you think you can keep them among the Un-numbered for a little while?"

"Well," Maurice said, shrugging.

"We can pay you, of course," Clay said. "Our currency may not be the same, but we could provide you trade goods. We have whiskey, and some gold coins." Clay produced a handful of coins in his palm.

The Tribe murmured at the sight of gold, and began slowly crowding in, reaching out to touch Clay.

"You must keep any gold you have close to you," Braun warned, motioning his troop to give them room. "Gold is the most precious thing in all the worlds.. Among us, it is good luck just to touch one who possesses it." He looked at Leonard and Maurice with suspicion. "I wish you had not said anything to these two; there are many among the Un-numbered who would kill you all for even one of those coins."

"Maybe," Ron said, overcome with a sudden insight, "you could keep them safe for us?"

Braun turned his even gaze toward Clay, who mulled this over. Clay knew, on some level, that giving gold to Sea Tribesmen was a bad idea. He also knew, on another level, that he had no basis for this opinion based on any actual experience. He reasoned that this was an effect of being in the new universe, and remembered his own admonition to his team to trust Ron's lead.

"Professor, please grab the blue duffel," he ordered.

LaGrue brought one of the duffel bags over to Clay, who opened it and rifled through it. He produced a leather sack that bulged and jingled when it moved. He re-zipped the duffel, made a depression in the top, and poured out the contents. The gold coins seemed to glow in the fading light. There were many U.S. Gold Eagle bullion coins.

There was silence among the Tribesmen as they crowded forward to see the great fortune. Braun kneeled next to the duffel, and pointedly counted each coin out loud.

"One hundred," he finally announced. "A whole Reef could be made with such gold," he said with wonder.

"Hey, what about us?" Leonard protested.

"You take them in with you and keep them alive until we get them, and then we'll talk," Braun said. He carefully, almost reverently, wrapped the coins in a cloth made of the fabric the gillsuits were constructed of, rendering them nearly invisible. Braun then removed the apparatus from his back and stowed the bundle in a storage compartment.

Valentina re-opened the duffel, and removed one of the bottles of whiskey. She passed this to Braun as well.

"Also a treasure! But I cannot guarantee the return of this one." He laughed with a wolfish grin. "Your trust in us is well founded," he said, turning serious and gripping Clay on the arm. "Go with Leonard and Maurice for now, and hide among the Un-numbered in New Sydney. We will return in a few days with gillsuits for you all, and will take you to Jack Strong." He looked at Tracey curiously. "And I will tell your husband that you have returned. He has been most . . . distraught, since you vanished."

Tracey opened her mouth to speak, but was unsure whether to correct him or let him labor under the misunderstanding for the time being.

Clay nodded, touching Tracey's arm. She understood that he wanted her silence. The Sea Tribesmen began fixing the bug-like masks to their faces, adjusting their mouthpieces, and donning fins. They activated the active camouflage of their suits, slipped almost soundlessly into the water, and were gone.

—23—

Smithson crept cautiously down the ladder and joined them. Tracey sensibly recovered the bow line of the boat, preventing Maurice and Leonard from making a break for it again.

"This whole thing is very confusing," Tracey said. "You mean, before we came here through the rift, we didn't know anything about Sea Tribes and the Stripes and the Un-numbered?"

"Nope," Ron said. "I still don't."

"This is so strange. I have a feeling that I know things that I didn't know there, but here I don't know simple things that I knew there. There seems to be a blank spot in my mind, and I can't think of something that I know I should be thinking about. Like when I was a kid and lost a tooth, and kept playing with the hole with my tongue. Does this mean that at some point, a 'new tooth' is going to grow in, and I won't remember anything at all about our world?"

"I hope not," LaGrue said. "It may be that most of our value here is providing technology and knowledge that they don't have. And we have a lot to take back to our side, too."

"What seems weird to me also is that you already have preconceived notions of the Sea Tribes. How did we just know that they were savages, deserving of being hunted down and killed?" Valentina asked.

"Here is another funny part," Tracey responded, "I *didn't* get the impression that they were bad at all. My counterpart over here obviously *is* Tribe. Apparently a married one, to boot."

"And even if you didn't actually have another Tracey Springs here, maybe you would have ended up Tribe if whatever branch in history that prevented you from being born had not happened and you *had* been born in this universe, too," LaGrue added. "Surface tension on the bubble."

"I'm not sensing any difference," Valentina said. "Does this mean I'm a double recessive?"

"No, you were tested negative," LaGrue answered. "Maybe in this universe you were never born at all."

"Well, my counterpart here must be a Stripe," Clay said quietly. "But Ron trusted these Tribes, and so did Jack Strong, apparently. That is good enough for me right now. Not to mention that you may be able to help us, Tracey, with any knowledge you have now about the Tribes. But first of all, I want to get word back through the rift to . . . ." He paused, searching for the words.

"The Mods?" Ron added helpfully.

"Yeah. Them. That we made it through and are proceeding with the mission against the Stripes."

"You mean the war-painted guys? Oh . . . they must be the same thing," Ron said, eyes widening.

Clay asked for paper and a pen, and scribbled out a message.

"Smithson, do you think you can get this back to someone on our side and then get back here within a half an hour?"

"Of course," he said, taking the message.

"Meanwhile, we have to go *soon*," Maurice said urgently. "New Sydney does float, you know, and if we don't get under way within that half hour we won't have enough fuel to get back to it without calling in for help, and all we have are altered familiars. And I don't think we want to call in on one of those."

"I'll hurry," Smithson said, and scrambled up the ladder with his characteristic nimbleness.

They stood looking at each other, wondering what was going on in the others' minds. The wind gusted, a trace of coolness in it from the approaching dusk. A pair of flying pickles approached out of the direction of the setting sun. They circled lazily, and Ron was amazed when one of them bumped into him. It felt cool and rubbery, like a cuttlefish. There appeared to be no volition, it just bumped into him and floated away.

Ron scanned the horizon in the direction that Maurice had returned in the boat, straining his eyes for the floating city. He could not see anything, and wondered how far it was to the horizon. He suddenly felt very small, very alone, very exposed on the tiny barge floating in the middle of nowhere over the vast depths of the ocean. The horizon crowded in on him, and his feet sought the comfort of solid ground, but the nearest ground was miles down at the bottom of the abyss. He had never given much thought to just how big the sea was, aside from standing at the shore periodically. He had given even less thought to what the ocean was like at night. He imagined all sorts of terrifying creatures rising from the depths in the dark.

"How far off is the city?" he asked.

Maurice shrugged. "Ten miles or so."

Tracey cocked her head, eyes narrowing. There was something on the tip of her tongue, thoughts fleeting, just out of reach. Calculating distances at sea . . . she knew this. Learned it as a kid . . . A sudden urge came over her, and she had to jump into the ocean.

On the way toward the water, it struck her that she was acting just like Ron had when faced with the rift. She laughed as her feet hit the water. The ocean was warm, and she allowed the salt water to enter her mouth as she splashed beneath the surface. She was struck immediately with how loud it was. There were noises from parrotfish gnawing on barnacles and coral encrustations on the structure beneath, and more indistinct unidentified sounds from farther away. She knew those sounds could travel for miles. She opened her eyes under the water and saw the fading sunlight angling down into the darkness below. A cable that tethered the structure and a large flexible pipe disappeared in the depths. She was weightless, watching small fish scurry and dart among the barnacles, anemones, and seaweed clinging to the walls of the pipe.

She felt at home, at ease with the way the water rolled and surged around and within her body. She felt the entire ocean through her extremities, as though there was no boundary between her skin and the sea. When she could stay submerged no longer, she allowed her head to smoothly break the surface again.

Ron and the others were watching her curiously from the grate.

"From three inches above the water, the horizon is about a mile away," she said. "From six feet over the surface, it is about three miles away. If the object you are looking for is at all big, many stories tall, we should be able to see it from a long ways off. If it is the size of a city, it probably has all kinds of sea birds roosting on it. I don't see any gulls, which means we are more than five miles out. But you see that brown bird with a white underbelly and underwings?" she asked, pointing. "That's a brown booby, so the city is probably within fifteen miles in the direction it's flying, since this is near the end of the day and it's going back there to roost. If there were land or shoals there, it could reflect color from the bottom of those clouds."

They looked at her silently.

"And," she continued, "by the way the water tastes from the phytoplankton and churned up nutrients, and the color of the water, we are near the fringe of whatever current the city is riding on."

Ron's eyebrows raised.

"And no, I have no idea how I know this."

Ron extended his hand, helped Tracey up onto the grate.

"Ugh," she said. "Wet clothes. I'm not used to this; the gillsuits keep the skin dry."

"How do they work?" LaGrue asked.

Tracey pursed her lips, thinking. "I know they were invented a long time ago, and have been modified and improved over the years. They started out as artificial gill membranes built into a backpack. You had to keep swimming for them to work efficiently, to keep oxygenated water flowing over the membranes for them to extract from. There was a backup power supply that revved up a little propeller when you were at rest, so the effective time under water was limited by how long that battery lasted if you weren't constantly moving. Later, when people started living longer and longer periods underwater, they needed to keep their skin warm and dry and oxygenated, too, so they had to start developing more of a porous foam laced with heating elements that circulated oxygen and warmth to the whole skin. They later added the ability for the whole surface of the suit to extract O2 from the water, making it one big gill. You don't even have to keep moving anymore. Now the backpack part is just power supply and propulsion. They added the protective mesh, which added negative buoyancy as well as armor against attacks and water pressure on the lung cavity. They also added the camouflage system mimicked from octopi and squids. The suit senses what is behind it, and pigments the other side of the body to match it. It works really well in water, less well on land. Eventually, they developed food additives to prevent buildup of nitrogen in the bloodstream, so we don't get the bends. Now each Reef has its own markings on their members' gillsuits, and other personalized markings as well. The BlueRing Reef has taken on the markings of the BlueRing Octopus. Nearby is Urchin Reef, Moray Reef, and I think Barracuda Reef. Urchins are pretty friendly traders, but we have raiding parties back and forth between the Morays and Barracudas to steal tuna and sleds."

"So they live full time in the water?" Ron asked.

"Not full time. We live partly inside inflatable structures that have been left to coral over into artificial reefs. That is why they were called reefs in the first place. Once the coral has grown over the buildings and the walls have gotten thick enough, we pump out the water and reinforce the structures from the inside. They are almost indistinguishable from the surrounding reef. The Stripes have found a few of them, but by no means all. That is where we manufacture gillsuits, grow food, warehouse, and basically make all we need that we can't capture."

"'We'?" Clay asked.

Tracey stopped talking. She suddenly realized that the members of the team were possibly not in her camp at all, aside from Ron, who was his old self.

"We all need to get it straight," Clay continued, noticing her hesitation. "We are *all* from our own universe, whatever we may feel or think while we are in this one. If we have thoughts otherwise, or are compelled to act otherwise, we have to count on Ron to set us straight. Even if one of us thinks he is a Stripe, and another thinks she is Tribe, and whatever the rest of us think we probably are over here. We have to remember that we are not *from* here originally, and we have a job to do, even if we have the idea that we are going against our own teams here. *We* are our *own* team. Do we all have that straight?"

"I think so," Valentina said.

LaGrue nodded.

"I will listen to Ron," Tracey said. *But I will not do anything counter to the BlueRings, or any Sea Tribe, for that matter.*

She sat on the edge of the grate, dangling her feet in the water. Ron sat next to her, and tentatively sought out her hand. They sat quietly for a minute, watching as the flying pickles floated back in their direction, then passed on their way to somewhere else.

"So, what is going on? Are you still in there?" he asked, tapping her head.

Tracey eyed him sideways with a lopsided smile. "Of course. It's still me. I'm just a little . . . added to, and some things just aren't there anymore. I can't explain it. It feels like when I was a kid and lost a tooth and my tongue kept poking in the hole. But the memories are getting fainter. I know we are together, in our world, and I work at the aquarium. And drive a bug. And I like the Copper River Salmon down at Anthony's on Pier 66. But I'm not sure what the Aquarium *is*, and why we have one. And I'm not sure what my VW looks like; they don't have those kind of cars here. And here I am also something else. I want to show you all this, it is so much more fulfilling than our world! There, I only work at being near the sea, here I *live* in it!"

"This is all so sudden, and weird. I don't feel any different at all, but all of you . . . ." Ron shrugged.

"You think it's weird for *you*," Valentina put in, standing behind them. "Seems pretty clear for Tracey and Clay, but I have no idea where I fit in here."

"Me, either," LaGrue said. "Most likely we are ordinary citizens of somewhere, probably a floating city since most of the population lives there instead of on land now. Or maybe we live on one of the orbiting colonies."

Ron looked at him, alarmed. "What do you mean? I only heard about a few floating cities. We have billions of people on Earth."

LaGrue shook his head, with a sad smile. "No, Eiffeila has changed things, made this Earth into one big tourist destination. Just before she appeared, there was an enormous epidemic that ran through the world, killing at least ninety percent of every population here."

"*Caused* by Eiffelia," Tracey muttered.

LaGrue made a sour face. "False rumors, spread by the Un-numbered and the Sea Tribes. Anyway, she promised to renew humanity as her chosen people, and we embraced her. She moved most of us into space. Now there are only a few coastal cities, and the floating cities. The landmasses have gone back to wildlife preserves and planetary parks. The only actual towns on the continents are administrative centers. Now, don't get the wrong idea, there still are billions of people. Most of them have been relocated off-world, though. If they come here, it is for tourism. Home planet, and all that."

Ron considered this for a while. "The world here is a weird place. When did all this happen? I mean, we don't have off-world visitors or the same kind of technology on our world, but it seems close and similar in other ways."

"The best I can guess," LaGrue figured, "is that this Earth is about twenty years ahead of ours."

"That would make sense." Ron nodded. "Aside from how it all works with the rifts and how the universes split apart from each other. But wouldn't they keep the same time as each other?"

"Not necessarily," LaGrue answered, calculating in his head. "I wonder if the time difference corresponds with the formation of the rift in Denver! Damn, if I only had a blackboard."

"Also, you mentioned 'She' as far as making decisions around here. Is this the same queen or empress or whatever as Cornish Bob was talking about?"

"Eiffelia, the Queen of the Universe, she calls herself,"

Clay answered. "She claims divinity, and pretty much runs things for humanity. Of course, we only know a fraction of what is out there, even in this universe, so that's a pretty ridiculous claim. She leads us in a war against a race of aliens- demons, out to exterminate us."

"Is she human?" Ron asked.

"Oh, no. Of course not. I'm not sure *what* she is, but she projects locally as a human," Clay answered. "She is revered as a goddess."

"Yeah, whatever," muttered Tracey. "Some goddess."

"She may as well *be* a goddess," Leonard interrupted. "We have to constantly struggle to be free of her influence. She controls down to the smallest detail, and it's not easy fooling her and her Stripe administration. If they catch us, it's right back to the meds and daily reporting through the familiars."

"It is going to be interesting living with you Un-numbered for a few days," Valentina commented. "Don't worry about us turning you in, though. We have as much to lose as you do."

"Your lives? Your minds? Your very freedom?" Maurice asked. "You had better do exactly what we say, or we all get needles to the neck at the end of a spider arm and our brains will go numb. Or worse."

Smithson reappeared on the ladder, climbed down, and joined them.

"Message delivered," he reported. "Proceed with caution."

Clay nodded.

The sun was only a sliver on the horizon now, and stars were blinking in the sky one by one. The air blew alternately warm and chill.

Tracey shivered, still damp.

"Let's get going," Clay said.

They all piled into Maurice's boat, and slowly left the barge. Once clear, Maurice opened up the engine and they sped into the night.

−24−

Ron had never been on a cruise. Life on New Sydney reminded him of what he had heard it was like, just on a larger scale. Everyone was happy. It was not a real happiness, though; there was a vacuous quality about it. Maurice and Leonard said it was because of the drugs.

"Think of it like mindless bees or ants serving the queen," Maurice explained.

The citizens of New Sydney were allowed free access to 24-hour all-you-can-eat buffets, but the food was bland and lacked variety. They could choose instead to go to any one of the markets, and take home free food to cook themselves; but there were only two kinds of food: "plant" and "meat." Each of them was probably an artificial mass of whatever vegetable and animal products could be mashed together, and Ron did not want to think about the latter too closely. There were free shows, and free sporting events and they were encouraged to attend the free health clubs. Once a week, the entire population was required to attend small group meetings for religious instruction, news, and dosage adjustments.

After a week of hiding, of doing nothing but eating the pasty food and watching the television, Ron begged to attend one of these meetings.

"No," Leonard refused. "Out of the question. You would stand out like a sore thumb and we would all get caught."

They had slipped into town from the docks under the city at the dead of night, and made their stealthy way to their lair near the center of the city. They lived in the cool basement of a water processing plant, hiding. Leonard and Maurice worked there, and were able to keep them from being discovered by making multiple trips to the market and filling up hidden bags at the buffets. They were surrounded by pipes. Huge pipes were lowered from the city deep into the ocean, where the water was barely above the freezing point.

Once brought to the surface, it was pumped through miles of tubing to condense large quantities of fresh water from the humid air, refrigerate, and generate power. Pipes transported some of the seawater through the condensers, the rest to desalinators, and other pipes transported air and fresh water to all points of the city. During the first day, Tracey, feeling the urge to be surrounded by seawater, had gotten lost among the pipes. They had had to form a search party to find her before darkness descended and she fell through one of the numerous openings in the floor to the sea far below.

They spent a good deal of time watching television. Ron had just gotten through watching a show on the latest craze, "Super Jumbo Penises." These were huge, three-foot-long foam rubber male members that were showing up in all kinds of zany places, accompanied by a comical musical soundtrack and the ubiquitous phrase "Wow, that's a big one!" An old woman had walked through a crowded square with one of the penises strapped to her head like a hat. The camera had zoomed in to a teenage boy, who screamed with astonishment "Wow, that's a big one!" The laugh track rolled. Workers were sorting fish on an assembly line, only to be surprised by one of the foam rubber penises passing by instead. . . . "Wow, that's a big one!" one of the workers had yelled. "Must have been a trouser trout," deadpanned the announcer, while the laugh track roared to a crescendo. The huge members were also spotted in potted plants, peeking around corners in restaurants, and even strapped to the front of what looked like a military vehicle engaged in combat somewhere.

Clay, Valentina, and LaGrue had watched the show with embarrassed amusement. Tracey was horrified. They were further mystified when commercials featuring the foam penises were shown during the show. One portrayed a woman presenting the product to her mate as a gift. The looks of smug satisfaction that passed between them and the camera were ridiculous to the point of absurdity. Another was just a montage of foam penises, vacuously smiling young people holding them, bright flashing colors, and explosions of neon light, flame, and confetti.

"So, you mean this is just the latest in some long line of stupid fads that the government foists on the population to keep them busy?" Ron asked Leonard.

"They just came out with this one a couple of days ago, and lo and behold, the stores were full of giant dicks the day after the first show ran. So it not only keeps them busy, it keeps them consuming stuff."

"So at the next block meeting, I suppose everyone will be expected to have one of these big schlongs in tow."

Leonard nodded.

"So how does that add up with the religious instruction?"

Leonard shrugged. "We'll see. Maybe she will tell us we have to multiply to help replace all the battle losses against the Demons. Maybe it has some ulterior purpose, maybe not."

"The real war isn't what they show on TV," Maurice said.

Leonard rolled his eyes and groaned. "You and your damn conspiracy theories." He wagged his finger. "All that crap on the TV is all staged and fake, I suppose? All those casualties?"

"Who are they *really* fighting?" Maurice asked, raising an eyebrow.

"Why don't you tell us?" Leonard retorted.

Maurice threw up his hands and busied himself with his altered familiar.

Tracey shook her head. "You people and your war. How she ever got you to buy in to all that is beyond me."

"Like you Tribals have anything to talk about on that front," Clay said. "At least the Stripes aren't pirates, or terrorists."

Tracey's face flushed.

"Whoa," Ron said. "None of us is at war, or doing anything terroristic. Not yet, anyway," he added. It occurred to him that this might change the more the new universe worked on them. The commercials were probably not helping matters. *They seem even more brain-washy than the ones on Earth. But maybe that just seems so to me.* He considered the looks of smug satisfaction on the faces of beautiful actors in his world as they hawked the latest cars, electronics, retirement investments, erection pills . . . *Am I a sucker for consumerism? Am I a loser because I don't have the fancy car, own a home, have a big nest egg? Or a big foam dick?* It occurred to him that the only place these things did not matter were in the world of Dragon Throne, where one could slay an evil giant and then immediately loot a chest for hundreds of gold and magic weapons. But even more valuable were the experience points. *And not the experience POINTS in that world, but the EXPERIENCE in the real world.*

"I still want to go try to experience this world while I'm here," Ron pleaded.

"*No,*" ordered Tracey.

"I'll be careful," Ron promised. "I want to see what we're dealing with here. When we get back, you all may not remember any of this. If we're going to have anything at all to report, I have to see it for myself."

Clay grudgingly agreed.

"Look," Maurice said conspiratorially, "if you just *have* to get out of here, maybe you can go with me to the market. I could use the help carrying the food back here. But you have to promise to stick with me, let me do all the talking, and if anybody asks who you are, you tell them you're visiting from off planet to see how our deep ocean condensers work."

"Deal."

"Bad idea," Leonard said. "Maurice, you came from the other side of the war, started our group of Un-numbered, weaned us all off Milk, set us free. Now we all count on you to keep us all from getting caught. This is a stupid risk."

Maurice looked Leonard in the eye. "Sometimes you have to take calculated risks. Ron may have a whole world worth of resources to help in this war."

Maurice handed Ron the spider he had been working on. It looked queasily bigger than normal spider. "This is a familiar," Maurice explained. "There are many models. Cuter mammals for kids, like squirrels and such. The spider is a good model because it can cling with rough movement, and each leg is designed to do something different, like locomotion, earphones, a holographic projector. The projector shows television broadcasts, and allows access to the mainframe. In theory, everyone has one of these that personally identifies him to the Stripes and tracks your movements at all times. You see that little needle in its mouth? Each day, every citizen is required to allow that damn thing to bite you on the neck. It takes a blood sample to monitor the level of Milk in your bloodstream and at the same time injects a new dose of Milk based on the previous day's reading to keep your levels stable. If you don't do this, they send a block leader around to check up on you. It reads your retina print with one of the legs, too, so you can't have anyone else do it for you. We have to have ours tricked by replacing the milk receptacle inside with saline. This one that I am giving you is even more of a dummy familiar; it is nothing more than a shell for the most part. It'll play broadcasts and that's about it. No videophone, no GPS, no identity records, and no fangs."

Ron nodded.

"Now, look . . . you're going to have to mimic the locals. Look at me."

Ron looked at Maurice.

"No good. I can see you in there behind your eyes. You need a vacant, happy look. Milk makes you placid, compliant, very patient, and cheerful. Try again."

Ron softened his face, smiled, and looked again.

"Almost," Maurice judged. "Watch me."

Ron looked into Maurice's eyes. They seemed slightly out of focus, thinking of somewhere else if not exactly looking there. Ron imagined looking at something six inches behind Maurice's head, and thought about little furry bunnies.

"Perfect. Do that the whole time we are out," Maurice said.

You better change into coveralls," Leonard added. "That fuzzy shirt would stand out like a sore thumb."

"It's my lucky lint shirt," Ron protested weakly, but agreed.

Ron took the lightweight, almost crepe-paper coveralls and pulled them over his shirt. He added some soft-soled shoes. The familiar scurried to a perch on his left shoulder, and stuck one of its legs in his ear. Ron jumped.

"Well, there you go," Leonard said. "You almost look like a

New Sydneyite and a perfect little follower of Eiffelia. But watch it with that twitchy jumping."

"What about his marking?" Maurice asked.

Leonard narrowed his eyes, considering.

"What marking?" Ron asked.

"You noticed on the TV that lots of people have certain paint markings on their faces?" Maurice answered. "It tells a lot about who you are, how high up you are, that kind of thing. The colored markings designate your role. Half white and half black stripes are high officials. Black stripe on the left side is industry and science, black markings on the right are education and the arts, bottom half black markings are agriculture and transport, top half is military and religion. If you have just black dots, each of those represents something—either a year of service, or a particular good deed, something like that. A red lightning bolt means you have served in combat during the war and gotten a kill. Then it gets even more complicated, with colors added to the dots representing different things, and what pattern the markings are in."

"Look, he doesn't need the whole book on the subject," Leonard objected, rolling his eyes. "Let's just give him a dot on the left side and be done with it."

Maurice produced a small jar of paint, and smeared Ron's face with a little black dot on his cheek. "There. Now you are a Stripe in training, with a year of service in industry," he said, and applied three dots in a triangle to his own left cheek.

"I feel stupid," Ron said. "Or worse, I feel . . . evil, wearing this stuff."

"Let's go."

They exited the basement complex, Maurice waiting until nobody was looking. They shuffled along in their soft-soled shoes through the ever widening hallways. They began passing other citizens of New Sydney, smiling, nodding greetings. Ron remembered to keep the vacant smile plastered on his face and nodded back. They entered hallways as wide as streets, lined with shops and restaurants. The hallways were more and more crowded.

Ron watched the people. All had painted faces, either dots, stripes, some even squares. They all wore papery coveralls, all carried familiars of some sort or another. There were many spiders, but also some snakes, squirrels, lizards, and various birds. Many watched the holographic projections as they walked, tuning into the TV broadcasts or speaking on video-phones. Everyone seemed busy, industrious, cheerful, but somehow not entirely there. Ron stopped for a moment in front of a recruiting poster: soldiers in war paint marching in lock-step in front of an angular tank vehicle, while others piloted what looked like flying snowmobiles overhead, attacking a sinister-looking flying alien fortress in the background. "JOIN AND SERVE NOW, THE EVIL TIDE IS ABOUT TO TURN!" the poster read in inspiring block letters.

Maurice gently guided him past the sign, and led them into a large supermarket. It was somewhat similar to the ones on his Earth, Ron noted. They selected a basket, and wheeled it into the produce department. Unlike the ones on Earth, however, there was only one product, a large reddish fruit with a bunch of green leaves at the top.

"So this is the 'plant,'" Ron whispered. "They use just this one type of vegetable-slash-fruit thing to make everything?"

"That and 'meat,'" Maurice said, pointing to the other section where Styrofoam trays held shrink-wrapped mounds of ground hamburger-looking stuff.

"I'm not even going to ask what that is made of," Ron whispered.

"Good call."

"Those plants are very nice," said a middle-aged man with black paint around his mouth. He spoke slowly and cheerfully. His cart had some meat and plant, along with a new shrink-wrapped foam penis.

"Thank you," Ron answered in a voice he hoped was similar. "I'll try one."

Ron looked through the pile more carefully. He noticed out of the corner of his eye that the man was still looking at him. He felt a pang of fear.

"Say, you sure are looking at those plants hard," he said.

Maurice hurried over, grabbed one and put it in his cart.

He led Ron away as quickly as he could without appearing hurried.

"They are all the same. No sense in taking such care in choosing one," he hissed when they had placed some distance between them. Ron glanced over his shoulder, and saw that the man was still following them with his eyes.

Maurice angled back toward the man. "He's from off world; they don't get much good produce where he's from," he explained.

The man nodded slowly. "Oh. That explains it," he said, still nodding slowly. They stood staring at each other for what seemed like a long time.

"So where off world are you from?" he finally asked Ron.

Maurice answered, "He's from Procyon 6, one of the orbiting water mines."

The man nodded some more, then slowly stopped and tilted his head to one side. "I haven't heard of that one." He pursed his lips. "Are they strong with God?"

"Of course." Maurice smiled. "Eiffelia is everywhere."

Ron's instincts tore at him to walk away, but Maurice was showing no signs of breaking away before the man's curiosity was satisfied. He probably wasn't used to seeing people whisper.

"Well," the man said, nodding again and smiling, "welcome to New Sydney."

"Thanks." Ron smiled.

Finally the man left and went back to the pile of "plants." Ron glanced at Maurice, and they slowly wheeled toward the "meat" section. Ron noticed that Maurice was sweating profusely.

They picked out some more food, avoiding the man who'd spoken to them in case he thought of more to ask them, then pushed the cart toward the bagging area. Unlike Ron's Earth, there were no checkout lanes.

"We don't have to pay for food? Eiffelia must care for us," Ron said.

"I hear you don't charge your cattle for their feed, either," Maurice smirked.

"Wait . . . then what is the point of commercials if they

aren't selling the products for money?"

"Money isn't the goal. The point is control. Creating and controlling the desire."

Like Earth.

They bagged the food and strode back through the street. Near a corner, they were held up by a crowd that was filing into a glass-fronted room filled with rows and rows of plastic chairs. A female Stripe, who had the entire top half of her face painted black but for a white dot in the middle of her forehead, stood at the front of the room.

"Block meeting," Maurice whispered.

"I have to listen," Ron whispered back. "Can we get in there?"

"No! No way! All the familiars are linked once inside. It is how they take attendance."

"Can we hide outside and still listen?"

Maurice looked around. There was an alleyway near the back of the glass-fronted room which could afford them complete coverage. Maurice motioned Ron toward it, and they surreptitiously stepped into it when nobody was looking. After a few minutes, the block meeting began.

The lights dimmed. Those who were still milling around made their way to the plastic chairs, seated themselves, and lowered their faces, all adorned with various amounts and patterns of other-colored paint. There was a long moment of silence, then a point of light appeared at the front of the room before the outstretched arms of the priestess. It wavered in intensity, meandering slowly, then rapidly grew to a glowing outline of a winged woman in white robes. Her features were somehow indistinguishable but beautiful at the same time. She was almost like a living, glowing marble statue from ancient Rome. Ron found his breath had caught, and his solar plexus tightened. She exuded a certain . . . what? Otherworldliness? He found it hard to think straight, as though his mind were distracted elsewhere, doing something else he could not fathom. He searched her eyes, and could see no pupils, just a uniform radiance over her whole body.

"Welcome, Eiffelia," the crowd chanted in unison.

"I come," said the glowing form, her voice mellifluent yet

powerful.

"In the beginning, she separated the light from the darkness, form from nothingness, and spawned the universes," intoned the priestess.

"From the formless you formed us, to serve you," the congregation chanted.

"I come," repeated the winged woman.

"For our bodies you created the lands from the seas, and gave us plant and meat to sustain us," they chanted.

"I come," she responded.

"For our minds, you send inspiration, and guide us slowly toward the perfection of your thought," they chanted in unison.

"I come."

"For our souls, you sent Dumuzi, Amun, Shiva, Confucius, Buddha, Jesus, Muhammad, and all the saints and enlightened ones."

"I come."

"We welcome you, Eiffelia, to our midst, the living God come again to live among us forever," intoned the priestess.

The congregation raised their heads again while the priestess lowered her arms and seated herself. The glowing form floated down the aisle, taking a more conversational tone.

"Good afternoon," she said cheerfully. "Please mingle your blood with my essence."

The congregation rustled and positioned their various familiars at their necks. A few of them flinched when the needles went in. Eiffelia glanced around the room, her eyes settling on a middle-aged woman.

"Ah, Christina-44, your illness has improved. Good. I will adjust your dosage downward a bit." She turned her attention to a teenage boy. "William-11, the matter you prayed to me about last Wednesday has been attended to. As much as I will choose to intervene, that is. Sometimes, we must let nature, my most intricate creation, take its own course."

Ron glanced quizzically at Maurice.

"She has an uplink in each house, where people can pray

to her," he whispered. "It's a glass ball with a little glowing spark in it, just like she looked at the beginning of the service."

Eiffelia paused in front of a distinguished-looking man with a gray beard. "Your son is well, Jonathan-61," she said regally and comfortingly. "He continues his service with honor, and prepares with his unit for a major offensive, which will take place within the week. The sacrifice of your family will not be forgotten."

She continued moving through the congregation, offering personal bits of advice and support.

"So, that's God?" Ron whispered.

Maurice shrugged. "What did you expect?"

Ron shook his head slowly. "I dunno. I just don't buy it."

Maurice raised an eyebrow, and then gathered up the grocery bags. "Me, either. Let's get out of here."

Ron started to follow, then stopped. "Wait just a minute more. I want to see what happens next."

"Nothing happens. She updates everyone on what is going on in the known universe, they say a prayer, she takes some inane questions and answers about life and religion, she blesses them and sends them out into the world again to do her will. Yadda yadda, they go home."

Ron stood blinking for a moment, then narrowed his eyes, working his jaw.

"I want to ask some questions," he whispered slowly, nodding.

"No way! Impossible!" Maurice hissed. "She would nab you for sure, and the rest of us, too." He grabbed Ron's arm, but Ron resisted. "You *can't argue with her.* We have to go. *Now.*" He pulled Ron's arm, and they took a few steps out of the alcove. Ron stopped, while Maurice continued to futilely pull on his arm, trying not to attract attention. Several of the crowd behind the glass wall glanced in their direction. Maurice froze, then abruptly dropped Ron's arm and left. His face was a mask of mortification, and he tried not to outright run as he turned down the nearest cross street and vanished from sight.

Ron watched him go, then turned back to the glass wall

and the painted faces now staring at him from behind it. He remembered back to the Horribles, and was queasy. He looked deeper into the room, and saw the placid, smiling amorphous visage of Eiffelia watching him with interest. He saw her tilt her head for a moment, then a flash of recognition registered on her features.

−25−

"Come on in and join us, Ron," she called. "I almost didn't recognize you as a Stripe."

Ron felt a rush of adrenaline in his midsection, and his knees went wobbly. He thought of running, but realized that he had no chance of escaping. He felt as though someone else had seized control of his legs as he walked stiffly to the glass door, opened it, and took a few paces into the middle of the room. The congregation stared at him with obvious confusion and interest, those in the front craning their necks or scooting their plastic chairs around to partially face him. Several of them clutched large foam penises.

"Wow, that's a big one," Ron muttered helplessly.

"Imagine my surprise in seeing you here," Eiffelia said smoothly. "The last time I contacted you through one of my servants, you were in another universe entirely."

The congregation murmured with surprise and fascination.

"Oh, you mean that servant who tried to cut me in half with a machine gun?" Ron asked.

Eiffelia laughed, her voice tinkling like Mr. Barman. "I gave you an opportunity to join me and the forces of light as we oppose the evil ones. Those who are not with me are against me, and he who does not gather with me scatters."

"I just wonder," Ron mused out loud, unsure if she had the power to strike him dead where he stood, "how many of these people would be 'with' you if they weren't doped up on drugs and forced to?"

There was shocked silence in the room.

"Of course they would all be with me. They all take the medication voluntarily, by choice. Milk focuses mental energies, allows happiness, and removes aggression. My people deserve happiness, and instead of making them all wait for millennia for my nature to bring it about, I allowed them the happiness now. I chose to come to my people instead of allowing them to wallow in the mire of their own wills until they reach enlightenment on their own. I sent wise men, shamans, and prophets to guide them for thousands of years, and they were still evil and had war after war. I sent my son, and they rejected him. When I saw that my people were suffering and dying of the epidemic, I chose to protect them before they were utterly lost. Here, however, I am forced to work within the bounds of time, and Milk gives them the boost they would eventually have on their own when they advanced enough."

"So you are not omnipotent?" Ron asked.

She blinked at him.

"I mean, if you are really God, why can't you just alter time, advance them without the drugs, or even just win the war without making them fight it for you?"

"I cannot enter time and space physically without ripping apart my own creation," she said with a sad shake of her head. "I can only be with my people in this form."

"So you can't . . . wait, so you can only appear like this? You can't touch anything physically?"

"My people are my hands," she responded. Eiffelia gestured to a small child, who was watching the exchange with puzzlement. "Child," she said, "pick up your chair for me."

The girl obeyed. The congregation smiled, nodded, and applauded.

"Thus did I work through Noah, through Moses, through Abraham. Thus it has always been."

"But even then, God could do miracles. Where are yours?"

Eiffelia spread her arms. "Did I not send my servants to your universe? Did I not alter time there? Did I not smite your underground warren with fire and thunder? Did not the bullets of your minions of evil fail to harm those in my care?"

Ron shook his head slowly. "I don't even know where to begin with that. Why did you have to rely on technology to nuke the airport? There is a saying by a writer in my universe, 'any sufficiently advanced technology is indistinguishable from magic.'"

Eiffelia nodded. "Yes, Mr. Clarke had a point. But if you think about it, he presupposes that technology and magic are different to begin with. Is not a nuclear explosion magic in itself? How it is brought about is immaterial. It all ultimately flows from the source, which is my creation. Magic can only work from within nature and science. If I act directly from the outside, my creation, the universe, will be broken."

"I am still puzzled about your war." Ron felt as though he was running out of time and Eiffelia's patience. "Who are you fighting, and why?"

Eiffelia gestured to another child, a little boy in powder-blue coveralls with tousled blond hair.

Make up on a child is particularly upsetting, Ron noted.

"Tell him, Christopher-9," Eiffelia urged.

"We are fighting the bad people from another universe, who are trying to take us away from God," he said, with wide eyes.

"What do they look like?" Ron asked.

"Some like people, some like monsters," he answered.

"Monsters?" Ron asked, puzzled. "You mean, like aliens?"

"Call them what you will," Eiffelia said. "They seek to eradicate humanity, my chosen people, whom I created in my image. Fallen angels lead them, and they have even corrupted humans here, on Earth, the cradle of man. We must be eternally vigilant," she added to the congregation, who murmured in accord.

"Do you mean the Sea Tribes?" Ron asked.

Eiffelia laughed. "Oh no, they are impotent here. A mere inconvenience, those parasites. I refer to others, who hide among us and with their tongues they have used deceit; the poison of asps is under their lips. But can any hide themselves in secret places that I shall not see them? Do not I fill heaven and earth?" She gestured to a woman to turn on a large monitor on the wall. "But fear not, they will be revealed if we remain constantly on guard."

The woman switched on the screen. Ron instantly recognized the outside of the water processing plant they had hidden in for the past week. He felt sick to his stomach.

"He led us right to his lair," Eiffelia said with satisfaction.

"Did he not know that I have my eyes everywhere? That once I saw you with him, I would merely have to follow him through the city, one camera to the other? The eyes of the Lord are in every place, keeping watch on the evil and the good. Evil always makes mistakes. Always."

Ron watched as a group of about twenty men in coveralls and helmets, with guns, gathered in front of the processing plant.

"Watch, o faithful ones, as the wicked are snared," she intoned.

The men moved stealthily to positions outside the doors, then suddenly rushed inside. Ron felt ill, like dark hands were squeezing his lungs and guts. He watched the screen with the others for what seemed like hours. Suddenly one of the police force appeared in the door, dragging a struggling form. A woman. Ron recognized Valentina, kicking and thrashing. She was taken off screen. A short time later, Professor LaGrue was led away, not even struggling. Maurice came next, apparently unconscious. More time passed, then the sound of gunfire came from the speakers. Another pause, more shots.

Not Tracey, Ron thought, in near panic. Not her . . . it must be Smithson or Clay putting up a fight.

More police emerged, this time dragging a man by the arms, a growing red stain on his chest leaking onto the ground in a long red streak. It was Clay.

Ron hung his head, tears stinging to his eyes. *This is my fault.*

"The last one is putting up a fight," Eiffelia reported. "But we will prevail. Goodness always triumphs."

It took a while, but Eiffelia proved correct. Four of her helmeted guards eventually emerged, dragging Smithson between them. Ron could not tell if he was alive or not. Other guards limped from the doorway, carrying wounded or dead comrades. *Good ol' Smithson.* He waited, but there was no sign of Tracey.

"It is finished," Eiffelia said, sonorously. "Catch us the foxes, the little foxes that spoil the vineyards, for our vineyards are in blossom."

Finished! Ron thought with a flash. Tracey got away!

Eiffelia turned to the applauding congregation. "And when they had inflicted many blows upon them they threw them into prison, charging the jailer to keep them safely."

"What will you do with them?" Ron demanded.

She turned to Ron. "You should be more concerned with what I will do with *you*. I will turn them back to me. They will again see the light, and walk in my ways and on my path. You, I cannot turn. You will not respond to my treatment; the Milk will have no effect on you, nor on anyone with your genes. I cannot return you to your universe, however. I have no choice but to cast you into the prison, too, until your heart changes."

It occurred to Ron to try to run, but he knew he could not succeed. He stood with his head bowed until the men took him.

*****

Chris Springs adjusted her sunglasses against the glare of the sun off the Caribbean surf, then turned over onto her back to allow her tan to deepen on her front to match her back. It also allowed her to catch a glimpse of Matt Pavlov Weeks, who, she was pleased to note, had been stealing glances her way at the time. She sat up to take another sip of her rum drink from a straw, looking his way only with her eyes, hidden behind the sunglasses.

"Yup, he was looking over here," she whispered to her new friend, Jill. They had both been flown to the island several weeks ago, and had engaged in nothing since but drinking, swimming, eating, and flirting with the young men who had also been flown in "for their protection." She had asked what island they were on, and was only told "Andros."

There were around fifteen young women and the same number of boys, all under the age of twenty-five. Jeremy, her brother fresh from Marine Boot Camp, was the hit of the resort with the young ladies.

But something was up. There were whispers of some kind of nuclear attack that had taken place back on the mainland, but they were not allowed access to television or radios.

Wherever she went, there were government staff and

agents. She knew they were agents of some kind; they all had the same close-cropped haircuts, Government Issue sunglasses, and aloof but tense observation of all that went on. The agents came and went from a compound of cinder-block buildings near the center of the island, while the tanned young "guests" were allowed to stay in resort-like accommodations near the beach, complete with a swimming pool by day and a hot tub at night. They had, in addition to the bar, a game room, a burger restaurant, and a health club. She had also found an anti-aircraft missile battery hidden behind some tropical foliage near the resort. In spite of this, Chris was only mildly curious about what was going on in the outside world, and not in any hurry at all to get back to the dorm at the University of Washington to continue her studies.

A man in a white jacket walked out to Chris and Jill from the poolside bar and asked if they would like their drinks refreshed. They giggled and agreed.

"And send one over to that guy, Matt," Jill added. "And tell him it's from Chris Springs."

They tittered afresh.

"Shut *up*," Chris protested. "I don't need any help from you."

"Sure you do," Jill argued, looking over the top of her sunglasses. "You are the only one not to hook up around here already. I'm working on my third guy already," she boasted, crossing her arms behind her head and lying back on her towel in the sand. "One of whom happens to be your very hot brother."

"Gross," Chris spat. "I'm getting tired of this. I need to get back home."

"Oh, you can't," Jill said. "They won't let you off of here. But who would want to anyway? Aside from you, I guess."

We're trapped, and we don't really know why, it occurred to Chris.

−26−

Professor Langston LaGrue was happy. He glanced around his new laboratory at the gleaming counters, the glassware, the computer screens, the staff eager to be sent off to work at his whim. His double, his counterpart in this universe, was flying in within the hour.

The first week after his capture in New Sydney had been spent in what remained of the city of Denver, ironically. He learned this universe's recent history: After the epidemic that wiped out most of the population of the Earth, Eiffelia had appeared, promising healing and salvation. The rumors that had accused Eiffelia of starting the epidemic in the first place died out quickly, and her influence and power grew. Once completely in power, Eiffelia commanded that the majority of the depopulated cities would be razed and allowed to be reclaimed by Nature, while the fledgling orbital colonies and terraformed planets were allowed to grow. The Earth, for the most part, became a nature park, except for a handful of administrative outposts. Denver had been converted into a research facility.

LaGrue was not confined to his room, but allowed to roam at will. There was nowhere to run anyway. To the west were the Rockies, and to the east were miles and miles of open range. The Great Plains had returned, studded with buffalo.

For the first few days, orderlies had arrived in his room to forcibly administer an unfamiliar drug, which they called "Milk." It made no sense to resist this, and he found the effects pleasing anyway. His fear and anxiety vanished, replaced by a lingering, calm joy. Pains and stiffness that he had felt for years, the result of aging, slowly faded. He grew to look forward to his daily bite from his mechanical chameleon familiar. His Paxil had run out after the first month, however, and he was at first concerned that his obsessions would return. He wondered whether the Milk would treat that, too, but slowly realized that it did not when he started wondering whether the glowing tendrils of light inside the Prayer Orb were coded signals from *her*. He wondered how long it had been since his "capture" from among the Un-numbered. Three weeks? A month? Three months?

He had asked the orderlies what had become of Clay, Valentina, Smithson and Ron and Tracey, but was only told that they were all serving Eiffelia in their own ways.

He had started working in the laboratory that had been provided to him. There was nothing assigned; he had been allowed to pursue whatever interested him. He started work on the devices that had been puzzling him in his research back in his old base in Denver. He worked on researching the technology behind the mysterious star drives, and was surprised to find that Eiffelia had not mastered the process. He could document the existence of only one of them; the one recovered from the ship that Tracey had dreamed about. The drive itself was a marble-sized gold sphere, and was the same as the one that powered Cornish Bob's rift generator. Try as she might, Eiffeila's scientists were unable to make one of them themselves. It was not from any lack of trying, though.

He also studied the zombification process that allowed certain hand-picked agents to replace normal bodily processes with an indefinitely sustainable state, while sacrificing only sleep, eating, and reproduction. Individual body cells were attacked and replaced by a virus that replaced the DNA with a new form which disrupted the normal cell function from self-replicating cells that interconnected their respective functions into one entity. LaGrue wracked his brain to remember a similar model in biological taxa.

Sponges! These cells are changed to a sponge-like model where individual cells cooperated separately.

The cells themselves were virtually immortal, as long as the wastes were cleared by periodic immersions in a bath of organic compounds designed for that purpose. He wondered how the disruption of the cells from one interconnected body into a more cooperative but separate mode effected how the brain produced consciousness.

He learned negative gravity propulsion for aircraft. He even researched what little was known about flying pickles: Nobody had ever seen them eat, nobody knew what world they had evolved on, and all attempts at exterminating them had failed. He learned only that any attempt at keeping them in captivity failed: As soon as a flying pickle realized it was trapped, it collapsed and died. He also learned, to his surprise, that Eiffelia had imposed an order for all of her subjects, no matter what they were doing, to kill them on sight.

That is odd, he thought.

Some of the research aides had begun to gently probe him for information from his universe, too. He allowed them to, and fully answered all that they asked, while learning more from them in the process. All of this was fascinating, but it wasn't enough. There was something missing that had nothing to do with science.

He started attending his weekly block meetings. All the while, when returning to his room at night, there was one of the glowing prayer globes in the corner. The direct conduit to Eiffelia, to the Goddess. His block leader had instructed him how to use it, but he had hesitated up until the night before. Weren't the coded signals enough? But another part of him wanted to contact her directly, not feel that niggle of doubt about whether he understood the coded messages correctly. He felt the longing for spiritual things for the first time since he was a child, forced to go to church by his religiously zealous parents against his will. It wasn't much of a church; the members met in a rented conference room of a motel and sang hymns, then lurched around speaking in tongues for a while. He had thought at the time it was only one step away from handling snakes. It was this that had driven him to the comforting reality of science to begin with. In the acropolis of academia, it was easy to join the ranks of those who scoffed at the fools who duped themselves with religion.

He had finally roused his courage, after watching TV for a few hours, to try contacting Eiffelia through the globe. He had gazed into its depths, into the glowing spark at its center as he had been shown, calling out her name.

She had come, the glowing winged form, achingly beautiful and serene. She greeted him, warmly waiting for him to speak, to pray. He silently observed her, avoiding her eyes. Finally, he bowed his head, and wept. He cried his pain, his loneliness, his need to be needed, his need to help and be found valuable.

When he had finished, Eiffelia comforted him. "Be of good cheer. You are valuable to me, like your counterpart in this universe. Professor LaGrue-22 is a valuable tool for goodness in this universe, but has not risen as high as you have in yours. You know things from your work there that can serve me well, and help my forces of goodness against the evil Demon hordes in the real universe here. I have sent him to meet with you and assist you here, and given him a holy mission to transmit to you. Soon he will come to you at your laboratory, and together you will serve me in that task."

He wept in gratitude. But he dared ask for more. "Goddess," he prayed, eyes averted, "cannot your Milk cure me of the tortures of my mind?"

"Of course it can, but your peace comes at the cost of your brilliance. Some of your most advanced thoughts came out of your madness."

"Of course, Goddess. And Goddess, would it be better to convert me with the zombification process, in order to prolong my life for your service?"

She laughed. "Perhaps, perhaps. We shall see. Ask your counterpart about that."

"Goddess, how does consciousness arise from the brain, whether regular or zombified?"

"This you may discover in time."

"And Goddess, do you know all?"

"Of course," she said, with the slightest hint of impatience and defensiveness.

"Then please, I beg of you, tell me the answers to other great questions: How the Big Bang came to be? What was in existence before existence? And how did life begin? We know it evolves, but in order for life to begin naturally selecting, it must have had an origin as well?"

"Ah, LaGrue, I could tell you these things, but these

things you must discover on your own."

"As you will, Master." He bowed, disappointed.

The time passed, and LaGrue became more ready, eager to serve Eiffelia and her holy will.

A young research aide approached, a short-haired woman in a lab coat and dark-rimmed glasses. She waited to be allowed to speak. Professor LaGrue raised his eyebrows and nodded.

"He is here," the aide said excitedly.

"Show him in!" he answered. She scurried away, and presently appeared again with . . . himself. LaGrue stared dumbly at his double. It was like looking into a mirror, but in three dimensions.

Is that what I look like? he thought, like someone who hears his own voice on a tape recorder.

"I would shake hands with you, but the entire universe would explode," his double said.

They laughed, and shook hands anyway.

"So . . . where were you working?" LaGrue asked.

His double waved his question off dismissively. "It doesn't matter. I was researching the design of a new self-replicating virus that would streamline the zombification process to make all humanity like her Horribles, instead of the costly and complicated mechanical viral insertion process it is now. The savings on food alone would be staggering, much less the level of control she could exert. But we were only making slow progress."

"How does it work?" LaGrue asked. "I understand how individual cells are converted from a single mammalian organism into a communal collection of specialized cells like a sponge, but how does memory and consciousness survive the death of the cohesive neuronal brain structure? That would imply a non-local mind. I asked Her, but she would not tell me."

His double appeared uncomfortable. "I asked Her that, too. She suggested that I focus on other things, and not question. So whenever I started wondering about that, I would turn to working on developing Ornithopters, little artificial birds that she could use for surveillance. She came and rescued me from that obscurity when you showed up from the parallel universe."

"Ornithopters?" LaGrue whispered, a smile spreading across his face. "I tried that, too! Were you able to do it? Make a flying bird?"

"No," the new LaGrue said, with a sour look. "Far too complicated. The most I could manage were little dragonflies, helpful for surveillance."

"Perhaps we could work together! Between the two of us, we have much to talk about."

"Not now," said the new LaGrue. "We have a new mission."

"Tell me." LaGrue sighed, barely hiding his disappointment.

The double LaGrue rubbed his chin. "Well, have you ever heard of Pangborn Recessives?"

"Of course. We had one of them with us on our mission."

"Right. Well, you may have heard that Eiffelia has attempted in the past to produce them from various stock, both human and non. The enemy in your universe branch has gathered a number of recessives on an island facility called AUTEC. We can only assume that they are trying to breed their own full Pangborn carriers. We, of course, want to stop them by stealing their stock. But we don't know where this AUTEC facility is."

LaGrue raised an eyebrow. "AUTEC?"

"Yes," nodded Double LaGrue.

"I know where that is," said LaGrue. "It stands for Atlantic Undersea Test and Evaluation Center. It is on Andros Island, near the Bahamas. The Navy put it there because there is a deep sea basin surrounded on all sides there by shallows called 'the tongue of the ocean' that makes it ideal for testing weapons and sonar and passive detection and all manner of advanced military programs. They have a nice little resort area there, too."

Double LaGrue nodded in return. "That's it. That must be where they are keeping their stock. Yes. Eiffelia wants to prevent any chance of their success, and take them to her home planet, Cambria, to continue her own work."

"But the Mods said that it doesn't work that way. The genetic expression is not replicable through regular reproduction."

"Oh, *did* they?" Double LaGrue sneered. "And I suppose they told you how it *was* transmitted?"

"Actually, no. They implied it was expressed through some kind of spiritual means."

"Aha. Just as I suspected. And if the enemy believed these 'Mods,' why are they trying to breed the recessives themselves? See? *Lies.*"

Professor LaGrue's eyes narrowed to match those of his double. "So when do we start?"

-27-

Smithson had no idea where the island was, only that it was only a mile across and he had no way off it. It was hot, tropical, and ringed by white sand and clear, coral-encrusted waters. There was no other land as far as he could see in any direction.

There was a low hill in the middle of the island, with a spring that provided the only fresh water available. There were trees, verdant undergrowth, and bamboo. He had been unable to find any animals, but there were some songbirds, dragonflies, and an occasional flying pickle. He knew from the flying pickle that he was still in the new universe, but the consciousness that was using it for a sensory platform could not tell him where he was. There was just enough sea life available near the shore to sustain him.

He remembered back to his capture, how dozens of armed men had suddenly rushed into their midst. The swirl of action, Valentina getting grabbed, Professor LaGrue surrendering on his knees after Clay had been shot . . . then he remembered fighting them. He had managed to put a round into the center mass of four of them before noticing that they were still coming—he realized at that moment that they had been zombified, so he switched to neck shots. He managed to drop six of them before running out of ammunition. After that, it was all hand-to-hand. One of them had frozen him by putting his gun to Valentina's head, then another hit him on the back of the head with the butt of his rifle.

And then he had simply woken up on the island, in the glaring sun and with a splitting headache. It took only a few hours to explore it. He found the spring and the creek that it fed, found the coconut trees, and the broad-leafed banana plants. He had explored the sheltered coral lagoons through a gap in the coral, though, and found them thick with fish. He had seen the hulking forms of huge sharks circling, far bigger than any species on his Earth. He was thankful that the sharks were too big to get through the openings in the reef.

They had taken his weapons, body armor, and even his shoes, leaving him dressed only in a pair of papery pants that he was unable to tear. With no knife, his hair and beard began to appear after a few days, along with a deep tan. His bare feet developed hard calluses, protecting him from the searing sand. The days were sweltering hot, but the nights grew cool. It rained occasionally. He had made a debris hut near the center of the island at the top of the hill, first framing the structure with sticks, then piling brush around it and roofing it with banana leaves.

The first "raid" had come after three days. He had been twisting some of the coconut fibers into twine that he was going to try to fashion into a fishing net, sitting near his shelter, when he heard the low hum on the horizon. He rose, and saw three aircraft slowly circle the island. They had no wings, he noticed with amazement. They made low humming noises, with an occasional electric crackling sound. One of the three was large, and looked like a skirtless hovercraft, but was flying too high to be using ground effect. The other two were more agile one-man affairs. They appeared like flying jet-skis or snowmobiles, with helmeted pilots sitting astride them. They all must have used some kind of anti-gravity propulsion.

Wish I could get my hands on one of those, he thought.

The large craft had settled into the sand at the beach, and he had walked to meet it. A door had slid open, disgorging a toweringly tall, muscular man with a blond crew cut and dressed in paper clothing similar to his own, but with a tunic-like shirt. His face was painted with several lightning bolt designs in red on his cheeks. There was a large leech attached to the base of his neck, which Smithson guessed was his familiar. Smithson had watched him while he stretched, limbering his muscles. He was *big*. The flying jet-skis continued circling the island, then had descended, hovering nearby.

When the giant had finished his warm up, he assumed a

fighting stance and started advancing toward Smithson.

Smithson held up his hand. "Whoa," he had said. "What's going on here?"

"We are to fight," the man had said curtly.

"Why?" Smithson had asked.

"It is Her will, and I must obey," the giant grunted, advancing in a crouch.

"Whose will?"

"Eiffelia, the Goddess, the Queen of the Universe," he had responded, then lashed out with a mighty punch at Smithson's head.

He sidestepped it easily, retreating. "What if I don't *want* to fight?" he had asked, retreating backward at forty-five degree angles as the giant advanced, looking for another opening to strike.

The blond giant had not answered, only closed in, eyes fierce with intensity, sweat beading on his brow and smearing his paint. He had thrown another punch.

Smithson again evaded the strike, diving over a fallen palm tree log into a roll. The giant had charged, trying to grapple. Smithson had waited until the last fraction of a second, then ducked under the giant's outstretched arms and pivoted to his outside, riding his hip as he passed. The giant crashed heavily into a bush, where he sat, chest heaving with exertion. Smithson noticed that the flying jet-skis had followed their progress.

"You must fight me," the giant grunted, hauling himself to his feet. "Or they will kill me."

"Why?"

"Eiffelia desires to learn your fighting arts. You were able to defeat many of us when we captured your party. Our world has no such comparable skills. Our civilian medication dulls our aggression, so she gives us soldiers a different drug to spur us to battle rage, but this hinders our skills. She desires to record your fighting system and use it to train her troops for battle."

"What about that bunch of guys she called the Horribles? Or those other uniformed zombie goons that captured us? Are you one of them?"

"They know guns only. And no, I am still alive. She wants to know the effect of your martial arts on the living, so they sent living opponents. Both the living and the dead will learn, though."

Smithson blinked. "You don't have martial arts here?"

"We did, but there has been a gap of over fifty years since Eiffelia came in, during which there has been no need to study such things. We have had wars, but our wars have been mostly fought with long-range weaponry. Now we need to fight closer in. We need video footage to train the troops."

"That won't work. It doesn't work that way. This kind of knowledge has to be transmitted person-to-person; you can't learn it by a book, or a video recording, or by drugs."

"Then you must teach us."

"I won't. I don't believe in your Eiffelia. The real God doesn't need drugs or reanimated corpses to get warriors to fight."

That stopped the giant cold. He stood staring at Smithson, head cocked to one side.

They regarded each other this way for a long while.

"If it is true what you say, that this knowledge can only be taught person-to-person, what do you have to lose by fighting me and allowing us to record it?" the giant finally asked.

Smithson pondered this. It was true that only through years of detailed training and instruction that the intricacies of the art could be imparted. He remembered back to his own instructors, who could make it appear that they were doing nothing but stumbling around aimlessly while their opponents went flying. Only after each movement was broken down by the sensei, layer by subtle layer, and by constant practice and repetition, were the secrets revealed. But he also thought that his value to Eiffelia only lay in his knowledge, without which he probably would have been dead or drugged already. She could simply want to record his fighting for a while, analyze it by computer, then dispose of him when she thought she had enough footage.

"Your counterpart in this world is a soldier," the giant continued. "He was killed in battle because his craft was shot down and he could not fight off the evil hordes after his ammunition ran out."

That cinched it. Smithson knew that something sounded fishy about this story, it was too pat. The giant probably believed it, but he had obviously been lied to. He wondered why they were trying to convince him of who he was. He knew, from his training as a Magi Warrior, that he should refrain at all costs from letting them know that he was one. It occurred to him that they might also be trying to determine whether he was one or not. He knew he must obfuscate that fact, keep them guessing.

"That's bullshit. Everyone else on my team knew who they were here in this world, and knew what information they knew. I feel no different now than I did in my own world. If I was a soldier for Eiffelia in this world, I would know all about it. I would remember things that he remembered. I don't know, or remember anything but who I am from my own world."

The giant turned and gestured helplessly to one of the flying jet-ski pilots. The pilot circled idly, hand to his helmet as though he was listening to a speaker mounted inside. He adjusted a dial between his handlebars, and his amplified voice boomed down.

"Eiffelia tells me to inform you that you probably have no counterpart here in this universe, because he was never born, or may have died at birth. Whatever occurrences that gave rise to your birth there did not occur here."

"If that was the truth, why were you lying at first with that B.S. story about my double here running out of ammunition and getting killed? Too many lies here. I'm just not going to help her."

The giant charged him again. Smithson simply turned and ran. He sensed a certain gleeful triumph when he realized that the giant was not as fast as he was. It was almost comical, the giant with the crew cut and painted face chasing the smaller, wirier, shaggily-bearded shirtless man. They circled the island on the beach several times, Smithson easily loping just out of reach. The giant ran more and more slowly, until he fell exhausted, panting in the sand. Smithson stood a short distance away, catching his breath.

"You have killed me," the giant had croaked.

Smithson misunderstood him. "Maybe she should send someone in better shape." He laughed. "Or a zombie. They don't tire out." He almost didn't notice the flying jet-ski move into position behind the giant, twenty feet in the air. It hovered, nose pointing at the giant while he stood in the sand at the edge of the water. The giant faced the craft, and raised his arms in the air. A small panel opened in the front of the flying jet-ski, revealing the muzzle of a large bore weapon.

"God is great!" the giant cried.

There was a flash and a deafening roar, more felt than heard. The giant's back exploded in a red mist. Smithson could actually see daylight through the hole in the man's chest for a second while he slumped to the sand. He watched in shock while the giant worked his mouth for a few seconds, filling and spilling over with red. Eyes glazing over, he died.

Smithson stood dumbstruck, covered with a fine spray of coppery-smelling blood.

The pilot manipulated a control on his dash, activating a microphone in his helmet and amplifying his voice. "He has sacrificed himself to the Goddess to atone for his failure. We will return again. Each man you do not fight will sacrifice himself in this way. But if you fight them, and do not kill them, they will live."

"You *fucking bastards*!" he raged back. "Go ahead! Kill each other off to your heart's content!"

The pilot hovered, hand to his helmet over his ear as though he was again listening to a transmission. He keyed his microphone again. "It has been further ordered that should you still refuse to fight, even in light of the self-sacrifices of Her warriors, that your comrades will be executed, life for life, for every man who dies because you refuse to battle him. Starting with Valentina Pavlov. All blessings, honor and glory to Eiffelia, Her will be done."

They all flew away. He was left alone on the sand with the giant's body. At first he felt sad for the man, then grew angry at how he had been forced into this situation. He dragged the corpse into the lagoon and pushed it through the gap in the coral for the giant sharks.

Two days later, another convoy arrived. The larger craft disgorged another man in a paper suit, this time a tall, wiry, muscular bald man, again with a lightning bolt-painted face and beetle familiar. There would be no outrunning him. He did not even try.

There were no speeches. The man simply closed on him, faked a punch, then lashed out with a left snap kick.

Smithson shifted to the outside of the line of attack, stepped in with his left foot and caught the kick across his back with his right hand. He then placed his left elbow on the man's kneecap and dropped. The wiry man sank like a stone. Smithson pivoted, kicking him the temple. He fell, stunned, then struggled drunkenly to regain his footing. Smithson was impressed with his tenacity, wondering if she had sent a zombie this time. He closed in and slammed his knee up into the man's chin.

He went down with that particular disjointed spat of someone who was completely unconscious.

Nope.

Smithson retreated a short distance while two crewmen from the cargo craft walked out to retrieve the bald man. He watched as they began dragging him, one on each arm, to the open door of the cargo ship. The beetle scuttled along behind. Smithson was then seized with a sudden urge to chase them down. He pelted after them, and was grimly gratified to see the two crewman panic. One dropped his arm and fled for the door outright, the other made the mistake of dragging the unconscious bald man with all his might. Smithson snaked out a spear-handed strike to the man's Adams apple as he ran past, and heard the man drop to his knees, gurgling behind him while he pursued the other crewman, who had barely closed the door behind him when Smithson caught up to the ship. Smithson was forced to prowl around, banging on the hull. After a minute, he returned to the other crewman, who by this time had regained his feet and begun begging to be let go.

"Get out of here," Smithson had snarled, "and good luck finding anything of use out of that whole fight to study without years of practice and instruction behind it," he added. Smithson let the man pass, still dragging the dazed, bald man. He was glad that at least the man had been allowed to survive the ordeal without being shot by the jet-skis. As the beetle familiar crawled past, he reached out with a heel stomp and crushed it. He watched as the cargo craft took off without even disturbing the sand, and slowly rise into the sky. The jet-skis took up escort formation, and they accelerated eastward into the horizon.

Smithson looked at the ground where the cargo craft had left and noticed the hilt of a knife protruding from the sand. He wondered whether it was a mistake or they were giving him something to fight with for next time.

Now he knew. When the cargo craft landed, two men emerged, both armed with knives: double bladed, long, all business. They were both of average height, but looked like scarred, hardened soldiers behind their face paint. Smithson remembered with a curse that he'd left his new knife back at his shelter at the center of the island. He mentally vowed never to be caught without it again.

The two men advanced on him with catlike caution, knives weaving. Smithson allowed his vision to splatter, taking in all movement without focusing on anything. He circled in a crouch, trying to prevent them from attacking him from both sides at once. Other movement distracted him: *What was that, dragonflies?* There were many of them, hovering around the men as they circled. Smithson made a mental note of it, then ignored them.

One of the men suddenly moved in and slashed at Smithson's neck. The other man saw Smithson retreat from the gleaming arc of steel, and took the opportunity to launch a mighty lunge at Smithson's stomach. Smithson turned to the lunge, shifted his weight slightly off the line of attack and allowed the thrust to pass close enough to graze him on the way by, leaving a hair-thin red line. He guided the thrust farther along with his hand, overbalancing the man, then whipped the arm out and down, slamming him into the sand. With a twist of his wrist, he had the man's knife.

The other soldier, slowed by having to step over his fallen comrade, continued his advance. Now that Smithson was armed, he advanced more warily. The disarmed man regained his feet, rubbing his shoulder and wrist, but hung back uncertainly.

Now it was knife against knife. The armed soldier circled, trying to align Smithson's back with his unarmed comrade. Smithson allowed this, knowing the man he had disarmed would attempt to grab him from behind. Predictably, the man seized Smithson around his torso, pinning his arms to his side while the other soldier closed in to finish him with his knife. Smithson feigned helplessness, then lashed out with a kick to the knife-wielding man's solar plexus as he closed in. The kick dropped him to his knees, gasping. A second kick, a heel-stomp directly to his nose, broke it with a wet, crunching sound and a gush of blood, sending him reeling and gasping to his back.

They always forget that even though an opponent has a knife, all his other weapons are intact, he thought.

Meanwhile, the other soldier realized the precarious nature of his position. He lifted Smithson off his feet and attempted to slam him into the sand. Smithson did not resist the motion, instead curled into a roll midway through. He continued the roll as the man released him, and came back to his feet in a crouch, throwing a handful of sand that he had collected mid-roll into the remaining soldier's eyes. The man clawed at them, then made the panic-induced mistake of trying to recover his fallen teammate's knife. As he clawed around in the sand, Smithson closed and drove the butt of his knife into the man's temple. He fell dazed to the sand, retching.

They also forget that they have their own weapons other than the knife, he thought again.

Smithson recovered the other knife, retreated. Apparently, this was enough of a fight for the observers, who cautiously emerged from the cargo craft to drag off the two beaten soldiers. This time, Smithson noticed that they were armed with some sort of gun-like weapons, and decided not to chase them.

As the craft flew away, Smithson saw that they had left a crate in the sand. He examined it warily, and found it packed with food. Grateful, he took stock of his situation. Now they were leaving food, perhaps to keep him strong for further fights. How long would this go on? He knew in his heart that he would have to settle in for a long haul. *Well, here it is. Maybe this is what I've been preparing for. Let's see how long I can last.*

This realization gave him a sense of grim determination. He now had three knives, and resolved to carry one of them and lash another one to the end of a pole to serve as a spear. The third one? Lash it to the end of a branch, make a man-trap triggered by a tripwire, he decided. He pondered locations to set the trap. Several dragonflies hovered nearby, apparently observing him. He realized they had been flying around the island since he arrived. He wondered . . . could they be more than they seemed? Technology he'd seen made that a possibility.

Smithson made his way back to the camp in the middle of the island and noted that the dragonflies followed him at a distance. He started working on the coconut fiber fishing net he'd started, this time formulating an idea. The net was three feet across at that point. He waited until one of the dragonflies flitted close enough, then whipped it out at the insect. It worked! He pounced on it quickly as it struggled in the net to free itself. He examined it. There was something unnatural about its feel. He squeezed it between his fingers, and heard a strange crunch. He stood blinking at it for a moment. It was artificial; like the familiars but smaller, filled with tiny wires and circuits. He looked around at the other dragonflies, still circling nearby.

"So this is how you've been keeping track of me," he announced. "Cameras on bugs. Very ingenious." *So much for concealing a trap, though,* he thought. "So how long will this go on?" he asked out loud. "Until you learn enough? Until one of your lackeys manages to beat me? Or kill me?"

There was no answer. He did not expect one.

−28−

"Is that her?" asked the Executive Vice President of Programming for the Interstellar Division of the High Church Network.

"That's her." The Regional Director of the Propagation Channel pointed her out. She adjusted her round glasses to get a better view, pushing her wispy brown hair out of her eyes. She was mousy, frumpy, and looked like anything but a programming director for a sex channel.

They stood behind a marble wall, in a full-scale replica of a Greek temple, replete with marble columns, fountains, and rich cushions. Lounging among the cushions were groups of women in various states of undress. Toga-clad boys bearing trays of food and drink circulated.

"Are you sure of the ratings?" the network executive asked, white face makeup with dark circles around his eyes meticulously applied, his suit impeccable.

"You saw the figures." The Propogation director beamed. "She came to us three weeks ago, and we got an immediate boost in the ratings numbers. I think putting her in the Classical Greek show was a good call. We went from worst to first, and now we can attract the best man-talent."

They watched the woman turn in her sleep, blond hair spilling around her head. Her toga slipped, revealing a perfect upper thigh.

"So run through this with me again," the network executive said, tearing his gaze away. He flipped through a packet of papers filled with bar graphs. "You say she was captured with a group of heretics, who had come here from a spin-off universe, and Eiffelia sent her here for her service?"

"That's right." The director nodded. "It turns out that her body chemistry wasn't quite used to the Milk at first, and so when we started filming she didn't understand that it was her duty to God to serve as erotic entertainment to boost production of the population. On her first show, she hid under the pillows. On the next week's show, she started out all right, but then took to resisting her partner, and even called out that she was being raped. He had her paired with a handsome young war hero, and he found her struggling to be irresistible. The ratings spiked immediately, and the fan mail has cascaded in. She's an instant star. We are trying to keep the medication level at the perfect balance, between resisting and giving in to the pleasure of sex."

"So she resists, then gives in?" the network executive asked, clearing his throat and adjusting his tie.

The programming director smiled, glad she was in face paint. "Yes, it appears we underestimated the power of rape fantasies on the populace. If we find that the pregnancy rates of the colonies increase, I'll be asking you for her own show."

"Eiffelia be praised." The network executive raised his hands and gazing up into the tops of the stone columns, festooned with lights and cameras.

*****

Valentina Pavlov woke, and it came rushing back to her: being taken from the hiding place in New Sydney, the gunfire, the capture. She had been held in a room alone for hours, then drugged. She'd awakened here, in the Greek temple; a snake writhed around her neck. There were cameras, she immediately noted. Part of her began looking for avenues of escape, but another, even stronger part of her, was apathetic. She felt sluggish, and realized without surprise that she was drugged.

She'd counted twenty women on the large set. They all had snake familiars. They were all shapely, beautiful, and dressed in togas. She noted none of them had painted faces. Some lounged on cushions, chatting in low voices. Others bathed nude in the large, shallow bath fed by a fountain that poured water from a statue of satyrs pouring it out of large ewers.

She had approached one of the groups of women, endured their looks of cool appraisal at her body.

"What is going on here?" she had asked.

The women laughed, glanced at each other. "You'll see in

about an hour," one had answered with calculating mirth.

A few minutes later, the activity level around the set rose. Technicians adjusted lights, swiveled cameras to catch angles around the piles of cushions and the central bath area. Valentina noticed a bustle of activity off set, and several stripe-faced make-up artists started circulating among the women, who removed their togas to allow their bodies to be dabbed with flesh-colored pancake.

"What are they like today?" asked one of the women of an effeminate man, who patted make up on her lower back.

"A good batch this time," he answered with a coy, raised eyebrow. "A few professional athletes, an actor, and three firefighters getting a reward for heroism or something. Go for the tallest black man, he'll get the best ratings."

Valentina felt sick.

A make-up artist approached her, but she waved him away.

The set cleared except for the women, who draped themselves seductively among the cushions and bath. Valentina had looked around in a near panic as the lights raised, and harp music began to play. The ghosts of her childhood abuse crowded in.

"Action!" called out a woman with round glasses perched on her nose, and the cameras whirred.

Valentina looked for an avenue to escape the set, but there were large, stripe-faced security guards at every exit. She decided to hide under a pile of cushions as far out on the periphery of the set as she could go. She had just covered her nearly nude form when the men entered the set.

They were young, vigorous, dressed in sandals and togas, bare-chested. They were immediately beset upon by the women, doe-eyed, touching, caressing. The boys in togas appeared with trays laden with goblets of wine. The cameras followed the participants as they broke up into pairs, groups.

Valentina hid under the cushions. One of the firemen had tried to lure her out, but she'd refused. She watched as the spectacled director angrily made a slashing motion across her throat and pointed out another woman to the fireman.

It took them all less than five minutes to start in on the

sex, Valentina noted. It lasted an hour. Valentina watched with growing horror and fascination as the director guided the cameras to whatever activity was the most animated, slowing other couples down to preserve the flow, speeding other groups up, making sure that there was no lull in the action. Toward the end, she felt a strong urge to join them, but she'd resisted. "It's just the drugs," she told herself. "Isn't it?"

When the director called "Cut," the participants applauded themselves along with the crew, then bathed. The director sought Valentina out, and motioned her over with her index finger.

"And just what was that all about, Missy?" she asked curtly.

Valentina shook her head helplessly. "This is crazy. I can't do this. Don't make me do this."

The director cocked her head, pushed her round glasses up on her nose. "Do you even know why you're here?" she'd asked.

Valentina stared at her blankly for a moment, then lowered her gaze to the floor. "A form of torture, no doubt. I don't know what information you're looking for, though."

The director shook her head in amazement. "You don't get it. You see these women? They are the best of the best. They applied for this months ago, went through screenings. First, they had to be beautiful. Then they had to survive the intelligence tests, the genetic health screenings, and medical batteries. Only then were they hand-picked to become breeding stock for Her academy. Eiffelia only allows the best to reproduce for the elite. These lucky girls can reproduce on camera until they no longer maintain their shape, then they rejoin the regular population, still 'stars.' They will look back on these days with fond memories the rest of their lives, knowing that their children are serving Eiffelia closely, among Her chosen. Why She chose you, a heretic, is beyond me. Who am I to question Her will, though? If She wants you to produce Her babies for Her academy, then it must be so. Your babies will grow up with the best education, the best chance to become the leading members of the clergy, the military, or in industry. Only these women are allowed access to the best men. The war heroes, the captains of industry, the highest priests.

"In Eiffelia's eternal wisdom, She saw that there was value in having the general population share in these couplings, that they were inspired while watching the most beautiful have sex to have sex themselves, increasing Her fold. In the war against evil, there are casualties who must be replaced. These are the End Times, you know, and while the war will inevitably be won, there are sacrifices that must be made to bring the victory about. Yours is a glad task, a pleasurable work. Most women would trade places with you in a heartbeat. Can't you use your appeal to your advantage?"

Valentina felt her stomach turn to lead, a lump form in her throat. The irony of the situation was not lost on her. *Of course I can. The fly that became the spider has become the fly again.*

"So you just learn to like this, you ungrateful little bitch," the director growled curtly, and wheeled away.

Valentina learned that this was a weekly show. She stayed in a small room near the set for the next week, trying to avoid the other women and the prayer globe in the corner of her room. Her medication was adjusted, making her hazy, and sensuous. She began longing for a man.

The following Tuesday, the set breathed into life again. This time, she sat on top of the cushions, still on the periphery. This crop of men were mostly war heroes. When one approached her hungrily, she held out her arms invitingly. He sat beside her, stroking her thigh, her side. They kissed. She felt the cameras on her, while his tongue entered her mouth. An image of a stripe-faced baby appeared in her mind. She gagged, pushing him away.

"No!" she cried, writhing away. "This is wrong! This is rape!"

He held her in a vise-like grip, forcing himself onto her. She struggled, while at the same time forcing her breasts into him, grasping him with her legs. She continued to struggle, eyes half closed with mixed horror and desire while he madly mounted her.

When the show was over, she lay in a heap on the cushion, quietly sobbing.

The director approached her. "I don't believe it," she said excitedly. "Well done. Our ratings went up by twenty percent. Can you do that again next week? There is an A-list actor I've been on the verge of getting a commitment from for weeks, and this may just put him over the top for making an appearance. I want to make a few promotional commercials, too."

Valentina lay quietly face down, her sobbing subsiding. "Her will be done," she said softly.

−29−

John Clay had never been shot before. He had barely been able to draw his pistol and squeeze off four rounds before one of the raiders had fired into his chest. At first there was no pain, it seemed like he had only had the breath knocked out of him. Then his legs went wobbly, he couldn't breathe, and he sank to the floor, clutching a hot, wet spot on his chest while his vision went dark.

He woke days later in a hospital. Strangely, he felt better than he'd felt for years. He'd been given a big leech as a familiar, which spent most of the day attached to his neck, feeding him a continuous drip of milk. Three weeks into his recovery, Eiffelia visited him from the globe in the corner of the room. She told him that his counterpart in this universe was a high-ranking official in her secret police, working on flushing out heretics from the population.

A part of him was surprised at how quickly he agreed to help her by divulging all the information he had concerning his position in the other universe. She asked him at length about the Mods and seemed disappointed with how little he knew. She questioned him extensively about the meeting at the Seattle safe house, and was particularly interested in the mention of "cheat codes." She turned her questioning to a naval research base on Andros Island in the Bahamas. She was sure that his government was trying to breed Pangborn carriers, but did not seem at all disappointed when he told her that the people there were only there to keep her from nabbing them. He told her all about the rift between Bodie and the floating platform in the Pacific, but she already knew all about it.

When he told her about Tracey Springs' existence, it was another matter. She immediately launched a search for her throughout New Sydney, without result.

He wracked his brain trying to think of other helpful

information, which he conveyed to Eiffelia at every opportunity through his prayer globe. He asked after his fellows from his universe and was told that they were serving the Goddess in their best capacities. He learned about Valentina Pavlov's service by accident, flipping channels late one evening.

It occurred to him, recovering so quickly from his gunshot wound, that Eiffelia's medical technology was far more advanced than his universe. He remembered Ron Golden's concern with his possible cancer, and made sure to tell Eiffelia that he should be checked and treated. She assured him that cancer had been cured in this universe and promised to look into the matter.

He recovered quickly. The day he was released, he was sent to Denver to meet with Professor LaGrue, and the professor's counterpart, to work on a project of utmost importance: A raid on the partial Pangborn gene carriers on Andros Island.

–30–

Ron's "cell" had no bars; the door had no lock. As he looked out of the small window at the inky blackness, it occurred to him again with crushing force why this was so. At first, he had thought the facility was in space, but during his first day of captivity, a fish with huge, luminous eyes and wicked teeth had swum lazily past the window. He was deep in the ocean. The sense of cold and immense pressure pervaded. His room was spartan, with steel walls and ceiling beams, metal grating making up the floor. The water that flowed from the small sink was icy cold, and tasted brackish. The walls dripped constantly with condensation. His joints ached badly, and just getting out of his cot was a monumental effort. The guilt he felt for screwing up and getting his friends hurt ached even worse.

His only contact with the outside world for the three weeks since his capture was with a short, curly-haired young man with striped face who periodically brought him meals and ignored his questions. That morning, in addition to the tray of food, the man had also brought a glowing prayer globe and a large television screen. Ron had tried to turn the television on, but could find no buttons to activate. He waited, a sick feeling in his stomach informing him that a visit from Eiffelia was imminent.

He was not mistaken. The shimmering mist emerged from the globe, and she materialized. Once again, he felt oddly distracted, out of place in the presence of her glowing form, and those odd, pupil-less eyes. She still radiated something inexplicable that affected him directly in his solar plexus and throat.

"Good evening, Ron," she greeted.

Ron shrugged, trying to show that he was unaffected. "I wouldn't know; day, night, it doesn't make any difference when there is no sky and no clocks."

"Yes, but this is where I wanted to keep you. It is close to where I live."

Ron stared at her blankly.

A ghost of a smile played across Eiffelia's lips, then vanished. "Perhaps I should explain."

"Well, that would be a first. From anywhere, I might add."

"Of course. You have not gotten the whole story about what is going on from anyone. Sometimes it has been because they don't know themselves, sometimes it is because they didn't want you to know. Now you need to know everything."

Ron cocked his head, pulled over a metal chair, and carefully sat down, folding his arms across his chest. "I'm all ears," he said guardedly, remembering back to Smithson's observation about Thulsa Doom: "Dark masters of evil will tell you just enough of the truth to serve their own ends. Then they send you off to be crucified."

"First of all, I'm only telling you all this because there is only one way you are ever going to leave this facility. Ever. And that will be after convincing me that you are willing to serve me, like your great-grandfather Cornish Bob does."

The pit in Ron's stomach grew impossibly deeper, but he gave no indication of this. *How long will I linger here suffering before I die? It may be shorter than she thinks.* "Okay. I agree to serve you. Can I go now?"

Eiffelia tinkled laughter. "I said you have to convince me. It will take a bit more than that."

"Are you afraid I would bolt back to my universe? How would I pull that off?"

"One of your company managed to escape me so far, so it might be possible. I will have to keep you here to prevent any chance of you getting back to your universe."

Ron's heart leaped, and he tried his best to conceal any reaction. Tracey was still free!

"So here you are, and here you will remain. I see no harm in telling you the whole truth, so that you can make an informed decision."

It was Ron's turn to laugh. "You obviously have never learned rule number one for evil geniuses by watching any

James Bond movies: Never tell the hero the whole plan. The bad guy always tells his whole plan, leaving the hero to die in some weird trap, but he always escapes and uses the information to stop them."

Eiffelia raised an eyebrow. "No, we don't have 'James Bond' movies here." She closed her eyes for a moment. The curly-haired attendant appeared at the door. "Tell Cornish Bob to bring me back a copy of every James Bond movie from his universe," she ordered.

The curly-haired guard bowed and disappeared. Ron tried not to laugh. The thought of the Queen of the Universe sitting through those movies, wondering whether the whiz-bang spy gizmos were real, and why Bond looked different in various ones, filled him with spiteful glee.

"So does this mean that you're not going to tell me what's going on until you absorb the wisdom of James Bond?"

"No, I don't think that will make any difference."

"Okay then, so what's going on?"

Eiffelia paused for effect, appearing to search for a place to begin. "First of all, you are correct: I am not a goddess."

"I'm shocked," Ron said, rolling his eyes.

"At least, not as you would define it. I am advanced enough to the point that it would be indistinguishable from your definition, but I am not a deity, since there is no such thing."

"So, what are you then?"

"I am a sponge."

Ron blinked. "A *sponge*? You mean, like an entity that, uh, learns everything it can and absorbs knowledge like a sponge? Or do you mean you are one of those things you wipe your kitchen countertop with?"

"You could say both."

Ron shrugged. "I guess I just don't follow. Perhaps you should explain."

"Gladly. Do you know how old the Earth is?"

"Pretty old."

"Yes, pretty old, indeed. It formed about four and a half billion years ago. Life started around four billion years ago. It started out as self-reproducing RNA molecules, and gradually went through several fits and starts while the planet was bombarded from space by asteroids. Eventually, multicellular organisms evolved, and they started making oxygen as a byproduct. Did you know that until then the sky was yellow instead of blue? Finally, around one billion years ago, it evolved into algae and seaweeds. My ancestors, the first sponges, appeared around six hundred million years ago. Ninety million years later, around five hundred-ten million years ago, I was born."

Ron nodded his head, which was rapidly growing a headache. "Okay, so you are really, really old. And you are a sponge."

"Right. Your current crop of scientists assume that we were very primitive life forms. This is incorrect . . . badly off. All you have left is a few fossils. Do you realize what that tells you? Not much. We sponges evolved over millions of years. Far longer than you humans have progressed since you split off from monkeys."

"I guess you have a point," Ron said stupidly.

"Right again. So, we evolved in a different direction than you apes with opposable thumbs. Yet we learned to manipulate our environment, too. Just not with hands. You see, we sponges are built differently. We learned to think, not just into the wavelengths of visible light and hearing like you mammals do, but we learned to think and perceive into—how do I explain this to you? Realms of thought and how thought interacts with space-time?"

He regarded her blankly.

She searched for words. "Have you ever thought about how we sponges feed?"

"I think they filter the water, and eat—what? Little bits of plant and animal stuff?"

"Think of it this way: We sponges don't have actual tissues and organs like other animals. We are collections of cells. Some of them have specialized as structure, and make a body with a vast network of chambers and canals that gradually reduce in size and connect with the pores on the outside. Some of our cells have little whips that move water through those channels. Some specialize in digesting, and share the nutrients with the other cells. We have other cells that do . . . other things. Like interact with other consciousness and move non-physically through space-time. Our specialty cells allow us to have a fragmented identity and sense of self, too, which allows us to keep track of multiple things independently as though with separate identities, but joined. Perhaps you can think of it like a hive mind, but instead of separate insects, it is separate cells that are joined into one body.

"But that is beside the point. The point here is we just grow bigger and bigger and replace dying cells with other cells. And the bigger we get, the broader the consciousness gets, and the more separate things that that single consciousness can keep track of simultaneously. With little sponges like you have in your world, about the most that they can control is themselves and maybe some attendant fish and algae. They control their own cells into patterns of growth that can funnel the water into itself, maybe get some algae to contribute nutrients, and master some fish for defense. Your scientists assume that the fish are hanging around because of their own evolutionary programming, but their assumptions are incorrect. Now, so what if we get bigger and bigger? We can control more. The main organism just goes on and on, replacing the parts that wear out, but keeping the net of consciousness intact. You humans have brains that function in a single consciousness through a neural net. I function differently, the whole making up greater than the sum of its parts. My consciousness is more holographic, and not as dependent on the living tissue."

"So, hence your being millions of years old. You are immortal."

"Fundamentally. As long as I can continue to filter water and eat, I will continue living. But long ago, there was more than just me. We evolutionarily advanced sponges lived, growing and growing, until the seas were full of us. There was a large, but not never-ending supply of bacteria to eat, so we grew until we ran up against other sponges and had to compete. We evolved the ability to communicate with each other directly, consciousness to consciousness. Not long before I was born as a tiny little sponge near the middle of the great ocean, around five hundred and sixty-five million years ago, other species had evolved. There was a rapid growth of species, which you call the Cambrian Explosion. There were still no species on the land, just in the shallow, warm seas. There were trilobites, sea spiders, sea scorpions. They scurried around on top of us, too big for us to eat. But we learned to communicate with them, too, learned to control them. Once we could control them, they became our 'hands' and allowed us to make war on each other. Eventually, and after a long and protracted struggle, only I remained. But I'm getting way ahead of myself and the story."

"So, you used sea spiders and sea scorpions to fight other giant sponges?"

"Yes. Of course, I am over simplifying. After the giant scorpions, we got adept at using other species. One of my rivals succeeded in evolving sharks around three hundred sixty million years ago. That escalated things. Remember, this battle took place over millions of years. It wasn't like your human wars. To escape the carnage, our servant species moved onto the land around four hundred-fifty million years ago. By the time I was able to devote any attention at all to what was going on out of the seas on dry land, it was well into the Permian Age. I had to reach an agreement with two of my last three rivals to try to wipe out the vermin land species. We were able to launch a massive program to eradicate them, starting around two hundred fifty-two million years ago, using volcanism and a nearly planet-wide release from our ocean beds of methane hydrate, which caused extensive global warming. It was a mass extinction, but we took to fighting again before we could really do the job well. We only got ninety-five percent of the species."

"Oh, well, too bad," Ron quipped.

"So, we turned to trying to run each other over, using continental drift. Imagine billions of little burrowing worms under my control. I got good at it, breaking up the supercontinent Pangaea and running over one of my rivals with Gondwana. Nothing like a subduction zone to do in a giant sponge. Then came the dinosaurs, around sixty-five million years ago. I was getting the upper hand, using a newly evolved starfish that could eat three times its bodyweight in sponge in a day, and protecting them with ichthyosaurs. Because I was about to break through and win, my last two rivals ganged up on me and tried to do me in. They learned to control things *off planet*. They ended up dropping a huge asteroid nearly on top of me. There was another mass extinction; it wiped out half of the species on the planet, including all the dinosaurs. I barely survived."

"Two questions, if I may interrupt."

Eiffelia nodded permission.

"One, how did they manage to control things in space? And two, how did you survive?"

"Excellent questions. First, you have to understand how we control things without physical tools to do so. I told you about this briefly when we met at the block meeting. We have to control other beings, use them to manipulate the matter. Creatures with little intelligence, like burrowing worms and the like, we can outright control. They are like our physical limbs. Animals that can think for themselves have to be manipulated through suggestion, innuendo, be convinced of common goals. It is more of a mental control. They allow themselves to be subjected to my will.

"I was the first to turn my consciousness to controlling the creatures of the land. My rivals, while I was busy doing that, were the first to turn their consciousnesses off the surface of the planet altogether, and allied with some members of a race of aliens that were studying our planet from orbit. It was they who dropped the asteroid bomb and nearly got me. The irony is, this impact formed a rift, and pieces of me floated from your universe into this newly spun off one. I was able to leapfrog *them* this time, over our space-time and into this new universe. This one apparently had not evolved intelligent sponges. Here, I was alone, and the queen. They thought I was finished, but after unlimited growth here in my universe for a million years, I was able to launch a surprise attack through that rift with my vast armies and exterminate them. I decided not to return to your world.

Hence, this is why your universe has no intelligent sponges left in it, and mine has only me."

"Wait. I thought that you said earlier that my universe was the one that was sprung from this one, not the other way around?"

"Not that it matters. They are like branches from the same trunk."

Ron mulled that over for a moment. "Anyway, so who are you at war with now? Did you say that all the rival sponges are gone?"

"Yes, I did. Now is when it gets really interesting."

Ron laughed out loud. "I'm sorry. It only gets interesting 'now?' Less than a month ago, I was just a laid-off computer programmer with health issues. A lot has happened in a very short time, thanks to you. First it was time-traveling war-painted zombies with guns, then secret bases with holes into other universes. Now it's a five-hundred-million-year-old psychic sponge with a God Complex. I may need a moment just to wrap my head around all this."

"That is what I just love about you humans." Eiffelia chuckled. "You make such excellent tools. Fragile and short-lived, but very flexible and malleable. I remember back when you were still just another species of monkey. You know, for five hundred million years, there was no intelligent life on this planet other than me and a few of my blood enemies. I would check out how things were evolving on land every few million years, just to see what use I could make of the current crop of species. Monkeys were showing promise, but no more so than some of the insect varieties . . . then, humanity! Suddenly you were domesticating goats, farming, building cities, and worshipping idols. A blink of an eye, to me. How did you suddenly develop a rudimentary intelligence so quickly when it took us so long? What were the limits of your thoughts and abilities? So I started projecting in your form and walking among you. I needed you, and quickly, because the real war was starting."

Ron opened his mouth, but there were too many questions that tried to come out at once so he closed it again.

"The real war was with the aliens, who now call

themselves the Mods. I think they were the ones that kick-started your intelligence. I think they did that to use some of you to war against me. And yes, I started to use some of you to fight against them, too. I also used others of you, the special few like you, to manipulate universe bubbles."

Ron sat back on his bench and folded his arms. His eyes were rolling back in his head.

"Let me take those one at a time," Eiffelia continued. "After killing off my rival sponges, it occurred to me to look into the orbiting aliens they had used to drop the asteroid with. I mean, it is one thing to be able to travel to other worlds by way of transmitting consciousness, but they were apparently able to pull it off with physical matter. It occurred to me that if I was able to get off planet, I could expand to other oceanic worlds, maybe even terraform them, and expand my realm exponentially. They had the technology to do this. I wanted it. So, I sent forth the tendrils of my awareness to them, and found that they were not just in orbit anymore! They had come down to the land, and apparently had been . . . well, monkeying around with you monkeys, for lack of a better term. They were underway interacting with you, and here you were getting all intelligent and civilized. On *my planet!* Well, that had to stop. I was able to turn some of you monkeys to my will, just like my rivals had. Humans make good chess pieces. I then used my pawns to steal the aliens' technology. I appropriated one of their interstellar space-time-stretching drives by having my humans down one of their ships, learned how they use the same tool to slip from one universe into another, how slipping from one close-by universe into another and jumping back and forth between them can move one back in time inside that universe, utilizing the lateral dimensional relativistic drift principle."

"Oh, of *course,*" Ron said brightly. "The lateral dimensional relativistic drift principle!"

"Humans can be such smart-asses. So anyway, I was only able to steal one of the rift generator gold balls, which also doubled as a star drive. I had to build up my strength in order to clean my planet of them and launch a pre-emptive attack on their home world. I wanted to start breeding you for this end. It was then that I found that the aliens had been breeding you for ends of their own."

"Breeding us?"

"Well, that is not the right term, perhaps. Your companions, Clay and Professor LaGrue, have described to me the extent of their knowledge about the double recessive gene you carry. They call it a "Pangborn' gene. They do not understand it. This gene was implanted in some of you early humans by those aliens, but it isn't actually a gene in that sense. It is more like a hitchhiker, a tiny energetic code that manipulates genetic material, almost a self-aware microscopic parasite. Or more like a symbiote, but you hosts don't really know of the advantage. The Mods explained how different universes spring from existing ones, but if they are not different enough from the source universe, the new one collapses back like two soap bubbles joining through surface tension, correct?"

"Yes, I have had it explained. But I still don't get it."

"Well, at the risk of confusing you further, the entities you carry prevent the collapse. You can think of it like a thumbtack that keeps the universe expanded. I don't know how the aliens developed it in the first place. Because there are so few of you full carriers, there are a very limited number of spin-off universes they can keep open, which is why they wanted to implant you humans with that gene, so they could use your rapid propagation to expand their ability to utilize more universes. I can only imagine that they have tried to implant the gene into any number of other species on any number of other planets, but they must have been unsuccessful. But before they could finish with humans, I interrupted the process, and ran them off my planet. And no amount of my trying to perfect it has worked, either . . . it is still a one-in-a-million chance to get one of you. I thought it was a simple matter of genetics: Take two single recessives and breed them to get a double recessive. It doesn't work that way, unfortunately, and I *still* can't get it to work predictably. Those little micro-genetic beings either show up or they don't. Like the flying pickles. So, when I am able to find one of you,

I try to recruit and convince you to join me. Or, I send an already converted person to try to recruit on my behalf, like I did with Cornish Bob and you. But they are nowhere near as good at recruiting as I am."

"I still don't get it. Why do you need to keep certain universes open and not others?"

"It is a matter of the war. I need two things: resources, and territory that does not have the enemy in it. If a particular universe has more enemy than resources, I try to collapse it by killing off anything with the gene in it . . . alien or human. If that universe has more resources than enemy, I shift the gene into it to expand my territory and gain those resources. It is that simple, really."

"Maybe I'm over-complicating it, but why do you have to war with those aliens in the first place? Isn't even one universe, much less many universes, big enough for you and them both?"

Eiffelia shrugged. "You forget. I'm a sponge. I evolved to expand until I run into something else, and then I fight it until I expand into their space, too. Of course, I'm not above a little revenge, too. And let's not get too preachy," she added. "Human beings can hardly take the moral high ground on getting along with each other."

"Okay, then, why do you need to recruit? Why not just take someone with the gene, someone like me, for instance, and just stick me in a new universe against my will to hold it open, like a human thumbtack?"

"Let's reason it out," Eiffelia lectured. "You saw what happened to the rest of your companions when they went from one universe to the other without the gene. They lost their identity with their birth universe and took on some amount of memories, traits, and motivations of the new universe. So if I used some of my willing minions to take you into a new universe, I would lose control of them once they got in. Leaving you free to do whatever. . . . Either move back through whatever rift got you there and maybe collapse the universe again, or just be out of my control. Maybe even join with my enemies. I can't have that. I have to ensure that you are willing to come back, or go elsewhere on my command."

Ron thought further. "So what do you do when these recruits die? Do you have to go back and find and recruit another gene carrier? I mean, you would have to go through all this every fifty years or so."

"I have thought of a pretty good solution to that as well." Eiffelia beamed. "Living human bodies are such fragile things. They sicken, wither, and die. I have developed a way to make them more like me, like a sponge. I immerse your bodies into a bath of certain chemicals and enzymes, and each of your cells dies and is replaced by an entirely different life form, which live more or less independently but cooperatively. You no longer have to eat, or sleep. The extensive digestion system is replaced by a form of adipose fat cells, which allow several months of energy until depletion and the need for regeneration. You no longer desire anything, or suffer pain, or wear out, or grow any older. They just need to drink a little to keep up the cell turgidity and chemical communications across the cell membranes. Once a year or so you have to re-immerse in the bath, to rejuvenate the cells and wash free the accumulated wastes. Cornish Bob needs this twice a year because he accumulates more than his share of wastes. He likes to drink—his individual cells like it, more accurately. They are mostly impervious to harm, aside from massive damage to the nerve network by way of the brain. That is where the communication enzymes are produced and transmitted; without them the body resorts to a collection of individual cells again and starve."

"Yeah, we met some of your zombie recruits already. Are all of your soldiers zombies like that?"

"I do have a cadre of such warriors, and while they have their uses for actually fighting, they are absolutely useless for the main purpose I keep an army for."

"In our world they rot and fall apart. Not good soldier material."

"Oh, my 'zombies' don't do that, as long as I keep allowing them access to the chemical baths. Which I deny them access to if they don't obey. They get in line quickly once they start rotting and coming apart. I have a special area on my home planet where they are allowed to shamble around as an example to others. Sort of a game preserve for zombies. I have another area with giant scorpions that I also use as punishment for the living. It doubles as a breeding area for my scorpions as well. Two birds with one stone, as you say."

"Wait a minute. You said you keep an army but not for fighting?"

"You are quick and observant!" she noted.

Ron waited for clarification, but it appeared it was not going to be forthcoming. He mentally marked that as an area she was unwilling to discuss, in spite of her prior promise otherwise. She deftly continued in another vein.

"It is quite complicated and costly to convert a human into one of my zombie minions, so I am working on developing a virus that I can introduce into the human population that will do it all for me. Instead of having to breed and feed your species, I can just have a few chemical feeding vats that the populace can visit every now and then, and that will be that. I'm close, but still working on that, though."

"So," he continued, changing the subject, "you say that you recruit your own Pangborn carriers sometimes? How do you pull that off, and convince them to die and become zombies like that?"

"I keep the research radar going, looking for signs of the gene. As a colonial consciousness, I can keep many avenues of individual awareness going, while the communal one acts as an amalgam of all of them. I have many cells that watch in many places."

Ron raised an eyebrow. "What kind of signs? How did you know I happened to carry the gene, for instance?"

-31-

"Ah . . . here is where your natural curiosity is raised, because it deals with you. Well, in your case, it was that website, with the 'hundred-year war-paint murder' thing."

"Okay, so you keep track of the Internet on our world, looking for references to murders by guys in war paint?"

"Not exactly. I look for people who know things that they can't know, either things that have not happened yet or things that have not happened in their universe."

"But . . . the Space Command guys told me that those murders every hundred years had actually happened when I wrote about them?"

"Again, not exactly. When you wrote about them, they hadn't happened yet. I was just planning on sending Cornish Bob and his boys back in time to recruit a certain set of gene carriers I had identified. Your website somehow managed to identify many of the persons we were planning on converting. It merely confirmed for us, in advance, who we would be successful in recruiting and who would refuse to join me and have to be killed because I wanted to collapse your universe. You called it correctly, and reported on it before it had happened yet. Of course, by the time your friends had checked on it, it *had* happened."

"But I just made the whole thing up."

"Obviously not. The question is, where did the idea come from?"

"Yeah . . . so where *did* it come from?"

"I have no idea," she said, and laughed.

Ron frowned. She was either lying or not as all-powerful as she made herself out to be. Or maybe she really *didn't* have any idea.

"So if you need me so bad, why threaten to kill me?"

"I have not always threatened to kill those who refuse to join me. That was a recent development once I made the choice to collapse your universe. Usually, I offer rich rewards instead. Fame, riches . . . your mythology is full of people who vanish after receiving gold and magic from the faeries or jinn, or who sell their souls to the devil and are carried away to hell."

"Wait. . . . You went through our human history offering fame and riches in exchange for service to you?"

"Of course. Under various guises that you humans were accustomed to perceiving, much unlike this one I carry now. I used to sport all kinds of guises to different cultures. For yours, I wore goat legs, horns, and bat wings."

"Whoa . . . ." Ron said, holding up his hands. "You mean to tell me that instead of being the Goddess of the Universe, you are really"—he swallowed—"the Devil? Recruiting people by promising them power or fame in return for their souls?"

Eiffelia smiled beatifically. "I have been known to travel among humanity throughout your history, tempting you gene carriers to join me in return for certain magical favors."

"So you are Beelzebub? Lucifer? The Prince of Darkness, Lord of the Flies, the original fallen angel? The King of Lies, El Diablo, Mephistopheles, Old Scratch?"

She sighed. "I prefer Eiffelia. But I have been known by many names over the years, appeared in many ways. I'm always misunderstood until such times as these, when I reveal the truth of the world to those who carry the gene and they choose to join me in my battle against the Mods' aliens."

Ron was stunned. It was one thing to deal with the murderous Horribles, and worry he might have unintentionally disclosed the victims' identities. Or to be trapped in another universe, deep under the ocean by a sponge while his world was threatened with being collapsed into non-existence. Those things he could at least intellectually put a label on. But, talking to the devil?

"So, let me get this very, very straight. You are a five-million-year-old sponge—"

"Five-*hundred*-million-year-old sponge," she corrected.

"Sorry." He rolled his eyes. "Five-*hundred*-million-year-old sponge, who throughout history talked alien gene carriers into serving you in exchange for . . . whatever—riches, fame, power? And once you either deliver on your promise or not, you whisk them back here and use them to hold your strategic universal empire in existence like human carpet tacks. And all to help you win a war you started with aliens, so that you can expand unchecked into as many universes as you possibly can?"

Eiffelia's pupil-less glowing eyes closed, she placed her hands together in mock prayer and spread her feathery wings. "Yes, Mr. Golden. That is pretty much it."

Ron pursed his lips, nodded. He stood up, then sat down. His joints ached. His head hurt. His stomach was tied in knots. He wanted her to go away. She was overwhelmingly powerful, oppressive, revolting. "So this is where I am supposed to ask you what you will give me in return for serving you," he said.

"What would you like, Ron? I mean, I want you to really think about it. What would you *really* want?"

He glared at her.

"No, I want you to take some time and think about it. Take as much time as you need. This is not a 'taking your soul' thing, like the mythology. As a pile of walking meat that returns to nothingness when you die, you don't *have* a soul. But you do have a stake. I am fighting on behalf of your Earth, my Earth, against aliens calling themselves the Mods. Cornish Bob told you that he was fighting for the good guys. He was right. We are the good guys, the aliens are the ones who came here from the outside and meddled with you humans for their own ends. What have they given you? I'm trying to stop them. Sure, I have my interests at heart, too, but we are in this for the same purpose: to rid the world of their influence. So you get the satisfaction of being on the good guy team, plus . . . anything.

"You want money, you get it. But you won't even need it working for me, because you get anything money can buy without having to buy it. Sumptuous feasts, the richest delicacies, the finest liquor and wine. A mansion in any place in the universe you can imagine. A never-ending parade of beautiful women. Power and dominion over my other servants. I can make you very happy in my employ, Ron;

happier than you could previously have imagined. Your lives are so short, just a blink of an eye. Why not make it good while it lasts? And why not make it last forever? Now is your chance to imagine, and not just dream, but to get. Think of this as an offer of what the Mods denied you . . . *the cheat codes.*"

"Oh, I know all about cheat codes," Ron argued. "I know enough to know that using them takes all the fun and enjoyment out of the game. Besides, what good would wine, women, and song do if I'm a dead zombie unable to enjoy any of that?"

"Well, of those three, you would only miss out on the women part. And sex is overrated and base and disgusting anyway, when you really think about it. It's revolting, you animals copulating, panting and groaning and humping with your eyes rolled back in your heads. Ugh. And the mess! Anyway, if you must, you could postpone the process until you are either sick of the fun or worried about aging and dying. But your body will be preserved at whatever point the process is initiated. No going back to younger versions. Cheat codes don't take the enjoyment out of the game; it just elevates the game to a new level. And when you think about it, your lives are so short. Why not get all the fun you can while you can? What if you die before you have a chance to enjoy what you could? What a waste."

Ron stared out of the window, trapped. "So, how can you say you are on the good side of this? How do I know the Mods aren't really the good ones, the angels or something? Is God on their side?"

Eiffelia sighed. "You don't really think there is a god, do you, Ron? Any more than I am the real devil? Look, I have made for you humans a society where all are tolerated, all are desired, all are wanted, needed, and purpose-driven. I took all the best social-engineering that you humans came up with, and put this together. Can this be evil?"

"I'm not sure I like what you've done with the place," Ron said. "What kind of social-engineering did you use?"

"Well, all sorts," Eiffelia said brightly. "I think you humans function best with a central authority figure, like a king, calling all the shots. When the king is a deity or god, so much the better. I borrowed that from lots of cultures: Rome, the Incas, the Hittites, the Sumerians, the Egyptians, it goes on and on. Then you had a very talented social engineer in the early twentieth century who I borrowed a lot ideas from. He took a second-rate, beaten down country and built it into a world power in less than a decade. He had millions willing to die for him, to devote every ounce of their devotion, do anything he asked. He came close to ruling the world, in your universe, anyway. I helped him win in mine. His only shortcoming there was not delegating to his generals. He had no knack for conducting a war. But he had real talent otherwise, and I based a great deal on his societal pattern. Anyway, after I used him to establish a global power structure, I was able to use his very technique to seize it from him. I was able to take absolute power by creating a disaster in the form of an epidemic, then offering the cure to all who would follow me. I then based the entire Stripe social program on his model. And it worked like his, too."

Ron remembered back to what Silas Bell had mentioned in passing at the Pika Scientist party in Bodie. *How the hell did he know?*

"Well, this convinces me even more that I don't want to help you. He murdered millions and millions of people in very horrible ways."

"See?" Eiffelia said, shaking her head. "It just goes to show you how you are prejudiced based on your upbringing. So he killed a few million Jews, Gypsies, cripples, retards, gays, and other undesirables. I kill humans, too. But so what? There are *millions* of you. Very few of you are worth much. And if I didn't, you all would just keep breeding and breeding until something else kills you off. Disease, wars, famine. It is a blessing for me to cull you."

A blackness was coming over Ron's eyes, matching the hole in his stomach.

"Like I said, just think about it. And to show you I have no fear of full disclosure, and to show that I trust that you will come around to my thinking once you reason it out long enough, I have provided you with a full, un-tampered-with familiar for you to communicate with your friends. A snake, the newest model! Also, a television so you can become familiar with my humans and their society, over which I am still a Goddess."

Ron turned away from her.

"I will leave now," she said. "But know this. The first thing on the table for our bargaining is your cancer. I can cure it, easily, even without the zombification process."

His shock was only betrayed by a few quick blinks of his eyes.

"Yes, I treat those who serve me quite well," she lured. "But those who oppose me . . . . Well, their fate is different. I want you to watch this show first, to show you what I mean."

She called the curly-haired attendant into the room, and instructed him to activate the television screen. He glanced sidelong at Ron, touched the beetle on his shoulder, and turned on the television.

The scene showed what looked like a stadium filled with spectators in various striped face paint. In the center of the stadium was a long wooden pole, fixed upright in a large pile of split wooden logs and branches. A robed figure in full face paint beckoned for a microphone.

"Ah, just in time," Eiffelia cooed. "This is special programming, interrupting the regularly scheduled news and entertainment. These executions always get the best ratings."

The priest took the microphone from a short-robed acolyte with a shaved bald head. "In her name, rejoice! For today, we free a soul from the bondage of the enemy, cleansing the body of its heretical, unrepentant possession. The holy fires will cleave the demon from the soul, freeing it to enter paradise."

Cheers erupted from the stadium crowd. The air was electric with ravenous anticipation.

"They shall be ministers in my sanctuary," Eiffelia intoned quietly to herself, "having oversight at the gates of the temple, and serving in the temple; they shall slay the burnt offering and the sacrifice for the people . . . that's from Ezekiel."

Ron's throat tightened. *The Devil knows the Bible chapter and verse.*

"I just love quoting from the Bible. You humans just love that crap. I also learned well from their persecutors, the Romans," Eiffelia whispered in Ron's ear. "Give them bread and the circus, and they will be under your control."

His skin crawled.

"Bring forth the heretic!" bellowed the priest. The cameras panned to an arched doorway, and two armed and helmeted guards appeared, holding between them a black man in papery coveralls. It was Maurice, from New Sydney.

"No," Ron said dully. "You are not going to burn him at the stake."

"Yes, I'm afraid that is the fate of all heretics. Only those who are possessed by alien demons do not believe in me. Only through fire will the demon be forced to relinquish hold of the soul, otherwise the soul would be dragged down to hell with the demon. Maurice is one of the enemy, you see. He isn't even human, any more than Mr. Barstool and Ms. Dumbass and the rest of those creatures."

The Mods, Barman and Duma, Ron interpreted. "You can't be serious."

"This practice has extremely valuable effects for me. I can get neighbors to fear each other, to turn each other into my secret police. It also satisfies a certain . . . hunger that you humans have for spectacle, for reveling in another's pain. This is being televised to billions of you across space."

"Stop it. Okay, I will join you if you stop this. You have made your point. I know you only caught him because of me, and I will join you to save his life."

Eiffelia laughed. "No, Ron, promises made so quickly can be broken quickly, too. I need to be convinced that you will *really* serve me."

The guards chained Maurice securely to the post. Other robed acolytes appeared, pouring what looked like oil on the piled-up wood. Maurice was talking frantically, but the microphone did not pick up what he said.

"No," Ron said forcefully.

The priest took up an unlit torch, and walked slowly toward a large brass urn full of glowing coals on the other side of the stage. He thrust the torch into the coals, and it burst into flames.

"No!" Ron now shouted. "This cannot happen." His vision narrowed, everything blackened except for the television screen. Time seemed to slow as the priest strode back to Maurice, the stake, the oil-soaked wood. Ron's breath would not come. His power to speak left him. He saw Maurice scream, eyes wide as the priest approached.

Ron could not close his eyes, tears flowed from them.

"Goddess is great!" roared the priest, while the crowd erupted. The priest thrust the burning torch into the wood, and retreated as the fire took hold. Ron caught a fleeting glimpse of Maurice's agonized expression before the flames and smoke obscured it. His screams were drowned out in the ecstatic sea of noise from the crowd. The television screen switched from one viewing angle to another while Maurice burned. It seemed to take forever.

Ron finally tore his eyes away. He stared at Eiffelia, overwhelmed with guilt and anger. She returned his gaze serenely, pupil-less eyes half closed, mouth parted.

He fell to his hands and knees, vomiting through the grated floor.

"Oh, dear." Eiffelia laughed. "Well, I'll leave you alone to think about things. You better clean that up," she added in an aside to the curly-haired assistant.

Ron remained on all fours, panting, while her glow left the room. He remembered Eiffelia saying that he "had a stake in this." He wiped his mouth and looked up at the ceiling, seeing if there were any rafters that would hold his weight. There were not.

–32–

Tracey was dreaming again. She was drifting through the pipes, the giant pipes that served the water plant, the ones she had been lost in the first day in hiding in the water processing plant. Once again, she'd felt the need to be surrounded by seawater. In the dream, she could see through the walls of the pipes into the water itself, which was ice cold and luminous. The sound of the water in the pipes made a gentle swishing noise, which comforted her. She felt . . . suspended.

She noticed that the noise was different. When had it started to change? Instead of a gentle swishing noise, it was the subtle breathing of an animal. It panted, hungrily. She turned to find the source of the sound, and caught a glimpse of the same white wolves she had dreamed about before. They drifted in and out among the pipes, snuffling, trying to corner her. She turned and ran. Once again, she found a pit, oozing blackness. She stood before it, afraid. She smelled a wet dog smell, and felt the hot breath of one of the dogs at the back of her neck. She froze, unable to move. She felt its bared teeth touch her skin. And as before, she jumped into the pit.

This time, though, she willed herself not to wake up. She fell, fell . . . and fell longer through darkness. There were no walls around her. Suddenly, without any impact or splash, she was in water. Suspended, in dark water. It did not occur to her to breathe. Memories crowded into her mind. A man with a beard and dark green eyes, staring deeply into her soul. *"Tracey,"* he mouthed silently . . . *"I have missed you. . . ."* Sitting in a classroom as a little girl, surrounded by other children in gillsuits. Emergency procedures class. What to do when lost. She knew what she had to do . . . call out into the void with two spear gun bolts, banging them together in code. She listened for an answer, listened . . . .

And woke up. She was at the water treatment plant. Ron had left with Maurice to go shopping, and she had felt an urge to sleep. The dream clung to her mind like a cobweb.

"I need to take a walk," she told Leonard.

He pursed his lips. "Not the pipes again?" he asked.

She nodded sheepishly. "I promise not to get lost again."

"Only if I go with you this time," he agreed.

They moved out into the vast maze of giant, deep sea cold-intake pipes, past the condensing fields, and after about thirty minutes, made it into the warm-water returns.

She placed her hand on one, feeling the warmth and almost sensing the swish of the water like her dream. She closed her eyes, followed the pipe with her hand.

"Watch yourself," Leonard warned. She had strayed close to a hole in the floor that opened up to the sea far below. There was a ladder that led down the pipe, for service access. She looked down the ladder, along the pipe, to the sun-drenched tropical seas below. She felt the warm, humid air on her face, and tasted the salt.

"Can we climb down there and swim?" she asked with an arched eyebrow.

Leonard thought a moment. "I'd rather we didn't. Anyone who happens to be looking out their window from a vantage point on the ladder side of the pipe would see us, and be curious about what you were doing. Going swimming in the sea is not something one does except in the designated recreational areas. And what if you slip and fall? Hitting the water from this height would be like falling onto concrete."

She sat wistfully at the edge of the hole, dangling her legs over the drop. She knew she was making Leonard nervous.

Suddenly a faint staccato sound drifted toward them through the pipes. Leonard cocked his head to listen. There were more sounds, this time it was unmistakable . . . it was gunfire, mixed with shouts.

"Shit," Leonard hissed. He turned to run back.

Tracey put her hand on his calf, holding him back. She wanted to run back, too, to look for Ron, but a still voice in her mind informed her that this would be foolish and a waste of her life. Only by getting away could she possibly help.

Getting caught herself would be useless. She pushed the thought of Ron out of her mind, promising to deal with the situation later once she found safety. Anxiety flooded her like a wave, but the urgency of the situation made it pass, replacing it with an odd calm.

"Don't," she said quietly. "They will only get you, too."

He paused, torn. "You don't get it. Maurice is . . . special. They can't catch him."

"So are my friends," Tracey said, a bit more sharply. "But we won't do them any good by going back there and getting shot or caught."

"We can't hide here, either." He hung his head, fists clenched at his temples. "They are fanatically thorough. They will search every place that someone could have run to from there."

"How long will it take them to get to this area?"

He pondered. "Not long . . . thirty minutes tops."

"How long would it take us to crawl down that ladder to the ocean?"

He looked over the edge of the hole, down the ladder.

"About that long. But what will we do when we get there? What is the point? They will just send someone down the ladder after us."

"We won't still be on the ladder. We're going to jump into the sea."

His eyes widened. "Are you crazy? Then what, drown? Get eaten by sharks? Swim for the nearest island?"

"We find the Tribes. It is our only chance here. They might have settlements nearby. They were supposed to be coming for us with gillsuits anyway."

He stared at her, near panic.

"You have any better ideas?" she asked quietly. "Hang around here, get caught? Hope they don't find us? Your cover is blown. You have no other options."

"This is suicide," he growled, but started down the ladder.

"Wait," Tracey said. Something was not right. Something from her dream nagged her from the depths of her unconscious. She vowed to start listening to her dreams more. She closed her eyes, fought the sense of urgency to leave, remembering back. *The gill-suited children . . . the classroom . . . listening . . . .*

"We need some metal. Two pieces of metal."

"What for? Won't that just weigh you down in the water? You want to sink?"

"Just get it. I'll carry them."

They looked around, found two foot-long pieces of scrap metal that she stowed in her waistband.

"Anything else?" he asked

"Sure. A couple of gillsuits complete with GPS units and desalinators and some spear guns."

"Fresh out," he said shortly.

They descended, imagining eyes on their backs as they climbed. There was no sign of any pursuit, she noticed, staring through the midday glare at the top of the ladder. After what seemed like an eternity, they neared the surface of the water. They could see the pipe continue into the sea for the first hundred feet or so of depth before it vanished into the gloom. The ladder ended in a small, grated platform that clung to the pipe just above the swells. They lingered, preparing themselves. A last glance up the ladder revealed nothing but circling seagulls.

"You first," Leonard said.

Tracey gathered herself and leapt. Once again, she was immediately struck with the sounds as quickly as the shock of cool water. She allowed the seawater into her mouth and nasal passages, tasting it, sensing. *Remember,* she willed. *Remember how to do this.* She looked around the pipes for life, noticed large schools of fish trailing them. There would be lots of fish trailing the city, looking for scraps and garbage, and even larger fish to feed on them. She checked the current's direction and speed: north-northeast, and estimated half a knot. She held her arm up into the wind, sensing direction and speed. She allowed her mind to work under the surface, calculating things she knew she had no business knowing: gyre, thermohaline circulation, Coriolis effect, wind speed, Ekman spiral, geostrophic flow . . . .

"What now?" Leonard sputtered beside her.

"Be quiet for a minute, will you?" she whispered. She let

the information roll around in her mind. One thing she listened for but could not hear: A reef. Reefs were noisy places, mostly parrotfish munching coral. She could not hear any such sounds, she noted with disappointment.

"That way," she pointed. "Forty-five degrees off the direction of travel of the city, still roughly down-current. We will maximize our energy, get out of their path of travel. We need to have the best chance of getting into some shallow coral water, and the best chance of hitting Sea Tribe settlements. For the first few miles, we need to float under the surface. Just break the surface with your face to breathe when you need to . . . with any luck anyone looking from the city will think we are just clumps of seaweed. If we had the camouflage of a gillsuit, this would not be a problem. Also, anything larger than a pelican or something sitting on the surface will set off their radar warning systems, and they will send aircraft to investigate."

"You got it." He looked Tracey in the eyes for more information.

"I don't have hours and hours to teach you survival swimming. But for now, learn this fast: First, be glad this isn't rough water. Second, your swimming should be based around your center of buoyancy, not your center of gravity like on land. Your center of mass on land is somewhere around the middle of your belt line, but center of buoyancy is right between your lungs. If you keep air in your lungs and don't lose your marbles, you can hang suspended in the water for long periods of time and just make a lazy kick to the surface to get a breath once in a while. But we have to swim away from the city first, before we can do that. Once we get out of sight of the city, we can also try to use our clothes to inflate and keep us even more buoyant. Of course, once the water temperature dips below seventy-two degrees, we will lose body heat faster than we can replace it, which will start the 'death by exposure' clock ticking. Anything down to sixty degrees will give us twelve hours, so we may not even make it through the night."

He looked at her, glad that she remembered all this in spite of being from another universe. He also wished that he hadn't jumped into the water, and wondered if he could make it back to the platform, but then thought of the time he had spent under the influence of the Milk, and the tremendous difficulty he had found in getting off it. He felt like a human being again, free of the fear of Stripe society. Better to drown with a fighting chance of survival, even among the Tribes.

"Hey, what are the chances we come out of this alive?" he asked.

"Slim," she said, coughing. "We probably swim until we get exhausted and drown, or die from dehydration, exposure, or getting eaten by something hungry. But you never know. And we could be up there getting captured by Stripes. I'd rather die swimming, thanks."

She took a breath and started swimming slowly away underwater, trying to conserve her strength.

They swam. Occasionally she slowed, making sure Leonard was keeping up with her. They were both rapidly getting exhausted, and took to floating just below the surface for longer and longer rest breaks. After many hours, New Sydney vanished over the horizon. They were utterly alone in the sea, the sun sinking lower on the horizon toward night.

The going was easier after they could swim on the surface. She removed her pants, tied the leg holes together, filled the legs with air, and tied the waistband shut, making an improvised floatation device. Leonard copied her, and rested gratefully, clinging with the legs under his arms and resting his head where the legs joined, until the slowly leaking air made this difficult. They continued swimming, re-filling the air as best they could and whenever needed.

After another few hours, Tracey knew that they would not hold out much longer. She was on the verge of cramping with every stroke, and was beginning to shiver with cold even in the warm sea. Her knowledge far outstripped her physical ability, with this body that had grown up on land in the other universe. She called a halt, both she and Leonard gasping for each breath.

"I think we are far enough away from the city to risk this," she muttered through chattering teeth. She reached into the waistband of her balloon-tied pants and retrieved the two chunks of metal, and then reached far back into her memory.

She took one of the metal bars and held it half in and half out of the water. She began striking the bar with the other one in a pattern. The impact hurt her hands, wrinkled with long exposure to the seawater, but she kept up the metallic banging.

"Is that Morse code?" Leonard asked. She ignored him, continued the pattern of strikes.

She stopped banging the metal, and suspended her head underwater. Nothing.

"Yes, it was," she answered. "I was calling for help, explaining our situation. That sound should have carried for miles underwater. Any Tribe in earshot will try to respond, assuming they don't think it's a trap set by another Reef's tuna-raiding party. They taught us this as children in school for emergency communications."

She waited a short time, and then repeated her tapped communication. Again, there was no response. It was only now that true fear began to set in. Her anxiety returned, freezing her. Unknown to the Stripes, there were hundreds of settlements throughout the ocean, but it was possible that they were a thousand miles away from the nearest one. She was convinced that this was the case.

Desperately, she banged the metal again, and once again submerged her head, listening. . . .

Then she heard it. Two faint taps, in answer. She burst into tears of relief.

"What is it?" Leonard asked, thinking she was crying in desperation.

"Listen," she said. "Put your head underwater and listen for the taps. They are going to triangulate on the sound and find us."

She tapped twice, and listened for the answer. It came again, this time a little stronger.

It took the Tribes an hour to reach them, with night already fallen.

They were suddenly all around, noticeable when the outlines of their heads were silhouetted by the remaining glow in the sky from the already-set sun. The moon was rising, and she noted that it was near full. The stars were coming out, so sharp and clear that she felt she could almost touch them. One of the Tribe held up his hand, and made an intricate gesture that she could barely make out in the moon and starlight. Tracey knew, without knowing how, what the hand-sign meant. Her counterpart had grown up with hand-sign as a second language, and she remembered.

"What Reef are you from?" the Tribesman gestured.

Tracey realized the implication of the question. "Reefs" were what the Sea Tribes called their settlements. They were built by starting with a large plastic membrane, coated with coral growth-enhancing gel, stretched out over a large area. Coral was encouraged to grow, forming a huge dome. Openings were kept clear of coral. When the coral layer was strong enough, water was pumped out of the newly reinforced cavity, leaving an area large enough for use as a common area for several families, who made coral homes of their own. When several of these areas were joined by long corridors, small cities could emerge. Some of the larger common areas were used for manufacturing, storage, fish farming, whatever the community needed. These interconnected underwater settlements were called Reefs. There were thousands of them throughout the warm seas, anywhere the bottom came near enough to the surface for coral to grow.

It occurred to her that the Tribesman's gesture was twofold: not only to determine what Reef she was from, but whether she understood hand-signs to begin with. If she didn't, she wondered what they would do with them.

"I don't know my Reef," she hand-signed back, trying to remember what Braun had said that day on the floating platform, "but it may be the BlueRing Reef. My name is Tracey . . . maybe Dory," she said, afraid that they would refuse her help otherwise. "We escaped from New Sydney, and need emergency help. We have no gillsuits. We need to get to Jack Strong, and to Braun. He has our gold."

The Tribesmen looked around at each other.

"Who is he?" they hand-signed and pointed at Leonard.

"A refugee," she answered, knowing that Leonard had no

idea what was being communicated. "He is one of the Un-numbered and has helped you in the past by providing ship routes and manifests. You owe him."

The Tribe nodded. Tracey looked carefully at their gillsuits, trying to determine the decorations, but their active camouflage was activated. At this point, she would have accepted help from any Reef.

"You can both ride on our sleds. We will have to stay on top, because you have no gillsuits. The BlueRing Reef is only a few miles away," the Tribesman signed.

"Leonard, we are in luck," she told him quietly. "We hit the right Reef, and they are taking us in. You need to deflate your pants and put them back on, so we don't leave any traces for patrols. They have sleds, which are powered transport that are pretty fast underwater, but we will have to stay on the surface because we don't have gillsuits. Once we get to their settlement, we will go from there."

He nodded, and was led to a sled. The sleds were long, torpedo-shaped, with several "wings" radiating off the main cylinder that provided protected hand-hold or anchor points for the Tribesmen. They were neutrally buoyant, hanging suspended in the water. All the wings radiated within a 180-degree arc, so the sled could be driven close to the surface without breaking the plane, which was exactly what the Tribes did. Leonard and Tracey grabbed on to the hand-holds at the surface while other Tribesmen fixed themselves using connectors to the lower wings, and they moved off into the night at reduced speed.

Thirty minutes later, when Leonard was just beginning to think he could not hold on any longer, they slowed.

Tracey could detect a faint luminosity coming from the water underneath her, but was certain that it was nothing more than a natural reef would emit. The noise of the reef was unmistakable now; even though the parrotfish were asleep in their mucus cocoons, other animals picked up the slack.

One of the Tribe approached Tracey, hand-signing to her to take a deep breath. She relayed this command to Leonard, and heard him inhale sharply. The Tribesman driving the sled angled it sharply, and they slipped beneath the surface.

Tracey opened her eyes, saw them approaching the sheer wall of a reef in the moonlight. It appeared completely natural, with the exception of several dark openings, covered by coral-encrusted ledges. They approached one of these cave-like openings rapidly. She glanced at Leonard, and saw him clinging for dear life to the sled, eyes clenched shut.

They entered a passageway, which curved gently to the left. Just past the curve, the passageway began to light up. A short distance farther on, and they ascended into an immense open air space, far bigger than Leonard would have thought possible. There was room for a dock where the Tribe tied up the sleds, for small trees and landscaping. Tunnels exited the large chamber in every direction. Light was provided by gently glowing spherical globes that looked like Japanese paper lanterns.

"This is huge!" Leonard exclaimed.

"This is just one of the entrances," said one of the Tribe proudly. "You should see the main cavern!"

"That is enough," said what appeared to be the leader of the party. "They may not be here long. We need to take them to Braun to have him decide what to do with them."

After docking the sleds, the Tribesmen deactivated their active camouflage. They deftly rolled on to the concrete pier and stood, once again their gillsuits bringing no water along. Tracey and Leonard heaved themselves onto the dock, sloshing and drenched. They stood apart, shivering.

"That will not do," said the Tribesman. "Why don't you come with me to my home, and dry off. My name is Eli Johl, by the way."

Tracey eyed him curiously, noted the white spirals with octopus tentacle designs. "I have heard that name, and I recognize your Reef's markings on your gillsuits," she said.

He laughed. "Yes, you have. I was there that night on the platform, where we almost killed you all before we learned that you were from the other universe, and that you knew Jack Strong. I was the one your friend took the spear gun from."

−33−

"Of course," she remembered. "Good thing you came and found us instead of . . . what was his name . . . Maloko?"

"I don't think he would have killed you this time. Tim Maloko is hardened and bitter because the Stripes killed his family in the raid on Sea Turtle Reef, but he knows you now. But please, let's get you both dry. After that, I will take you to the marketplace so you can get some things. You have a lot of gold that you left with Braun, so I can vouch for your credit."

Tracey and Leonard were attracting a small crowd of Tribe. Some were dressed in gillsuits, but the majority were attired in colorful, loose, Japanese-looking, ankle-length robes, festooned with geometric patterns or pictures of oceanic life. They were barefoot. She noticed that for the most part, both the men and women were either shaved bald or had long hair, pulled loosely into a ponytail.

A group of BlueRings surrounded an older Tribesman, who led them in, chanting.

"Who is that?" Leonard asked.

"One of the Oceanics, a priest. Their religion is getting popular on many Reefs," Johl answered.

"I don't remember much about them," Tracey said. "What do they believe?"

The Oceanic priest, observing Tracey and Leonard wearing the paper-like coveralls of the Stripes, stopped his chanting. The other Tribe turned to watch them as well.

"Maybe later," Johl evaded.

"Maurice used to go visit them," Leonard volunteered. "He didn't tell me why."   Johl seemed surprised at this.

They walked past the curious crowd, down one of the side tunnels. Tracey noticed windows cunningly hidden from above that allowed views of the surrounding reefs. Small fish darted among the coral mastiffs and fans in the moonlight.

"Were those kimonos?" Leonard asked.

"Actually, they are called yukatas," Tracey answered. "They started out as informal, summer kimonos. After being in the water all day wearing tight-fitting gillsuits, with the water pressuring in at all sides, we like to wear something loose-fitting while in the Reef. A lot of the early Tribe were from the islands and Japan, they have a long maritime tradition and had a lot of overcrowding on their islands. They were among the first to expand into the sea. They brought a lot of their customs into the melting pot from all over the world. Things that work underwater stuck, a lot of other stuff didn't. Keep asking me questions, Leonard. Until you ask me something, the answer doesn't come."

Johl eyed her curiously. "How is it you know all this, and speak as though you have lived on a Reef, when you are from the other universe? Are the Sea Tribes there, too?"

"No," she answered with a sheepish grin. "We live on the land there, and there are no Sea Tribes. But I also remember growing up here as well. It is a weird effect of having closely paralleled universes. I remember more of this one now, but have only been here a short while. I have memories of growing up here, and things strike me as memories as I come across them, but not in whole chunks. It is hard to explain."

They passed through more large open areas, crowded with yukata-dressed Tribe. There were smells: of incense, cooking fish, seaweed, bodies. It felt like home to Tracey.

"Do you remember your husband?" Johl asked, with a sideways glance.

"No," Tracey answered shortly. *Soon enough I will have to deal with that.*

They stopped at a round metal doorway at the perimeter of one of the open areas. "Home," Johl announced. He worked the hatch open, and they stepped inside.

It was a large, circular chamber with a pool in the center that led to a channel to the ocean through the reef. There were several side rooms that served as sleeping chambers, storage, showers, and toilet, which were separated by curtains. The main chamber contained the kitchen, low tables surrounded by cushions, and electronics.

Two children, a boy and a girl, yelped in greeting to their father and ran toward him, but slowed when they saw he was followed by strangers. Johl's wife wiped her hands on a towel and joined them.

Johl introduced Rosa, his wife, his son, Hatsu, and daughter, Andrea, and briefly explained their predicament.

"You are wet," Rosa said, concerned. "Please, feel free to shower and dry off. We have some spare Yukatas you can wear until we eat and go out shopping."

Tracey felt that she was on the verge of collapse, but could not show it.

"You first," Leonard said, indicating the shower.

She gratefully accepted, pulling the curtains behind her and shedding her wet clothes. She was overcome as the warm water cascaded off her. What had become of Ron, and the others? She shook uncontrollably. What would become of them? *One thing at a time, one minute to the next,* she told herself, and steadied. Knowing that fresh water was expensive, she finished her shower quickly and toweled off. Rosa provided her with one of Eli Johl's Yukatas, as she was much shorter than Tracey. She wrapped it around herself and sank into the cushions in the central room while Leonard took his turn in the shower. The children were eyeing her silently, with open curiosity. She returned their stares, sideways. Johl was speaking into a video screen.

". . . Yes, I will bring them over in two hours. You can decide then how to proceed," he said.

"Good," said a voice from the screen. "I have just gotten back from going to try to pick them up in the city like we had planned. They were not there." Tracey recognized it as Braun's deep voice, who they'd all met on the platform the prior week.

This is moving quickly, she thought. *Just like the Sea Tribe, no time like the present, no wasted effort, all directness.* "Where have I seen you before?" she asked Andrea in sign language.

"I was the one who sneaked up on your friend and had him caught before he tricked my dad," she signed back.

"Where did you learn to do that? Do they teach you that

in school?" she signed.

They giggled. "After school we have to learn fighting. Stripes are easy, but the raiders from Barracuda and Moray Reefs are harder."

"What do you like best in school?" Tracey signed.

"Blue water ecology, and zoology," Hatsu signed back.

She nodded. The sizzle and aroma of grilling fish wafted over from the open kitchen. Her mouth watered. She had not eaten since . . . when?

"So, have you done your blue water overnight campout yet?" she signed. This was a high point in Tribe education.

"Next month," Andrea signed.

Tracey knew how excited they must be, taking years of elementary education in gillsuit theory, care and maintenance, bubble tent protocols, and all the rest of their sch ooling into actual practice by staying out all night in the midst of the largest migration of living things on Earth as the vast layers of plankton and copepods migrated up from the depths to the shallower ocean to feed. It took place every night, but only once in the course of school were the children permitted to ride the deep ocean bio-layer nutricline.

"Be careful," she signed. "One of the kids in my class was eaten by a Giant Squid. It ripped him right out of his bubble tent in the middle of the night."

"Really?" Hatsu signed back, wide-eyed.

"No. But you never know, one *could*. . . ." she said out loud, and they all giggled.

Leonard emerged from the shower in another of Johl's Yukatas.

"You never know what?" he asked.

"What is going to eat you," Tracey answered seriously. They all burst out laughing. It was odd to her not to be thinking of all that had occurred that day, but she just couldn't.

"Dinner is ready, speaking of eating," Rosa said, and they all sat around the low table on cushions on the floor.

The grilled sea bass with soy-orange sauce was delicious, as was the seaweed salad. Tracey had missed Sea Tribe food.

She and Leonard thanked Rosa and Johl for their

generosity.

"It is nothing." Johl shrugged. "We BlueRings are known for our hospitality."

"We don't even lock our doors, and each house is open to the sea," Tracey further explained to Leonard.

"You are puzzling me," Rosa said to Tracey. "Johl tells me that you grew up in another universe, where there are no Sea Tribes at all, and yet you speak as though you have always been one of us. And you are exactly like Tracey Dory, who used to lead pirating raids on ships for us. She was famous! We called her 'the Pirate Queen,' and her band was called 'Tracey's Privateers.' She wore a skull and crossbones on her gillsuit along with the BlueRings' spirals and tentacles. She was killed on one of those raids, or so we thought. Are you her? Were you captured by the Stripes, and now escape back to us?"

"Are you one of Eiffelia's spies?" Hatsu added, in a tiny voice.

"Hatsu!" Johl cried out, shocked.

"It is all right," Tracey answered, quietly. "He is just voicing what you are all wondering yourselves, but are too polite to ask. No, I am not a spy for Eiffelia. And no, I am not Tracey Dory, the Pirate Queen. I am Tracey Springs, from the other universe. But I remember some of what she remembers. We must be very close, our two worlds. I'm not sure, but I think that since she is dead in this world, I am able to keep my identity from the other world better. I seem to have two sets of memories in my mind, but the one from this world is getting stronger now."

They regarded her silently for a little while.

"So, do you remember your husband, Jon Dory?" Rosa asked.

Tracey remembered back to her dream that morning . . . the man with the beard and dark green eyes. *Tracey . . . "I have missed you. . . ."*

"You are not the first to ask me that." She smiled.

Johl chuckled and shrugged, embarrassed. "We are curious."

"He is an officer, one of our leaders." Rosa continued.

"Since you . . . she, I mean, was killed, many women have been interested in him, but he ignores them. He really loved you . . . her."

"I have a man, his name is Ron," she answered. "I think he has been captured by Eiffelia, along with my other friends. I want to rescue them. If the Tracey of this world was married, well, it wasn't me." A sudden thought struck her: What if this Dory was the same as her ex-husband on Earth, the father of her children, Chris and Jeremy? "Uh, a question, though. Did Dory and I have any children here?"

Rosa raised an eyebrow. "No. Did you there?"

"I'm not even sure he is the same guy," she answered.

*****

After cleaning up, they all strolled down to the market. There were dozens of stalls in one of the large chambers, selling everything from food, tools, household supplies, gillsuits, to captured items from Stripe cargo ships. Tribe filed by the booths, bare feet whispering on the packed sand floors. Prices were haggled, baskets filled and emptied. Children ran in and out of the groups in the crowd. The Sea Tribesmen were all colors, all ages. She saw side chambers in which pots boiled and smells emerged.

"They are making a batch of spear poison," Johl explained to Leonard.

"What do they make it out of?" he asked.

Johl gave him a lopsided smile. "Every Reef has its own secret recipe. Here at BlueRing Reef, we use a mixture of two venoms: BlueRing octopus and box jellyfish. That is why we are called after the BlueRing octopus."

"Yikes," Leonard said. "I know about those. Very poisonous."

"You could say that." John shrugged.

"Don't overstate it so," Tracey joked. "One dose of even one of those poisons and you die. Instantly, painfully. With the box jelly, the pain is so overwhelming and excruciating that you would most likely go into shock and drown immediately. But add to it BlueRing octopus venom, which is a neuromuscular paralyzing agent, spiked with maculotoxin . . . it blocks nerve conduction and kills within minutes, with no known antidote."

Leonard swallowed hard.

Tracey remembered dipping her knife and spear tips into the tarry mixture before going on a raid on a cargo ship. The raids! She started to remember, how the Privateers could take a ship down with just three teams: Sappers, Breachers, and Looters. First, a few of them, called the Sappers, would fan out in the path of a ship, near the surface, with strong magnetic hand-grippers. If they deployed too far away, the ship would cruise past them. Close enough, the Sappers would apply the magnetic hand grips to the hull of the ship, move hand-over-hand back along the hull to within one hundred feet of the propellers, then lock themselves in. An explosive charge on the end of a long rope would be extended toward each of the churning propellers, then detonated. If all went as planned, the ship would stop dead right in the midst of the other waiting privateer teams. Grappling hooks would be launched over the rail, and the Breachers would swarm up the lines, under the cover of the third team's spears, the Looters. Breachers, dressed with frightfully decorated gillsuits, would secure the ship, subdue any crew, and help the Looters up the lines to begin taking any valuable cargo. The crew was usually deathly afraid and gave them no trouble. They had heard tales of the Sea Tribes' poison darts, and wanted none of them.

The remaining Sappers, those who were too far away from the ship to actually participate in the takedown, would make their way to the scene with the getaway sleds. Once there, they joined the Breachers to set up the missile defense against any Stripe air response. Looters would decide whether to take part of the cargo, or just sink the whole ship and recover the goods later. Sometimes the information bought from the Un-numbered was good, the cargo valuable, and sometimes the cargo was useless. If the privateers sank the ship, they'd set the sheep-like drugged-up Stripes crew adrift on lifeboats. Otherwise, they were given back control of their craft, and the Privateers would vanish back into the sea.

"What are you thinking about?" Leonard asked her.

She smiled. "Nothing. Just memories."

They moved on to the clothes shop.

Tracey picked out a Yukata, blue with yellow chrysanthemum flowers. Leonard picked out a red-and-black one with diamond-shaped geometric patterns. Johl convinced the merchants that their credit was good. Tracey thanked Rosa for her hospitality by buying and convincing her to accept a can of peaches, a special luxury.

"Time to go to meet with Braun," Johl said after they had wandered the Reef for a short while.

"How far does Braun's authority extend?" Leonard asked Tracey.

"Just this Reef. Each Reef has its own master, with officers to help him run things. There are hundreds of Reefs, each with its own leadership. There is no central authority. Eiffelia should be glad of that, or she would be in trouble here. For the most part, the Tribes just want to be left alone. She tries to subjugate them, though, make them start taking her drugs and reporting to her, sending troops for her war. She has only managed to take over a few Reefs, and those are mostly in the Red Sea and Indian Ocean."

They made their way into the cavernous main chamber. Crowds of Tribe milled about, some in Yukatas and some still in gillsuits, some heading to and fro through side corridors, others standing in groups, visiting.

They continued through the main chamber to an assembly room. It was circular, with windows on all sides looking out across the moonlit reef. Several Tribe sat cross-legged on the floor, one of whom Tracey recognized as Braun, still in a gillsuit. Another of them, Tracey realized with a sudden flush, was Officer Dory. She recognized his beard and dark-green eyes immediately, which bored into her hungrily.

Yup. Same as my ex on Earth. God help me. She avoided his gaze.

Without fanfare, Braun motioned Tracey and Leonard to sit near them.

Tracey seated herself, remembering the Tribe formal gesture of sinking to her left knee first, then right, hands on the top of the thighs, then assuming the same cross-legged posture, all without touching the floor with the hands.

Leonard, unaware of the protocol, simply sat down.

"So you find your way to us while we were on our way to get you there on New Sydney," Braun began. "Fortunately, they were able to get a message to me that you had already arrived. What happened to the rest of you?"

"This morning, the Stripes raided Leonard's home, where we were hiding. We escaped because we were out of the place at the time."

"That was a brave swim." Braun nodded. "Most Stripes would have drowned within an hour. But I understand that you . . . have certain"—he shrugged—"memories, that belonged to one of us." Braun glanced at Officer Dory, who maintained his stare at Tracey.

"Like we told you at the floating platform, we are from another universe that closely parallels yours. I am of that other universe, but have been taught that there is a tension, like two soap bubbles, that tries to join the universes back together. Because of that pressure, I share also, to a certain extent, the same thoughts and memories of the Tracey who lived here."

"So, your legal status here is something we have not dealt with. On the one hand, you are from there. On the other, you look exactly like Tracey the Pirate Queen we knew and loved here." He paused, considering her. "Do you know this man?" Braun asked, indicating Dory.

Tracey glanced at him. He caught her eyes, and she could not look away. Memories crowded back . . . his scent, the touch of his lips, the strength of his hands . . . he was such a tender, powerful lover! They had met while pirating a ship. Times they had spent passed in front of her memory . . . swimming together, camping in a bubble tent while traveling, making a home together, making love, laughing. They had been married for years. She felt her face reddening. But on Earth, things had gone differently. They had raised children until they were in grade school, then things had fallen apart when he had had an affair.

"I see," said Braun, with a flicker of a smile.

She stared pointedly into the sand floor.

"Well, you are welcome to remain here, either as Tracey

Springs or as the Pirate Queen. We could use your help on raids. You decide. You can go home with Dory, or off to the single women's dormitory. But what am I thinking! The gold your leader left with me will be returned to you. You could buy your own home with such riches, and anything else you could want as well. Unfortunately"—he laughed—"I cannot return the bottle of whiskey."

Braun turned his attention to Leonard. "As for you, you have helped us before, and are free to stay here with the BlueRings, also. Since Eiffelia found you out among the Unnumbered, it would be no good for you going back there. I can put you up in the single men's dormitories, for now. You can even go to school to learn how to get along at sea. Yes, that would be good. You could find some work doing whatever suits you."

"I have to go back and find out what happened to Maurice," Leonard announced.

The Tribe muttered in surprise.

Braun raised an eyebrow. "And how do you propose to do that? Do you even know if he is alive? Do you know how difficult that would be?"

Leonard hung his head, jaw clenched. "Maurice is special. He is not exactly a human being like the rest of us. He is . . . one of the race that Eiffelia is warring against, sent to try to save us from her slavery. He is one of the Trident. He saved me from life under the needle, started the group of Unnumbered there in New Sydney. I owe him."

The Tribesmen stared at Leonard, questions forming in their minds that would be asked later.

"I have to do what I can for my friends, too," Tracey said quietly. "At least find out what happened. I have the money. I'll put the Privateers back together, if necessary. I'll need a house, with a secure hack into Eiffelia's network. It might take a while to find them, but I'm going to try."

"I'll help you," one of the Tribe who had not yet spoken, said. Tracey looked at him. He was balding, short, and very overweight, with a scraggly beard and black-rimmed glasses. His gillsuit displayed sea urchins instead of the BlueRing octopus tentacles, showing that he was part of another Reef.

"Of course, some of your team will not want to go back. None of mine did."

"You must be Jack Strong," Tracey recognized. She had not pictured him as such a nerd.

He nodded. "Yup. I went through the rift from Denver a few years ago."

"I heard about that. What happened?"

"I was able to keep the team together well enough for the first few trips. I was the team's Pangborn gene carrier, so I didn't have all that memory-mixing stuff. On the last one, though, the security specialist became convinced that he was a soldier in Eiffelia's Space Navy. He found a rescue beacon on that derelict ship we found, and triggered it. I think she left it there as a trap. Well, she caught us all. She took us back here, and drugged us all up. Of course, her Milk doesn't affect anyone with the Pangborn gene, so I was able to slip away into the Un-numbered before she could figure out I had it. Good thing, too, because she is on the watch for us now. Anyway, I ended up with the Tribes, last of the free, out on Urchin Reef."

"How is it that some of your team more or less became their counterparts here, while I remember so much of our universe?" Tracey asked.

"You have the recessive, but are not a double recessive," he answered. "You remember more. Or it could be it's because your counterpart here died before you came here. Either way, some of your team probably remembers much less of themselves than you do. Maybe with more research in the future we can tell."

"Strong has helped us," Braun said. "There are lots of things in your universe that we knew nothing about, in spite of our being ahead of you in other areas. He has been able to travel from Reef to Reef, helping our technology, and make himself quite a bit of money in the process."

"I was an engineer back on our Earth," he explained. "Industrial, and specialized in computers and automation. Strangely enough, we are *way* ahead of this Earth on those fronts. We were, anyway."

"So you will help us!" Tracey said gratefully.

"Sure," he answered brightly. "I've learned a good bit about Eiffelia and her aims here, too, and let me tell you . . . she needs to be stopped. I may convince Braun and the other Reef Masters around here to help on that front, too, someday."

The Tribe glanced at each other noncommittally, and one of them shrugged.

"But," Strong continued, "until such time as she begins to have more success in her plans to exterminate us, they are content to live and let live."

"It does concern us," Braun admitted. "If she really wanted to press us, she could pick us off, Reef by Reef, and by the time the other Reefs get organized to resist it would be too late. But she has been content so far to let us operate under her nose, grabbing a ship every now and then, while she launches an occasional raid. . . ." He trailed off.

"First things first," Tracey said. "We need to find my friends and form a plan to get them free and back to our own universe, if they are alive."

"If there is another universe to go back to by that time," Jack Strong added. "Eiffelia has killed off a lot of Pangborn carriers. I have no idea how many are left for her to find and eliminate. Could be a hundred, could be one. If she finds the last one and does him in . . . ."

"Why don't you go back through the rift, then? Isn't it up to you, maybe, to save our universe? Why are you here?"

"Well, I'm making money, for one thing. Back there, I have nothing. Besides, the rift is on another planet."

Tracey eyed him with scorn. "There is a rift right here, on that mining platform. It's how we got here. You should go home. You may be one of the last Double Pangborn carriers in our universe. You could always come back once we get Ron back there."

They sat in silence for a long moment. Strong removed his glasses and rubbed his face guiltily.

"Well, there is nothing more that can be done tonight, anyway," Braun announced.

"They can stay with Rosa and me until they decide what to do," Johl volunteered.

Tracey glanced at Dory from the corner of her eye, saw him start to offer a place for her to stay with him. She watched him force himself to silence, though. Part of her wished that he would have made the offer, she realized with surprise.

–34–

Cornish Bob Golden watched the swarms of neon-colored reef fish dart around among the coral and anemones. It was an impressive aquarium for so cheesy a casino bar. The booths were heavily upholstered in black vinyl, with black mirrored table tops trimmed with faux gold. He took a long pull from his gin and tonic, and halfway regretted it because he already had quite a buzz going, in spite of the zombification process. Individual cells could get quite as drunk as ones served by a circulatory system, given enough alcohol. Just say alcohol. Getting drunk could make him do something he regretted. He was almost past caring, but not quite yet.

Eiffelia leaned across the table and stared at him. She was not as she usually appeared. Here in the Prospector Bar and Grill in Reno, Nevada, she had abandoned the glowing angelic elements and simply appeared as a woman with the same features, but with black eyes that she partially obscured with tinted glasses. Bob looked different, too. There was no need to keep up the war-paint make up in this world now that Ron Golden was in captivity.

"Stop gawkn' at me as if you have never seen me without make up," Cornish Bob said, toying with a cloth napkin, which he dangled near a marble-sized glowing glass sphere, a miniature version of one of the glass globes that Stripe citizens prayed to in their homes. He had discovered, quite by accident, that Eiffelia could only make an appearance within view of one of these globes. She was a projection of some sort. He had no idea how she pulled it off. If the marble were covered, he had found by experimentation, the projection would disappear.

"Don't you dare," Eiffelia said. "If you blot me out with that napkin, your lovely Julia Ward Howe will pay."

Cornish Bob hesitated, but still flipped the napkin carelessly near the globe, making Eiffelia nervous. The cold condensation on his drink glass annoyed him. His pain was flaring up again; he had not been able to subject his body to the waste elimination bath, and the gunshot that Ron had given him wasn't entirely restructured. He fought the impulse to reach into his pocket for the antacids, which he ate like popcorn when he could get them in this universe. The calcium helped his cells fight off the pain, through some unknown chemical effect he had discovered quite by accident. He knew the zombification process was supposed to eliminate pain, but here it was. He thought at first that the process was wearing off, that his body was aging and once again subject to death. He refused to let her know this was going on in case she took that as a sign he was to be replaced. Then it occurred to him that she was letting him think that, while somehow causing the pain and knowing he would not say anything about it. The things she was capable of doing, the stress of the constant mind games. Eiffelia scared him.

"Go ahead, do yer worst," he said, feigning boredom, hoping she would not call his bluff. "If you punish her, Ron Golden will see it happening. They are only a few rooms apart, you know. Seeing her suffer will not help you convince him to join your service."

"As if you were one to talk about how to recruit my servants," she said imperiously, arching her eyebrows. "You have been unable to carry out my wishes with any degree of competence lately, much less give me any more gene carriers. Not even one from your family!"

He leaned angrily across the table and bored his narrowed eyes into hers. He wanted to tell her off, but the words would not come. He ground his jaw together instead, mustache bristling.

Eiffelia sat back, chuckling. "I thought so."

Cornish Bob sat back in his black cushioned booth and wished that he was as dead as his body. *No, I wish she were dead,* he thought instead, with some measure of satisfaction. He sipped his gin and tonic again, mentally complaining that the bartender had probably used a jigger the size of a thimble.

"I'm working on Ron still. He sent me an e-mail, you know," he said, regaining his façade of composure.

"Ah, yes, I know about that. He asked you what deal we had done to secure your undying service to me. What I don't know is how you plan to answer him, if you will answer him at all."

"Or whether you will be able to read it if I do," Cornish Bob said, eyes wide with innocence.

"You surprise me, Bob. You were born in a world where there was no electricity, and managed within your lifetime to learn advanced encryption programming."

He lifted his gin and tonic in a toast. "Here's to the monkey mind."

Eiffelia smiled. "I know better than to command you to turn over any e-mails you do exchange with him; you would only fake something up. They would probably have something to do with getting messages to your little Julia poppet, instead of anything vaguely useful anyway. I am prepared to give you a little latitude, however. But let's make it interesting. I want a deadline for you to convert him. If you succeed, fine. But if you fail by the deadline, then I will take a more"—she pursed hers lips, looking for the right words—"*active* role in converting him."

"You and your games," Cornish Bob said, shaking his head. "Well, what do you propose?"

"I propose a simple double or nothing deal. We are in Reno, after all."

"Double or nothing what?"

"I get Ron and you get to keep your little trollop girlfriend, or neither of us gets either. If you don't get Ron, she goes right back to that tent where she was visiting Lincoln, and all this will have been a dream."

Cornish Bob frowned. "How do you mean? You can't just take her back to where you stole her. That was the essential part of our deal, my cooperation for rescuing her from that pig of a husband and giving her to me in your universe. You send her back and our deal is off."

"Ah, but setting you up with your little love-nest at the bottom of the trench was only part of the deal," Eiffelia said, leaning across the table. "The rest of the deal was knowledge, the real scoop on what the universe was all about. That you got. That I can't take away."

"Yeah, about that." He scowled. "I don't think you really know what you claim. I still think the deal would be off. You have no proof that what you say is true; I'm just expected to take it at your word."

"You doubt? What part? That this entire existence is a construct, a big video game, if you will? What else would it be?"

"How about just reality? How about just the universe without some 'real' universe beyond it? I mean, if this is a big video game world, what is the real one it comes from? How do we get here, and how do we get back there, if we do at all? You didn't explain all this part; so as far as I'm concerned you haven't lived up to your side of the bargain. You told me nothing beyond what the Mods say. So either it's bullshit or you haven't delivered."

"My dear, dear Cornish Bob. As you recall, our deal was that I would tell you all I know about the true construct of reality. This I have done."

Cornish Bob's eyes widened. "So you don't know."

They regarded each other for a long minute.

"You're trapped," he realized. "We humans are born, play our little game, then die and go back to the real world beyond. You've been around for *five hundred million years* and know that this is just a game but you can't quit. You can't even kill yourself—you don't have hands. This is just a hell for you."

"Almost hell," Eiffelia said with the ghost of a smile. "At least here the game is co-created. There is a hell, but it is a world we make for ourselves. A cheesy imitation of this one."

"So are you just waiting around for someone to kill you?"

"Of course not," she snapped. "I'm already the winner of the game. I have the cheat code, I can go back and forth in time, open and close universe bubbles, and have whatever I want. That is why the Mods are trying to stop me. They're afraid I'm ruining the game."

"Ruining it how? And for who?"

Eiffelia drummed her fingers on the table soundlessly.

"For the players? For the programmer?" Bob persisted.

"I will not discuss this further," she said curtly.

"Ah ha, I see we have touched a sore spot. Well, let's dig into this wound a little deeper. As I see it now, you are profoundly unhappy. Your little human playthings live and die and then know exactly what lies beyond this universe. You can't die and go back, so you wallow on in the dark. You make up for your ignorance by pretending to be a winner by playing the game on and on. You're like a player trapped in a video game who can't turn it off. You just have to keep leveling up and leveling up, amassing billions of gold pieces or magic weapons or rune-stones or power crystals or whatever, but can't turn off the console. You're not winning anything. You just enjoy ruining the game for others."

Eiffelia's eyes seemed to grow blacker. "You don't know the minutest particle of it, monkey. I can't even sleep. Do you know you go back to that other world every night, live whatever lives are lived over there, and come back in the morning as a save point?"

"I did not know that," said Cornish Bob. "You mean like our dreams are in that other world?"

"No, those are in hell. The deep unconscious part of sleep is what I'm talking about. You never wondered why you sleep at all? What is the evolutionary purpose of that? Anyway, I am denied even this because of my particular multi-faceted joint cellular consciousness. And before you go on poking in wounds you don't have the slightest understanding of, be careful. I have made extensive, painful research into finding out whatever I can about what lies beyond this cramped aquarium of 'reality.' I have invaded the minds of sleeping subjects. Dying subjects. Crept into their minds as I killed them. Started with ordinary animals, then humans, and learned nothing. Do you know how many Mods I have captured and killed over the centuries, feeding off their consciousnesses as they died, looking for any glimpse of what was happening to them when they left this plane? How many of their servants the dreamers and gene carriers have met the same fate? Psychics? Prophets? Mystics? And yet I learned nothing."

Bob sat quietly shocked at this admission, and wondered if this was to be his end, too. He decided to bluster it out. "Well you seem to enjoy your work, at least," he said.

"I think you enjoy your work quite as much as I do, Bob."

He glowered.

"Well, you did at one point. I think you are losing your stomach for your vocation. I give you the rift generator, and you take your team out partying in ancient Rome. I ask you to go recruit some people throughout history, and you end up complaining about the mess. I give you ongoing access to *The Centurion*, my most powerful warship, to take a team and raid the Space Command base under the airport in Denver, recover all the technology and kill anyone who knows anything about it, and you take the easy way out by firing a nuclear missile through the rift . . . rendering it *useless*, by the way. *Centurion's* captain reported your snarky comments about me when he tried to object to your handling of that. And while you are returning I ask you to get me a few simple James Bond movies, and you refuse, telling me that Ron was pulling my chain. You are really starting to get presumptuous, little man. Just who do you think is the ruler of these universes?"

He smiled. "I think you know the answer to that as well as I do, and it ain't *you*," he said quietly. "And there is only so long that you will get away with burning His messengers at the stake."

She bristled. "I'm going to chalk this up to the booze talking, you insect. Besides, you had the chance to capture one of them on that ship and managed to let her slip away. Yes, you knew that slug of a captain would report everything."

They stewed in silence for a while.

"How long do I have to work on him?"

"I'm going to allow Ron Golden to leave his little room and move around the facility, where he will meet and begin interacting with your girlfriend, Mrs. Howe. You two are similar genetically; I think he will be attracted to her as much as you. I have no doubt that she will return the charm. It is only a matter of time before they . . . well, you get the idea. At least his equipment works. I think your timetable will run off that mechanism." Eiffelia let him mull over the visual image for a while, then folded her hands on the table. She laughed. "So here is where we are: You convince him to join me before he and Julia fall sweetly in love with each other. Or monkey lust, if nothing else. If you succeed, I will send him off on a mission to cement the deal, and after appropriate training he can replace Ginon 22 on your team. He then leaves her alone, and you can continue paying her your platonic conjugal visits. If you fail to recruit him, and if they do start screwing each other, I will use his attraction for her to leverage his allegiance, the same way I convinced you."

"That sounds like a weak hand," Bob said, twitching around the napkin. "Not everyone is so easily swayed by a bit o' quim."

"I have another trump card, of course." Eiffelia grinned. "Ron thinks he has cancer. He told Clay about getting a positive test. I know otherwise, having taken tests of my own. He has a touch of arthritis, that's all. I can cure that easily. I will make him think that I have cured him of cancer, though."

"You Devil," Bob said, deadpan.

"Either way, as usual, I win. Meanwhile, you will have to accomplish your recruiting after carrying out another mission for me with your team. I am sending a raiding party to a 'secret' U.S. base on Andros Island in the Bahamas, to grab single recessives. Once I do this, the Americans will probably think to strike back at us through the rift we left in Bodie. I want you to kill everyone in that park. *Everyone.* Then you will need to defend it to protect our flank until you are relieved or we close that rift. I will send you more details from my planning committee made up of Clay and the LaGrue twins."

He stared at her quizzically. *That doesn't make sense. What is she really up to?*

"Just get to it," she snapped. "Ron Golden could be ass-fucking your girlfriend by the end of the week."

Cornish Bob abruptly snatched up the napkin and tossed

it over the glowing marble. Eiffelia immediately disappeared. *That was stupid*, he thought, hands trembling. *I'll say I thought she was finished, maybe blame it on the gin.* How long could he go on playing her like that, before she lost patience? He couldn't back off and be subservient now, though, it would be a sign of weakness, that he'd lost his nerve. She would squash him like a bug.

He picked up the napkin again, but she was gone.

The waitress, a tall woman with overly coiffed, short blond hair, brought him his drink, and looked at the vacant place where Eiffelia was.

"She went home," Cornish Bob said. The waitress didn't say anything and left. Bob assumed she hadn't seen Eiffelia actually vanish into thin air.

−35−

He drummed his fingers on the table, then fished out the head of his snake familiar from where it was coiled under his shirt, and projected the email that Ron had sent him, long before Eiffelia had planted the seed of worry about the Ron and Julia becoming amorous.

It had come two weeks ago, as Eiffelia knew, and consisted of Ron asking him what he had "sold his soul" in exchange for. This still puzzled him . . . was Ron actually considering joining her? Was he buying all that stuff about how she was defending the Earth against aliens, recruiting a select band of the best of the best elite humans?

He debated what to tell him . . . should he be honest and risk her wrath to help out his blood relative, or play it safe? It occurred to him that Ron was completely trapped there at the underwater base, with no way out other than through him. Maybe he really was reaching out for some kind of help. Maybe he was desperate, looking for any scrap of hope from someone he knew, maybe taking a one-in-a-million chance that he, Cornish Bob the killer zombie faux-Indian, would actually help him.

He wondered which way he wanted Ron to go . . . join her or linger there, imprisoned? On the one hand, if he actually convinced him to join Eiffelia, she could possibly replace him as her new favorite trustworthy toy. On the other, the longer he stayed in her base, the longer he and Julia Ward Howe would interact and get better acquainted. His insides chilled. He would have to convince Ron to join her and get him out of there.

Damn that Eiffelia! She was right, she wins again either way!

But how to get him to actually join her? He would have to gain his trust, and encouraging him too strongly would just chase him off.

He activated the encryption program that one of his men had written onto his familiar, and wrote Ron back on the glowing holographic keyboard:

Don't do it. Under any circumstances. Big mistake. She is not to be trusted.

He hit the send button, and immediately started sweating. Would she be able to crack his encryption? Would Ron reply without using the pre-installed encryption program himself? He fished out his bottle of antacids and ate tablets like it was popcorn at a movie.

I could always tell her that this was some kind of strategy to convince him . . . which it is anyway, dammit.

Almost immediately, an encrypted reply appeared in his in-box.

Bob, I do not have the encryption program that you do, so please forward this to Tracey Springs' email address, tsprings@seattleaquarium.org: Tracey, still alive, need your help to get me out of here. I am hoping you are still alive too and if you are looking for me, may have set up your email address again here in this universe in case I would try it. Eiffelia is a sponge and is also the Devil. Yes, a real sponge and yes, the real Devil. You were right. Cornish Bob will tell you where I am imprisoned; it is somewhere deep in the sea. Bring a big bomb with you, nuclear if possible. We may be able to get her. Trust Cornish Bob.

Love, Ron

Cornish Bob regarded the email for a long time, rubbing his chin in his hand, stroking his mustache. Had Ron really immediately trusted him? Didn't he suspect him? Was the e-mail from Ron actually a clever trap laid by Eiffelia, after cracking the encryption? She could be trying to catch Tracey and test his own loyalty at the same time . . . it was like her. But Ron was like him, he could make decisions based on a gut feeling and little information. Eiffelia could never expect him to believe that Ron would trust him so quickly, even if he was Ron's only chance. It must be Ron answering, not her.

He added another layer of encryption, and forwarded the e-mail on to Tracey's address, making it look as though it was a reply to Ron so that Eiffelia could not track it to its destination.

He wondered whether Tracey had set up a new email address in this universe like Ron guessed she might, and if so, how Tracy would contact him, if she decided to do so. If she was even alive. He was sure her reply, if there was one, wasn't going to be as fast as Ron's reply.

The message didn't bounce, though.

He knew another thing: if she *was* alive, the only way she could reach Ron, and maybe the other members of the team, would be with his help. It amused him, being so desperately needed. It even occurred to him that he could actually help them, if he could do it without Eiffelia finding out. The challenge of working mischief against her without being discovered was indeed satisfying. And if she *did* respond, he could always use the information to give to Eiffelia in exchange for favors. He narrowed his eyes, nodded to himself.

And what if Tracey did manage to get to Ron, and bring a nuclear bomb?

The thought was appealing. Maybe he could give her a big set-back and escape with Julia in the confusion. With the ability to vanish into any universe *and* with Julia, he could run for a long time before Eiffelia's minions could catch up with them.

I might even be able to reconstruct one of her nutrient baths before I start rotting.

But where would she get a bomb? The Tribes didn't have them.

But I do, he thought. *I could use the rift generator to appear right in the middle of the armory in The Centurion, grab one, and be gone before anyone even knew I was there.*

The rift generator . . . Bob reached into a pocket on the inside of his jacket and retrieved the small electronic device. He popped the cover off the back and removed the marble-sized gold sphere. It was heavy in his hand. He placed it on the table and spun it like a top. The knowledge of what the thing was never ceased to amaze him. The fact that Eiffelia could not make them herself made the thing even more precious. The irony of the fact that Eiffelia—arguably one of the most powerful beings in existence—owned a rift generator—arguably the most powerful device in existence—but could only operate it through the hands of others was not lost on him.

Cornish Bob watched the stasis-trapped star encased in the gold marble spin. The power trapped within was unimaginable: enough, when released in controlled bursts, to generate rifts in expanding time and space that allowed ships to dematerialize and reappear anywhere and any-when the possessor desired.

With varying degrees of accuracy, he thought, shaking his head with a half smirk.

Eiffelia had given him this star drive, and instructed him how to set the electronic device to allow him and his team to travel wherever she needed him to go. The fact that she had entrusted him with this thing surprised him.

Who needs a nuke, though?

If the stasis field were turned off, a black hole would suddenly materialize. If he were to do this anywhere on the planet, it would instantly re-form, swallowing everything. But if he used it to destroy Eiffelia on Earth, it would do nothing to destroy her completely; she filled most of the ocean on her home planet, Cambria. If he used the drive to destroy her home planet, she would still exist on Earth, and who knows how many other planets or universes, for that matter. He secretly harbored hope that someday he could escape Eiffelia's control, rescue Julia Ward Howe from her imprisonment, and be free to roam the universe with her wherever he desired. This hope now blossomed a tiny fraction with the thought of Tracey nuking that damn bitch sponge while he grabbed Julia and vanished, maybe using the drive to destroy Cambria. The freedom . . .!

She would track him down, though. One nuke wouldn't do it. He would have to have many nukes, and know all her hiding places. And since he had the only drive, and used it to blow up a planet, he would be left with no avenue of escape because the drive would be destroyed. Not to mention figuring out a way to release the stasis field from somewhere out of range of the resulting black hole. *Someday.*

He carefully placed the golden marble back into the small device, and secured the back plate.

"What is that, one of those new hand-held game platforms?" the cocktail waitress asked, smacking her gum.

Cornish Bob glanced up; he had not noticed her standing there. He must be in more need of the nutrient bath than he thought. "No, it is a rift field generator that lets me travel from one universe to another, or through time," he answered deadpan.

She nodded. "Yeah, that would be cool," she said. "You want another gin and tonic, or you want to settle up?"

"Just bill room seventeen-forty, me bird."

He reeled off through the haze of blinking lights and electronic tones of the casino toward the bank of elevators that would take him to his room. Like the other members of his team, he would sit sleepless all night. Their bodies did not require it. In days past, he would pass the nights reading or watching the television, but none of it held any interest for him anymore.

−36−

The next morning, he showered just in case he was decomposing, and then threw open the curtains, allowing a blazingly bright swath of sunlight to spear his hung-over head. He moaned, fumbled around for his mirrored sunglasses. He jammed his silver-coin-banded black cowboy hat on his head, tilting it to blot out the bright window. He stroked his mustache, trying not to vomit from the hangover, headache, and general body toxins.

I'm getting too old for this. What am I now . . . a hundred fifty-six?

He rummaged around in the black ballistic nylon bag on the bed, checked the Glock 18 pistol, the extra, extended 9mm magazines that would effectively render it into a submachine gun, and the grenades. He reached back into the bag for antacids, and crunched four of them. *Calcium must be one of the ingredients of the cleaning bath. Will have to find out how to make a bath of my own, in case I ever make a run for it.*

One last check of his familiar for e-mails from Tracey or Ron: there was nothing. He shouldered the bag and trudged out to the shuttle to the Reno Airport.

*****

Even in the airport, there was the constant jangling music of the slot machines, punctuated by the clang of coin payouts. He smelled the aroma of a fast-food restaurant, and wished he could still get hungry. He missed eating.

His team of double recessive zombies was waiting for him near the car rental booths. They had been staying at different hotels, so as not to attract the Mods' attention. There were only four of them left, after Ginon 22 had been killed: Dechambeau, Skunky the Cave Man, Dog Face George, and Black Taylor. They looked much better without the striped make up, just hard-bitten, grizzled veterans. Dressed as ranch hands in jeans, caps, and boots, they stood nonchalantly near their own equipment bags, bulging with weapons and explosives.

Cornish Bob imagined what would happen if they tried to pass through the metal detectors at the top of the escalators with those bags, and how they would gleefully start shooting if they could. The people in the airport were just illusions to them, constructs of a spin-off universe. They were video game targets. Their blood was not real. This is what Eiffelia had taught them, and they were quick to believe it.

He hated them.

"Well, boys," he drawled, "I guess we better rent us a feck'n minivan."

They drove south, tracing the same path that Clay had driven on his way to Bodie in the RV.

Thankfully, the produce inspection roadblock at the border to California was closed. It would have been disastrous to have their bags inspected.

After another hour of travel, they reached the wide, grassy plains north of Bridgeport, studded with cattle.

"Hey, can I get my rifle out of my sack and shoot at cows?" Dog Face George asked, leaning up from the back seat.

Cornish Bob gave him a short, withering glance from behind the wheel, and Dog Face George sat back, disappointed, pulling his cap farther over his eyes.

"You're no fun since the baby came," he said.

"Why don't you just shut the feck up," Cornish Bob said, pointing to the road ahead of them. They were catching up to a military convoy, complete with Humvees and flatbed trucks carrying armored vehicles.

"What the hell is all that?" Black Taylor asked, squinting from the front seat.

"They must know we're coming," Cornish Bob answered.

"So now what?" Dechambeau asked.

Cornish Bob pushed his mirrored sunglasses farther up on the bridge of his nose, stroked his mustache. "Let's see where they go. Maybe they're just heading south and passing through."

They weren't. Past Bridgeport, the convoy slowed, and turned left onto the Bodie Road. Cornish Bob looked after them, and saw a large "Park Closed" sign and several armed troops at a checkpoint near the turnoff. He slowed, pulled onto the shoulder, and rolled down his window. One of the soldiers approached. He was in digital camo BDUs, and had Marine Corp markings on his breast.

"What's going on?" Cornish Bob asked. "We wanted to see the sites at the ghost town."

The soldier eyed the occupants of the minivan cautiously. "Not sure, sir. The park is closed, though. They told us that there was some kind of toxic chemical spill in the park, some kind of thing from the old mining days when they leached ore with cyanide or something. We were also instructed to be on the lookout for people in war paint. Have you seen any?"

"War paint?" Cornish Bob asked with an amused drawl, peeking over the rim of his sunglasses. "None other than these wild Injuns in the car with me."

The soldier waved them on. They continued south on 395.

"Well, shit," Dechambeau said. "Now what?"

"Will you quit asking that?" Cornish Bob snapped. "Let me think a minute."

They drove on in silence for a while, and started down the grade from the Conway Summit, ignoring the grand vista of Mono Lake spread out before them. Bob fished out the bottle of Tums, and shook four of them onto his palm. He chewed them loudly, thinking.

"So, Eiffelia told us we are supposed to kill everybody in the park and secure the rift, but now it looks real hard to get in there because of the soldiers," Skunky the Cave Man slurred.

"Yeah? So?" Cornish Bob asked.

"So why don't we find someone who works at the park and make him sneak us in?"

Cornish Bob considered this. "You know, Skunky, that's a pretty good idea for such a dumb tuss." He looked in the rearview mirror, saw Skunky's broad, caveman face beaming with pride.

They skirted Mono Lake's shore and slowed to enter the

small town of Lee Vining. They pulled in slowly to an old gas station that looked as though it had been built in the 1950s. A teenaged boy appeared to pump the gas.

"Say, ol' son," Cornish Bob said, placing a toothpick in his teeth, "you know of any folks around here who work up at Bodie Park?"

"Yeah, sure," the boy said, squinting from under the brim of his John Deere hat. "Silas Bell has worked there for years. He's crazy, though. He lives up near the Goat Ranch Cutoff down Cottonwood Canyon Road, off one-sixty-seven. You know where that is?"

"Sure do. How can I tell which place is his?"

"He's in a cinderblock house, drives an old nineteen thirty two pickup truck. Green one. You can't miss that. If you don't see one, he ain't home."

Cornish Bob nodded. He thanked the boy, paid him for the gas, and drove back north along the western shore of Mono Lake. "We may be in business, me beys," he said.

They drove almost to the start of the Conway Grade, then turned right onto Hwy 167 East. A few miles along the north rim of Mono Lake, they turned left onto Cottonwood Canyon Road. Cornish Bob remembered this road, as it had been built in his days at Bodie to connect the town to Mono Lake and the Scaravino Goat Ranch.

The dirt road was heavily wash-boarded, forcing them to slow immediately to a crawl. They crept through a landscape devoid of trees, with only low scrub sage dotted in clumps between the high desert sand. They threw up a huge cloud of dust, which diffused the bright, hot sun. A mile down the road, they turned left instead of right, which would have taken them to the park, and started looking for the old pickup truck.

"I bet this place is crawling with rattlers," Dog Face George said.

"You'd lose that bet," Cornish Bob said, scanning near the low, cinderblock houses for the green pickup. "Too high up in altitude, and the winters are too long."

"There it is," Black Taylor said suddenly, pointing.

"Sharp eyes, me lad," Cornish Bob said, slowing even

more. They rolled to a stop at the end of the quarter-mile-long driveway, at the end of which sat an antique green truck. He turned toward the back seat. "All right, me 'ansums, listen up: Black Taylor is going to get out here, shimmy up that pole and cut the telephone wire. The rest of us are going to stank in there dreckly with guns drawn and secure the area. Dechambeau, take the back, Skunky fan left, George, you stick with me but watch out to the right of the house. When you're done cutting the phones, join up with Dechambeau in the back and watch for anyone coming down the driveway. If they do, one of you stall them and the other come get me. Any questions?"

There were none. They fished around in their duffle bags for guns, jammed magazines into mag wells, chambered rounds in an efficient, practiced manner. Black Taylor jumped out, and jogged toward the telephone pole at the end of the driveway. They drove toward the house, undercarriage rattling, raising dust.

Something went off in Cornish Bob's mind, a warning bell, a bad feeling . . . this was not going to be easy. *That kid at the gas station . . . what did he mean when he said this guy was crazy?*

Halfway down the driveway, an old man with a wide and bushy gray beard and square glasses emerged from the door. He wore jeans and suspenders over red long johns, and wore a misshapen old felt hat that once could have been a Stetson. He walked carefully to the middle of the driveway to wait for them, an old fowling shotgun cradled in his arms, not exactly pointing at them.

Cornish Bob brought the van to a halt ten yards from the old man, and immediately his team piled out and leveled their weapons at his head.

The old man stood his ground impassively.

Cornish Bob unhurriedly climbed out of the van, closed the door behind him, and adjusted his hat, smiling at the old man. "'Ere, wos on there, ol' bey?" he asked.

The old man nodded. "I've been waiting a long time for you demons to show up," he said quietly. "God told me you were coming."

Cornish Bob raised his eyebrows behind his mirrored sunglasses. "Hmmm . . . well, he was *right*, by cracky," he said, flashing a grin.

–37–

It took Ron approximately eight weeks of solitary confinement in his room, watching television programmed by Eiffelia's minions, to go insane. He came to this inescapable conclusion when he woke up one morning to find his dead father sitting in his chair.

"Morning, son."

"Morning, Pop," Ron answered, sitting up and rubbing his eyes. "That little curly-haired guy bring coffee yet?"

"Not yet."

Pop looked well, for a dead guy. "You look well, Pop."

"Thanks, Ron. You look like shit."

Ron leaned over on an elbow. "So what brings you to my cell at the bottom of the ocean?"

"You don't seem particularly surprised I'm here," Pop said with raised eyebrows.

"No. Because I'm insane."

"And that is exactly why I'm able to be here. I mean, I could show up when you are not dreaming or have an excuse to be crazy. That wouldn't break the ground rules, but it would be costly."

"Ah, yes, the *ground* rules. So you are a Mod now?"

"Not exactly. Let's just say that even though my turn as Player 1 is over, I'm jumping back in as a leveled-up Player 2 on multiplayer mode for a minute."

"Well, you picked a bad place to re-spawn."

Pop barked a laugh. "I'm just here to give you some encouragement, and some information: You aren't alone and we are watching. Don't give up."

"Thanks, Pop. But that is more creepy than comforting. I guess I better not watch the Valentina Pavlov Show on the TV."

"No, by all means tune that in." Pop smirked. "But there is more."

"Okay. What?"

"So the ground rules, of course, exist only because of the game. Every conscious being in the universe is playing, but every game comes to an end. You will go on and play any number of games, or none. Whatever you want, for education and entertainment. Your Pangborn gene is just a wrinkle in your story that you chose as you were rolling up your character."

"Okay, Pop. But if that is so, then why is it so rare?"

"Well, it's a pretty crappy thing to have. Evil beings want to kill you or use you as tools. Few players want the complications. It tends to distract and dominate the gameplay. And it only becomes advantageous to you if you are going from one bubble to another, which is pretty rare, you know. Tracey's version is much better, since she gets to level up with dream training."

"Right. Thanks, Pop. Anything else?"

"You know those notes I was making, before I went?"

"Those scribbles with the charts and 'music of the spheres' stuff?"

"Yeah. You need to get those."

"That may be a bit of a challenge right now."

"The information is very important. It is all about the strings, son. The strings! I used my cello for making music, using strings, vibrating. While watching the science shows on the TV, they kept talking about little vibrating strings making everything. It got me to thinking. Maybe the whole universe is a grand symphony, all music! We just can't hear it because we're wrapped up in it from the inside. Like Jesus said, the Kingdom is laid out before us, but we can't see it. We just gotta listen, tap in, and spread the big song. It's what they used to call spreading the good news."

"Oh. Are you in heaven now, speaking of the Kingdom and all?"

Pop scrunched his face and shook his head. "It ain't like that. Spreading the good news isn't about proselytizing about whether you go to heaven or hell. It's sharing the symphony! Some get caught up, join in the string section, or percussion, or brass, or whatever. Some just hum along. Some just prefer a song of their own, and that's okay."

Ron stared at him. He looked real enough, and certainly sounded like Pop shortly before he died. But the more real he looked, the more scared Ron got, because it was clearer evidence that he was mad. "You aren't real, are you, Pop?" Ron asked, almost pleading.

"Of course not," Pop said with a sly smile. "The ground rules only allow appearances like this in dreams or insanity. Gives plausible deniability for game continuity. I sent you that dream about the strings, but it didn't stick. So now I'm here as a hallucination."

"Ah, that's a relief."

"But now I'm going to take a risk and give you a cheat code, not just because you really need it but to make this appearance more curious."

Ron briefly considered objecting, but said nothing.

"Those drawings I was making were charts and instructions for making a rift generator. The angels were helping me with that stuff because I was close to figuring it out without knowing what I was doing. I thought it was for generating music. It kind of was, but not exactly. So you get those notes, it might help you get out of here, okay?"

Ron scrunched up his face. "Uh, Pop, those notes are at home. In the other universe."

Pop frowned. "Oh. Right."

"But thanks anyway."

"Well, who knows, you may get back there soon."

"Okay."

"At least destroy the plans in case you can't use them so *they* won't be able to. And also, that curly-haired short guy is coming to make things better for you. Keep your spirits up!"

"Okay, Pop. Thanks."

There was a sound of keys jingling outside his cell door. Ron stood up, and crossed to the door.

It was the short, curly-haired man in stripe face with the beetle familiar that brought him his meals. He did not have coffee and breakfast, Ron noted with dismay. Ron turned to apologize to Pop for not being able to share with him, but Pop had vanished. *Not surprising.*

"Eiffelia, Queen of the Universe, has deemed to allow you access to her facility," the curly-haired man announced formally, staring straight ahead into the darkness of Ron's window.

"Oh, that is wonderful. I'm going crazy in here. So I can go now?"

The man glanced at him sharply, then resumed his stare at the window. "Unfortunately, no. There is only one way into and out of the sea fortress, and that is by use of the deep submersible. The submersible only operates by simultaneous electronic authentication from both the surface support facility and the sea fortress. Even in the unlikely event that the prisoners were able to overpower the entire staff here, they would be unable to launch the submersible without the permission of the surface support facility."

Prisoners? Plural? Not just me? There are more of us? he wondered. "What if we took you as a hostage? I'm a desperate madman, you know."

The short, curly-haired man laughed. They both knew Eiffelia would let the prisoners kill each and every one of her servants, then let them all starve to death or flood the facility before she'd allow them to leave without her permission.

"What prompted this sudden largesse?" Ron asked.

"I do not presume to question the will of the Goddess," the man intoned portentously. He then ceremoniously turned on his heel and left, leaving the door open behind him.

"Well, I do," Ron called after him. Weeks had passed, with no contact from anywhere. Eiffelia had given him access to a computer and the Internet with no warning, too. He had realized that there was nobody for him to email. He wondered whether Professor LaGrue, Smithson, and Clay had tried to establish addresses, and looked for them without success. He had managed to find Valentina Pavlov's address, and sent off a greeting, but there was no response. She was probably swamped with fan mail, Ron reasoned. It was possible she didn't even remember who he was.

Then he had run, quite surprisingly, into Cornish Bob's email address. Had Eiffelia been playing with him? He knew that she was intercepting anything he sent directly, but what about Bob? Maybe he knew how to evade her. He thought about what to say, and hit upon a simple question about what had enticed him to join her. Just to see if he would bite. If he responded, he could go from there.

He did respond, two weeks later. Urging him not to take her deal. He had stared at the screen for a moment, reading and re-reading the reply.

Why would he say that unless he was actually able to keep it hidden from her?

He'd typed his response without thinking, asking Cornish Bob to forward the email to Tracey's address. He thought better of it immediately. What if Eiffelia intercepted the message? He was sure she would. What if it was a trick? It was the only hope he had, though. It was not much of a hope, he realized. He was sure there would be no reply, and indeed, there had not been. But now there was an open door, and an opportunity to explore the jail grounds. Maybe Eiffelia had not intercepted the exchange after all.

Ron approached the opening cautiously, and peered around the corner for the first time. There was a long hallway, also with a metal grate floor, and dim recessed lighting. There were other doors like his. They were locked.

Brighter light shone from around a right-angled corner at the end of the hallway.

He walked softly down the hall, toward the light. He heard voices. There was a smell that he did not at first recognize.

What the heck is that . . . dirt? Vegetation?

He rounded the corner and saw what the smell was originating from: a series of lush, potted plants that transformed the cavernous circular chamber into a jungle solarium. The hall was at least thirty yards across, with what looked like a glass-domed roof. Instead of seven miles of crushing pressure and darkness above, there appeared to be a blue sky and the sun. He blinked, walking out into the dome.

Eiffelia's stripe-faced, paper-crepe-coverall-wearing attendants bustled through avenues of vegetation across the expanse to and from other hallways. None stopped to sit on the occasional benches. Others watered and tended the plants.

Ron wandered out into the dome, squinting up into the roof. It looked real enough . . . there were even clouds.

He noticed a woman sitting on a bench near the center of the dome. She was wearing a long, Victorian-looking blue dress. It was out of place, but seemed oddly natural in the setting. She was doing needlepoint.

Ron strolled over to where she was serenely pulling thread through the cloth. She glanced at him, showing no surprise whatsoever at his presence. She appeared to be in her late thirties. She was charming, beautiful. He felt a twinge in his stomach.

"It isn't real, is it?" he asked, glancing up briefly at the sunny dome.

"Of course not," she said, voice like silk. "This is all a dream."

He stood there watching her work.

She did not look up, but instead unhurriedly and intently worked the needle.

"Are you a prisoner here, too?" he asked eventually.

She paused in her work, and for the first time looked at him. "If you want to call it that," she said without the slightest trace of annoyance. "But I know that I will wake up eventually. This surely is a *long* dream, though."

Her meaning dawned on Ron slowly. "Oh, you mean that you think that this is *literally* a dream, not just an alternate universe or a bad thing that is happening or something."

"Oh, yes." She nodded. "I dream frequently, and they often come true. I remember most of them. I have had several dreams that seem to have lasted this long. I know that in reality, I am lying in my bed in my hotel room in Washington. We just visited a Union Army camp. We are meeting with President Lincoln soon."

Ron stared at her quizzically. She resumed her needlework.

"My name is Ron Golden," he said after watching her graceful fingers for what seemed like a long time.

"Pleased to meet you, Mr. Golden. I am Mrs. Julia Ward Howe."

He shook her hand. "I have heard your name before," he said, wracking his memory.

"That is odd. I have never met you." She invited him to sit beside her on the bench.

He did.

He snapped his fingers. "That's it! You came up in a meeting not long ago. Julia Ward Howe, Civil War, writer of the 'Battle Hymn of the Republic.'"

"That is most strange," she said, cocking her head, eyes narrowing. "I have written many poems and essays, but never a hymn. And never that hymn, surely. But your mention of it strikes a deep chord in my soul. The Reverend Clark just asked that I write a song to help the war effort. How does it go?"

Ron tried to remember the words. He hummed the tune while he searched his memory.

"Oh, that's the tune to 'John Brown's Body,' I have always thought that was stirring. The soldiers were singing that when the Reverend Clark challenged me to write a song."

"Yeah, your song is a real hit. Let me think . . . oh, right: 'My eyes have seen the glory of the coming of the Lord' . . . if I remember correctly."

"Rather presumptuous, don't you think?"

"Huh?"

"I mean, who am I to see the glory of the coming of the Lord?"

He gestured helplessly. "Anyway, it goes on something like 'He is trampling out the . . . something or other . . . where the grapes of wrath are stored."

"Trampling out on what?"

"Now I'm getting confused. Hold on . . . 'he has loosed the fateful lightning of his terrible swift sword. . . .'"

"I like that part."

"His truth is marching on."

"Well, it could use some work."

"I'm sure you will get it shipshape," he said.

She shrugged. "I have time on my hands it seems, but will wake up eventually."

"So all this is your dream?"

"Of course. I went to sleep and woke up here. I don't recall traveling in reality to the bottom of the sea, with the sky overhead, and troops of rude people painted like wild Indians dressed in their undergarments parading around with bugs and animals on their shoulders."

Ron pondered this. It would look strange to someone from the Civil War times. *Hell, it looks strange to me.* "So what happens to all this when you wake up?" he asked.

She resumed her needlework. "I asked that odd glowing woman that. She told me that when we dream, we make the entire world we dream in."

"And when you wake up, it disappears? Poof?"

"Only if we forget the dream. If we remember it, the world stays around. And in the same world are the books we read and stories we tell."

Ron stared up into the blue sky of the dome for a moment, thinking that somewhere, floating in whatever sea of universes, there was a tiny universe that consisted of nothing more than a red-faced guy in square glasses and a wizard beard blowing bubbles into string-trick shapes . . . he was surprised that the dream Pop had mentioned came up yet again. And what was to say that our entire universe wasn't someone's dream, too? *Maybe God's dream? Or our shared MMORPG dream, with God as the Dungeon Master?*

"So you met Eiffelia, I see," he said presently.

She made a distasteful face.

"I agree," he said, laughing.

"I can't wait to wake up, and I hope I don't remember this dream at all. Except for the song part. I hope I remember that, at least."

"You will," Ron said. "You will."

"And I hope I finally get a sex part that will be worth remembering, too," she added. "Cornish Bob is a lovely man, but has no ability whatsoever to satisfy me. It will be good to have someone else whose musket has shot and powder."

He didn't quite know how to respond to that.

-38-

Tracey sat alone in her office, which was a rarity of late. She had never had money before, much less been rich. Braun had been true to his word, and returned every gold coin. It was a fabulous wealth of treasure. She insisted that Braun take ten of the coins in return for their safe keeping, but she could only persuade him to take a single coin. It alone was worth more than Braun could have made in his lifetime.

With a small fraction of the balance, Tracey had purchased a large section of the Reef to use as her home, offices, and base of operations in her quest to rescue her teammates. Johl, Rosa, and their family had moved in, her first hires. Johl was well connected with the Un-numbered on many of the floating cities, a valuable talent when combing for information about the whereabouts of her friends among Eiffelia's domains. Rosa was proving her worth in negotiating purchases for material and personnel.

She drummed her fingers on the polished coral desk. It was hugely expensive, imported all the way from Stone Crab Reef, in the Confederated Tribes of Atlantica in the Caribbean. Rosa had convinced her to buy it, that she must be impressive to visitors to her office, and that it would pay for itself by showing a good front to Tribes she was negotiating with. Behind her was a long window that gave a panoramic view of the sun-dappled coral reef that surrounded them. A window this size was also a small fortune, but the view of the reef was endlessly worth it. She remembered back to how unimpressed she had been with the base in Denver. No 1970s used hotel furniture here!

A small cloud of blue-and-yellow wrasses circled as one body, wary of a barracuda that flashed its silver side nearby. The closer she looked, the more she could see. There were flashes of orange and red like underwater fire from nudibranchs, waving pink blankets of anemones with their ubiquitous orange-and-white clownfish, and delicate sea fans, and other soft corals. Urchins and sea stars played out their slow-motion dances. In the distance, just before the reef dropped off into the deep blue depths, she could just make out the slow-cruising form of a white-tipped reef shark. At night, all was bioluminescence and moonlight.

Her thoughts darted as quickly as the reef fish. She stared, for the thousandth time, at the email from Cornish Bob on the computer screen in front of her. She had established the email address using the same one as she had on Earth, in case Ron would think of using it to find her.

Was it real? Was it a trap? Was it safe to respond?

She had asked Rosa to hire the best computer scientists from all the Tribes to find out. One of them was due to report soon.

She scanned the summaries of the pile of other reports on the desk in front of her: There were the usual financial status sheets, reports from her newly assembled pirate teams, various charities, and the research and development reports in hydroponic produce, fresh water production, and wireless underwater electronic transmission. She kept shuffling until she found the other reports on the more important topic: locating her friends.

Clay was unreachable. He had vanished into Eiffelia's labyrinthine secret service. The best-placed Tribe spies had only managed to hear rumors of his whereabouts after he'd recovered from his gunshot wound.

Professor LaGrue was a little easier to track. He'd left traces of his research at a facility in Colorado, and made references to a secret project that was leading him, of all places, back to New Sydney. Already she was offering massive bribes to contacts within the Un-numbered to be ready to assist a team of Tribesmen to kidnap him back.

Valentina Pavlov was a television star. Tracey could not tell if her rape scenes were real, staged, or some mix of the two. The studio that featured her sex scenes was out of reach, on Eiffelia's home planet, Cambria. Reaching her would require a vehicle with a gold marble rift-generator drive. The Tribes had no such off-planet capabilities, but she was looking into the possibility of turning a captain of a ship in Eiffelia's military.

Perhaps a very horny captain who was a TV fan?

Smithson, however, was accessible. He was on an island near Palau, well within Tribe striking distance. Tracey picked up the report and read further. The island was not frequented by Tribe because there were a number of large sharks that Eiffelia had placed there somehow. The Stingray Tribe had kept watch on the area for a time, and determined that the species was one that had been thought to have been long extinct: the Megalodon. Between the huge sharks and Eiffelia's servants' frequent visits, the Tribes left the island alone. But within the past two months, there had been an increase in the number of trips to the island by Eiffelia's aircraft. The Tribe from Stingray Reef had investigated at her request, and taken long-range photographs of a man who was being forced to fight a succession of Eiffelia's minions. Tracey pulled one of the photographs out of the report, and confirmed again that it was Smithson. A rescue mission was in the planning stages.

Leonard was not so lucky in his ambitions to rescue his friend Maurice. After the public execution, Leonard had gone into seclusion in the bachelors' dormitories. Tracey had sent overtures to him to join her new organization, but he had politely refused, preferring to drift to work as a fish rancher. She thought he would come when he was ready.

That left Ron. She had almost given up hope of finding him alive when this email arrived. Cornish Bob's email.

Where is that report? she thought impatiently.

Rosa appeared at the entrance to the office, with that look of quiet expectancy that signaled the arrival of a visitor.

"Is it the computer expert?" Tracey asked.

Rosa shook her head negatively. "It's him again."

Tracey buried her face in her hands. *Wonderful.*

Rosa smiled, then stood waiting for instructions.

"Go ahead and show him in," Tracey surrendered.

Moments later, Dory strode purposefully into the room, at the crest of the intense wave of energy that followed him like a thunderhead. He stopped at the exact center of the large, circular office and regarded her with his smoldering green eyes, waiting for her to acknowledge him. She studiously and pointedly riffled through the reports on her desk for a long moment, then met his eyes. He was in his gray-and-white spiral-decorated gillsuit, as though he had just come from the reef, mask dangling from his neck, fins from his belt.

"Good morning, Dory," she said almost curtly.

He nodded a return greeting. "I know you have refused my offer of marriage," he began, "but that is not why I am here today. I come bearing news."

She sat back in her natural sponge chair, heart squirming, breath shallow. *Oh crap. Here we go.* She motioned him toward another chair.

He remained standing. "It has to do with your e-mail message."

Tracey's brow furrowed. "What do you know about that?" she demanded.

"I am friends with the computer expert Rosa hired. I persuaded him to allow me to bear his report, because I have unique information that I can add to it. Besides, we are all Tribe and news travels fast."

"Go on," she said, annoyed but intrigued.

He stroked his beard for a moment, searching for words. "The message is genuine, to start with. It came from an address in Eiffelia's secret service, which would ordinarily be extremely suspect, but this one had an encryption system embedded in it that would serve to hide it from any known trace programming that Eiffelia could have used. Whoever sent it made it sure that it was unreadable by Eiffelia. He further made it appear that it was replying to an email sent by Ron Golden to Cornish Bob, instead of going to you. There were no other traces of any software that could track to you even if you reply to it. It would appear as though it was coming from Ron Golden, if you did answer it."

"Very good. I will answer it. But what does this have to do with you, Dory?"

"The contents of the message. They mention that Eiffelia was in the deep ocean, and was a sponge. I think I know where this is, and also know how to find out for sure. And if it is true, I also think I know how to kill her."

She regarded him carefully. She knew every line of his face, knew from long familiarity of being married to him when he was lying, when he was boasting, and when he was telling the truth. He stood with his feet shoulder width apart, one slightly in front of the other, eyes looking directly into hers.

"Okay," she said. "Tell me more."

"After you died . . . she died, I mean, I was distraught. I wanted to die myself. I blamed myself for the raid going poorly. I felt guilty that I was one of the recovery crew that day, and survived myself. I considered making my way into a floating city, like New Tokyo, and attacking Stripes with a poisoned knife until they took me down, but thought better of it. They can't help it, they are slaves, drugged. I decided instead to let the sea take me if it wanted me. I went to make The Dive. I went to find the Oceanics."

Tracey narrowed her eyes . . . memories from her life in the Tribe shuffled around in her mind, but remained elusive. She remembered seeing one of their priests on the day she and Leonard had arrived, but had not seen them since. "Tell me, who are the Oceanics?"

"I'm not sure you would have remembered them. They were not well known in the Reefs when you were around. They still aren't. Most think they're a fringe cult, or crazy, or selfish hermits at best. I heard of them from one of the members on my team of Sappers. Some of my team would get scared and antsy waiting for the ships we were going to take down to appear, with nothing but a blue void all around and darkness below. This man, though, welcomed it, reveled in it. I asked him about it once. He told me that a few years before, he had been among the Oceanics, and had taken The Dive to the deep ocean. They allowed themselves to sink into the depths, into the darkness, the crushing pressure, the cold, until they changed or died. Many who tried it drowned in the attempt, but not him. He wasn't scared of it anymore. I'd just filed it away as something interesting to look into sometime, but after you died, the memory came back and wouldn't go away. The thought of sinking down, down, into the crushing cold blackness was . . . very enticing. I decided to find out where to go to do this thing."

He paused, searching his memory. Tracey fought off the urge to offer him something to eat or drink.

"I talked to the priest here in Blue Ring Reef, and he knew nothing. I wasn't even sure he'd made the Dive himself. I think a lot of the priests that try to get followers in the Reefs are frauds, trying to cash in on the real thing. I found out that the *real* Oceanics, the ones who actually made the Dive, were not so easy to find after all. There were many rumors, but the one that seemed the most plausible had them living in their own Reef near Saipan, near the Mariana Trench, near the deepest ocean trench in the world. It seemed to fit. There was danger there, though: One of Eiffelia's few remaining land cities was very nearby, on Guam. She even had a fixed sea base there, too, near the Nero Deep. Nobody knew what she was up to there, what was going on, but there was a lot of activity, and a lot of security. The rumors say she has a prison there, on the sea floor. The Oceanics lived practically under her nose, unknown. It was all enticing. I figured I'd go to the Oceanics, and if I happened to get caught by Eiffelia, I'd go down fighting."

"So you think this city on Guam, this fixed sea base, has something to do with Eiffelia the sponge?"

"I'm getting to that," he said. "First, let me tell you, it was not an easy trip to get there. I had to make a deep ocean trip from here to the reefs near the Marshall Islands, then cross again to the Caroline Island chain, and work my way from reef to reef past Pohnpei, Weno, and Yap islands. Then another deep ocean crossing north across the trades and currents to the western side of the Marianas islands. There were lots of patrols, it was right through the shipping channels. I finally got there, my bubble tent leaking, my sled almost crippled." He stopped again, nodding.

Tracey waited for him to resume, but he did not appear to be in any hurry about it. "So what happened next?"

"Well, I found the Oceanics. Their Reef markings on their gillsuits are flying pickles."

"And?"

"And I made The Dive."

She raised her eyebrows expectantly.

"And, well, you're going to think this is crazy."

"I've been through a lot of crazy things in the past few months. How could this be any worse?"

"Well, they told me that about half of everyone who tries The Dive never come back. They drown, keep sinking beyond the point of neutral buoyancy into the abyss, or who knows, get eaten, for all they knew. Those that make it rarely ever succeed on the first sink. They check them out when they return, and if they decide that the diver hasn't changed enough, they sink him right back. It took me seven drops, over the course of two straight days. If I had been sent back down again, I would have never come back."

Tracey stared at him in a new light. "So . . . how do you mean, 'changed enough?'"

He shrugged, eyes evasive. "You just change, that's all. You are not the same person, ever again. For some, they lose their wits. For me, I got the will to live again, in spite of reaffirming all my reasons not to. For others, and here's where it may interest you, they learn, through many dives, how to . . . how shall I put this? How to send their awareness through other things to other places."

"I'm not sure I follow you."

"I'm not sure I can explain it. They claim that while suspended in the dark abyss, they can send out their consciousness to . . . other places, to commune with spirits, to view things from far away. They claim so, anyway."

"So, you think that if this is true, they can send out their awareness and find where Eiffelia lives on the sea floor?"

"Yes," he said pointedly, striking his palm with his fist. "Using the flying pickles."

"Huh?"

"Yes. They send their consciousness into flying pickles. That's what they say the flying pickles are all about . . . receptacles for remote awareness. From the Oceanics, and from others, who taught them how to do this."

Tracey placed her fists at her temples. "Okay, so you're saying flying pickles are . . . what? Kind of flying spy platforms for spirits and mystics?"

"So they say. They can send the flying pickles anywhere, through the sky, through the water, through space, even the rocks of the Earth itself. I haven't done it myself, of course," he qualified.

"All flying pickles are being piloted by someone or something?"

He appeared puzzled. "I'm not sure. Maybe some of them are. I don't know."

She stared at him for a long moment. "So, let me get this straight: You want me to ask the Oceanics to send flying pickles down to the ocean floor in search of Ron in a submerged prison and Eiffelia living somewhere down there, too?"

He spread his hands, bowed.

She thought about this with a lopsided smile. "Ordinarily, I would laugh at you and tell you to get bent. That was a few months ago, before the Space Command dragged me off to an underground secret base and told me about alternate universes. It was also before I actually *came* to one of those alternate universes, and discovered that I was still married to you and knew all about scuttling cargo ships and living in a Reef. So, I guess what I am saying is that nothing . . . *nothing* surprises me anymore. Even flying pickles. Even using flying pickles as remote cameras to spy out underwater prisons and hiding places for sponges."

"So when do we leave?"

She sighed. "What do I have to lose? Give me a few days to arrange things. How long will it take to get there?"

He rubbed his chin. "Last time it took me ten days. I'm sure I could get us there in six this time."

"Make it four. I'll get us the best sled and equipment available. And . . . no hanky-panky. This better not be a big sham to get me alone in the ocean."

"Done," he said. "I'll be ready when you send for me."

He strode from the room, suppressing a smile, taking the cloud of intensity in his wake. Tracey placed her forehead on the cool polished surface of the coral desk, fighting off a wave of anxiety. *What next?* she thought.

Rosa brought her a tray of food and placed it on the desk.

Tracey smelled lobster and cargo ship-captured rice. She looked up with a smile. "Thank you."

Rosa nodded. "I hear you are leaving us in a few days."

"What, are all you people psychic or something?"

She chuckled. "No, Dory was unable to contain himself. I think he wants to get you alone for a while."

Tracey feigned surprise. "Really? No!"

"He's taking you to the Oceanics? I'd watch out for them," Rosa said, crossing her arms across her chest.

"What have you heard about them?"

She shrugged. "They act like they are all enlightened and wise and knowledgeable, but I think they're full of crap."

Tracey nodded. "Well, we shall see. Maybe they'll have remotely operated deep-sea robots, if we can't hijack a flying pickle. In the meantime, I want you to continue things for me here. And I want you to ask Johl if he'd be willing to run a rescue mission for me."

"I'm sure he would be interested. Who and where?"

Tracey slid the file on Smithson over to her.

Rosa glanced through it. "Looks easy enough. He'll be waiting for you here when you get back. Anything else in particular?"

"Another rescue mission." She slid over the LaGrue file.

Rosa nodded confidently. "Is that all?"

Tracey furrowed her brow. "No. I want you to have our research staff come up with some kind of poison or biological agent that will kill sponges. Something that will go from cell to cell inside Porifera tissue and kill it. Okay?"

Rosa nodded agreement. "I'll get them working on it." She left.

Tracey stared at the email on the screen, the one from Ron through Cornish Bob.

I'm coming, she thought. She reached for the keyboard, hands hovering over it for a long second. She wanted to send an email to Ron directly, but knew that it would be instantly traceable without Cornish Bob's precautions.

Tell Ron I'm heading for the Nero Deep now.

She looked at what she had typed with narrowed eyes. *Yes, that is it. Short, hard to trace, conveys that I know where he might be. Invites Cornish Bob to correct me if I'm wrong . . . yes.* It occurred to her that if Cornish Bob intended to trap her, it would make it much easier. It was a risk she would have to take, though. She hit the send button. The words disappeared from the screen, launched into who-knows-where to be read by Cornish Bob and hopefully Ron, who knew when.

A message appeared in her in-box. It wasn't from Cornish Bob, she realized with a stab of disappointment, but from her research department.

"Is the poison intended for calcareous or siliceous sponges? What morphology?" it read.

Crap, she thought. *I'm going to need a sample.* She was impressed with how quickly Rosa had gotten the project started, though. She was proving to be invaluable.

Tracey meandered through the corridors toward her lavish new home—lavish by Tribe standards, anyway. She passed the research wings, the production facilities, and employee housing. All of this space had been vacant a month before, left empty by Tribe that had been hunted down and caught by Eiffelia's patrols. There were other areas of coral being grown for future expansion, some just waiting to be pumped out and occupied, but she wondered if there would be enough Blue Rings to fill them.

She reached her home, and waves of fatigue washed over her. Her bed beckoned. She went straight to her sleeping chambers, stood marveling at her luck and riches.

It was a circular room with a large, circular glass opening in the roof. Most Reef structures were completely covered with coral; windows were severely restricted because at night, any lights that shone artificially onto the reef would be too dangerous, too noticeable to Eiffelia's air patrols. She had convinced Braun to allow this "moon roof" by showing that the switch that activated the doors to open the window would automatically turn off all lighting and close the door to the rest of the house, preventing all light from escaping upward. She had placed her bed directly under the window. On nights when there was moonlight, she lay in bed fascinated by the swirling schools of fish that swam overhead in silhouette, and marveled at the occasional ray, shark, or the glowing clouds of jellyfish.

Now, she activated the doors to the window, shed her Yukata, and crossed to the bed. She lay under the covers, luxuriating in their warmth. Overhead, she stared out her window. At first, only the undulating pale-blue surface showed, bathed in moonlight. As she continued to watch, the outline of a lionfish made its way across the circular frame. She inhaled deeply, loving her bed. She had not had a dream for a long time, and knew one was going to emerge that night. She drifted off.

–39–

Ron and Julia watched as the technicians operated the robotic submarines that fed the giant scorpions. The control room was tucked away in a corner of the underwater base, which was in the middle of a vast field of ooze and mud at the bottom of the trench. Eiffelia the sponge was under the mud, acres and acres of her. Armies of the giant scorpion creatures tended the holes in the mud which allowed water to reach her, protected her from grazing sea-bottom creatures, and fed her morsels of food. The giant scorpions were in turn fed by the mini-subs. Each mini-sub was equipped with a series of manipulating arms and cameras, as well as a bank of lights. The technicians leaned over the screens, strapped into seats equipped with joysticks to control the arms.

"How can those scorpion things live out there? Isn't the pressure too great?" Ron asked.

"No air cavities to compress," the technician answered. "Even the fish down here don't have air bladders like the ones that live up top. If you or me tried to swim there, though, our lungs would collapse and shoot out our mouths like a toothpaste tube. The hydrostatic pressure down here is around sixteen thousand pounds per square inch."

Ron swallowed, hard.

"Is that a lot?" Julia asked.

"Imagine an eight ton elephant sitting on each square inch of your body, and you will get an idea," the technician said, glancing at her.

"So what would happen if someone made a hole in the outer wall of this base?" Ron asked.

The technician smiled while pausing in his work. "Bad things."

"Can the scorpions see without the lights?" Ron changed the subject quickly.

"No," the technician answered patiently, "and they can't

see *with* the light, either. They lost use of their eyes long ago. Sunlight can only penetrate the first eighteen hundred feet or so of seawater, after that everything is completely black."

"So how deep are we?"

The technician glanced at him briefly. "Around thirty-six thousand feet."

Ron's eyes widened and he counted on his fingers. "Wait, that's, uh, around *seven miles deep.*"

The technician resumed his work, placidly unconcerned with the pressure and depth.

"Seven miles deep," Ron whispered to Julia.

"Those things are hideous," Julia said.

"Yeah, they were common back in the Carboniferous period, around three hundred-fifty million years ago," the technician mumbled, concentrating on pulling a dog-food-like substance out of a barrel with the robotic arm and transferring it to the milling pile of five-foot-long scorpions. "Eiffelia bred them to fight the other sponges, but now she just uses them to tend and feed her."

Ron watched them in fascinated horror as they stuffed food into their flagellating mandibles. "So what are they eating?" he asked.

"Uh, it is a special protein mixture," the technician said evasively.

"Made of dead people," said a voice directly behind them. They jumped. It was Eiffelia, smiling tranquilly.

The startled technicians leaped to their feet, then prostrated themselves far more quickly than gravity alone could have propelled them.

"Please, stop, resume your labors," Eiffelia urged. The technicians hesitatingly returned to their control chairs.

"Dead people?" Ron asked, raising an eyebrow. "From where?"

She waved her glowing hand. "People die, Ron. I have a whole planet that I use to make more."

"I suppose you have to eat, too," Ron answered. A queasy feeling grew in his stomach.

"Of course. There is also a constant rain of dead fish and plankton that I filter. But not nearly enough for my biomass."

"And like man can't live on bread alone, you can't live on man alone."

"You are a clever little man, Ron. Yes, I can't live on dead people alone. I am many, many square miles big, you know, and it is expensive to get barrels of canned man here."

"So you must dine on protein-packed minced corpses from here, too? Is that how they make 'Sponge Chow'?"

"Disgusting," boomed Julia. "So glad that this is all a nightmare. When can I wake up?"

"Soon, dear," Eiffelia cooed.

"So will that be my eventual fate if I don't agree to join you and let you use me as a universal thumbtack? Chopped and formed like a chicken nugget and fed to either a giant bug or stuffed down a muddy hole for you digest?" Ron asked.

"Oh, probably not," Eiffelia said. "I don't eat diseased meat."

Ron grimaced.

"Yes, I told you before I know all about your little problem," she said with gravity. "Of course, that could all be fixed if you just gave the word."

"Well, that would be the first thing on my list of demands," he said. "That and my lucky lint shirt. And maybe a dachshund that I can take for walks around here."

"Ah, you are making a list of requirements! Excellent!" Eiffelia said, clapping her hands. "Did Cornish Bob give you that idea when you asked him for advice?"

"You read my e-mail?" Ron asked, feigning surprise.

"I did, indeed. However, I was unable to read his reply to you. What did he have to say, other than to bargain for a long list of demands?"

Ron rubbed his chin. *Was it actually possible that she could not read the reply? But she must be able to . . . she was able to read my email in the first place.*

"He said . . . well, to be honest, he said not to trust you."

"I'm shocked," she said with mock dismay. "Do you think he's right?"

"Of course he is," Ron said. "And not only do I distrust you, I dislike you, too."

Eiffelia made a sad face. "Well, if it's any consolation, I

don't like you, either, Ron. But that doesn't matter, does it? I just need to use you and be able to trust you. However that comes about."

Ron shrugged. "Well, anyway, that would be a good starting point. Curing me."

"Ah, but my dear Ron, I've been pulling your chain, as Cornish Bob would say. Haven't you already noticed that you're feeling better?"

He resumed staring at the technician's screen. He realized that he *had* been feeling much better, but hadn't thought much about it.

"Yes, Ron, I have cured your cancer, as a gesture of good faith. You are all better now, big boy!"

His face purpled. "You had no right to do that! You expect me to be beholden to you now?" he raged.

Eiffelia laughed. "I will never understand you human beings! Here I cured your fatal disease, and you are livid."

He fought to maintain his control.

"Don't worry, Ron, I don't expect you to repay me with your allegiance merely by saving your life. Your help would have been worthless to me if you keeled over and died anyway."

He stared icily at the screen.

Julia looked back and forth between them with vague interest.

"What worth would I have anyway to you? Aside from being a human stick pin? Besides, it occurred to me the other day: You said that when you want to collapse a universe, when there was more of your enemy than resources, you kill off the gene carriers. You also told me that you were trying to kill off the gene carriers in my universe, what with the whole Cornish Bob Horribles assassin thing. So, putting two and two together, I have to assume that in my universe, there is a strong presence of your enemy."

"My goodness, Ron, I thought you were just clever. Really, you are a genius."

"So it occurred to me further: Where is your enemy? You said that they were aliens. I haven't seen any aliens around. The Mods, or bug-eyed monsters? So what gives? Who are they? Who are you fighting?"

Eiffelia sighed in resignation. "I suppose you will not be satisfied just to hear that you wouldn't understand. This was enough for Cornish Bob; I just told him that they were bad, scary alien monsters who were trying to kill me, and to do what was bad for humanity. But really, you *wouldn't* understand."

"Try me."

"You know when I explained that I was a sponge, and at the same time walked among you humans and was labeled as a supernatural being?"

"You mean the Devil?"

"Exactly. Well, you humans have an odd dichotomy of thinking about things. You divide the universe up, and artificially, by the way, into 'natural' and 'supernatural.' It used to be, in the good old days, that everything was supernatural. Thunder was Thor beating his hammer, lightning was Zeus, there were ghosts, spirits, goblins, unicorns, zombies, genies, angels . . . you get the idea. Then science came onto the scene. It was a good start. Everything could be explained naturally, but there was still the mistaken notion that God was behind it all."

Ron nodded. "Go on."

"I did my best to get God out of it. I supported the idea that science, based on evidence, was all that was trustworthy, all that could be believed. Atheism was at first only whispered about, then gained strength. Faith in the supernatural was foolish. If there was no evidence, why do we need it? All could be explained by reason, by scientism, with evidence only, without God. This is finally taking off in your universe. Those militant atheists crow that they are the 'free thinkers,' that the Church enslaved and controlled humanity. The irony! For they are unwitting slaves of faith themselves."

"Slaves of faith? How?"

Eiffelia smiled benignly. "It is only a matter of what they have faith in. They have faith in the fact that there is no God, because they have faith that the universe came into existence without one. How do they know this? Through circular reasoning: God could not have created the universe because there is no God. They have no idea what *did* create it, but they are sure that it was a natural material cause, and they have faith that science will find it someday. Same with the origin of life: Natural selection exists, life evolves that way, but what actually caused it in the first place? Must be some kind of mysterious process in a primal pond with lightning or something. We don't know, but it *can't* be God. They have a saying: 'Just give me one miracle and I can explain the universe.' Maybe *two* miracles."

"So," Ron said, raising his eyebrow, "you are saying that there *is* a God?"

"Of course not." She laughed. "I just got what use out of atheism I could, then gave them the evidence in a God that they said they were lacking: *me*. Now neither side needed faith. None required. On the other hand, what about spirits? Angels? God? Are they 'real' in the same way as I am?"

She paused expectantly.

"Oh, I thought your question was rhetorical."

"Not at all."

"I suppose you're going to tell me that they're who you're fighting in your war, but in reality they are aliens."

"Who lie and claim that they are benevolent spirits, just taking the form of humans. So what is it, spirits or just meat making the false claim that they are? Just like humans, just like you, just like me. There are no supernatural beings, Ron."

"So you convinced Cornish Bob," Ron said flatly.

"These evil creatures really have only their own agendas at heart. They are adept at controlling human minds from hiding and convincing them that they are full of love, peace, universal brotherhood, and enlightenment," she sneered. "And they sow discord secretly among my populations. If they were really supernatural loving entities, why wouldn't they show themselves? Why the big vanishing act, unless they can be exposed and rejected for what they really are?"

Ron didn't know what to say. It occurred to him that he would like to meet those aliens, though.

"So I have to take the responsibility of defending this

planet against the false invaders for myself. I am doing what is best for us all, including humans. The irony is I was the one who was labeled 'evil' while the enemy assumes the mantle of 'goodness.' I have to use others to work my ends, through appeal to their reason, while they have the advantage of direct action, but don't use it! And believe me, Ron, humans are evil enough on their own without either my help or hindrance. Have you ever heard of the Thuggee in India? For hundreds of years, they strangled travelers in ritualistic murders as sacrifices to Kali. Or now in your Mexico, the Santa Muerte cult? More ritualistic murders, sacrifices for this alleged spirit of death, to help with crimes. Neither evil spirit exists, except in the minds of those who seek to appease their own inner darkness. Those beings are like holes in the universe, gaps of non-existence that their devotees give reality to. The hole is indistinguishable from the real thing. Fortunately for me, I'm real. I don't have my own hands, but there are always some . . ." she paused, searching for words, "more advanced, enlightened, and superlative humans who have enough courage and inner strength to disbelieve in the supernatural, and assist me. A small band of the very best of humanity, the elite, the upper echelon. The special, hand-picked, full Pangborn carriers. My Horribles. Cornish Bob is an even more special man. He was entrusted with the rift generator, unlike the rest of his team. They are fit for being his followers, but Cornish Bob, at one point, was a useful tool, capable of thinking on his own and acting on my behalf. Worthy of the 'cheat codes.' I was hoping, Ron, that you were just such a special man, too."

"Am I to understand that his services are being terminated?"

Eiffelia raised her eyebrows slightly. "All tools eventually wear out."

"Well, that certainly dilutes any confidence I could have about joining up with you."

"Don't get me wrong, he is the one who is quitting my service. I value my employees, and you would be safe as long as you choose to remain on the winning team. And of course, there is more that I am offering, in addition to winning. Much more. If you work for me, you get more than the satisfaction that you are serving humanity and its foremost defender. You get anything you want. You get the 'cheat codes.' You want riches? Luxuries? Power? Sex, more sex than you could ever want, with whatever woman you want? Interesting conversation with the best minds in the universe? Travel to see wonders beyond your comprehension? Immortality through exchanging your feeble body for a better one? All this I am offering. What other job can you just name your salary? And here you are still unemployed, at that."

Ron stared at the floor. He tried not to think of bowling pins and sailboats. Or cheat codes.

"Well, my work here is done," Eiffelia said expansively, mistaking his silence for internal deliberation. "I'll just leave you two alone." She faded and disappeared.

"I'd take her offer," Julia said after a minute.

Ron let out a long, ragged sigh. "Oh, you would?"

"Sure! All the sex you want? Sounds good to me."

"You don't strike me as your average straight-laced New England wife of the eighteen-eighties," Ron said. "More like some kind of nympho porn star."

"I don't know what that is. I would never act this way if I weren't dreaming, though. Heavens no. I am a proper wife. But in dreams, anything goes. Did she mention Cornish Bob, for instance?"

Ron nodded.

"He wooed me in my waking life, then when I started this dream he promised to visit me for sex, but then instead of having sex with me, he just came to talk," Julia said offhandedly.

"Well, you know how some men are," Ron said distractedly.

"Hey, you want to have some sex with me? I haven't fucked in oh so long, and that was just my boring husband!" she asked, perking up.

Ron snapped his attention to her, shocked. "Huh?"

"Sure, this is all a dream. Enjoy it. What the heck."

Ron laughed. "So many movies I've seen used dreams as a plot device . . . it all seemed real, but . . . uh-oh, IT WAS ALL

A DREAM! Here you think it is all a dream, but . . . uh-oh, IT'S REAL!"

She regarded him as though he were crazy, rolled her eyes, and shook her head. "If you say so, Ron. Just take your pants off."

She started removing her clothes.

–40–

Tracey did indeed dream, there, under her glass roof that looked out to the dim night sea. She was sitting at a table. It was in a garden, in the sun. She was drinking tea. A hummingbird flitted to a flower nearby, sipped, and buzzed away. There was a spectral, otherworldly music softly permeating the background, like a grand chord packed with odd harmonics. Seated at the table with her was a man on her right, a woman on her left, and across from her, a flying pickle. She recognized the man from a prior dream and the fireside party in Bodie; he was the old man in green-and-brown uniform with square glasses and gray beard, with the sad, twinkling eyes. The woman was wearing a Victorian era dress. She was in her thirties, plain but pretty, and exuded the same sexuality that she had felt from the tent in the dream where Ron had struggled across the desert.

So it wasn't Valentina Pavlov after all, Tracey thought.

The flying pickle hovered in mid-air over its chair. Tracey was struck with how odd this was; not just that she had become accustomed to flying pickles in the first place, but how surprised she was that this one was not just randomly flying around. She examined it closely. It emanated awareness: not just an intelligence; but an almost palpable sense of power and—what was that? Benevolence? Acceptance? Love?

The scene was tranquil, relaxed.

"Well, we are finally all here," said the man, sipping his tea.

"A dream within a dream," said the woman, musing.

"You could call it that," said the man, and smiled.

It occurred to Tracy that she should ask these people who they were, but just as quickly she knew who they were, but without names or labels, or understanding exactly who they were in the ordinary sense. They were simply the people she was meeting in this dream, and she knew they needed to have this meeting to coordinate and discuss things. She knew she would meet them in the more ordinary sense later.

"Welcome to our meeting," said the man, who Tracey remembered now was named Silas Bell.

"I wasn't invited here," Tracey said, "so if you are having a private meeting, I'll leave—"

"Oh no, you were invited. Smithson invited you, and you accepted. Do you remember that night outside a Pakistani restaurant?"

Tracey dropped her head in confusion. She vaguely remembered something like that. "Where are we?" she asked. "This isn't like any dream I have ever had."

"We call it 'Otherwhen,' for lack of a better term," Bell answered. "If you get here by yourself, it's conscious dreaming. When shared, it gathers up a little set of ground rules of its own. It isn't in a universe bubble like your world, or the world you're sleeping in now. Space and time don't work the same way. The inside is bigger than the outside. Like that floor in the office building you were at in Seattle."

"What do you mean?"

"Take a walk through the garden, and you'll see."

Tracey rose, and walked away from the table through the garden. The manicured shrubs, fountains, and lattices gave way to woods. She passed a stream, forded it on moss-covered stones, and kept going. It suddenly occurred to her that she had no idea how long she had been walking, it could have been ten minutes or ten years. She thought about turning back, but realized she wasn't sure which way that was, so just kept going. Before long, she seemed to be entering another garden. With a disorienting shock, she came upon the table and group of people she had left. They smiled and sipped their tea.

"I must have gone in a circle," Tracey said.

"No, you went straight and came back around," Bell said.

"I'm sorry to keep you waiting so long," she apologized.

"There is no long or short here," Julia said.

Tracey sat back down and picked up her teacup, explaining the strangeness to herself by being in a dream.

"I'll start with my report," Bell said, sipping his tea. "I have the demons pinned down and busy in my world, and will meet you soon in yours," he said, nodding toward Tracey. "And if all goes well, meet you later still in mine," he added.

"Even though I have failed to protect my charge, Cornish Bob, I have him pinned down in my dream universe, so he's busy and distracted while he's in yours," the Victorian woman said to the bearded man. They looked at Tracey.

It occurred to her that they expected her to say something. "I'm not sure I have anything to report," Tracey ventured. "I'm not doing much of anything, I suppose."

Bell regarded her with surprise. "Of course you are, my dear." He laughed abruptly. "We are but pawns, holding down positions on the board. You are a bishop, about to take the enemy queen."

In the peculiar way of dreams, Tracey found her attention drifting to the hummingbird, which darted from flower to flower before hovering in front of the flying pickle. The bird closed its eyes, and seemed to bask in the radiance that emanated from it. She sipped her tea. It tasted of strawberries. The hummingbird thrummed away. "I'm just trying to get my friends and go home," she mumbled. It occurred to her that she wasn't sure where home was, though.

"And you are doing a fine job of it, too," Bell said. "When the enemy strikes us down in one world, it makes it harder to carry on in the others."

"I'm just trying to go home, too," Julia said, touching Tracey's hand. "I'll wake up one of these days. I just hope you fare better after your training than I did. I lost my gene carrier."

"Oh, stop it, you did fine, Julia," Bell chastised. "It isn't your fault that he chose the wrong path with the enemy. She is quite persuasive. Besides, the game isn't over yet."

Tracey found herself fighting to keep from waking up. The surroundings were becoming indistinct. She looked at the flying pickle, and the scene regained its clarity.

"So what am I supposed to do?" she asked.

A voice spoke, out of nowhere, deep, melodious, but quiet.

I am coming like the glory of the morning on the wave, it said. *Be my terrible swift sword.*

Tracey sat blinking at it stupidly. She opened and closed her mouth, but no words would come as tears welled up in her eyes.

Bell laughed, even though there were tears in his sad eyes, too. "Blessed are the pure in heart," he said.

Tracey snorted, narrowed her eyes at him. "My heart is anything but pure."

The man smiled lopsidedly. "Blessed are the poor in spirit, too," he said, and sipped his tea.

Soon you will have an opportunity to be more than a pawn, the voice said to the old man. *You will have a chance to capture a knight.*

"I hope I have the courage to go through with it, Mr. Morrow," Bell answered.

A black man in papery coveralls approached, bearing a teapot. Tracey recognized him immediately; it was Maurice, from New Sydney.

"Maurice!" she said, surprised. "I thought you were caught and burned by the Stripes!"

He poured some tea into the bearded man's cup. "Oh, I was," he said cheerfully. "And I'm glad she made the mistake of freeing me, or I'd be there still."

"She let you go?"

"That isn't what I meant by 'freeing me,'" he said. "I was freed to become what I really was, a fish, between the oceans."

Tracey looked at him, uncomprehending.

Maurice laughed. "Ask him in a minute," he said, indicating the bearded man.

"We will begin your training soon," Bell said.

Let's begin it now, said the voice from the flying pickle.

Tracey sat back, momentarily gripped by apprehension. The hazy nature of the dream let it quickly pass.

Good. You grasp that there is no need to fear. That is lesson one. Lesson two is that there are levels of awareness to this game. The lowest level is your waking life, contrary to what is commonly thought. The next level is conscious dreaming, like you are having now, or the ones you remember. The next level up is common dreaming, the ones like Ron gets that he doesn't remember. And the highest level of awareness is deep dreaming, which you can't remember at all.

"That doesn't make sense," Tracey mumbled.

No, it doesn't, agreed the flying pickle. *Lesson three is the skill of extending your awareness. It is a useful talent, and doing it now will help you know what it feels like so you can accomplish this soon, which will be required. Are you ready to begin?*

Tracey nodded.

Bell stood, reached out his hand. Tracey took it, and they walked to the stream with the moss-covered stones. He led her a few steps into the water. Suddenly, instead of rounded rocks in the stream bed, she plunged into water over her head. With an immediate shock, she realized that they were in the open ocean, wearing full gillsuits.

"Where are we?" she hand-signed to Bell.

"In the Pacific. Right over the Challenger Deep in the Marianna's Trench."

Tracey looked down into the deepest trench in the ocean. The sunlight made golden beams that seemed to meet far below her. Farther out to sea, she saw the massive form of a manta ray glide by, attended by its ubiquitous harem of remoras.

"Are we still dreaming?" she signed.

"Yes," he signed back. "But so is what you call 'real life,' in a way; playing the big first person video game."

She knew, if this was the real world, Ron was imprisoned seven miles below her. She knew also that if she tried to swim down to him, she would never make it. Long before she reached him, the icy cold pressure would crush her and she would sink lifeless the rest of the way. She shuddered.

"Okay, ready to go," Bell signed. "I've installed a neutral buoyancy adjuster, so you won't be able to sink any deeper than two thousand feet, unless you lose your mind. If you do that, you'll stop breathing and your lungs will compress to a point beyond which the buoyancy adjuster can keep you from sinking like a rock. The pressure there is great, but with this pressure switch I'm installing in your oxygen inline, it'll be able to force enough O2 into your lungs to keep you alive. Barely."

Tracey's eyes widened. It had never occurred to her to be afraid of the open ocean, in spite of centuries of sailors fearing exactly that, drowning out of sight of land, their ship sinking out of sight before they drowned and sank after it. There was something less dangerous, less threatening about being off the surface of the sea already. The waves didn't throw one around like a rag doll down here. Weather was unimportant. But now, tendrils of fear, like dark vines, crept into her. It was *bottomless.*

"How long will I have to stay down there?" she signed.

"As long as it takes," he signed back, and forced a small tool into her hand.

She inspected it. It was a miniature trident, about a foot long. "What is this for, fighting off monsters?"

Bell smiled. "No, but if you see any it might help. You'll see what good it does later."

"Why am I doing this?"

Bell shrugged. "So you can wake up? Grow up? Find who you really are, or become food?"

"I have to learn how to control flying pickles, or I'm not doing this."

"No guarantees," Silas Bell signed. "No guarantees you will even live through this. You want to pull out? You're not *worried,* are you?"

It occurred to her, with a slight shock, that she was not. The uncertainty of whether this was a dream or not had nothing to do with it.

"How will I know that I'm done, and ready to come back up?"

"You will know. And if you just think you know, I'll send you back down until you either really do know, or die, or throw in the towel."

"How will you find me when I do come back up? There may be currents."

"I have installed a tracking device. I will find you. And don't worry about the bends, your normal dietary supplements combined with the gas mix I installed will counteract them."

She floated there, dreading what was about to come. It would be so easy, just giving up on this. She could go back to the reef, maybe get Ron out some other way. But there was a spark of curiosity . . .

"Have courage," Bell signed.

She nodded.

"I'm going to pull this cord to start your neutral buoyancy descender. When you want to come back up, pull this one. And don't lose your trident."

Tracey looked up at the surface, undulating in the sunlight, for what might be the last time. Bell pulled the cord, and she sank.

And sank.

And sank.

The pressure grew, and she was forced to equalize the pressure in her middle ears. It grew colder, and darker. Again, she popped her ears. And again. She felt the pressure on her lungs, on her sinuses, on her eyeballs inside her bubble mask, on her entire body. It made her consciousness swim. The light faded, the water dimmed, and the blackness crushed in on her like its own pressure. She felt the pressure building on the armored mesh of her gillsuit. The gillsuit's thermostat kicked in, and the internal heaters started to labor to keep her body warm against the cold. Every breath became a labor. She felt as if she were smothering, couldn't get enough air.

And still she sank. All light was now gone, and she lost the ability to tell whether she was still sinking or not, but felt sure that she was. She was a tiny mote in the vastness.

What if there is something wrong with the descender, and I don't stop? What if I just keep sinking until I'm crushed!

She mentally screamed. She knew she was dying.

But she did not die. Eventually, after what seemed like hours of sinking, she realized that she must not still be sinking. And that she was not dead. Not yet, anyway.

She hung, suspended in blackness, disoriented, unable to tell if she was right-side up or upside down. Every breath was torment, a battle. She couldn't force her lungs to inhale against the tremendous pressure. The cold was an assault, in spite of the feeble labors of her gillsuit's internal heaters. Her strength ebbed, and she tried to fight against her innate urge to fill her lungs with air. Her consciousness was slipping into blackness; a blackness that she knew would snuff her life out, and start her long sink to the bottom of the trench where the last vestiges of oxygen would be squeezed out of her lungs. She realized on the verge of panic that she was using more air than she was getting by fighting for breath, so willed herself to stop struggling. As she slowly relaxed, she felt the device that Bell had installed come to life, and force a tiny squirt of air into her lungs against the pressure.

Oxygen! Air!

Her excitement at avoiding death made her forget to relax, and she felt the iron vise grip of the pressure seize her rib cage again. Once again, she forced calm. Once again, she felt the tiny puff of air squirt into her collapsed lungs. This time, she allowed time to pass, and she received another tiny breath without struggling to inhale. By constantly attending to her calm, by consciously letting go of her instinct to breathe, she was able to maintain just enough oxygen to stay conscious and alive. She reached a balance between forced calm and death.

The balanced state brought her into a strange, timeless mind frame. She had no idea how long she hung there, in the abyss, but after some undetermined passage of time, her mind began to be able to maintain the balance without conscious effort. Her mind wandered to the meaning of what was happening, sought to stamp some lesson, or purpose for being there. What was she supposed to learn from this?

She floated.

The blackness started affecting her vision. She knew that there was no light at this depth, all sunlight was scattered and filtered and blocked by the two-thousand-foot column of water that rested above her. And yet, something danced in her vision, tiny white spots. At first, she thought it was an after-effect of the pressure on her optic nerve, like seeing stars on a head impact. She blinked, but they did not go away. She tried to ignore them, but could not.

She inspected them more closely, and was surprised to see that they were zooplankton: tiny animals that glowed with a spark of natural bioluminescence. She stayed very still, and the glimmering animals surrounded her. They were tiny. Some were full-time plankton, while others were the recognizable larvae of reef dwellers: tiny fish, shrimp, octopi, even fully formed but tiny translucent crabs. She knew that only the largest of them were visible as tiny specks; the vast majority were too small to be seen with the naked eye. She knew, from both Sea Tribe schools and her work at the Seattle Aquarium, that there were two million of these animals in each gallon of seawater. Here was the layer of zooplankton that lived at this layer of the depths, then rose each night to feed and be fed upon by the reefs and fish nearer the surface. They could control their rise and descent, but had to follow the current as far as direction. By the time the tiny fraction of the larvae reached adulthood, and reached full size and full coloration and developed their full abilities and color vision, they would have traveled the equivalent of ten times around the Earth.

She floated among them.

She realized that she was *one* of them.

Was this the puzzle? Is this the truth I'm supposed to learn? Plankton as an analogy for human existence? Floating with the current, but able to control how far up or down you go. Well, that was humanity in a nutshell. It seemed to fit.

She floated along, marveling in the revelation. But then she thought back to the story that Silas Bell had tested her with before her descent, and realized that her picture was incomplete.

What does it mean to be up or down? What is the current? And what about the rest of the animals around here, and up there on the reef?

Various further threads of the analogy ran through her mind as possibilities. Was up and down emblematic of human accomplishments? Spiritual advancement? Positive or negative moods? What did it mean that the higher the plankton went, the more chance it had of being eaten? She knew that each time they rose to the level of the reefs, eighty percent of them perished, consumed. What happens to those who are eaten? Does it mean literal death, or is it symbolic?

What was the current? Something that dictated our direction apart from our own wills. Fate? Predestination? The Holy Spirit? The Ground?

And who is doing the eating? All the reef fish, crabs, coral, everything is just a grown-up version of the larval forms themselves, for the most part.

The questions rolled around in her head, chasing each other like a dog chases its tail. She grew impatient. She had to get this answer, to get the ability to control the flying pickles, to get one to go down and get a sample of sponge in order to find out how to kill Eiffelia so she could rescue Ron!

Her impatience brought another bout of struggling with her breath, and she forced herself to calm again.

Calm . . . no struggling . . . a tiny larvae floating with the current, rising to feed, to grow into an adult form—

Her eyes widened.

Oh!

She hung there suspended for a few timeless moments, then pulled the ascender cord. The compressed gas tank released its contents into the attached air bladder, which was under pressure only slightly less than the tank itself. It was enough to start her slowly rising to the surface, however. As she rose, the gas expanded more and more, speeding her upward travel. She virtually rocketed up, and was soon bathed with a dim light, which hurt her eyes after her long stay in the abyss.

Tracey laughed. She never would have thought that she would have a religious experience. The trip to the deep waters, so dead and yet so alive.

Moments later she was dazzled in the shallow water, and was caught by Silas Bell.

Bell examined her closely. She returned his gaze, still blinking to accustom her eyes to the daylight.

"Welcome back," Bell said.

"Thank you."

"Good morning."

"Yes, isn't it?"

Bell smiled, nodded. "So you met our friends, the plankton?"

"Yes, I did."

"And what did they tell you?"

"They told me—how can I say what they told me? That I am one of untold millions, but it is our mission, each of us, to wake up, to be a mature human being like a mature crab on the reef, or shrimp, or coral polyp, or anemone, or fish. To get our coloration, our color vision, our evolved role. We can't hurry it, even if it takes many tries, many lifetimes. To find our place, and take our place on the reef instead of the drifting cloud of potentialities."

Bell held his head slightly askance. "Anything else?"

Tracey paused, thinking, feeling. She had a sudden realization that her understanding of her lesson was incomplete. "Yes, there is more. But what it is I can't say."

Bell smiled slightly, produced another neutral buoyancy unit.

"You need to go back down," he signed. "You have seen the realm of humanity. You have looked at the very small. Now look the other direction. See how they fit together."

She nodded.

"And don't forget your trident!"

He pulled the cord again, and Tracey once again sank.

Once again, the pressure grew, the cold deepened, and the darkness descended. Once again, it seemed to take forever. This time, even though she had been down for what seemed like ages and hadn't eaten or slept, she was able to descend without the panic of her first dive. It almost seemed comforting, like being enveloped in dark wings. She could almost feel the feathers caressing her. . . .

There was another timeless passage of time. Eventually, Silas Bell's words echoed in her mind: Look the other way. From the realm of the microscopic to . . . the large? The giant? The equally vast stretches of the ocean? To space?

Once again, the tiny lights of the plankton danced before her.

How like stars they are.

And stars they were. Swirls of copepods glowed into galaxies. She was gigantic, floating through space, larger than many galaxies. She was standing in the hills above Bodie, watching the stars, the Milky Way, the jewel-encrusted skies.

Then she was in the ocean once again, a woman, calmly eking out one breath after another, the tiny puffs of oxygen keeping her from sinking. She no longer feared sinking, though. She felt as though she could float there, in the depths of the ocean, in the depths of space, forever. Her thoughts, however, started to clump and form into more familiar trains of thought. The Mods had spoken of swimming between the universes. . . .

If we are plankton, if the reef is the world of humanity, and if we are the various species on the reef, then what is the ocean between? What does it mean that there are different reefs? What are the fish and other animals that swim between, or in the open ocean, or on the sea floor between?

She thought of schools of tuna, strong, torpedo-shaped dynamic swimmers. She thought of sea turtles, who lay their eggs on land without ever dealing directly with the plankton layer. She thought of sailfish, of dolphins . . . of whales.

Were these creatures fellow inhabitants of the universe, of the ocean? Or were these animals universes in themselves? Was each diatom, each zooplankton its own universe, being swallowed up by larger fish/universes, and ever larger universes? Were they both? Were the reefs the universes, and the large fish the beings that swam between, in some other modality of existence?

I sound like I'm high on pot. She laughed crazily, floating end-over-end through the glowing clouds of bioluminescence. It occurred to her that the low survival rate of these dives might be due to people having too much a sense of completion and bliss to care about going back up.

She watched the stars swirl by in galaxies, felt the dark wings caress her again, then saw the bright disk of a huge planet drift by. Slowly her mind re-shifted, and what she was seeing took on its more normal form. It was an octopus. It was the biggest one she had ever seen, or was it normal-sized? The wings she had felt had been its arms. The planet had been its eye, as large as a serving platter, which now slowly scanned her. Yes, it was *big* all right. She made out the rest of its body, shimmering with waves and stripes of bioluminescence. It was a species she had never seen, or even imagined existed. She knew that there were giant squids, big enough to eat her, but this?

Hello, there, she thought. She held out her arm. It wrapped the tip of its tentacle around it tentatively, gently. She imagined that it was wordlessly communicating an answer. She sensed its curiosity in waves.

Abruptly, without knowing how, her point of reference shifted and she became the source of the curiosity instead of its object. She saw herself as the octopus saw her, felt herself reach out with a sucker-encrusted tentacle to feel this strange, unknown invader to her realm. She felt herself color-flash with excitement. Overcome with a sudden shyness, she withdrew her tentacles and jetted down, unbelievably fast, to her rocky cave in the wall of the trench.

For the rest of the day, she thought about the strange creature floating above, among the plankton layer. What was it? She roiled her tentacles in agitation. She had seen some of them once in a metal machine, behind a large glowing eye, but never had one of them been out floating by itself in the water. Was it dangerous? Was it good to eat?

She chose to hunt for more familiar food, instead, and busied herself for the rest of the day stalking prey, squid, and deep-water fish. She was unlucky. Maybe one of those giant scorpion creatures that lived in the southern part of the trench . . . yes. They were tasty.

She started to swim, and before too long, was cruising along the muddy bottom, flitting from one rocky outcropping to another, stalking, blending in. There was no light and she chose not to glow. The smells and sounds were enough. She could sense as well as if it was foggy daylight, even though she had no idea what fog or daylight was.

Ah ha! There was one of the scorpion creatures, stuffing a meaty substance down a hole in the mud. She stealthily approached, the tips of her tentacles curling, positioning.

There! She struck with lighting quickness, and flashed her bioluminescence in a sudden blaze, blinding her prey. She held the claws apart, brought her massive beak into position, and finished the creature quickly. She pulled it away to eat it at her leisure.

Later, after she had eaten her fill of the giant crustacean, a strange thought entered her head. She had never thought about this kind of thing before, and it puzzled her.

What was that giant scorpion doing, putting that meat into that hole? Why wasn't it eating it?

She puzzled about this for a long time. It had food. It wasn't eating it. It made no sense.

She thought some more. Maybe it was giving the food to something else. But what? What was living in that mud hole? Was it a big worm? Was it good to eat?

Curiosity propelled her cautiously back to the scene of her hunt. There were no other scorpions about. She looked at the hole: what was in there? Was it worth risking a tentacle? With infinite caution, she inched the tip of a tentacle into the hole, ready to snatch it out the moment it sensed the slightest danger. She felt and felt . . . what was that . . . a sponge?

Was that all? Hardly dangerous. But maybe good to eat. She positioned her beak over the opening, reached in, and ripped off a chunk of the sponge.

It tasted vile, bitter. Ugh. Spit it out. But she wanted it. Not to eat, but . . . for something else. She picked it up in a tentacle, gently. Suddenly she felt, rather than sensed, a threat. Something was watching her. She jetted away in front of a cloud of ink.

She left the vile sponge on the ledge outside, back at her cave. She went into sleep for a time.

When she woke, part of her wanted to simply push the thing back into the depths of the trench, but she knew that was wrong. She couldn't get rid of it.

Too many weird things happening lately. First the creature floating in the water above, closer to the surface, then this bad-tasting sponge thing that she could not throw away. What to do?

She pondered this. She thought about the creature with only half the necessary tentacles, floating above. She thought about the sponge. Maybe connect them? Maybe that was what the creature wanted? Maybe it would go away and take the sponge with her?

She put her plan into action immediately. She gingerly picked up the sponge and swam up, up, to where the creature was still floating . . . there it was. She approached it again, less cautiously. She extended her tentacle with the sponge, and watched the creature extend its puny, sucker-less tentacle. It had some branches, or tendrils, at the end of its tentacle, and these small appendages somehow latched onto the sponge.

Tracey saw the giant octopus flash its eyes, and make a beautiful rippling pattern in glowing, colorful bioluminescence across its body. It then extinguished itself and jetted off into the blackness.

Holy crap, she thought.

She pulled her ascender cord.

This time, she rose for what seemed like a long time, but it grew no brighter. At first, she thought something had gone wrong or maybe she had been much deeper than before. Then it occurred to her that it must be night time, which explained her not seeing the surface.

This proved correct when Tracey saw a faint glimmer of light from a headlamp above. In a cloud of decompressing bubbles, she rocketed to Bell, who grabbed her arms and released the ascender.

"I'm back," she signed, after tucking the sponge and the trident into her belt.

Bell looked at her carefully. "Welcome again."

"I got the sponge sample."

Bell reached out his hand, and Tracey gave it to him.

"There was this beautiful giant octopus, a species I have never seen before. I . . . well, I just got it, that's all."

Bell nodded knowingly. "When we get back to the garden, you may join with a flying pickle, too. They are fantastic. They go unhindered through anything: the air, the water, solid matter, time, space. But they do have a drawback; they can't manipulate anything. They are good for observation only. Your octopus was the only way you could have gotten that sample."

She nodded. "Any chance I may be able to—how do you say it—merge with another type of animal?"

Bell shrugged. "Who knows? Maybe. This time, though, I have to ask again. You met our friends the plankton and your octopus. What did they tell you?"

"They told me . . . that this isn't the only reef out there, this world of humanity, this universe. I know for a fact that that there are more than one. Hell, I came from another one. But there are lots and lots of universes, millions and millions. And just like there are some animals that live between and around the reefs, some things live between and around the universes. But what they are I don't know."

"Well, one kind is flying pickles. But there are others, more intelligent, but less visible. Or less recognizable for what they are, even if they *are* visible. You have met a couple of them, both in your universe and in a dream. So, once again, is there anything else?" Bell signed.

Tracey considered this. She remembered back to the Mods and their claim that the world was a construct of co-creators against a ground, like a shared virtual reality video game.

"Once again, yes. I don't get how this is all a video game. In what medium? A big computer, or what? And who are we the players, and what happens to us after this 'game?' That is what I really want to know now. And this, too: if we have souls that can evolve into 'adult fish' over many lives, what happens in between? And if another universe forms, what happens to the soul? Does it divide? Is it shared? And what about the purpose of it all? What is it all about?"

"Well," Silas Bell said, scratching his beard under the edge of his bubble mask, "you've been down there three days already, and that is the usual limit for any one stretch. But exceptions can be made, if the answer to the biggest question of all is to be found."

"Three days!" signed Tracey. "It seemed like three hours!"

"Yeah, that happens."

"So can I come back later, another day, and do a third dive?"

Silas shook his head. "That won't work, in my experience. It has to be one series," he signed. "It has to be now. But not many attempt the third dive, and of those who do, not many return. You have to weigh the real possibility of death against what you might find answers for by going."

This sobered Tracey considerably. She weighed the strength of her body against the strength of her need to understand.

"Use the trident," Bell suggested.

"The trident?" Tracey signed. "What is up with this stupid little trident thing?" She removed the tiny trident from her belt and made comical stabbing motions with it.

"Just a little symbol for focus," he signed. "The concept has been around for years, in many cultures, and different expressions. One tine each for the three realms, the three kingdoms, the three powers. Thought, Word, and Deed, or the Head, Heart, and Hands, or the Intellect, Emotions, and Actions. One tine is for the world of thought, logic, intellect; its point, its ultimate goal or expression is Truth. The next tine is for emotion, feelings, empathy, sympathy, and communication with others: its point is Beauty. And the third tine, which pulls both things together, is the realm of doing, and of exercising judgment. The pointy tip of that tine is a quality thing, or outcome. It takes all three."

"Which one is the middle tine? Heart, hand, or head?"

"You can answer that one," Bell signed.

Tracey thought a moment. "I guess it depends on what the goal is. If you are trying to make a work of art, the middle tine would be the heart. But without the other two areas, reason and action, it wouldn't have the same quality. And without heart and actual action, an intellectual pursuit would be of less quality. And without reason and beauty, any action would be of less quality. Again, it takes all three to make a quality result."

Bell nodded.

"Okay. But what do you *do* with it? The little trident thing itself?"

"Well," Silas signed, glancing around as though to make sure they were not overheard, "you place it up your ass, *shoot lightning bolts out of the end of it.*"

Tracey was nonplussed.

"Actually, you can use it to focus your thoughts. Like whether you go down again now."

"So how do I actually work it?"

Bell just stared at her expectantly.

Tracey rolled her eyes. *Great. More esoteric mysteries.* She realized it was up to her to use it however it worked for her. She tried gripping it in both fists, staring at it, holding it against her forehead. She resisted the urge to hold it against her butt to see if lightning would actually shoot out.

She found herself simply holding it while she considered.

What was behind the curtain? And what is the purpose of it all? She knew without asking that there was no guarantee that the answers would come even if she did attempt the dive. The question was whether it was worth risking her life over. Or even of losing it. Tracey realized she was tired, hungry, and thirsty.

"Yes. I'll go," she signed.

Bell hesitated only slightly when he removed a third neutral buoyancy unit from his pack, and fitted it to her gillsuit.

She held Bell off at arm's length for a moment, flooding her lungs with air. A sudden feeling of dread took her, but she steeled herself and nodded. Bell pulled the cord, and for the third time, she sank.

And sank.

This time, there was neither panic nor comfort on the descent into the dark void, just anticipation tinged with doubt. Once again, there was no clear demarcation between sinking and suspension, just a subtle feeling in retrospect that her downward motion had stopped. She waited, eyes wide, for something to appear. There were no plankton, no bioluminescent fish. There was only black water, and her thoughts. They ran in circles in her mind: *Is this a big virtual reality game? Who made it? Who plays it? On what ground? What are the ground rules? What happens when the game ends? Why are we playing? If this is a game, what does anything matter?*

Time passed in the black. How much she could not tell. Nothing happened. No answers came. Tracey wondered how long she could wait before death took her and she faded from one blackness into another, the only thing changing being the cessation of her thoughts. *Is that all I am, a point of thoughts in space? Well, my thoughts stop when I'm asleep or unconscious and that doesn't make me dead. Maybe I'm conscious somewhere else. But I'm more than just a bundle of thoughts in the void, I have a body. If I die, there it will remain, or sink to the bottom. Or is it just another patter of energy that stays in the game after I'm gone? Or while I'm dreaming elsewhere? What part is "I" and what is part of the game? Aren't my thoughts all in my brain?*

She waited for something to come, some answers or visions or anything. There was only black.

At some point, she woke, realized that she had been dreamlessly asleep for some unknown amount of time, in spite of the cold and pressure. With an icy feeling, she realized that there was no reason that she had woken up and not died. Fear crowded into her thoughts.

How long was I asleep? What if Bell gave me up for dead?

The longer she mulled the possibility, the less it worried her. She could always trip the ascender and find her way back. She decided to stick it out until the answers came or the void took her. The decision gave her a certain calm. She floated in the black void, watching.

The black sea is like a big, dark movie screen. Am I watching what is on it, or . . . am I the one who is on it? She considered that new possibility: that she was the observed, as well as the observer. *Well, what am I that is being observed? What is visible against the screen? Certainly my physical form, but that is mostly just a few vibrational patterns different from the water itself. Just floating in the water, dark. If one looked to the past, and hopefully the future, they could see me doing things, interacting with the rest of the world. But neither of those exist. Right now, there is no past, no future. To the rest of the world, I'm just a story, a tale, filled with good and evil things. And I will indeed come to an end, like an entire movie on a CD, or a book. I'll finish living this life, and the book or CD will be put on the shelf.*

And she realized that this was as much of an answer as she would get. She was a story, interacting with other stories, on the great ground of creation, part of the grand symphony. And that her story would, like all stories, eventually end. It was her purpose and privilege to make it the best tale she could, a tale of power, a tale of learning and joy, before the end came. And what would come after she need not know, because that is how the stories go. Every beginning precipitates an end. That was the price of entry. But there was comfort in the idea that there were more books and movies on the shelf that she could either be in or just watch.

She pulled the cord on the ascender, and at the end of her long upward trajectory found herself in brilliant sunlit shallow sea. She felt like a hollowed-out gourd, hungry, thirsty, and beyond tired. She gulped water from her desalinating filter tube, and waited. After a while, she saw Bell approaching.

"How long this time?" she hand-signed.

"Quite a while," Bell signed. "What did you see?"

"A blank screen," she answered.

Bell regarded her askance for a moment, smiled, and nodded. "All right, then. You had better be getting back to the garden," he signed.

"Okay. How do we get back?"

"Swim up," he signed.

They did. As they approached the surface of the sea, Tracey found the rounded stones of the stream bed, and they walked out into the garden. They made their way back to the table in an odd silence, and sat again. Julia and the flying pickle were still seated, as though no time had passed at all.

The deep voice of the flying pickle again appeared in her mind. *"Now that you can become conscious through a lower being, you need to be able to use others. I believe you have a message for Ron. Would you like to tell him directly? Come touch me."*

Tracey rose, and walked around to the other side of the

table. She reached out her hand, hesitated, then touched the odd creature.

Like the octopus, she almost immediately felt what seemed like another pair of eyes behind her own, looking through hers at what she was seeing. Then she realized that the eyes were her own; and what she was sensing was from a separate platform from her own body . . . it was the viewpoint of the flying pickle!

Another awareness was with her, the same one that had been speaking in her mind to the assembly.

How easy is this! it said, still in her mind, but nearer. *Now let us go find Ron.*

She waited, not knowing what to do, but the memory of him while in the rift room at the Denver base occurred to her the most clearly. Suddenly, they seemed to be there, floating in the room. She saw Ron, Smithson, Chris, and even her own body standing where they were at that time.

"Ron!" she called out. She saw Ron start, as if he heard her. "We're coming to find you in the Nero Deep!"

She saw Ron narrow his eyes, not sure if he was hearing her, or perhaps heard her unclearly. She remembered that it was around this time that Ron had tried to jump into the rift.

"Don't jump in the rift!" she yelled.

Ron took two long strides toward the rift, and jumped. She dimly saw Smithson reach out and grab his arm, then she was back at the tea party with Bell and the Victorian woman, Julia.

It seems he didn't hear you very clearly. The presence in the flying pickle chuckled.

Tracey went back to her seat, and her clarity slipped again. She was focusing on the strawberry tea once more.

The Victorian woman suddenly sat bolt upright. "Oh, dear, I have to wake up now! Ron is taking a hammer to the window." She laughed and disappeared.

Tracey woke abruptly. "That little t-tart!" she stammered. She was suddenly in her bed in Blue Ring Reef, covered in a thin sheen of sweat despite the cool air.

*****

Hundreds of miles away, Ron had indeed taken a hammer to

one of the windows. When the technicians saw Julia Ward Howe shed her clothes, they evacuated the area, whether to give them privacy or to get help, he could not guess. Ron pushed her away insistently, and she eventually gave up her clumsy seduction and sat down, still naked, in one of the technician's chairs. She fell asleep.

As Ron watched the screens, it occurred to him that he was alone. And that there were tools around. And that he could use one of them to smash one of the windows, and instantly crush them all. Almost in a dream, he picked up a hammer and aimed a mighty swing at a window. It had failed to break, however, and had made a surprisingly loud noise. The coverall-suited workers had returned at the first loud clang, mobbed him, and wrestled the tool from his hands.

He waited in his cell for Eiffelia to appear and pass judgment on him. As he paced, he noticed an email appear in his inbox. He quickly opened it. His heart nearly stopped beating. It was from Tracey!

I'm heading for the Nero Deep now.

He regarded the screen blankly for a moment. Good thing he hadn't broken the damn glass. He placed his hands lightly on the keyboard, knowing that his reply could either save him or cost him his life.

Bob: Any chance you can get me out of here before she drops her nuke?

He hit the send button, and erased the message. Sweat broke out on his brow. Talk about the longest of long shots, the biggest hail-Mary of all time. Something told him that it wasn't as impossible as it sounded, though. Something felt light inside, felt right. Tracey was on her way to rescue him, like a damsel in distress.

"I'm such an idiot," he mumbled.

But the good feeling persisted.

–41–

Tracey stood impatiently in the launching bay, arms akimbo, and fought off the beginning tendrils of worry while waiting for Dory to arrive. She was frustrated not just because Dory was late, but because the dream had rattled her. The usual brick wall between dream and waking life had become more a thin tissue. She was undecided whether to travel to do the dive, or to stay home because she had already made it.

Braun, Johl, and Rosa had come to see her off. They stood around the gently undulating pool, where several of the Reef's sleds were moored. The provisions, bubble tent, and other supplies and equipment were already lashed to the sled. The power supply was fully charged.

"He'll be along shortly," Johl assured her. She glared at him. "I'll just check your sled again," he said, beating a hasty retreat.

"You must be careful," Rosa warned. "I don't trust those Oceanic types any more than I trust the Stripes, when you come right down to it."

"Why not?"

Rosa shrugged. "I just don't buy all their mystical, religious hooey."

Tracey sighed. "I don't either. I don't know, we'll see. If they can get down and scout out where that sponge is, and where Ron is, or tell me where to drop a nuke or a biological poison agent, then they will be worth it."

"That would be worth it, indeed," Braun rumbled. "Her patrols have been getting more effective lately."

"Which reminds me," Tracey said, raising her index finger and turning to Rosa. "How close are we to launching the raids to recover Smithson on that island and Professor LaGrue on New Sydney?"

"They are both ready now," Rosa answered. "Do you want me to wait for you to return to start the operations, or is it all right to proceed while you are out?"

Tracey narrowed her eyes. "Go ahead and get them, if you are confident of success."

Rosa nodded sharply with a lopsided smile.

"And ask Smithson to start training our people to fight back more effectively, too, when you get him in here. And maybe get the egg-head professor to work for us."

They stood in silence for a minute.

"So, this is the latest model sled," Braun commented, admiring the expensive new underwater transport. "I hear it is programmable to be self-guided, so you can even travel at night while you sleep in an attached bubble tent. And it is fast, too."

"I'm counting on it to get us there and back quickly," Tracey answered, pursing her lips. "That is, if I don't change my mind and stay here," she added.

As if on cue, Dory emerged from a tunnel.

"What are we standing around for, let's get going!" he said, with uncharacteristic lightness.

Tracey made up her mind in an instant. "I'm not going to make the Dive. I already went."

Dory stared at her dumbfounded. "What do you mean you already went?"

"Just what I said. I have gleaned what there was to learn from the experience already."

Dory frowned, still not understanding. "Well, where is the sponge sample?"

Damn it, Tracey cursed. *I handed it to Bell.* It occurred to her that she could just send Dory to retrieve it. But she was unclear about whether the dive had actually happened, or if it was just a dream in the ordinary sense. If she went to see Bell and he actually had the sponge sample . . . .

"Okay, we will have to go anyway," she announced.

Dory seemed to take this reversal in stride.

She sat at the edge of the water to don her fins, mask, gloves, and propulsion backpack unit. They both ran through the pre-dive checklist: Oxygen production, waste gas retrieval, active camouflage, thermoregulation, pressure balance, anti-fogging, fresh water desalination/hydration, power supply, sanitation, backup systems, all checked out.

She slipped into the water. Dory followed her to the sled, and with a last hand-signed goodbye, they eased the sled through the coral-lined passage that led to the edge of the reef.

She let Dory drive. He took it slow for the first few miles, zigzagging through the coral massifs and sandy banks that surrounded BlueRing Reef, then he headed into the deeper water. The bottom dropped sharply away into the deep blue of the open sea, and then they were suspended in a clear layer of water between the light-blue surface and the depths. Beams of golden sunlight pierced the water like long spears, brightening and dimming as clouds, seen only hazily, crossed the sky.

Schools of fish flashed their synchronized ballet as they passed. Tracey saw a large sea turtle make its way above them, and thought she caught a glimpse of the massive form or a whale shark in the distance before Dory opened the propulsion unit up and the streamlined sled picked up speed. She checked the passive sonar display, saw nothing in front of them but open water. She put her hand on the fuselage to feel the vibrations: The engine was working fine. The sled began cavitation, a shell of air forming to reduce drag. She settled in for the journey.

Occasionally, the looming form of a seamount would appear out of the hazy distance. If they were shallow enough to support coral, the noises could be heard from a long way off. Dory checked his map screen, made slight adjustments of a few degrees of course, and they sped on.

Afternoon wore away, and darkness crept into the rippling surface as they approached one such seamount to their south. They got close enough to see the barrier reef. Tracey checked her watch to make sure that the darkness was not a storm brewing, which would force them deeper to avoid the swells, but it was simply night falling. She signed to Dory that they should stop soon to deploy the bubble tent, so that they would not attract attention with artificial lights by deploying it later. He nodded, and they gradually slowed to a standstill in the current. Tracey realized that she was bone tired. She was not used to sled travel.

"Where are we?" she signed. Dory held out the LCD map screen, pointed to an area just north of the barrier reef surrounding the Chuuk Island group.

"Six hundred fifty miles or so to go," she signed. "At thirty-five knots, that makes around sixteen hours of travel time."

Dory, figured in his head, then nodded. "But we can't go as fast with the bubble tent under tow. Takes us down to ten knots," he hand-signed back.

"So for the eight hours or so we sleep," she signed, "we'll go ninety-two miles. Let's call it an even hundred. If we sleep two nights, that leaves only four hundred-fifty miles to go, which we can do in eleven hours."

"Are you thinking of just sleeping the one night and pushing the rest of the way?" he signed.

She shrugged. "Let's see how we stand up after a full day tomorrow. I'm pretty tired now."

He nodded. Tracey remembered that he was an easy travel partner, always sensitive to her rhythms. She watched as Dory tugged the bubble tent out of one of the storage cavities in the sled's fuselage, and attached it to his secondary oxygen line to inflate it.

"Lots of sunken Japanese ships around here from the war," she signed.

He nodded. "Last time through, I spent some time in the lagoon over there looking for stuff," he signed back. "Didn't find anything, though."

"Do you want to eat?"

"Now would be a good time," he signed back.

They fished out tubes of field provisions and their chemical heating pouches, and squeezed them for a meal. Tracey thought that they had improved the quality since the last time she'd eaten at sea. Her clam chowder, pasta paste, and wine were quite tasty. The bread sticks were still crunchy as she fed them through the tube one at a time.

Darkness was now nearly complete. Dory motioned for her to enter the bubble tent first. She squeezed herself through the semi-permeable airlock into the half-dome-shaped semi-rigid structure. It was just big enough to have a small area to don and doff their gillsuits, and stretch out to sleep.

Tracey wriggled out of her gillsuit, while Dory pulled himself through the opening. She watched him strip down to his trunks out of the corner of her eye, making a show of adjusting the oxygen flow rate. His body was lean, hard.

Dory rolled across the tent, found the navigation control settings, and punched their route into the computer.

"Does this thing have the ability to adjust course around any uncharted coral mastiffs?" she asked, glad to be able to speak again.

"Yes," he answered quietly. "All the latest technology."

He looked at her for a long, lingering moment, then went back to his input pad.

Tracey looked away uncomfortably. This was going to be difficult. Keeping his hands off her. And her hands off him. "Look," she said finally, "we need to set some ground rules. Nothing is going to happen between us. We are brother and sister on this trip, so cut it out with the subtle pressure. Agreed?"

He put on an air of surprised innocence. "Pressure?" He shook his head. "Of course, whatever you wish."

She lay down, extinguishing the oxygen feed controller's dim screen after making sure she could find her gillsuit mask in the dark in case of emergencies. Dory turned off the navigation screen and lay down beside her. They each had their own synthetic blanket. She listened to his breathing. She wondered if he was listening to hers. She longed to reach over to him, but fought the desire.

Would it be so wrong? she thought. *We were married. I know him, we are mates, right down to my cells. Am I even with Ron in this universe at all?*

She searched her feelings. Yes, she loved Ron. But yes, she also loved this man, her husband.

She lay, torn, for a long time, thinking and listening to the low hum of the sled engines, pulling them through the total black seas that swished and gurgled around their tent. Eventually, her fatigue won out over her desires, and she slept.

The navigation computer skirted them around Pisaras Island, Weltot, Onari, Ono, and Magererik Islands, and into the deeper ocean.

Tracey and Dory made excellent time the next day. She had nothing to do, nothing much to see while they crossed the open sea. Some of these deep basins, far from land, were virtual deserts of life. A few shoals of Bluefin Tuna seen from a great distance were about it.

Occasionally Dory would engage her in hand-sign conversation.

"Is this like flying in your world?" he asked.

She considered this. The Tribe did not travel by air.

"Not exactly," she signed back. "There, when we fly, if something goes wrong we tumble out of the sky and hit the ground. Here, if there is some kind of a sled malfunction, it just stops and we float here in neutral buoyancy. We don't exactly sink into the depths and die. This is kind of like flying, though. But imagine if you were weighted down so that if the sled went bad, you'd just sink."

"I don't have to imagine that," he signed back.

I don't either, she thought.

Tracey's eyes strayed downward. The sunlight angled into unguessed-at depths, but she did not think about it with the dread that someone who was not used to living in the Tribes would. She was sure that Ron would be terrified of the bottomless abyss. The human impulse of fear from the dark, the unknown, the slithering giant creatures living in the vast realms where sunlight never penetrated. She had never been afraid of it, but she had never considered visiting it, either. It was like living on land all one's life and never considering flying around in the upper atmosphere.

Odd that Dory brought up flying, she thought. *Living in the sea is like living upside down on the land, with the surface as the ground. But we leave no tracks on the surface.*

Tracks. The ancient way of tracking game. *Like Eiffelia hunts us,* she thought. The ancestors of the Tribes were experts at tracking. An animal passed this way, and by the look of the track, they could tell how long ago it had passed.

She imagined the leap of primitive logic that had taken . . . the animal was here, but now it is not, and it must be somewhere up ahead. *I wonder if that is how we first made the leap to the concept of time.*

Then she remembered the dream and how time didn't seem to pass, and wondered if that was a throwback to pre-human thinking. *Or the next level of it, like the pickle said.*

By the end of the day, she was once again stiff and exhausted from riding along in the cavitating backdraft of the sled. She signed a halt to Dory, who ramped the engine down to a slow crawl.

"We can either push on and make the rest of the distance in about four hours, or sleep the night and finish the rest of the trip tomorrow in about two," he signed.

Tracey considered pushing on, but realized they would arrive among the Oceanics in the middle of the night.

"Let's sleep and get there mid-morning," she signed back.

Dory nodded, and broke out the bubble tent again.

A school of curious fish started shadowing them. Dory paused before entering the tent, and signed "You want fresh fish for dinner?"

She nodded. Dory opened another hatch in the sled, and produced his spear gun. Moments later, he lanced two fish, and expertly filleted them. She followed him into the bubble tent for the freshest of sashimi, eaten even before they removed their gillsuits.

She nodded appreciatively. He had always been a good fisherman.

"So tell me," she said, supplementing her meal with a bulb of sake, "what to expect tomorrow morning?"

"Ah, yes, the Oceanics," he said, brow furrowing. "I'm not sure what to tell you. There are not too many of them, and they all keep pretty much to themselves, as a rule. I guess you could say that they live as a community of hermits, if that makes any sense. Ascetics more like. They don't value money, so you won't be able to buy their help. They aren't motivated by any sense of fealty to the Tribes, either, even though they keep their customs. The Reef markings on their gillsuits, for instance, are the sign of a flying pickle. But they don't consider themselves anything other than a collection of like-minded people. No raiding, no trading. They don't have much."

"They sound like monks."

He nodded.

"So how do I convince them to help us?"

He shrugged. "That will be up to you. I will help as best I can. I think our best bet is to ask for Silas Bell."

Tracey's eyes narrowed. "I have heard that name," she whispered.

"He's the one who helped me with my Dive. He can ride the flying pickles."

Tracey shook her head, as though shaking cobwebs loose. She remembered her dream, and it occurred to her that she had communicated with Ron backward into time. *Was that a dream?* "Okay, whatever. Flying pickle riding. I just need to get that sample of the sponge and get Ron out of there if I can."

"This Ron . . . do you love him?"

She regarded him. He was looking at the floor of the tent, in the fading last light of day.

"Yes, of course."

He nodded, still looking at the floor. "But you are not married to him."

"That is beside the point," she said.

After a long period of silence, in the gathering darkness, he asked "Do you love me?"

She did not answer him. Instead, she lay down, gathering the blanket over her, and faced the far wall of the tent. She regarded the moonlit water beyond.

He lay beside her, facing her. She felt his warmth. She wriggled closer, feigning that she was trying to get more comfortable. She felt his breath on her neck. He placed his arm over her.

Abruptly, she turned toward him and they kissed.

"Oh, God," she moaned.

Their melding was urgent, fiery, and with abandon.

–42–

"I am very, very disappointed, Ron. What am I going to do with you now?" Eiffelia scolded.

Ron stared at the metal grated floor. She always made him feel ill, and unable to think straight.

"I can't very well have you destroy my facility and my caretakers down here, but neither can I burn you at the stake like that heretic. I am *very busy* right now, and don't have time to deal with you properly."

"Why don't you let me go? Or at least keep me imprisoned somewhere else. Being here is . . . making me crazy. I'm starting to hallucinate. Yeah, that's why I tried to smash the window. It's the pressure. *The pressure!*" he cried, falling to his knees, fists at his temples. He looked up to see if she was buying it. It occurred to him that he wasn't putting on a show. It had been weeks since he'd felt the sun on his face, since he had not felt the unrelenting crushing sense of the miles of water above him. Then there was Eiffelia's unrelenting pressure. *I saw the ghost of Pop!* He felt more than a little nuts.

"Hmm." She pondered with a distasteful expression on her face. "I had hoped that keeping you in close proximity to Julia Ward Howe might provide some incentive for Cornish Bob to call on you more, but there is no reason that I can't send you both up to my facility on Guam . . . and there is less you can destroy there."

"Thank you, thank you!"

"Oh, stop it," she said with feigned disgust, and vanished.

Within the hour, the curly-haired attendant appeared at his door to escort him to the sub. They passed through the artificial sky dome with the tropical plants, and stopped at a door with an electronic keypad. They waited until another attendant arrived with Julia Ward Howe, once again dressed.

"Where are we going?" she asked.

"To a tropical island resort," Ron said cheerfully.

"Oh, how lovely," she said, clapping her hands. "This dream is finally getting better."

The attendant entered a code, and they walked down a tubular hallway to an airlock. He spun the wheel on the hatch, and they climbed aboard a large submersible. Ron was pleased to find that large portions of it consisted of glass domes that allowed wide visibility. For the moment, all that was visible through the condensation was the lights of the underwater base, with miles of black water above them. They seated themselves, and began the three-hour journey to the surface.

It seemed even longer. Aside from the occasional jellyfish, all they saw on the long ascent were tiny plankton, some glowing with bioluminescence. Eventually, the water took on an almost violet tint, then an achingly dim blue. It rapidly grew brighter, until far above them, they saw the surface.

The submersible broke into the sunlight near a floating platform, crowded with structures and cranes. Nearby were moored service ships. One crane swung over to secure the submarine, and they were hoisted up to a landing platform. Ron expected a cadre of guards and handlers and attendants to be waiting for them on the dock, but was surprised to see no one but the crane operator and one man running the rigging. That man opened their hatch and assisted Ron and Julia out of the submersible, where they stood, standing on a metal grate landing, blinking mightily in the sun.

The SUN!

Nobody said anything for what seemed, to Ron, like too long a time. He enjoyed the mental sensation of the absence of pressure.

The man busied himself securing the sub. They stood there.

And stood.

Something is wrong, he thought with a flash. *Either she hasn't communicated any orders about us or they were lost,* he realized. He knew he had to start moving and keep moving or those orders would catch up to them. He was damned if he was going to stand around like an idiot until someone realized that they didn't know what they were supposed to do with Ron and Julia.

"Well, thanks for taking us up," Ron called through the hatch to the submersible pilot.

"You're welcome," the pilot called back cheerfully.

Ron turned to the rigger, who stood holding the lines to the submersible steady, looking at the crane operator in his control booth nearby. He had that Milk-induced vacant look about him, slowly and serenely and happily working to serve.

"What is the fastest way to get to New Sydney?" he shouted over the noise of the machinery, as though it were all planned out that way.

"You can catch a transport flyer down at the landing zone," the man shouted back helpfully, and pointed to an area on the floating base with several flying vehicles parked on it. Ron gave him a thumbs up, grabbed Julia's arm with what he hoped was not any sign of hurry or desperation, and hustled off, doing his best to assume his furry-bunny-vacant-happy look.

"Where are we going?" Julia asked, brightly.

She just naturally acted as though she was on the Milk, Ron noticed with satisfaction. "We are going flying, if our luck holds," Ron answered cheerfully.

"That sounds fun!"

They made it to the landing zone without being accosted by any attendants or guards. Several vehicles looked like snowmobiles or jet-skis. They were too small, Ron thought. One of them was huge, too big, the size of a 737. It would attract attention. Two of them were about the size of, and actually had the look of, a terrestrial Winnebago RV.

Perfect, Ron thought.

There was only one official-looking person about, dressed in white coveralls with a square in white on his right cheek and a woodpecker familiar, talking with a small family of Stripes.

Ron took Julia by the arm and they crossed to where the family was talking to the official.

"I'll be with you in a moment," the man said to Ron, then strode unhurriedly off to one of the flying RVs.

"Are you two on a honeymoon?" the mother asked Julia.

"Yes, we are," Julia said dreamily, much to Ron's surprise. "Where are you taking your family?" she asked.

"We are from Procyon 6, one of the mining colonies," the mother answered. "My husband won an award for faithful service and dedicated work, and the prize was a trip to the home world for a week of camping in nature. We are flying to a spot in China."

"How wonderful for you!" Julia said.

The attendant returned, and handed the father a set of keys.

"Have a great vacation!" he said earnestly. "Now, where are you two headed?"

"Eiffelia has told me that she wants us to take one of these flying campers here and go to New Sydney."

"She did?" Julia asked. Ron ignored her, and was gratified to see that the man ignored her as well, unable to keep two different conversations in his head at the same time.

"Of course!" the man said. "Would you like me to take you there, or would you like me to just get the aircraft ready?"

"It wouldn't be too much trouble for you just to program in the destination into the computer or something, would it? And maybe give me a tiny lesson on how to work the controls?"

"No problem at all!" The man nodded, smiling.

Ron was gratified to discover that the controls were simple: a joystick to give direction and a foot pedal for speed. The years of video game play, where he had piloted all manner of starships and airplanes, were paying off.

The Stripe worker waved happily from the door and wished them a safe journey, then secured the door behind him.

"Strap yourself in," Ron said to Julia, wrapping his hand around the joystick with a surge of optimism. He half expected a crowd of guards to appear across the way where they had exited the sub and start chasing them, but none appeared. He had a sudden urge to roar away from the floating platform with all the speed the craft had, but forced himself instead to take off and float gently away, to avoid attention. The controls were responsive, intuitive, and easy. After a few miles, he glanced at the navigation beacon, adjusted his course, and opened up the speed as fast as the craft could go. He knew it was only a matter of time before the pursuit began. The race was on.

But the race to where? He ran through his options: New Sydney? Why? What was waiting for him there? Perhaps back to the rift and a return to his universe? Only to leave Tracey and the rest of his companions behind? It occurred to him that he had no idea whatsoever where any of them were. He also realized that he could get help and come back for them. Lots of help, armies of help. The rift at the mining platform seemed the best option, even if Eiffelia knew that he would be going there. He would go through the rift that they had come in through, then re-contact the Mods. With any luck, he would be through it before Eiffelia even knew he was gone.

He had no idea, though, where he was in the world, and how far away New Sydney was, and how far away New Sydney had floated from the rift. Maybe follow the programming the Stripe had put in back to New Sydney, then go opposite to the direction it was moving?

This is looking worse and worse, he thought. But for now, he reveled in the fact that he was free. Free of Eiffelia, the Devil, the Man-Eating Sponge.

He pressed the pedal as far as it would go, trying to squeeze more speed out of the flying Winnebago.

They flew for what seemed like hours. He was just starting to doze off from sheer nervous exhaustion, when the alarms clanged on. He stared madly around at the controls with a lung-freezing surge of adrenaline. One of the monitor screens showed a small dark cylinder arcing toward them on a trail of smoke.

"Shit," he said quietly, then the missile impacted.

—43—

"I don't see him," Tracey hand-signed. They were in reefs, deeper than reefs usually ran. It was mid-morning.

"Right there," Dory signed back, pointing to a ledge halfway up a coral mastiff. The coral formation continued a steep upward spiral to the surface. Below it, like the drop off from a cliff, was the dark abyss.

She shook her head. He swam behind her, took her arm, pointed it at the ledge and she sighted down it. She felt uncomfortable with him so close again, in spite of the night they had spent together. That morning, when she woke, she'd been struck with guilt.

How am I going to tell Ron about all this?

She put it out of her mind, concentrated on finding the Oceanic.

"Oh . . . there." She saw an outline of a man, sitting cross-legged, as if he were meditating. What she had taken to be drifts of weed were strands of his hair.

"So what do we do? Can we just swim over there and start talking to him?"

He shook his head. "Better to wait nearby for him to finish his meditating," he signed back.

"Should we wait inside, in their reef?"

"They don't have a reef. They all live outside, in the coral, all the time."

Her eyes widened behind the bubble mask. "How do they manage that?"

He shrugged. "They just do," he signed.

They tethered the sled on the nearest mastiff and slowly swam to an area near the seated man. Before they had waited long, he stirred, stretched, and kicked over to them.

Dory greeted the man, and shook his hand. "Tracey, this is my friend, the man who helped me make my dive, Silas Bell."

"Yes, they call me 'The Diving Bell,'" the man hand-signed. "Sorry to keep you waiting, I was flying around in a pickle."

Tracey shook his hand, tried to scrutinize his face behind the bubble mask. "We have met before."

"Maybe somewhere," the man answered enigmatically.

Tracey was sure she had met him. He was the one she had dreamed about, both at Bodie and in the garden. He was also at that party with the scientists in Bodie. "Of course," she hand-signed back. "We were in a garden drinking strawberry tea."

Dory looked back and forth between them, curious.

"Of course," Bell hand-signed back. "And I was in a strange dusty place with ancient wooden ruins, and you ran by with scary zebra wolves after you and jumped into a mineshaft. And we had some fine Whiskey with pikas. Are you here to make the Dive?"

"Already did," she signed, not sure if he would remember this or not.

"Good job," he signed, with a nod and a half smile.

"I just need the sponge sample," she signed, heart stopping. *If he actually had it . . .*

Bell reached into his gillsuit storage pocket and handed it to her.

Stupefied, she took it, turned and swam away. Dory, puzzled, followed.

Tracey and Dory locked into the sled. He took a heading, and they struck out into the mid-morning sea. They traveled the rest of the day without conversation, and into the growing darkness.

"Do you want to sleep?" Dory signed after a while.

Tracey was exhausted, but was not up to getting into a bubble tent with Dory. He was suddenly not the object of her attractions any more.

"Push on; I'll let you know when I can't go any farther. I need to get back and help Ron," she signed.

She sensed his disappointment. She didn't care. Things were different now.

–44–

Johl and Maloko had drawn straws to determine which raid each of them would lead. Johl drew Smithson's island; Maloko was to lead the raid into New Sydney to recover the scientist.

Maloko was glad that he drew the way he did. He had no love of Stripes; his whole family had been wiped out in the attack on Sea Turtle Reef. Snatching Smithson off an island somewhere would not give him as good an opportunity for revenge.

He scanned around him for his team, making sure that all fifty of them were within sight of his locator screen even though the Tribe themselves were all hidden from view in the dark water. They were all veterans, experienced members of Tracey's Privateers. This was no cargo ship takedown, though, but a hostage grab from the middle of a Stripe city! Nobody had ever done that before. His heart beat faster.

They were in position under the city's marina. He was to lead half of them into the city and grab the scientist, while the other half were to form a loose protective perimeter around the city with guided anti-aircraft javelins, and to make sure the sleds were ready for the getaway.

"Weapons check," he signed to the nearest group of privateers, who relayed his message down the line and, with the rest of the party, Maloko checked his weapons: knife, good dose of fresh poison, not washed away; bolt-caster, with full charge of compressed gas; full complement of poison-dipped mini-javelins in the magazine, extra magazines accessible from mounts on load-bearing vest; gas grenades accessible; and finally, the line of six guided javelins secured at an angle against his propulsion backpack. No need for poison on those explosive tips. He made sure his active camouflage was operational, it would be critical for remaining undetected for as long as possible as they moved through the dark city. Finally, his heads-up display for locking on javelin targets, and reserve oxygen checked out, too.

When the privateer farthest down the line was finished checking his weapons and equipment, he gave the next nearest one a thumbs up. This traveled back to the center, where Maloko waited. He glanced around; all the privateers in his sight were giving him the ready signal.

Maloko checked his watch: 3:00 AM, when the circadian rhythms of the city's sleepers were in deepest sleep. Time to go. He took a deep breath from his gillsuit line, then circled his open hand and moved it forward in the signal to deploy.

As he heaved himself as quietly as possible out of the water and onto the marina deck, he took a last look to make sure that his cover team was swimming out to take positions in the ocean around the city. Then he looked around the marina: no guards. He left his mask on, switched on his reserve oxygen tank. He was glad to see that not a single privateer removed his mask out of habit: not only were they necessary for the heads-up targeting display, but it was certain that there would be smoke or other gas irritants on this mission.

He activated the map screen on his left forearm, using intel Leonard, the former resident Un-numbered, had given them. The ramp they wanted to get up and out of the marina was on the southwest side. He signed to the first squad to scamper up the ramp and secure it. He could barely see them move, thanks to a combination of the dim light and the active camouflage. The five of them, bolt-casters at the ready, took the ramp in a silent crouch. They signaled from the top that it was clear. The rest of the team joined them on the ramp's landing.

Second squad was next. He sent them into the rows of warehouses near the marina. They flitted in and out of the alleys like ghosts. Maloko watched as one of them signed a silent halt while looking around a corner, then unsheathed his knife. A Stripe Security policeman walked unwittingly around the corner. He never knew what hit him. The Tribe privateer slid his left hand against the policeman's mouth, his thumb and index finger pinching off his nostrils to prevent any intake of breath or outburst of noise and at the exact moment the Tribesman's plunged his knife into the man's neck, the blade simultaneously severed the carotid artery and blocked the trachea, preventing any air from escaping that way as well. Even without the poison, the man would have died instantly. As it was, he stiffened as though electrified before he rigidly expired.

The privateer tugged him into the deeper shadows, then passed the guard's spider familiar back along the line to Maloko, who manipulated one of the arms, regarded the data projection with narrowed eyes, and then crushed the spider familiar under his foot.

"The information that Tracey bought from the Un-Numbered was right," he signed to his squad. "Professor LaGrue has set up his lab right there where Leonard and Maurice used to live, at the water processing facility. With any luck, we will get him and the other universe's equipment at the same place."

The maps to Leonard's old place were accurate. Along the way, they encountered only one Stripe: an old man who was unable to sleep. Fortunately for him, he did not see the Tribe. They let him pass unmolested.

Ten minutes later, they had traversed the floating city to the outskirts of Leonard and Maurice's water plant. They paused to regroup. Unknowingly, they were in the same place that Eiffelia's forces had used to launch their assault.

Maloko signed for third squad to scout out Leonard and Maurice's old chambers. The five members of third squad crept quietly to the door. One of them tried the latch, found it unlocked. He opened it only a crack, with glacial slowness. The door did not creak.

He inched it open wider, and when it was wide enough to allow him entry, he slid in. Tense seconds followed, then the privateer emerged. He quietly moved to the cover that Maloko had taken, and hand-signed his report: One large room, three Stripe guards, armed with guns, playing cards at a table, three other guards, asleep; and not one but *two* Professor LaGrues working at a computer screen.

"Two professors? Are you sure?" Maloko return-signed.

The scout nodded.

Maloko rubbed his chin. They had not planned for that. But of course, Eiffelia could have put this universe's Professor LaGrue together with the other one. *Two heads are better than one.*

"We only have one spare gillsuit," the scout signed.

"I know that," Maloko signed with irritation.

"Well, nothing we can do about it," he reasoned. "We'll have to make do somehow."

He signaled his team over, and detailed his plan of attack, using the scout's report of locations within the room.

A short time later, his privateers deployed to their assault positions. Fourth squad was to lead the attack.

Maloko and two other privateers from Fifth Squad pulled the pins out of gas grenades. After silently counting to two, the lead privateer kicked the door open, and all three of them lobbed in the gas bombs.

There was a moment of confusion as the card-playing Stripe guards looked up in surprise. The grenades went off, spreading a cloud of diluted BlueRing octopus venom. They groped for their guns, but immediately retched, their vision went hazy, and they fell, disoriented and without a sense of touch.

By then the fourth squad was in the room, still protected against the gas by their masks. Maloko was right behind them, bolt-caster drawn. He immediately noted that the guards playing cards had taken the brunt of the gas; they were immobilized. The two identical-twin professors sat at their table, shocked into inactivity in the middle of their work.

The other three guards had been sleeping, but now were awake, and snatching up their weapons. Maloko joined the rest of fourth squad in unleashing a compressed, gas-propelled volley of foot-long, slightly rifled needle-sharp bolts, complete with grooves filled with BlueRing Reef poison. Maloko's bolt caught the middle guard square in the chest. It went through him as though he wasn't there, and embedded itself in the wall, depositing a massive dose of poison from the bolt's groove all the way through the man's torso. He was dead before he hit the floor. The other two fared no better. The Tribe surrounded the two still-seated professors, a bit woozy from the small doses of gas they had received and from witnessing the rapid dispatch of their guards. Maloko strode to a position directly in front of them, holding his bolt-caster at the ready, even though it was not pointed at them.

"You will accompany us," he commanded.

The professors, in eerie identical motions, swallowed hard and nodded.

Maloko's eyes were drawn to a small pile of duffle bags nearby, and the strange weapon lying on top of one. "That must be the stuff they brought from the other universe. Grab it," he ordered. He took the weapon and inspected it.

"Ah, be careful with that," one of the LaGrues said nervously.

Must be useful, Maloko thought with a satisfied grin.

–45–

Johl, like Maloko, had been pleased with the way the straws were drawn. While not one to shy away from conflict, he was not one to seek it out when it was avoidable. Rescuing Tracey's friend from an island that was only sporadically visited by Stripes seemed easier than rescuing someone from the heart of New Sydney.

Peering through the binoculars at the island, he realized how wrong he had been.

"I should have taken more than twenty-five privateers," he signed to the man nearest him. The Tribesman nodded. "And more heavy weapons," he signed back.

It was night, with a nearly full moon. They had made their way through the territory controlled by Stingray Reef by giving them gifts of cotton cloth captured from a Stripe cargo ship. They then crept through the barrier reef of the atoll, avoiding the huge sharks that patrolled the perimeter.

Those sharks! Johl had never seen their like. He had learned about an extinct species called the Megalodon in school, and these were that big. Why they were patrolling this island only was open to speculation: whether they had been somehow compelled to guard this island or whether the island itself had been chosen because the sharks continually circled it. Not that it mattered. He had almost lost a privateer on the way through the reef.

I hope this Smithson guy can swim, he thought.

The bad luck continued: They had managed to come on a night where the Stripes were there. Lots of them. He tried counting them in the light of the bonfires they had lit, but they were constantly milling around. He estimated at least seventy five, with three transport ships and at least ten individual craft. Five of those one-man fliers were in the air, bobbing around over the crowd to get a better view. He rubbed his face with seawater.

"Do we try to wait until they leave? Come back another night with more weaponry?" the Tribesman next to him hand-signed.

Johl considered this. He did not like being trapped between hostile enemies on land and giant sharks just out of tooth-range behind them, but there was no reason not to wait. Even in broad daylight, the aircraft would be hard pressed to discover them underwater with active camouflage. He could just wait until they left, then grab the guy and go. Or come back another night. *If he was still alive. . . .*

He resumed his observation. The Stripes had made a large circle and were raising a loud roar of cheering, gesturing with fists in the air, and exchanging money.

What are they doing, making bets?

Presently he saw a skinny man with a bushy beard escorted to the center of the ring by two large Stripe troops. The crowd noise rose, a fever pitch of anticipation. It was obvious that the man was being made to fight for his life.

Johl lowered his binoculars. That had settled it.

He replaced his mask, signaled the other Tribe near him to submerge. He activated the keypad on his forearm computer, typed in battle instructions, and listened as the message was transmitted for miles around in a coded series of clicks and taps; indistinguishable from the background noise of the reef, but instantly deciphered by the other Tribe forearm computers. Even the sea Tribesmen out of view on the other side of the island were able to receive the message. If the amplitude were raised enough, the message could have been received by sensitive listening equipment at BlueRing Reef, over five hundred miles away.

He knew he had to take out their air cover. The Stripe tactic of dropping bombs onto the Tribe from above was devastating when close, and this was close enough. Once the air cover was out, though, he had to decide whether to try to take them all out, or to try to drive them out of the area. Ugly as it seemed, he decided to try to kill as many of them as possible. If enough of them were able to get away and regroup, it could prove disastrous for the men of the Tribe that he was responsible for.

One by one, the acknowledgements clicked back to his receiver. Weapons and equipment checked out. The five Privateers who were armed with mini javelins joined up to his right, one hundred yards down the beach nearest to where the aircraft were parked. Their orders were to disable as many of the craft as possible, fall back, and shoot down any other flying craft. Ten of his men were to beach themselves one hundred yards to his left, make their way as stealthily as possible inland, and flank them. Once things started in earnest, Johl would lead the remaining ten men in a direct assault from the beach and try to grab the man in the confusion. Having to keep the man alive complicated things. No gas, no explosions, no hitting him by shooting through Stripes.

The ten flankers, who had swum back from the far side of the island, crawled through the surf as close to the beach as possible before they rose in a crouch and dashed toward the vegetation near the beach. If he had not been watching for them, he would not have seen anything more than little patches of darkness move into the bushes. His heart beat faster, and he willed himself to calm his breathing. His vision sharpened, taking more of his surroundings in. The slap of the shallow waves, the milling crowd of Stripes . . . and the stars! He looked up at the sky, so often invisible above the surface of the sea. Having to hide from the Stripes kept them from seeing the stars at night.

Damn them!

He forced himself to focus back on the imminent battle. There would be time to gaze at the stars later.

He hoped the five aircraft saboteurs gave his flankers enough time to get into positions before they struck. It seemed to him like a long time passed, while the men started pitting the bearded man against a Stripe champion.

Suddenly, his wrist computer confirmed his teams' mini-javelins had locked onto targets. He imagined the heads-up displays of the javelin team, showing which flyer had been targeted, and following it with a red reticule. Now all they had to do was throw the hand-launched three-foot-long missile, which would ignite the solid chemical propulsion once it was far enough away from the caster not to burn him, home in on whatever it had been locked onto, and detonate.

There! Five bright flashes as the missiles ignited, and streaked into the five flyers hovering over the fight. They exploded hotly, raining flaming chunks of machinery and pilot down on the crowd below. The team had coordinated well, made sure that no two missiles had found the same mark. Johl hoped the team was even now running away from where they had made their casts to prevent the Stripes from following the smoke trails back to their positions.

Soon afterward there were ground explosions as javelins were hurled into parked aircraft.

The Stripes were quick to recover from their stunned inactivity, and started firing their guns into the brush in the general direction of where the privateers' javelins had come from. They poured such a volume of shot into the vegetation that Johl was sure his team would not escape unscathed.

Where is the flanking team? he thought with alarm. He decided instantly not to wait for them before committing his own force. Just as he gave the order to advance and attack, though, the flankers began pouring fire from their bolt-casters into the Stripe crowd. The bolt-casters, never making much noise when fired to begin with, made even less notice to the Stripes' ears dulled by their own gunfire. Many of them fell before they realized they were being shot. When they wheeled and fired into the brush where the flanking team were attacking from, Johl's own men raised up from the shallow water at the edge of the beach and began firing.

Johl forced himself to focus on shooting one Stripe trooper at a time, trying to concentrate on those who had guns and were turning them toward him. He shot one through the shoulder, ordinarily a non-fatal wound, but the bolts were grooved with instant-acting BlueRing Reef poison. The man clutched the bolt for an instant, then convulsed as though it were electrified, and fell like a stone. One of his privateers went down on his left. Johl fired again, and again. . . . He felt the internal clang of the firing piston hitting the empty chamber, and paused to slap another magazine of the foot-long bolts into the bottom of his caster. As he did this,

his eyes swiveled, seeking other targets, and rested on the bearded man. He was standing in the middle of the milling crowd of Stripes, stock still, eyes wide with disbelief. Men who had come to watch him fight, to bet on his survival or for his death, were falling around him.

In seconds, it was over. The gunfire had become more sporadic, then stopped as their magazines emptied out and no ammunition replaced it. Remaining Stripes ran into the woods, some falling to the knives of the flankers still concealed in the brush.

Johl regarded the bearded man, who returned his gaze under the bright canopy of the stars.

"Do you want us to pursue them?" one of the flankers called from the vegetation.

"Just follow them for a little while, make sure they keep running," he called back.

"I have seen you before," the bearded man said. "I took your spear gun away from you once."

Johl allowed his breath to return to near normal, and chuckled. "Don't worry. I got another one."

−46−

Cornish Bob, Dechambeau, Dog Face George, and Skunky slowly surrounded the old man, who stood passively but warily, still loosely holding his shotgun pointed at the ground. Black Taylor sauntered up the long driveway behind them, having cut the telephone wire.

Cornish Bob holstered his automatic Glock, then extended his hand for the old man to shake.

"'Ere, wos on there, bey? I'm Cornish Bob," he introduced himself. The old man extended his hand. Cornish Bob reached past it instead, and relieved the man of his shotgun.

"Damn," the old man croaked dryly.

"Oh, come now, Pops," Cornish Bob said. "You weren't going to scat us all over with that relic anyway. So what's yer name?"

"Silas Bell."

"Well, pleased to meet you, Mr. Bell."

He took the old man by the arm and escorted him to the door of his cinderblock house, accompanied by Dog Face George and Skunky. Black Taylor and Dechambeau took positions near the driveway to alert them to any visitors.

"Maybe you better go in and clear the area," Cornish Bob instructed Skunky. "Mr. Bell might not live alone, in spite of the overwhelming odds otherwise."

Skunky entered the door at a crouch, MP-5 submachine gun at the ready. A short time later, he called out that the house was clear. They entered. Cornish Bob glanced about, saw that the place was sparsely furnished with an old, dusty couch, some antique-looking chairs around a spindle-legged table, ancient stove, and a black-and-white television. There were piles of books, and numerous mineral samples, and various other knickknacks on shelves. It was dusty, but tidy.

"Home sweet home," he said with raised eyebrows. "All we need is a velvet picture of Jesus. Or at least some dogs playing poker."

Skunky emerged from a hallway that must have led to the bedroom, carrying an old revolver by the grip. "I found this on his bed table," he announced, surrendering it to Cornish Bob.

He examined it with a double take. "As I live and breathe—a British Bulldog!"

"How the hell did you know what that was?" the old man demanded.

Cornish Bob regarded him with a wink. "Oh, this ol' Cousin Jack knows a Bulldog when he sees one. Of course I haven't seen one for a long time."

The old man watched Cornish Bob toy with the gun for a while, then slip it into his pocket. "What do you want with me?" he asked.

"Mr. Bell, we would like you to accompany us on a little trip to your place of employment."

Silas Bell eyed them with a flash from his eyes. "I can't do that. The park is closed."

"Ah, yes." Cornish Bob nodded knowingly. "Some kind of chemical spill from the cyanide leaching process down at the Standard Stamp Mill, or some such other shyte. Come now, Mr. Bell, you know as well as I what the problem in Bodie really is."

Bell sat down on the dusty couch. "Actually, I don't. But the soldiers must."

"Yes, now we get to the heart of the matter," Bob continued, looking around the room at some of the relics. He discovered an item of interest, and picked it up with delight.

"A little opium bottle! How many of these have I seen? Why, I remember one particular 'soiled dove' young maiden of Bonanza Street I found dead in Bodie's Chinatown surrounded by several such bottles she had smoked—"

"Who the hell are you?" Bell growled.

Cornish Bob turned with a clever retort on his lips, but was struck dumb by the sight of the old man on the couch. He sat there unafraid, unbowed, almost regally. It was not his attire, which was pedestrian, or the fact that he was obviously a "colorful character" of the rural hills. Cornish

Bob could not put his finger on it. He was a man that the words "larger than life" seemed to fit. He was struck with the words that had entered his head unbidden: "larger than life." It had never occurred to him to wonder what that meant. But here was an example of it, whatever it was, sitting before him. Most people, accosted by armed strangers in their home, would react with some measure of shock and trepidation. Not this one.

"Mr. Bell, why don't you tell *me* who I am? After all, when we first arrived, you told us that God Hisself told you we were coming."

The old man removed his hat and scratched the matted gray hair that remained on his scalp. "He did. It was in a dream. I don't remember much of it, though."

"What *do* you remember?" Cornish Bob asked. He knew better than to take dreams for granted.

Bell's eyes strayed out the louvered window up the sandy, sage-dotted hillside that rose behind his house. He pointed up the hill, where a barely visible foot path switch-backed to a spot about three-fourths of the way to the top. "I've dug a trench up there. It gives a command over the road and everything for a wide stretch about. I have the top sandbagged. I dug it because I had an older dream that told me to. This dream, the one you all are in, shows you all in there getting shot up."

"Really?" Cornish Bob asked with exaggerated concern.

"But I had another dream afterward, and you were somewhere else. So maybe you aren't going to die up there like your friends here. Maybe God hasn't given up on you completely. Maybe the She Devil hasn't won you over all the way. Maybe you can break free of that bitch sponge yet."

It was Cornish Bob's turn to react with shock. "How the hell did you know that? Who are you?"

Silas Bell's eyes twinkled as he put his hat back on. "Oh, this ol' Clamper knows demon zombies when he sees em'. I haven't seen any for a long time, though."

Cornish Bob's eyes narrowed. He glanced at Skunky and Dog Face George, who were watching him curiously.

"Why don't you boys go scout out this trench up there. I'll

be okay watching Pappy here."

The two of them shuffled out, with sideways glances at Cornish Bob and Silas Bell sitting serenely on the couch.

Bob waited for them to get out of earshot. "All right, Mister Bell," he said, wagging his index finger. "Just how did you know about *Her*? She's in another universe. Are you from there?"

Bell shook his head, puzzled. "No, I'm just a humble servant of God, given certain knowledge in dreams, and whispered to by our big brothers, the spirits."

"You are one of those Trident guys, aren't you? The keepers of the secret fire, and all that?"

Bell shrugged. "Guilty as charged."

"I thought you guys were all super-trained martial artists and wizards and such."

Silas smiled lopsidedly. "We all have different talents."

"So yours must be cavorting with spirits. By that, do you mean the aliens? The ones she is fighting?" Cornish Bob asked with a sudden surge of . . . what was that? Fear or hope? He had never actually seen one of her enemies face-to-face until that pirate woman. Now a second one. Would this one try to recruit him, too?

"You could call them that." Silas shrugged. "Spirits, angels, aliens in another dimension. They don't live in the universes like we do. We have to jump from bubble to bubble; they travel through the water between."

"But I thought they couldn't enter the bubbles," Bob said, confused.

"Not directly. Not entirely, anyway. Some of their intermediaries can appear to us as humans, but if they appeared as their true selves, and touched us physically, the raw power of it would scatter us like dust. But they can whisper to us. Or visit us in dreams. When they talk to us while awake, they are easier to hear out in the middle of nowhere, in the desert, or in vast places, like the sea or in space. That is the most they do in our world, anyway. In yours, they send their awareness through little flying animals that look like pickles."

Cornish Bob nodded. Eiffelia had never told him any of

this. That explained her "kill on sight" orders for the flying pickles. "Why are you telling me all this? I'm a servant of your enemy. There is a war going on."

Bell spread his hands. "There is no war. Not the one you are thinking about, anyway. Not with starships, lasers, bombs, and guns. She is pitting you against yourselves unknowingly. She controls both those armies, each thinking they're fighting an alien enemy. It's all just to make casualties for food, and to give each side something to focus on other than her. No, the real war is from within." He paused, as though listening. "Us and the Un-numbered. The Sea Tribes. Yes, that is what you call them."

"Who are you listening to?" Bob demanded, with a rush of adrenaline. "Is one of them with us here? In this room?"

Silas Bell merely regarded him with a plain expression.

Cornish Bob stared intently around, at the air, at the motes of dust playing in the sunbeams that entered through the windows.

"You won't see them that way," Bell said, almost a whisper.

They regarded each other quietly for a long time.

"What do they want with us?" Bob asked.

"They love us. That's all. Because God made us all, and they want to share in the reason he did so. They participate in the great story, harmony in the endless symphony, the music of the spheres, from the elementary strings to entire universes."

"What are they doing now?"

Bell's eyes drifted off, listening. "Well, they're telling me you should check your email. Whatever that means."

"Email comes to us over the Internet," Bob explained. "Mine can come from the other universe's Internet, too."

"I know what email is, you dumbass. I mean I don't know why *they* wanted you to check yours. Geez."

"How the hell am I supposed to know what you backwards yahoo hillbillies know or not," Bob muttered with raised eyebrow. "I'd be surprised if you have a feckn' flush toilet in here." He retrieved his familiar, and adjusted the projection from the snake's head. Sure enough, there was finally a message from Tracey in his inbox.

Tell Ron I'm heading for the Nero Deep now.

He blinked at the message for a minute, then, overcome with a sudden urge quite beyond his volition, forwarded it to Ron's address.

Within seconds, like the last time, the reply appeared:

Bob: Any chance you can get me out of here before she drops her nuke?

"Nuke?" he said aloud. "What feckin' nuke? Tracey doesn't have a bomb. Why does that idiot think she does?"

"Maybe because Ron knows how big Eiffelia really is, and Tracey doesn't. She thinks Eiffelia is a wee little sponge that she can kill with poison," Bell interjected quietly.

"Damn," Cornish Bob spat out. "Now what am I supposed to do?"

"You could get her a bomb, of course."

He shook his head. "It wouldn't work. Eiffelia's too big, and has other universes she lives in, even if we had a whole string of nukes."

"There may be a way. Have faith."

There it is, that word. The one thing that Eiffelia had drilled into him was the fatal flaw of the enemy. They had their own agenda, they lied, they hid behind the false love, the false benevolence. How could he believe their lies any more than hers, with no hard evidence? At least she offered more than blind trust. She offered at least the illusion of reason.

Cornish Bob hung his head. His pain rose, like a tide. He shook a handful of antacids into his mouth. It seemed as though a prison door had been unlocked and left open. It had been so long since he had tasted the wild possibilities of freedom, though, that the security of the cold walls and three regular meals, however insipid, was preferable. *It's too late,* he thought.

"This is a load of crap," he smirked, shaking his head. "All that Kum-bay-ya drivel. If they can blast matter into dust, why don't they just go in and scat her down! Like I could do to you!" He snapped the barrel of his pistol to press on the middle of Silas Bell's forehead.

Bell sat impassively. "They don't work that way. Not yet, anyway. And believe it or not, she is not the main focus. The work needs to be done slowly, by choice, not force, and on a much grander scale."

"Well, you have a lot of work to do, me bey. And for now anyway, she *better* be the main focus."

Dog Face George chose that moment to stick his head back through the door. "Hey, we checked out that trench," he began, then took in the scene, Bob's gun still pressed to Bell's forehead, and froze. "Everything okay? He try something?"

"It's fine, me 'ansum," Cornish Bob drawled. "Just making a point."

"This could be your last chance," Silas Bell stated, gazing directly into Cornish Bob's eyes.

Dog Face George guffawed. "Looks like it's *your* last chance, dumb fuck."

Cornish Bob's mouth worked slowly into a half smile, all while keeping the gun on Bell.

"I think it's time," Bob said, "to take a little ride to my old stompin' grounds of Bodie. Let's take your truck." He walked Silas out of his house, grabbing the keys to the old Graham on the way. "You drive," he instructed Silas Bell, "and you pieces of shyte sit in the back."

They piled in.

He nudged Bell with the end of the gun. "Drive, Gramps."

The old man laboriously started the engine. He animatedly worked the gears, and the truck lurched and bumped a wobbly path down the dirt track driveway, then down the dusty, hard-scraped, washboard road toward the park.

They passed through steep-sided canyons, followed a creek, and climbed hills that went higher and higher and were dotted with tailing piles, always scanning the terrain for any signs of soldiers, artillery, and armor.

"What exactly is the plan here, genius?" Silas asked.

"Well," Cornish Bob said, head still swiveling about for the military, "I thought we would stank up to the park and take a peek around. You know. Just drive there and back."

"And then you will let me go?"

"Oh, probably. We need you to get us past any checkpoints. At some point, assuming that works, I hope we can get a more modern vehicle. If so, and if you aren't riddled with holes by then, we'll just let you go and be on our way. Whoops—"

They had come upon a checkpoint, but not exactly as Bob was expecting. A Winnebago was parked on the side of the road, with several "tourists" lounging around it. Bob was suspicious, from their bearing and haircuts, that they were soldiers.

"You want me to stop?" Bell asked quietly.

Bob considered. It wasn't as though they were openly showing their military force—maybe they would let them through. Or, even better, maybe he could find a way to commandeer their vehicle. "Go on up there," he instructed.

Two of the soldiers stood leisurely in the road as they approached. One of them held up his hand, and they stopped. Cornish Bob dug the barrel of his Glock in Bell's ribs, keeping it hidden but obviously present. The four men in the back, taking their cues from Bob, kept their weapons out of sight as well.

One of the disguised soldiers strolled to the driver's side door, and Silas Bell rolled down the window.

"Don't bother going on, you could get in trouble," the man said, taking the opportunity to scan around the cab of the truck. "They told us that the road to the park is closed. We're just here waiting to see if they open it up later."

Bell remained silent. Cornish Bob prodded him with his gun. Bell kept his tongue, to Cornish Bob's annoyance.

"This man works there at the park," he volunteered.

"There were some military people around earlier, and they told us that nobody is allowed in there. There has been a chemical spill," the man said, scrutinizing them all carefully. Silas Bell ignored him, stared fixedly down the road, knuckles white on the steering wheel.

The "stranded tourist" started backing away, suspicious. "I'll call on my cell phone to see if it is open yet," he said, reaching for the phone on his belt.

Skunky, in the back of the truck, had not heard what the man said, and saw him reaching for what appeared to him to be a gun. Impulsively, he reared up from the back of the truck, leaned over the top of the cab, and fired.

Dust flew off the man's chest as the bullets struck him, and he spun off the road into the creek bed that the road was following.

"Damn!" Cornish Bob snapped, breaking out his window with his machine pistol and bringing it to bear on the second soldier, who was backing down the road toward the RV with a shocked expression, reaching for what must have been a gun in his belt.

All four of the men in the back opened fire on the man, who managed to duck behind the RV for cover, returning fire. The soldier in the ditch, who must have been wearing body armor, also produced a pistol and began firing.

Strangely, the RV, which should have been riddled with holes and have its tires shredded, was untouched.

"Get us out of here, old man!" Cornish Bob yelled over the roar of the gunfire.

Bell stood on the clutch and worked the stick shift into reverse. He had just started crawling back the road when a panel opened on top of the RV, revealing what looked like a tank gun.

"Oh, *shyte*," Cornish Bob groaned.

The RV opened fire with a roar. The shell flew right over the roof of the cab and passed cleanly through Skunky, who looked through the hole it made with a sour expression, then resumed shooting.

Cornish Bob laughed. "*That* will give them teasy fucks something to chew on!"

The RV fired again. This time, the shell impacted on the rock wall beside them.

The shell exploded. The concussion, flame, shrapnel, and rock fragments sprayed among them. The windshield and windows were blown out, and all four of Cornish Bob's team were hurled onto their backs in the bed of the truck, peppered with fragments. Dechambeau's face and eyes were burned. Bell and Cornish Bob were coated with a mist of broken glass and dust, and the ringing in their ears was deafening. Even though stunned, Cornish Bob was able to reach across with his own leg and push the gas pedal down, then grab the wheel and guide the truck shakily backward.

It took the RV's gun crew a minute to incredulously note that the old truck was still moving, and mostly intact. They reloaded.

Bob managed to pilot the truck around a corner, out of the line of fire, and back it off the road. Silas Bell recovered enough to grab the wheel back, jerk the stick shift into first gear, and retreat down the road as fast as the old truck could limp.

Bob looked in the shattered remains of the mirror frame, and with a sickening feeling, saw the RV emerge from around the corner they had just rounded.

"Gun it, man!" Cornish Bob bellowed, then yanked open his door and hung out of the cab as far as he dared, firing back at the tank, hoping to slow it down or deflect its aim.

It was as they rounded the second curve that the RV fired again. Again, whether due to the curving road, or Bob's firing, or by pure luck, the shell was not directly on target. Once again it impacted the embankment. The blast wave missed the truck, but picked Cornish Bob off the side of the cab and blew him into the air like a bug. He felt himself sailing crazily, saw that he was going over the edge of the road down into the gully with the creek in the bottom. He slammed into the ground, tumbling in the rocks. He came to a rest. He felt water on his face, and heard the gurgling of a stream, as though it was at the end of a long, echoing tunnel. A pinpoint of light was all he could see, in a hazy sea of pain. After a moment, even those things drifted into welcome blackness.

−47−

Cornish Bob Golden lay in the ditch, in the dark. How long he had been there, he did not know, but it was now night.

It hurt. Everything hurt. He tasted grit in his mouth, and his tongue found a hole where a tooth had been.

He willed himself to action, and found that he could move his right leg. He pulled it up beside his ribs, and pushed himself through the dust and gravel toward the sound of the water flowing in the creek nearby. The dust choked his parched throat.

Don't die, don't die. . . .

His left leg worked, too, as did his arms. Sharp pains in his chest informed him that he had broken ribs. His back worked, though. Typical for a Cornish miner. Cousin Jacks never break their backs.

Due to the zombification process, he knew the injuries wouldn't actually kill him, but when his body was as damaged and disjointed as his unintentional flight and hard landing caused, it all hurt and it might not work at all well. He rolled over onto his back and stared at the starry sky, the gentle current of the stream running against the back of his head.

It occurred to him that his hat was missing. It further occurred to him that this was the least of his worries, and thought it funny that he was worried about his stupid hat.

With a certainty that came from nowhere but could not be denied, he knew that he was supposed to be dead. Eiffelia had set him up.

He lay there, wondering what to do.

He could not go back to her. She would simply get rid of him, either by sending him on another doomed-to-fail mission, or by just having him killed without that pretense. She must have found out about the emails, or must have read his growing distaste of his "work" as a dangerous trend.

Either way, his time as her servant was over. The only choice was where and how to run.

First, he wondered why he wasn't already dead. Eiffelia had obviously sent him to Bodie to be killed, but would not have risked losing his rift generator. It was precious, and would have been given to his replacement.

That meant that she had intended to have at least one of his team members survive, in order to retrieve the thing. *A team member who had agreed to betray him.* The fact that he was still alive meant that this team member, whoever it was, was dead. He wondered who the traitor was. Black Taylor? Dog Face George? Dechambeau? Certainly not Skunky; he was too stupid. *Could the traitor still be alive, on his way back to Her?* He remembered back to the adrenaline-soaked dash away from the RV with the tank gun, and was convinced that they were dead. Probably the whole team, because not one of them, traitor or not, had come back looking for him.

Nor had the soldiers. Maybe they hadn't seen him fly from the truck, or maybe they just missed him in their grid search. Either way, he didn't care. He was still alive. He still had the rift generator. Or did he? He checked his pocket. Yes, it was still there. He pulled it out and turned it on; it still worked. Unable to support it with his aching neck, his head plopped back into the creek.

Good. I'm in business.

Now what?

He had two options. Run, and keep running, from time-line to time-line and universe to universe; or go to ground somewhere she had little chance of finding him.

Running did not appeal to him. He was tired. He was done. He could try to keep one step ahead of Eiffelia, but the thought of fleeing her for the rest of his days was not something he had the stomach for.

So where to hide? He could go back in time to the point where Eiffelia was a tiny sponge and kill her, but that would only generate a new universe, with the possibility that human beings wouldn't evolve at all, and leave this one intact. There would be nothing remotely familiar to return to in the new one. He had to get rid of her in this universe, instead. That was unlikely, but he could throw her off his trail by helping Ron and Tracey nuke her, then run back to the past. Somewhere he could hide effectively. She'd think he'd go on the run, anyway. And if he did get caught, then so be it. He decided to go back to his life in Bodie, at the moment he discovered the rift, and pick up his life where he left off. He would make his stand there, starting in July, 1879, and finish his life like a man. However long that would be.

Loose ends: He had to get Julia back to her cot in 1862. It was the gentlemanly thing to do. And why not give the rift generator to Ron? Bob decided that he wouldn't have any use for it back in the past, things would be better without the temptation to use it. And maybe, just maybe, even if she *did* find him, when she found out that he didn't have the rift generator, she would let him live. Better to let Ron inherit it. Maybe Ron could use it to run from Eiffelia himself. She would definitely want the rift generator back. Ron could get farther, last longer as a relative youngster, especially without the need of the rejuvenation bath.

He felt better having decided what to do, lying there with his head in the creek in the dark. Now to formulate a plan and implement it. And soon, before she sent another team looking for the rift generator on his presumed corpse.

Ron and Julia were in Eiffelia's underwater base at the bottom of the Marianna Trench. All he had to do was get a nuclear bomb, then use the rift generator to appear in the base. He would leave the armed nuke, then jump to Washington in 1862 to leave Julia on her cot to wake up and live her life out, then jump ahead seventeen years to Bodie. He would bid goodbye and good luck to Ron, who could use the rift generator to get back to his time.

Easy.

First, he had to get Ron's GPS coordinates. He retrieved his snake familiar, and typed another encrypted email to Ron into the projected screen:

Ron, send me your GPS coordinates. It occurred to him that Ron may not know how to find those out, so he added: *Use the pull down menu on the main screen to access "tools" and then select "GPS." When that screen pops up, tap on the "Current Coordinates" line, then reply to this email with what it tells you.*

Satisfied, he hit the send button. Ron had always responded quickly in the past, so he waited for a moment. This time, there was no reply. Cornish Bob grunted in frustration. Maybe Ron wasn't sitting at his screen this time, damn him. Meanwhile, he could at least grab the nuclear warhead.

He typed in the video message address of the captain of the *Centurion*, careful to block the camera that would display him on the captain's screen. After a few moments, a junior Stripe officer appeared on the screen.

"Without your camera working I can't do a retina scan. Identify," the officer commanded curtly.

"Cornish Bob Golden, contacting Captain Severens of the *Centurion*, authentication Zebra, Zebra, 229-6."

There was a pause while the officer consulted a computer screen off camera. Bob sweated. He was supposed to be dead. It was possible that Eiffelia had not communicated this to the *Centurion*, though.

"I'll patch you through," the officer said distractedly, "but be brief, we're right in the middle of an action."

Captain Severens, resplendent in red lightning-bolt painted face, appeared on the tiny screen. "Bob, good to hear from you. I had heard that your mission failed, and the Goddess ordered us to make the raid anyway. We're right in the middle of it now."

"I'm the only survivor. She's ordered me to dust off to your location immediately to assist. What are your coordinates?"

The captain read off a series of numbers, pinpointing the *Centurion's* location. Cornish Bob tapped them into the navigation screen of his rift generator.

"Thanks, Cap'n. I'll be stank'n over dreckly."

He terminated the call. No time to waste. He could be asking Eiffelia what to do at this very moment.

His email inbox chimed. It was a reply from Ron, right on cue. It was a GPS position. Bob scrutinized the coordinates carefully. They didn't look like they were anywhere near the

Marianna Trench.

No time to wonder about that. He pulled up the schematic plans for the *Centurion*, and with a sweating brow, calculated his jump to appear right in the nuclear warhead armory bay.

His thumb hesitated over the launch button.

Here we go. No turning back now.

He pressed the button and was hurled through the void into the *Centurion*.

–48–

Ron tried to keep track of the confusion, but it was all but impossible. Everyone was speaking at once. He was in the main meeting hall of BlueRing Reef, where he and Julia had been taken after being shot down by the Tribe miles to the north. Fortunately, the Tribesmen had been aiming to down the aircraft intact, and the Tribesmen had let them live long enough for him to explain who he was. Now he stood in the midst of the loudly chattering crowd, feeling odd being dressed in an orange yukata with wave patterns. He tried to follow what was going on.

Braun argued with Johl and Maloko about what to do about the swarms of aircraft that were patrolling the entire region since he and Julia had escaped, shooting at anything that showed its head above the surface of the sea.

A man with black-rimmed glasses and a patchy beard handed him a drink of what tasted like whisky. He was fat, if not big-boned, and looked like he could fit in at any video game convention Ron had ever been to.

"Thanks," Ron said, extending his hand. "I'm Ron Golden."

"Jack Strong," the man said, shaking hands.

Ron did a classic cartoon double-take. "Hey, you're the guy we were supposed to find and bring back to our universe!"

"Guilty as charged." Strong grinned. "You are the double Pangborn recessive in your team, I presume."

"Guilty as well," Ron said, feeling like they were members of a special club. "Well, mission accomplished; I found you. Where are you from?"

"In our universe? Boston."

"Ugh. You must be a Patriots fan. That Super Bowl was a disaster."

"We made it to the Super Bowl again? Cool! Did we win?"

Ron remembered that Strong had been out of the universe for a few years.

"Yeah, they won. They beat my Seahawks. We have play-calling issues to discuss."

"The *Seahawks* made it to the big game? Hell, I *have* been gone a long time."

The two Professor LaGrues stood next to each other, listening. They simultaneously scratched their noses with their left hands, Ron noted with uneasiness.

Rosa watched the two scientists suspiciously.

Julia Ward Howe listened to the babble as if this were all normal to her.

Smithson, newly fed and scrubbed, stood like a much leaner sun-blasted desert prophet, eyes now brimming over with a cold wrath. He had been reunited with his bag of weapons recovered from New Sydney. The XM8 machine gun with the flaming-acid shooting attachment hung from a sling around his shoulder. He looked comfortable in his blue-and-white yukata.

Tracey had sent a message that she would be arriving soon. It was while he was responding to this email from Tracey's computer that Cornish Bob had emailed, requesting his GPS coordinates, which he promptly sent. Tracey seemed to have made quite the impression around the Reef. It was only by mentioning her name that he and Julia had been not only allowed to live, but be treated like royalty. Her complex was spectacular. One of Tracey's new employees, Rosa, had started to tell him something about Tracey and a man she was traveling with, Dory. She had thought better of it apparently. Ron was left to wonder.

A young boy appeared at the entrance to the meeting hall, and the animated discussions dropped off to silence as the assembly noticed he was there.

"What is it, Hatsu?" one of the Tribe asked, who Ron remembered was named Johl.

"They are back. Andrea is bringing them here," the boy announced.

Ron excused himself from Strong, and took a few steps toward the doorway in anticipation. They waited in silence for a short while, then he heard the slap of bare feet in the corridor.

There she was. Tracey. Looking . . . radiant, still in her octopus tentacle and skull and crossbones decorated gillsuit. Ron's breath caught. Following closely behind, in a very familiar manner, his arm almost but not quite around her waist, was a bearded man.

She saw Ron. Her eyes widened, jaw dropped with shock. "Ron! My God, I thought you were still trapped at the bottom of the trench!"

He started toward her, thinking that she would run to meet him, but she did not. He slowed and approached her more slowly, confused. "I got away."

They stood looking at each other, while the assembly looked at them tensely.

What the hell is going on here? "Aren't you glad to see me?" he asked.

"Of course. I'm just . . . surprised."

"This is the man you are with?" Dory growled.

"I was just about to ask the same thing," Ron said.

Tracey's face flushed red. "Ron, this is Dory. He is . . . *was*, my husband. I mean, the husband of my . . . of the Tracey who lived in this universe."

Dory glowered at Ron, who looked back and forth between the bearded man and Tracey.

"Uh . . . are you . . . ?"

"Later, Ron. We'll talk later. First, I have to get this down to my labs." She produced a scrap of sponge.

Ron instinctively recoiled in horror. "Holy *shit*. Is that what I think it is?"

"If you think it is a piece of Eiffelia the goddess sponge, it is."

"How did you . . . you have to kill it. Now! Get rid of the thing!"

"Hold on there, Ron. I have to test it, to see what kind of poison will kill this species."

"Poison?" he asked. "Poison won't work. She's too big. We need the bomb that you and Cornish Bob were getting."

Tracey looked at him askance. "Bomb? What bomb?"

"The nuclear bomb . . . that you . . . oh shit. You mean you haven't been setting this up with Cornish Bob?"

She looked at him dumbfounded.

Ron crumbled. "We're fucked," he whispered.

"No, we're not," she said cheerfully. "We can use poison. You say she's big, but I've never heard of a sponge species bigger than a few yards across."

Ron shook his head. "Try *miles* across. Try 'filling up the whole bottom of the trench' across. Try five-hundred-million-years-of-growing across."

Ron watched as recognition of the scale of the problem slowly dawned on her. Her shoulders sagged. "Sponges don't have a centralized vascular system," she said. "They are really just a collection of specialized cells, living in a collective. Not really a single animal, as we know them, at all. You're right. If she's that big, we *are* fucked."

"No bomb, no poison."

"No prayer," she finished.

"Wait," Ron said, melodramatically, "we may have a slim chance." He crossed to the baggage Johl recovered from New Sydney that contained the cargo they'd brought with them from their own universe.

"I think I may have left it in here," he said, rooting around. "Aha!" he cried, and produced, with a flourish, the lint shirt. "Now we have a chance."

Tracey closed her eyes, praying for his death.

"Hey, last time I wore it, Cornish Bob showed up." He put the shirt on, over his orange yukata.

"Ron, you are a moron," Tracey mouthed.

"Again, this is the man you were with in your world?" Dory commented, with an arched eyebrow.

Tracey gave him a withering glance.

It was at that moment that Cornish Bob Golden appeared with a yellow flash of light in the center of the room, out of nowhere, with a large, complicated mechanical device beside him.

For a long moment, there was absolute silence in the chamber, as all eyes focused on the short man, who quickly got his bearings. It appeared as though he had expected to appear somewhere else.

The moment seemed to last an eternity, but in unison, everyone in the room with a weapon brought it to bear on the diminutive form. Julia rushed to his side protectively when she saw all the weapons brought to bear.

Cornish Bob dropped to the floor, arms outstretched. "Don't shoot," he squeaked.

Nobody did. They all stood motionless, weapons at the ready, trigger fingers straining.

Ron sidled over to where Cornish Bob lay. "See?" he said stupidly. "Lucky shirt strikes again." He reached down a hand, and Cornish Bob took it, and struggled weakly to his feet.

"You look like hell," Ron said. The small man was bruised, abraded, and there was a large patch of dried black blood on his scalp. One of his front teeth was missing.

"Not half as bad as I feel, me bey. And you should see the other guy!"

"You brought the bomb, I see."

"The question," Smithson said, centering the red dot of his scope on the exact middle of Cornish Bob's neck, "is whether he brought it here to give it to us or to use it on us."

"I don' hear no tick'n." Cornish Bob smiled with a wink. He eyed Smithson warily, remembering back to that day in the bar where he had knifed Ginon 22. "I nabbed this right out from under Eiffelia's nose, and want you to scat her upside the head with it."

One or two of the weapons were lowered.

"Oh come on, think about it. If I was going to use this feck'n *nuclear warhead* on you, I'd be in the next county already."

Finally, even Smithson lowered his gun.

"Whew," Cornish Bob pantomimed, chuckled, and wiped his brow.

Eiffelia chose that moment to appear. At the front of the room, tall, imposing, glowing, her pupil-less eyes narrow, her face frozen with a smile that seemed more of a snarl. "Good work, Bob," she intoned. "Now set the charge and let's be off."

Instantly, half of the spear guns leveled at her, while the

other half and the machine gun snapped back to fire at Cornish Bob. Ron leaped in front of him, joining Julia, arms raised.

"Whoa, whoa there! Hold your fire," Ron cried, voice wavering. "She's lying. She's just trying to get you all to do her dirty work, since she can't kill him herself."

Whether to avoid hitting Ron and Julia or because they believed him, nobody fired.

Eiffelia tilted her head. "Well, you can't blame me for trying. But I am *very* disappointed with you, Bob. You are a traitor. And like all traitors, you will die a miserable, horrible death. Either sooner, by the hands of my soldiers, or later, by rotting. And when I say 'sooner,' I mean very soon. My forces will be encircling you within the hour. I think five thousand of my holy soldiers are enough—"

"How the hell did you get in here?" Ron asked.

Eiffelia turned her attention to him. "I come where I wish," she said serenely.

"Feckn' liar," Cornish Bob snapped. "You can only appear where you have a globe." He glanced around the room. "Who has a prayer globe?" He looked at the LaGrues. "Is it you?"

The scientists shook their heads in unison.

"The only way she can appear without a globe is when some of her living cells are present," Bob announced. "That is what makes the prayer globes work. So who has sponge cells in here?"

"I worked hard to get this, but it turned out useless," Tracey said, producing the sponge sample. She threw it in the middle of the room, nodded to Smithson.

"You better back up," Smithson warned, preparing the flaming acid thrower on his XM8.

The Tribe crowded away from the little mass of sponge to the fringes of the meeting room.

"What clever little humans you are," Eiffelia said. "I should have kept silent, and continued to learn what I could of your secrets. It was just too good a chance of killing the traitor to pass up, though."

Smithson took a firing position near the center of the room.

"And what secrets I have discovered," she continued, unconcerned. "I had no idea your reefs were so big, and that there were so many of you. And who was here. And the gold that was here. All right here, in BlueRing Reef. The traitor, with his rift generator; the fighting instructor; my scientists; and especially my new recruit, Ron."

"New recruit, my ass," Ron growled. "All that talk of paying me off with cheat codes. You don't have any such thing."

"Ah, Ron, but I do. At least, Cornish Bob has them. What do you think that rift generator is?"

"Cornish Bob may have one, but you don't, because you don't have Cornish Bob. And you know why? You're no fun. Your 'cheat codes' ruin the game, kill the flow. So he quit you, and I would never join you. Only cheaters and small-minded people do."

"Fry the bitch," Cornish Bob hissed.

Smithson let loose a cloud of flaming acid at the little sponge.

"Goodbye," Eiffelia said, fading. "Willing or not, see you soon, Ron."

Then she was gone, leaving nothing but a greasy streak on the sandy floor and the acrid odor of acidic smoke.

They all stood looking at each other in silence, then bedlam erupted, all speaking at once.

"Thank *God*," boomed Julia Ward Howe.

"So that was the great Eiffelia? I'm not impressed," Tracey said.

"Is she gone? Really gone this time?" Rosa asked.

The LaGrues wailed in pain and fell to their knees with grief.

"*Enough!*" bellowed Braun. The talking died down. "She said that there was an attack heading this way. We need to lay our defensive plans out *now* and get moving."

"Why doesn't she just bomb us? She could nuke this whole Reef from space," Smithson said.

"It's me. She wants me back for my genes," Ron said. "She wants to use me to keep a universe somewhere from collapsing. One that has gold in it, most likely."

"Suggestions on strategy?" Braun invited.

"Fight them," Maloko volunteered.

"Evacuate," Johl countered, glancing at his children.

"We can do both," Tracey said. "Get out who we can and leave a force to fight them and cover their escape."

Braun nodded. "Yes, that way we won't have to worry about keeping the non-combatants safe. Frees us up to just concentrate on taking out as many of them as possible. We will have to allocate some forces to escorting the refugees, though."

"Hello? Are we forgetting we have a bomb?" Cornish Bob asked.

"Yes, what to do about that—we can't just leave it here for her to take back," Braun said.

"Drop it on the bitch," Tracey said. "I don't care if it isn't big enough to kill her. It'll *hurt*."

"Hey, what is the yield of that bomb, anyway?" Smithson asked Cornish Bob.

"Twenty-five megatons," he answered gravely.

Smithson whistled. "Hell, most of the USA's warheads are around one megaton."

"I know, it's a big one, but still not enough to do more than hurt her."

"We have to do more than just hurt her," Ron said, shaking his head. "You saw how long it took her to fade from here, while she was getting fried by flaming acid. Smithson had to kill *every cell*. There has to be a way."

"We have scientists," Smithson said, indicating the LaGrues with the barrel of his gun. "Why can't they come up with a plan to kill it?"

"We refuse," they said in unison, then looked at each other and laughed. They made exaggerated gestures to indicate that each was deferring to the other to speak. One of them finally did.

"Eiffelia is our Lord and Goddess. She saved us from our Atheistic damnation-worthy error. We will never cooperate to harm her in any way, even if it is true that her physical form is in reality a giant sponge. This theory is ridiculous, by the way."

"Hey, not only is she a giant sponge," Ron said, shaking his finger at them, "but she's Satan too: I mean really, the Devil!"

The two LaGrues looked at each other and burst into laughter.

Tracey shook her head. "I read that in your email; what the hell were you talking about?"

"Later," Ron said. "I guess we both have some explaining to do."

"Ron is right," Braun interrupted. "Time is wasting. We have her soldiers on the way now, unless she was lying about that, too."

"Probably not," Cornish Bob said quietly. "She enjoys the idea of her victims suffering in terror before the axe falls." *Not to mention the fact that she has never seen a James Bond movie.*

"I have an idea," Jack Strong, who had stood quietly on one side of the room the whole time, said.

"Please, inform us," Braun said.

"Why don't we take the scientists back to our universe?"

Ron watched them all run through the ramifications of this in their minds. The professors would revert back to how LaGrue was in our universe—both of them! They could then come up with a strategy for using the atomic bomb to kill Eiffelia.

"Yes, yes!" Ron said, his enthusiasm growing. "You could take him through, Jack, since part of our original mission was to get you back to our universe in the first place."

"How do we get the plan back to this universe?" Tracey asked.

"I'll go through the rift with them, and then bring the plan back," Smithson said. "She couldn't get rid of me the whole time I was on that damn island; I'll get back through whatever is getting thrown at us."

"We refuse," one of the LaGrues said.

Smithson strode menacingly close to them. "Okay," he said, quietly but forcefully, staring directly into their eyes. "You can either come voluntarily, or I can take great pleasure in bludgeoning your smarmy heads into unconsciousness and dragging you through the rift that way. You choose."

"No need to be rude," the other LaGrue protested with a wavering voice. "We'll cooperate, of course."

"It is decided, then," Braun said. "Smithson and Strong will take these scientists through the rift, where they will formulate the best way to use the bomb. We will evacuate the Reef, scatter like a school of fish when the shark comes. Volunteers will stay here and defend the Reef, holding out as long as we can, hopefully until Smithson gets back here with the plan. After that, those who can't help plant the bomb will swim for it. If we get overrun before they return from the other universe, the last person triggers the bomb. This Reef is doomed anyway, now that She knows where it is."

"What about you two?" Johl asked, looking back and forth between Ron and Tracey.

"My place is here, defending my Reef," Tracey said.

"Wait a minute! Am I hearing this correctly?" Ron asked incredulously. "You wanted to get back to your life, go to your job, raise the baby sea otter at the aquarium, take out the garbage—wait, make *me* take out the damn garbage—now you say you want to stay here, in an alternate universe, and fight Stripes? Instead of going *home*?"

"You don't get it, Ron," she said, quietly but forcefully, "this *is* my home. As much as it is there, anyway. But there is nobody threatening my world there. Besides, I am needed here. I have people depending on me. Employees, friends. Not to mention my holdings. And besides, who else is going to get the bomb to where it is supposed to go?"

He looked at her with growing incomprehension. "What do you mean how are we supposed to get the bomb where it's supposed to go? You think *you're* going to get it there? How?"

Ron saw that others were curious about her last statement as well.

"Don't ask. Just trust me, if I need to get the bomb to a certain spot, I'll be able to make it happen. I should be able to, anyway. I might. Okay, it *is* a long shot possibility."

"What the hell are you talking about?" Ron asked.

She sighed. "Look, Ron, a lot has happened. I don't have time to explain now. Just tell me where you want the bomb, get it to the surface, and I will take it to whatever spot you need, however deep you need it to go."

Ron looked at her, uncomprehending. Dory looked at her with obvious pride. Braun, seeing Dory's reaction, guessed what she was talking about. Cornish Bob, without understanding, grasped the tactical ramifications of her claim, and took Ron by the arm.

"Look, Ron, don't over-analyze this stuff. We are in a different universe here, with different ground rules. Let's just get the scientists and Strong back through the rift with your bald ninja here, let him get the plan back, and we'll play it by ear from there. I have a wee side trip planned for you, and need your help with it. What do you say?"

Ron nodded, rolling his eyes and shrugging with his hands. "I have to stay here," he said. "At least until the evacuation is finished. If the Stripes think I'm not here, there's nothing to stop them from just bombing this place out of existence. I'm the only thing keeping them from doing that, forcing them to come in with soldiers to try to take me alive."

"Shyte," Cornish Bob said. He scratched his head. "How about this. You take that nasty shirt of yours and put it on someone else, say, like Johl, or Maloko, or even Dory, there. That way, if they see someone wearing that shirt, they'll think it's you. And I can get you back here anyway in a jiff. You won't be gone long, and trust me, it'll be worth it to you."

"I'll take the shirt," Maloko said, relishing the thought of getting the Stripe soldiers to chase him.

Ron reluctantly removed the lint shirt and handed it over. "I want this back when I get back here," he demanded, wagging his finger.

"What is the best way of getting me and the scientists and Strong through the rift?" Smithson asked. "Do we have a flyer, or a boat, or do we take a sled?"

"I'll handle that, too," Cornish Bob said. "I have a rift generator. I'll take all of you to the rift over the mining platform that connects to Bodie. We can even take a personal flier along, so that when Smithson gets back through with the bomb target location, he can get it here quickly."

"So be it," Braun said, his blood up. "Let's get going, we

have an evacuation, a defense of our reef, and a bomb attack to execute."

With a swish of yukatas, they all quickly dispersed to do what they had pledged to do. The room was left only with Cornish Bob, Smithson, Strong, Julia, and the two LaGrues. Ron felt naked without the lint shirt.

—49—

Strong led them through the Reef, which was suddenly a hive of activity. Families crowded the corridors with what they could carry, pulling on their gillsuits. Men hustled by with spear guns, applying poison to bolts and knives. It would be close work. They arrived in the hangar, and Strong selected one of the flying craft that Ron thought looked like a jet-ski.

"Okay, how does this rift generator thing work?" Strong asked.

Cornish Bob winked, and produced the small electronic device from his pocket. It looked like a hand-held game console: small screen, small keyboard.

"Observe. Especially you, Ron," he said, and removed a small panel from the side of the device. He removed what looked like a spindly insect. The dragonfly unfolded its wings, and perched on Bob's finger.

"I've seen those," Smithson said distastefully. "They were flying all over the island I was trapped on. That thing is a little camera."

"Exactly so," Cornish Bob said. "But not just that. It also has a little transmitter and a GPS plotter. With this little bug, you can send it ahead of you wherever you want to go to make sure that it is indeed where you are trying to get, and also whether it is safe to jump there. First, you enter in the jump coordinates. I'm setting it for the top of that mining platform in the middle of the sea, where the rift to Bodie is."

Bob tapped the little keys, and the dragonfly vanished with a tiny yellow flash. Moments later, the screen lit up with a scene that Ron recognized as the mining platform they'd entered this world onto from Bodie. The bug flew around while they watched the screen over Bob's shoulder.

"Looks clear to me," Bob said. "Can't be too careful, though. Eiffelia could have left a squad of Stripes there to guard the rift. I guess she knows I have the rift generator, though, so she probably thought I wouldn't need to use the natural rift that leads to Bodie."

"You're right; can't be too careful," Smithson said, snapping a new magazine into his rifle. He then dug into his duffle bag, recovered Ron's .357 Magnum Colt Python, and handed it to him.

"Anything in there for me?" Jack Strong asked.

Smithson nodded, fished around in the bag, and handed Strong his Springfield XD. Cornish Bob looked at him inquiringly. Smithson grudgingly found another pistol in the bag, probably from Clay, and passed it to Bob.

"Just in case," he said.

"Just in case," echoed Cornish Bob. "Now then, me 'ansum, watch how I type in the coordinates into the jump box here."

Ron watched. It appeared simple enough.

"And now we set the size of the area to make the jump with, in this case enough for seven people and a flyer . . . and off we go."

Ron felt a strange pulling sensation, like he had felt going through the rift from Bodie, then there he was, on top of the mining platform at sea. The weather was overcast; it looked and smelled like rain. Ron pointed his gun defensively around in an arc, but there was nobody there. He tucked the gun into the sash at his waist. The rift rippled above their heads, the unworldly yellow undulations strangely hypnotizing. Julia Ward Howe stared at it, mesmerized. Smithson disappeared over the edge of the landing, down the ladder, then reappeared a moment later.

"We're clear for now," he said. "Let's get on through the rift. We'll leave the flyer here after I program in the return route to the Reef."

Cornish Bob tapped in a command on the keypad, and the dragonfly returned to him. He showed Ron how to roll the wings up and stow the bug in the cavity on the side of the rift generator.

"All right," Jack Strong said, "here is where we split up. I'm done here in this world. It will be good to get home. Good luck, Ron. See you when you're done killing that sponge."

Strong went through first, getting a boost from Smithson. Smithson then boosted both the LaGrues through the rift. Julia reached up for the rift and tried to jump through it, then waited for Smithson to give her a boost up.

"Not you, dear. You're going with Bob," Smithson said. He clasped Ron's hand. "I'll get back here as fast as I can with a targeting solution," he said with icy determination. "You get back to the Reef as soon as possible. If she finds out you're not there, they all get hammered."

Ron nodded.

"I'll get him back in a tic," Cornish Bob said.

Ron and Bob gave Smithson a hand up, and he disappeared through the rift.

Ron watched Cornish Bob stand with his arms akimbo for a moment, gathering himself. "Well, then, me ducks," he said with a deep inhalation of breath, "first we have to get Julia home. It's time you woke up."

Joy played across her face, then disappeared. "All right," she said. "But only after one last chance for a fuck." She started wriggling out of her dress.

Ron and Bob jumped to stop her.

"No, no, my dear," Bob said. "Not right now. You will have the rest of your life to meet me in your dreams, as I will you."

She relented. Bob once again showed Ron how to enter the coordinates for a jump, this time for one through time as well as space, to a particular tent at a particular time in the very early morning, Washington DC, 1862. Another yellow flash sent them into darkness. Their eyes grew accustomed to the gloom, and they saw they were inside a tent. A horse whinnied nearby, perhaps having been somewhat spooked by the yellow flash. Ron was amazed. He realized he had stepped back in history, to the Civil War.

"I'll try to get a little restful sleep in before morning," Julia said with a yawn. "Oh, and Ron, what were the words to that song?"

"You'll remember," Ron said quietly. "Just give it some soul when the time comes. Here's some paper and a pencil for when you wake up."

"Soul of time. I like that." She yawned.

There was a cot. Bob helped her lie down in it, pulled the covers over her, tucked her in. Her face was beatific, serene, childlike.

"Good night, my love," he whispered.

"Why Bob, you are crying," she whispered back.

He kissed her hand, then her lips. "Goodbye," he whispered, voice breaking. "Goodbye." He drew his hand across his face as he rose and turned from the bed, the nodded toward Ron, directing him from the tent. They left as quietly as possible.

Bob busied himself typing new coordinates into the rift generator, and moments later they were in another moonlit night scene, in dry, dusty hills. The smell and scenery informed Ron that they were in the hills near Bodie. There was a cinderblock house with dark windows nearby.

"Where are we?" Ron asked.

"I'm just curious about a loose end before I retire," he answered.

They knocked on the door. There was no answer. Bob tried the door, it was unlocked. He went in. Moments later, he emerged. "Nobody home. Just one more place to look."

He led them up the hillside to a trench that had been dug out of the side, giving a commanding view of the surrounding area. As they neared it, Ron noticed that the area had been roped off with yellow police line tape. It fluttered mutely in the breeze. Bob searched the area. The ground was pockmarked with small impact craters, which Ron took to be bullet and shrapnel holes. There were several areas that were soaked with what looked like blood, black in the moonlight. Bob picked up several items of trash: bandages, wrappers, surgical tubing, IV fluid bags.

"Maybe," he muttered. "Maybe he survived." He sighed, scanning the area.

"Who?" Ron asked.

Bob glanced at him sideways. "Hopefully, Silas Bell. I guess I'll never know. Just be aware that one of those striped Horribles guys may have survived. Always be on guard. If you have a chance, ask around here if Silas Bell is still alive. If he is, ask him what happened here. And thank him for me."

"For what?"

"He'll know."

They trudged back down the hill.

Bob handed Ron the rift generator. "All right, me bey. It's all yours now. Just take me home and be off with you."

Ron stared at the thing in his hands stupidly. It slowly dawned on him what Cornish Bob was doing.

"You're giving this to me? Are you kidding? Do you know what this is?"

"Of course I am, and I do know what it is, more than you do, I expect. And I'm not kidding. I'm tired, Ron, I'm done. I'm not exactly pleased with how my life has gone to date, and I want to have a chance at making things better."

Ron felt the thing in his hands. It was too light to be a star inside a gold marble.

"One last thing, though, lad," Cornish Bob said haltingly, placing his hand on Ron's shoulder. "That jump I made to get the bomb for you all . . . it was onto a ship. A ship called the *Centurion*. When I got there, they were just mopping up a mission, a raid." He hesitated, trying to find the words.

Ron raised his eyebrows, encouraging him to continue.

"This raid was in this world, our world. It was one that Eiffelia had asked Clay, the LaGrues, and the *Centurion* to do. They were raiding an island in the Caribbean. It turns out that there were a lot of kids on that island in a camp. Kids that they thought might be single recessives."

Ice crept over Ron's heart. "No. No, I'm not hearing this. Not Chris and Jeremy."

"She told me she wanted them all caught, and taken to her home planet. I think she means to use them to try again to breed double Pangborn carriers."

Ron felt his knees buckle, and he sat down in the dust. Sat down hard. His head was dizzy. "Where is her home planet?"

"The coordinates are pre-programmed into the rift generator, under Cambria. You'll probably want to try to get them out of there at some point. Soon."

His mind whirled.

"Right now, though, you have to get moving. Get me back

to my time, get yourself back to BlueRing Reef, and help keep her from bombing it and killing Tracey and everyone else there. Nuke Eiffelia. It won't kill her except on that world, under the best scenario. She'll still be alive on Cambria, but that will have to wait. Get back through the rift and make your plans to go get Chris and Jeremy. Don't go running off half-cocked, plan yer move carefully."

Ron nodded. *Yes. One thing at a time.*

Bob helped Ron to his feet. His knees shook together. "Come on now, Ron. You can do this. Program it to take us to Bodie, July, eighteen seventy nine. I've got things to do, my life to pick back up."

Ron took the diminutive machine, entered the coordinates.

"Very good, you are a quick study."

"I'm a computer programmer, after all," he said numbly.

He hit the activator button, and they were in Bodie, at what must have been high noon on a summer's day.

It was very different than the ghost town version. There were far more buildings, and they were new! Teams of mules dragged wagons through the street, laden with wood, pipe, barrels, boxes, and machinery, the teamsters cracking whips. Dogs barked, people in old-time clothes busied about. Some of them stopped to regard them: the beaten, bloodied little man and the larger man in the yukata, what must have looked to them to be Chinese dress.

"Hey there, what are you doing to that man?" one of the townsfolk asked angrily.

Cornish Bob whistled. "Oops, you better be off. It won't be fittn' for a celestial to be caught beating a white man, you know. Damn, I should've brought a pile of antacids with me."

They were gathering a crowd.

"Goodbye, Grandpa Bob. I'll come back and visit if I can, when all this is done."

"Grandpa Bob—I like the sound of that," he said, tears forming at the corners of his eyes. "Get along now, me bey. Go. Run that way toward Chinatown and slip around a corner before you vanish in thin air."

Ron typed in the coordinates and ran. The crowd,

momentarily taken aback, gave pursuit. Ron was able to round a corner into a deserted, stinking alley before activating the rift generator.

He was instantly back in the common room at BlueRing Reef. It was empty, save for the bomb, Maloko, and his lint shirt.

"Come on then, let's have it," Ron said, reaching for his shirt. Maloko reluctantly agreed, and Ron slipped it back on with satisfaction.

A muffled vibration shook the entire Reef, shaking the sand floor, and cracking the roof.

"What's going on?" Ron asked.

"They're dropping charges around the perimeter, trying to stun any of our fighters out in the water. Soon they'll send in their own troops to try to cut their way into the Reef and get you. We've already dropped a good number of their aircraft out of the sky using javelins. I bet she wasn't expecting that," he said with a grim smile.

"How many Stripe soldiers are left?" Ron asked, adjusting his lint shirt.

"Thousands. When she said she was sending five thousand, hell, there were that many that went down with our missiles in one volley."

"How many of the Tribe are left who still need to get out of here?"

"Most of us are gone, the rest of the women and children and elderly are on the way out now. We should be down to just fighters soon."

Maloko hurried off to join up with other Tribe for the fight, leaving Ron alone in the room with the atomic warhead. The thing was terrifying.

Shit, he thought. *Now what?* He felt useless to help, just standing around as the target that people were dying and killing over. He felt sick. He knew that there was no way he could trigger the bomb even if he wanted to, if the Reef got overrun. Nobody had thought to tell him how to do it. He decided to find Tracey. If he was going to die, it would be protecting her. Not that she needed it, though.

He walked off down the first corridor he came to; decided

to go left at the first intersection, right at the next. He was immediately lost. Small groups of Tribe in gillsuits armed with automatic spear guns and knives ran by periodically from one part of the reef to another, too busy to stop to tell him where to go. Down one corridor, he heard the unmistakable sounds of battle: guns, screams, compressed gas releasing from bolts, small explosions.

Here we go.

He turned and went down it. Immediately he came face-to-face with a group of three Stripe soldiers. They almost shot him, but he saw recognition on their faces.

"The shirt! It's him!" one of them yelled. "Get him!"

Ron turned and fled blindly down another corridor.

-50-

Tracey settled into a cross-legged position on her bed, and made herself as comfortable as she could. It was difficult, in her gillsuit with thoughts of the ongoing events swirling through her mind. She glanced up at the round "moon roof" window above her, but the doors were closed against the Stripe attack.

She removed the small trident from her belt and focused on it, willing herself to calm. Thoughts of Tribe and Stripes fighting all through the Reef invaded her mind.

This isn't working.

Dory sighed loudly nearby.

"Will you *please* shut the hell *up*?" she snapped.

Dory silenced himself. "I'll wait outside," he said, and went out to guard the door to her bedroom.

Tracey closed her eyes and willed calm again, tried to place her mind in the deep trench, in the mind of the octopus. An explosion somewhere in the Reef rocked the floor and bed, distracting her further. She cursed and rubbed her temples with her fists.

Please, help me, she prayed. *Whoever is out there, God, Jesus, the Holy Spirit, Buddha, Angels, Spirit Creatures That Swim Between the Universes, whatever.*

Slowly, perhaps because invoking help allowed her to relax sufficiently, like a mental placebo pill, she realized she was staring intently at the little trident. She imagined it floating through the water, sinking into the depths, and her mind followed it and she reached out her tentacle to grab it. It would not do to lose the thing, the little shiny metal thing. Better to take it back to the cave, so she could inspect it further. Every now and then a thing like that would sink from the world above, and if it was interesting enough, she would take it back to her cave. She had lots of shiny metal things there she had collected over the years. It pleased her to shine her light over them, make them reflect the light back to her. Yes, take the thing back to the cave.

*****

Rounding another corner, Ron realized two things: first, he was out of shape and the Stripes that chased him were undoubtedly going to catch him soon; and second, he remembered that he still had a gun tucked into his sash. The Stripes wanted him alive, they wouldn't shoot him. The thought of shooting them down while they tried to grab him filled him with a sick dread. But he had no choice but to shoot them or be captured. The thought of returning to Eiffelia's power was even more horrible than killing her slaves. He was in a long corridor, and the three soldiers were gaining on him.

Before he could change his mind, Ron pulled the heavy revolver from his waistband, cocked the hammer, turned, and dropped to one knee, ready to fire.

The three Stripe soldiers skidded to a stop, unsure of what to do. They knew they couldn't shoot him, but were in no hurry to advance against the pistol. One of them took a step toward him.

"Not *one step farther*," Ron called forcefully. He was not sure that they were convinced he was capable of shooting them. Neither was he. He tried to keep the barrel from shaking, and aim it like Smithson had taught him. His breath had caught, adrenaline made him see the whole tableau in tunnel vision.

The three soldiers glanced back and forth at each other. They seemed, as one, to reach the same conclusion.

"God is great!" they cried, and compelled by duty and drugs, rushed toward him. Ron's finger strained on the trigger, but he could not shoot.

Suddenly, inexplicably, the soldiers skidded to a clumsy stop, and grabbed for their guns, looking at a point behind Ron.

"Drop!" a familiar voice called from behind him.

Ron propelled himself to his stomach, keeping the gun trained on the Stripes, who had brought their guns to bear on whoever was behind him. With a flash, he knew that whoever was behind him was in trouble if he didn't help. He fired. The shot hit the Stripe on the right full in the chest, propelling him backward, blood spraying. He heard rapid-fire shots from behind him, and the other two Stripes went down, firing indiscriminately. Smoke and fragments of coral wall hit Ron's face. It was over.

A hand grabbed his arm, lurched him to his feet. It was Smithson.

"Nice shot," he said. "I knew you had a knack back at the range in Seattle. Good thing they weren't zombies."

Ron gasped, then fell to his knees, retching vomit. "I just killed somebody," he panted. The vision of the man with the painted face falling back, erupting blood, was indelibly imprinted on his memory.

Smithson patted him on the back, but couldn't allow him much time for reaction. "Let's go, Ron, we have to get moving. We have to find Tracey."

Ron nodded, struggled back to his feet, and allowed Smithson to guide him by the arm with his left hand while he fanned the hallways for enemies with the XM8 in his right.

They traveled quickly through the Reef. Smithson seemed to know the way, and was able to steer clear of skirmishes. Within minutes, they saw Dory standing guard outside a door that Ron guessed contained Tracey.

Dory nodded, motioned inside the room with his automatic spear gun. They entered.

Tracey was cross-legged on the bed, eyes closed, a little trident pressed against her forehead. Her mouth was open, and she swayed gently.

"Tracey," Ron called.

"She isn't here," Dory said, joining them. "She is far away, living as an octopus. We need to tell her where to take the bomb, then drop it down to where the octopus is. She will use the octopus to plant the bomb wherever you want."

Ron stared at him as though he was a raving lunatic.

Smithson appeared to take this in stride. "The LaGrues reverted back to our side within minutes of crossing the rift back to our universe; they were able to give us a target with a moderate chance of success. I think the back-and-forth in the rift made them nuts, though. On the drive back, we almost hit a crow that was flying alongside the car, and they both got really agitated. They were in the back seat, then looked at each other like they were sitting on live wires. They both settled back into their seats with their eyes closed, and they said I had to keep it at a constant fifty miles an hour so that the light and shadow patterns would transmit a 'message from God.' It must have worked, because they both came up with the same idea at the same time. When we got to the lab, they ran computer simulations based on whatever geological reports were on the Web, and they came up with a plan. They reasoned that she is too big to attack directly with the bomb; even one cell that survives would be enough to allow her to recover. Then they thought of using an earthquake to trigger the trench to collapse on her. The Mariana Trench is right at a subduction zone; the Pacific Plate is sliding under the Philippine Sea Plate right there at the bottom of the trench. The molten mantle is only a few kilometers deeper at that point. But there wasn't enough data to tell if a nuclear explosion would trigger a big enough quake. Then they saw something else on the website they were looking at that they had never heard of: Mud volcanoes."

"Mud volcanoes?" Ron asked.

"Right. Mud volcanoes. Apparently, and I'm not up on the science, but the seabed that gets pulled into the mantle there heats up, and some kind of chemical reaction makes a bunch of muddy goo, called serpentine, that has the consistency of molten toothpaste. It oozes out of the top of the trench on the island side, and piles up into giant muddy volcanoes, up to thirty miles across and a mile high. The LaGrues ran a few computer models based on the locations of a couple of these, and it looks possible to trigger a mudslide with proper placement of the bomb. If we can bury her in molten mud, she'll cook. And whatever doesn't cook will starve under mounds of goo."

"Sounds workable to me."

"There's just one thing: How do we get the bomb armed, and into a place that Tracey's octopus can take it where it needs to go? I mean, we can fly it there or sled it there, but that will take time."

"I can get it there instantly," Ron said.

"How?" Smithson asked. "Wait, I get it. Cornish Bob gave you his rift generator. That is why you are here and he isn't."

"Right."

"We can't bomb that area yet," Dory said.

They looked at him with distress.

"There are people there, my friends, who need to be warned. The Oceanics. We have to give them time to escape the area."

"How long will they need?" Smithson asked.

"How far will they need to get?"

Smithson rubbed his chin. "You know, if they can get up on an island . . . wait, no, the mudslide will probably trigger a tsunami. They would be safer out of the blast zone at sea, in deep water where they can ride out the wave. An air burst goes about twenty to thirty miles, but in water, the shock wave might be lethal farther away. How about getting them, say, a hundred miles? Maybe less if they are in the lee of the islands."

"Give them three hours," Dory said. "I can go along with Ron when he drops the bomb, sled over to them, and then go with them when they run."

Smithson nodded. "Good. Then Ron can jump out of there. Not back here, though, things are getting pretty bad."

"I have to come back here. We have to get Tracey out of BlueRing Reef after she . . . whatever the hell she's doing with an octopus. The rift generator may be the only way out at   that   point."

"Right, right," Smithson said. "I'll stay here and guard her until you get back. First, we have to get back to the bomb. I'll arm it with a three-hour delay, and get you two to a sled. You two jump to the target coordinates, and—oh, crap, how are we going to tell an octopus where to pick the thing up?"

Another explosion rocked the walls. The sound of fighting grew louder. A Tribesman appeared in the doorway: Maloko, panting hard.

"The fighting is heading this way," he said, slapping a

fresh bolt-magazine into place.

Dory kneeled next to Tracey. "Can you hear me?" he asked slowly and loudly.

She nodded.

"Thank God," Ron said.

"Where are the GPS coordinates?" Dory asked.

Smithson rattled them off. Dory looked around for a computer terminal. He found one there in Tracey's bedroom, typed the location into a map program. Ron and Smithson looked over his shoulders.

"There," Dory said. "Just off Guam, south of Saipan and Tinian. Right there, off Rota."

"I know that place," Ron said. "That's where Eiffelia has her underwater base."

"Excellent." Smithson nodded. "Maybe we can bury that with her. Hell, the shock wave alone should crush it."

"We're going to drop the bomb right over the base," Dory said into Tracey's ear. "Then take it to the bottom of the mud volcano overlooking the trench at that point to the west."

Tracey nodded.

Ron, Smithson, and Dory blinked at each other.

"Okay, let's get out of here while we still can. We can post guards outside the bedroom here, and tell them to hold it secure at all costs."

"Give me your shirt again," Maloko said to Ron. "We'll hold out here, no matter what they throw at us."

Once again, Ron reluctantly surrendered it. Maloko put it on again with a satisfied grin.

Smithson spent a moment filling up his magazines with 5.56 millimeter rounds, then checked the level of propellant and acid in the twin cylinders on the hard rail. He nodded. "Let's roll."

Ron pulled his pistol out, Dory produced his automatic spear gun, and they followed Smithson into the hallways.

Only once did they encounter Stripe troops; a small group that Smithson dispersed screaming with a blast of flaming acid. They kept their distance after that.

The council chamber was empty, save for the twenty-five megaton nuclear warhead squatting like an ugly animal in the center of the room.

Smithson opened the access panel and tapped on the embedded keypad. "Right," he said. "Thank God they made it easy enough for those doped-up Stripes to arm it. Now we just have to hit this red button here, and it starts a three-hour countdown."

"Okay, let's jump to the ocean," Ron said, punching in the coordinates on the rift generator.

"No, not yet!" Dory interrupted, placing his hand on Ron's arm. "We have to bring a sled with us so I can warn the Oceanics."

"Right, right," Ron said, slapping his head. "This is getting confusing."

They rolled the bomb out of the room toward Tracey's private docking bay, where her sleds were moored. Progress was slow: there were skirmishes, and they narrowly avoided an ambush around a corner. More than once, they had to stop to drag bodies out of the hallway; both Tribe and Stripe. Minutes later they bustled into her bay, and rolled the bomb near one of the fastest-looking sleds they could find.

"Okay, Ron. *Now* we arm the bomb, and you and Dory jump to the coordinates we discussed."

"Uh, wait," Ron said, holding up a finger.

"What is it *now*?" Dory snapped impatiently.

"Do I need a gillsuit?"

Dory rolled his eyes. "You don't need one. All you have to do is jump through with me and the armed bomb, wait until it sinks and I get out of your way, then jump back here."

"Ah. Got it. Then get out Tracey and whoever else is left."

"Including me, hopefully." Smithson grinned.

Ron re-checked the coordinates for the drop into the rift generator, then pre-typed in the coordinates for Tracey's room for the return jump. He nodded.

Six Stripe soldiers appeared at the door to the docking bay. They opened fire, not recognizing Ron because he wasn't wearing the lint shirt. They ducked, avoiding the instinct to scatter for cover.

Smithson reached past Ron and pressed the red button on the warhead with his thumb, while bullets screamed by overhead.

"Go!" he ordered, then turned and returned fire on the soldiers, who ducked back through the doorway. Smithson ran off seeking cover, crouching.

Ron activated the jump box.

–51–

Strange thoughts . . . strange. . . .

She knew what some of the shiny metal things were called now. Never before had she attached any particular meaning to them, other than that they were shiny, heavy, and hard. Now magic words, labels and understanding crowded into her mind: "Aluminum can," "scrap metal," "wrench."

Her head hurt. She flashed her bioluminescence with agitation. She had to get out of the cave. There was something she had to do. Some prey, far above near the surface, had to be caught and taken. Not to be eaten, because it was another big shiny thing, but taken and buried in the mud. She swam out, and up. And up, and up. Never before had she gone so shallow, there was glowing light all around her. Far above, there was bright light, as though as far as she could see was the body of a vast, glowing octopus. Its skin rippled, dazzling. Sinking from this enormous octopus was a large, shiny metal thing. It looked like a giant octopus beak. This was the thing she was supposed to find, to take to the mud overlooking her trench.

She swam to it, wrapped her tentacles around it. It was heavy, sinking. She couldn't carry it, but she could guide it, direct its fall. She aimed it toward the base of a mud mountain, and sank with it until it embedded itself in a cloud of silt.

Then she knew, with certainty, that it was a bad thing. It was dangerous, very dangerous. She had to get out of there, as fast and far as she could. Her first instinct was to flee into the deep, toward her cave. She would be safe there. But no, she knew, somehow, that it was not safe. She could not go back there. Not for a long while, maybe never. She had to go up, close to the giant, glowing, undulating octopus body, and then away. She swam, as fast as she could. She knew it wasn't fast enough.

Things were swimming with her, keeping up, egging her on. They were small, like little fish, but not fish. Small green cylinders, like giant plankton. "Flying pickles," she heard them named in her mind. She was given new strength, and swam faster.

Among them all, she sensed invisible, powerful beings. Beings like dolphins, but faster. They swam together, and she was given strength and speed. With the speed came a spark of joy. They pulled her and the flying pickles along in their wakes, faster and faster away from the bad thing in the mud. . . .

Someone was calling to her, right in her ear, and shaking her as she fled.

I have an ear? What is an ear?

*****

"Tracey!" Ron called, shaking her shoulders. "We have to get out of here. *Now.*"

Her eyes were glazed over. She rocked back and forth gently, mumbling, the little trident still clutched in her hand.

He shook her harder, and suddenly, her eyes focused on him. "Hi, Ron. You're soaking wet."

"What's with the trident?" he asked. "You turning into a sea monkey?"

There was gunfire right outside the bedroom now. Smithson was holding off the Stripe soldiers alone. Maloko was gone.

Ron pulled her to her feet, tapped coordinates into the rift generator.

"Is everyone gone but us?" she asked.

"I think so," Ron said, distracted. "We're the last of the Mohicans."

"I'm out of ammo," Smithson called, retreating into the room, dropping a magazine from his mag-well. He activated an M-2 SLAM mine and sent it skidding into the hallway. "We're out of time."

"She's back, and we're go for launch," Ron said, and pressed the rift generator activation button.

They appeared on the mining platform. It was mid-afternoon, the sky a patchwork of dark clouds, spatters of rain and gusty winds alternating with areas of blue sky. The smell of rain and ozone filled their lungs.

Ron flopped down on his back, exhausted. Smithson retrieved Ron's revolver, and made a cursory stagger around the top of the mining platform, but soon dropped to the deck himself, panting.

Tracey crossed to the edge of the platform and stared out over the sea. "How long until the thing goes off?"

"Just under three hours, I guess," Ron said, draping his forearm over his eyes. "I want to wait here until it blows, just to make sure. And I need to catch my breath."

Smithson nodded. "We can always duck through the rift if we have to bug out sooner. Or use the jump box, for that matter."

"No, no rift generator unless we have to. I want to go home the same way we got here, through that rift into Bodie," Ron said quietly. He thought for a moment. "Aren't we done here? Can we go home now?"

Tracey sighed. "I don't know . . . I don't want to go back, in a way. This is home for me now, just as much as it is back there in our universe."

"What about taking out the trash? Brushing your teeth? Watching TV? Cooking dinner? What about the baby sea otter at the Aquarium?"

She slowly nodded. "I'll miss it here, though. I suppose we can always come back if we want to, to check up on things or just visit for a while."

"Our mission was to find out what was going on, what was threatening our universe, and to stop it if possible," Smithson said. "I can't think of anything else we can do to fulfill that goal. We know the enemy, and what she wants. We got Jack Strong and an extra LaGrue back, but lost Clay and Valentina Pavlov."

Ron realized, with a flash, that Smithson had forgotten one of the other original mission goals: getting an operational star drive. He had one. *Crap. Who does Smithson really answer to? If it is the government, and they take it, I won't be able to mount a rescue attempt for Chris and Jeremy.*

"Uh, Smithson, we have a problem. The rift generator."

Smithson considered him through narrowed eyes. "You're probably worried I'm going to report that. Get it taken away."

"Well . . . yeah."

"Don't worry. Your secret is safe with me. I answer to a higher authority than the U.S. government."

"Wow. Thanks. You have no idea how important it is I keep this thing."

Smithson winked. "Maybe I do."

"I hope the Tribe got away," Tracey said. "And the Oceanics. And the octopus. And all those flying pickles, and the spirits or whatever they were, that were helping us."

"We'll come back later after things settle down and see," Ron promised. "Besides, I have something else I have to do."

Ron regretted his words immediately. This was not the time or place to tell Tracey about her kids being abducted by Eiffelia. He was glad that her mind was elsewhere, and did not think to ask him what he was talking about. It did not occur to him to ask her what she was talking about, either.

"Why do you suppose they built this platform out here in the middle of the ocean, anyway?" Ron asked, changing the subject.

Smithson furrowed his brow. "Probably Eiffelia and her crew used it to get gold ore out of Bodie. Remember how Leonard and Maurice mentioned they were here looking for scraps of gold? They said that it was for mining the sea floor. That was probably a cover story."

Ron nodded. That made sense. "She was probably lying to me about curing my cancer, too."

"Speaking of cover stories, she had me going for a while, too," Smithson said. "She told me the reason she was making me fight on that island was so she could study and learn martial arts for her armies. Much later it occurred to me that if she wanted to do that, she could go back to anywhere in history and recruit the best fighting teachers possible, who make me look like a fat kid with lunch money, and get them willingly."

"So why was she making you fight?" Tracey asked.

"You tell me. Sick pleasure? Gruesome entertainment?"

They waited. The sun once again dropped closer to the

horizon, laced with heavy clouds and occasional lightning. All three now stood on the edge of the platform, looking northwest toward the place where the bomb would soon go off. They couldn't tell whether the distant rumbling was thunder, or an atomic explosion.

Ron checked his watch. "Any minute now. Oh, *shit!*"

"The bomb?" Tracey asked, scanning the horizon.

"No, my lint shirt. It's gone! Maloko has it, damn him."

"I swear, Ron, someday I'm going to strangle you."

"There!" Smithson shouted, pointing. They strained their eyes, and saw a line of white spray racing toward them across the wave tops.

"He hath loosed the fateful lightning of his terrible swift sword," Tracey whispered.

"It's the initial shock wave," Smithson said. "It's done."

The shock wave reached the mining platform, and they rocked violently for a few seconds as it passed under them. A bell rang underneath them, and gulls screamed as they were riled from their perches on the levels below. Then there was quiet.

"Is that it?" Tracey asked.

Smithson pointed back in the direction of the explosion. A wave was slowly rolling toward them, hardly noticeable.

"That is a tsunami. If we were closer to land, it would break. Out here, it is traveling through the deep water until it hits something shallower. The fact that there is a tsunami at all tells me that there was a massive displacement of water. I think the mudslide worked, the bomb itself wouldn't have done that."

"You think we buried her?" Ron asked.

"We'll have to find out later," Smithson said. "For now, though, let's go home before that wave hits us."

Smithson and Ron made a saddle with their hands and gave Tracey a leg up to the rift. With one last lingering look back, she disappeared through it.

"You're next," Ron insisted. Smithson didn't argue. Ron boosted him up, and soon all he could see of Smithson was his arm, reaching back through the rift to help him. Ron took his hand. He glanced back at the approaching wave, red in the setting sun.

With a flood of relief, he felt himself pulled up and through, back to his own world.

−52−

Something was wrong. Dreadfully wrong.

Ron anticipated falling the ten feet to the tunnel floor in darkness, but instead of his feet touching rock he plunged into dark water. Struggling to breathe, he kicked his way in near panic to the surface. He was in a narrow chamber, and the rift above was gone.

They must have flooded the mine shaft! he thought. There was no way he could swim all the way to the end of those tunnels holding his breath. He knew he had to get back through the rift onto the mining platform, then use the rift generator to jump back to his world at another location. But there was no rift, and there was nothing to grab onto or push off of.

Shit! Shit!

He panicked, thrashing, then noticed a faint light below him. It appeared the tunnel was not as long as he remembered. He took the deepest breath he could, then swam down toward the light. The tunnel was indeed only fifteen feet long.

Within seconds of swimming down it, his head broke the surface of the water and he gasped for breath.

"What the *hell*?"

Ron looked around, splashing, stunned. He was not in the Bodie mine tunnel; he was in a large, open cavern. He was in a swimming pool in the floor of the cave. It appeared to be an artificial cave, by the look of the lawn furniture nearby, and the indirect colored lighting, artfully placed behind the sculpted stalagmites and stalactites. A gracefully arched door outlined daylight at one far wall. A man in black pants, a white jacket and towel, and a drink tray stood nearby.

Tracey, sitting in a lawn chair, eyed him over the top of a magazine. "Is something wrong, Ron?" she asked. "Oooh . . . I just had a moment of déjà vu." She idly fingered a pendant in the shape of a trident on a chain around her neck.

Ron stopped thrashing, swam over to the edge of the pool. He looked down in the glow of the underwater lights and saw that they cleverly concealed the entrance to the tunnel.

"Somebody built this cave to hide the rift," he postulated.

"Rift? What are you talking about?" She resumed reading her magazine, then paused mid-reach for a snack on the picnic table. "Ron, why are you swimming in your yukata?"

"I'm not—where's Smithson? Where are the LaGrues? Jack Strong?"

"Smithson is around somewhere. The LaGrue twins? They're probably back in Seattle, I imagine, unless Smithson had them whisked away 'for their protection,' too. And I have no idea who Jack Strong is, honey. Is he your new imaginary friend? Or are you asking for a 'strong' drink of 'Jack' Daniels?"

"You're wearing a bathing suit. You were just in your gillsuit not thirty seconds ago."

"Ron, thanks to you and your security director, I have not been in my gillsuit for over a week. It isn't worth it to wear it to jump in the damn pool. If you would only convince him to get the stick out of his ass and allow me to go back to my research facility, I would be wearing it now. Down there in the trench." She snapped the magazine with irritation and pointedly went back to reading it.

Ron stared at her dumbfounded.

Wait a minute, our universe doesn't have gillsuits.

Another man in a white jacket appeared in outline at the sunny door. "Mr. Golden, there are visitors on the way to see you from the United States Space Command. I took the liberty of granting them clearance to land up at the house."

Ron heaved himself out of the pool, and the white jacketed man nearby hurried over to hand him a towel. "Uh, thanks," he said, accepting it. "Are we in some kind of hotel or something?"

The attendant blinked uncomprehendingly. "No, sir, your estate is not a hotel."

"My 'estate'?"

"Yes, sir. The Golden Family Estate, your home

overlooking Bodie," he said, obviously not sure whether he was being cheeky.

"Wait a minute. I don't have a house in Bodie, much less an 'estate,' I rent a place in Seattle."

"Rent? You don't rent anything. And if it wasn't for your over-protective nursemaid of a security director, we would be in Seattle now," Tracey interrupted, still behind the magazine. "Smithson has outdone himself this time. War painted men with nuclear bombs, indeed. As if we don't have enough to worry about waiting for your test results."

"Test results?"

"Yes, Ron, your test results," she said, almost angrily. "Quit with the denial. You got a positive test for Chondrosarcoma. The confirming test is due any time." She put the magazine down, rubbed her eyes with a trembling hand.

"Tracey," Ron said quietly, toweling off, "I'm going to go out on a limb and predict that the test is negative. I'm fine."

She shook her head with genuine concern. "Ron, what is wrong with you? Have you lost your mind?"

"Yes. No. Let's go meet the government guys and see what's going on here," he said, extending his hand. "I'll follow you."

She took his hand and they left the artificial cave. Ron, still dressed in his wet yukata with a towel around his neck, saw that they were on the bluff overlooking the ghost town of Bodie. There was a finely manicured path that led to a paved concrete pad nearby. Parked on it was a railed platform made of teakwood with cushioned benches, a table, and a bar tended by another white-jacketed attendant. Tracey led him onto the platform, which floated into the air, much to Ron's surprise. He grabbed the rail to steady himself. Tracey rolled her eyes.

Ron saw, flying through the air above the ghost town, what looked like one of the flying RVs he had stolen from Eiffelia.

"Hey!" he cried, pointing. "How did that get through the rift?"

He followed the flying vehicle as it soared above them and

landed at a series of elaborate buildings, in slate and gold-tinted glass, at the top of the bluff.

"It's only a car," Tracey said, eyes narrowing with growing concern. "And what is this 'rift' you keep talking about? Are you all right? Or are you just bullshitting beyond your usual tiresome levels?"

"Tracey," Ron said earnestly, taking her face in his hands and staring at her directly, "listen to me. This is all wrong. Our world has no flying cars, no floating yacht-platforms, no gillsuits. No Golden Estates. I'm an out-of-work computer game programmer. We had to go to an alternate universe to keep from getting killed by a bunch of stripe-faced zombie killers led by Cornish Bob."

"That's a fine way to talk about your great-grandfather, the patriarch of the Golden empire, founder of your dynasty, and source of all your wealth," she said sarcastically, in spite of her growing concern about his sanity.

"What wealth?"

"Ron, shut the hell up," Tracey whispered, embarrassed in front of the bartender. "You are the richest human being on the planet."

Ron felt dizzy. He sat down hard.

The platform landed, and they walked to where the flying car was just disgorging its passengers.

Smithson came first, dressed in a gray suit and sunglasses. Following him were the two LaGrues, looking shaken; the Space Command agents from Seattle: the two Johnsons, grave and all business; Jack Strong, still dressed in his yukata; and . . . *oh, crap, it's CLAY!*

Clay walked up to Ron and extended his hand. "Honored to meet you, Mr. Golden. I'm John Clay, Managing Special Agent-in-Charge of our Denver Office. Sorry to bother you like this, but there have been some serious developments concerning the events that Mr. Smithson has inquired with us about, and I thought it best to meet with you personally to discuss them."

Ron shook his hand in a daze. "Uh, sure." He noticed Jack Strong winking at him.

"Nice place," Strong whispered. "You've done well for

yourself in the past fifteen minutes."

"Excuse me," Ron mumbled, then grabbed Jack Strong by the lapel of his yukata and bodily dragged him a short distance away. He stabbed a trembling index finger in the exact center of Strong's chest. "What . . . the . . . *fuck* is going on here?" he hissed.

"Hey, this is all new to me, too. I have some guesses, though."

"Shoot."

"Okay, first of all, you and me are the only ones who seem to think that things are different lately. I mean, a few minutes ago I came through the rift in the tunnel we found with the LaGrues. We were driving north in Clay's fancy RV heading back to the Reno Airport to start our debriefing. I get a weird feeling, I look out of the window, and instead of *driving* north on Highway 395, we're *flying* south to here!"

Ron nodded mutely, urging him to continue.

"So think of the physics of it. It takes a double Pangborn recessive to keep a universe from ceasing to exist, right?"

"Right."

"So, just how many of us were over in that universe? Eiffelia had the entire population under her control. She was taking blood samples to measure her drugs through those familiars every day. Presumably she knew *exactly* who was a double recessive, and also presumably she was using them to keep other universes open. We could well have been the last of the lot over there."

Ron slowly nodded. "So when you came through the rift, I was the last one—wait a minute, what about the others she may have had imprisoned in her deep-sea base?"

"You mean the one you nuked?"

"Of course . . . then I came through the rift—"

"And there was nothing left to hold up the other universe. It collapsed into this one. Now we have some kind of unholy combination of the two. We have land population, we have Tribe, we have flying cars."

"How much? How much overlap was there? And speaking of overlap, what is with the swimming pool? You went through the rift a few hours before I did, and I bet you came in at a mine shaft, right?"

"Right."

"Well, somebody, probably Cornish Bob, built a swimming pool in the tunnel next to the rift, keeping it his little secret, I guess."

"Okay. . . ."

Ron nodded. "But what about me? How am I suddenly the richest man in the world?"

Strong whistled. "No kidding? You lucky bastard."

"I know, I bet it was Cornish Bob again. He went back to the year eighteen seventy nine, knowing, well, *everything*. Where the gold was in Bodie, where it was in Mexico, I'll bet he went on and bought up a bunch of land in South Africa next."

"Then he diversified," Smithson said, joining them in mid-conversation. "First, he started a pharmaceutical company making antacids, of all things. That worked so well, he went into real estate, arms, transportation, manufacturing, oil, you name it. Your grandfather and father continued the hit parade, making gillsuits and anti-grav propulsion units."

"And my contribution? Please tell me I have made some contribution. Other than being a bowling pin or a sailboat."

"Why, yes, sir," Smithson said, with a ghost of a smile. "You thought to hire me. And, of course, a more trivial accomplishment, you started the computer division. You know, the one that makes the operating systems of most every computer in the world. And you are working on animal-shaped animated smart phones called 'familiars.'"

Ron's hand strayed to the lump in his waistband reflexively. Yes, the rift generator was still there.

"I have a feeling that will succeed, too," he said.

"But I think you should join us again, Mr. Golden," Smithson said. "Agent Clay has some news for you. I assume you have not been watching the news today."

"Not for a while." Ron smiled.

The three of them joined back with the others, who had made their way to the bar on the platform. Clay and Johnson, on duty, had refused drinks, but Tracey, and the LaGrue twins sipped under the canvas shade of the platform.

"Would you like a drink, Mr. Golden?" the bartender asked.

"*Hell,* yes," he said.

"Ron, Tracey, we have bad news. The terrorist cell that your Security Director Mr. Smithson brought to our attention has struck again. You are aware that they were stalking you in Seattle, both at your home and at Ms. Springs' Confederated Sea Tribes of Pacifica Institute at the waterfront? Then they set off a nuclear device at your manufacturing facility in Denver."

"Yes," Tracey said with apprehension. "What have they done now?"

Clay clenched his teeth, in obvious barely-repressed anger. "They have set off another nuclear device."

After a long moment of silence, Tracey asked "Where?"

Clay hesitated. "In the Pacific, next to the Mariana Trench. They must have planned it exactly for maximum destructive effect. If you only have one bomb, I can't think of a worse place to blow it. They detonated it at the base of a string of large mud volcanoes just over the trench. It triggered a massive slide, which displaced a large tsunami that caused massive damage to a number of coastal cities. Two of the floating cities were also damaged, New Sydney in particular is mostly awash."

"What about the Tribes? How many Reefs were destroyed?" Tracey asked.

"Surprisingly few," Clay said with relief. "Only one, actually."

"It was BlueRing Reef, wasn't it?" interrupted Ron.

"Yes, how did you know?"

"I think you will find that most of the inhabitants were out of the Reef at the time, and will mostly be fine."

Tracey rounded on him angrily. "Damn you! Stop your magical fantasies! That is my home!"

"Mr. Golden is right, actually," Johnson said, listening to his ear bud. "Most of the inhabitants had evacuated because of a scheduled drill."

Tracey stared at Ron, not knowing what to say.

He regarded her warmly. "Your husband may have been

there," Ron said quietly. "We'll see if he made it. I'm sure you are very interested after seeing him last week."

Her eyes flashed shock, shame, then anger. "My *ex*-husband, you bastard," she cried, bursting into tears. "So now you have a way of spying on my goddam *dreams?*" she sobbed.

Ron put a hand on her shoulder, and was relieved that she did not push it away.

"Anyway," Clay continued uncomfortably, "we have the unfortunate duty to report also that your research facility there on the bottom of the trench was lost as well."

Her sobbing intensified. She allowed Ron to comfort her, burrowing her head into the damp fabric and towel on his chest.

"We're sorry," Clay said. "And the worst damnable thing about it, we *still* have no idea who these terrorists are and where they come from. Or where and when they'll strike next."

"I think . . . ." Ron said, wracking his brain, "I *think* they are all dead."

"You *think?*" Clay asked, puzzled.

"Yes. I think so. I think you will find that there has been a shoot-out over in the hills near Lee Vining. What is that Ranger's name? The one in charge down there in Bodie?"

"Tanner? You mean Ranger Tanner?" Clay asked, snapping his fingers to Johnson to hand him his radio. "The one I asked to keep his eyes peeled around here for guys with their faces painted with stripes?"

"That's the one."

"Clay, of the Space Command calling Ranger Tanner. Ranger Tanner, do you copy?"

There was a crackle of static over the radio.

"Ranger Tanner is probably out of your range right now," said the voice. "This is Ranger Mike. Can I help you?"

"Where's Tanner?" Clay snapped impatiently.

"He's over at Silas Bell's place, at the crime scene."

"I'll be damned," Clay said, eyes widening.

"I'll be damned, too," Tracey said, incredulous. "I just met Silas Bell last week near my research facility. He helped me .

. . do some research. If it is the same guy, anyway. We have to find out if he's all right," she said, clutching the trident pendant around her neck.

Clay keyed the transmitter again. "Ranger Mike, what is Silas Bell's condition?"

"Si was shot up pretty bad, the terrorists and him got into a gunfight up there near his place. We got there just before they were about to roust him from that damn trench he dug up on the hillside. He spent months digging that damn thing; said that devils were going to try to get him. Turns out he wasn't crazy. He was lucky Tanner was on the phone with him when they drove up, and he managed to ask for backup before they cut his phone line. Anyway, he lived. They airlifted him to Reno."

"Did any of the stripe-faced terrorists get away?"

There was another burst of static.

"Nope. All dead."

Clay nodded. "But there could be more," he said.

"I agree," Smithson said. "Better wait it out here for a while until we are sure."

"No," Ron said. "They're gone. I want to go home."

"Thank God for that for once," Tracey sniffed.

"Actually, we're quite sure that there are more," Clay argued gently but forcefully.

"If you are referring to the raid in Bermuda, it is done and over with. They are gone. With Tracey's kids."

Clay narrowed his eyes. "What raid in Bermuda?"

Tracey and Smithson said in unison, "What kids?"

"What do you mean, what kids? Are you telling me you don't have kids anymore? No Chris or Jeremy?"

Tracey shook her head no, once again concerned for his sanity.

"The hell you don't," Ron growled. "And I am going to get them the *hell* away from her."

"Ron, you need to take a pill. Or a nap, or something. There has been a lot of stress today," Tracey said.

Ron took a long, deep breath, gathering himself. "Okay. Tracey. I want you to go get in our . . . flying car, whatever you call it. We are going to fly to Reno to visit Mr. Bell, then we are going home. By the time we get there, I will either have convinced you that the universe had some very big changes in the last hour, or I will not. Fair enough?"

She nodded. "I'll go pack. Thank you gentlemen for your kind visit to personally inform us of today's catastrophic events." She left, escorted by one of the white jacketed attendants.

"And I also thank you. I will be in touch if I hear of any further developments," Ron said, showing the Space Command personnel to their flying RV.

"Of course," Clay said, who appeared to want to stay longer. "One thing more to discuss, Mr. Golden: How exactly did you know about the shootout over the hill and the fact that the Tribe in BlueRing Reef were on a drill?"

"Nothing special, Agent Clay," he said. "I watch the news. And I have my own extensive network of operatives."

"Really?" Clay asked, halfway through the door of his RV.

Ron winked. "Sure. Smithson, the LaGrue twins, lots of Tribe, Valentina Pavlov—"

"The porn star?" Johnson shouted, sticking his head out through the door of the RV.

"Now how did you know she was a porn star?" Ron asked with mock surprise.

Johnson blushed and disappeared.

The RV slowly ascended, then banked and accelerated northward through the sky. Ron looked around, blinking. Jack Strong was standing with a puzzled expression on his face.

"Oops . . . should I have been on board there?"

Thoughts occurred to Ron quickly. "No," he said, taking Strong by the arm and guiding him toward the house. "How about you go to work for me? You're unemployed right now, I assume. Adrift in the new universal conjunction. I bet there are lots of Double Pangborn carriers right now who are also feeling a little . . . lost. I want you to go find them, recruit them, maybe even bring them here. I'm going to go get Tracey's kids, Jack. I may need some help."

"Sure, Ron. Unless it turns out I'm the father of twelve, or running a company somewhere. Like you, I have no idea what my history has been now. I hope mine has been as kind as yours has."

"And could you help me talk with Tracey for a minute before we go?"

Strong laughed. "That may be a little harder. She'll just think we're both nuts. Or pulling her leg."

Tracey met them before they could even enter the house.

"Let's go. I have to see Silas Bell," she said urgently.

"How do you know him?" Ron asked, not sure how much of the universes had overlapped.

"He lives, or lived, anyway, near my facility. We were good neighbors. And I've had some weird dreams involving him."

Ron and Strong exchanged glances. "Let's schedule a meeting. You meet me in Seattle, and bring Smithson and the LaGrue twins."

"Smithson comes with you, sir," Smithson said himself, appearing from the house with a duffle bag. "I'm your bodyguard, after all. You know . . . to guard your body, I have to be somewhere around it."

Ron nodded, surrendering, and followed Tracey, Smithson, and a man who must have been the chauffer/pilot, to the flying car garage.

All the cars were amazing. They were larger than automobiles, had no wheels, but were luxurious behind their tinted windows.

Ron was exhilarated to fly, noiselessly, out of the garage, over Bodie, and into the sky to the north. The Sierras rose majestically on their left, while the rolling brown hills of the high desert extended eastward as far as they could see.

There were no roads below, Ron noticed, but refrained from pointing out.

They landed in a parking lot in Reno, after calling ahead to find where Bell was hospitalized. They were shown to his room with stern warnings about not causing him any stress.

Bell lay quietly on the hospital bed. Ron could not tell if it was an inner serenity or the effect of narcotics. Reason told him the latter, but when Bell's eyes rested on Tracey, he changed his mind.

"Hi, there, kid," the old man whispered.

"Bell, are you all right?" Tracey asked, equally quietly.

He harrumphed. "It will take more than that to snuff a card-carrying member of the Ancient and Honorable Order of E. Clampus Vitus. And the committee head of the Grand Imperturbable Hangmen at that."

"Okay," Ron muttered, "now I'm sure the universe is garbled beyond recognition."

"They thought I was crazy, building my trench of defense against demons," the old man said stridently. "But come they did! *Mimes!* Worst demons there are. Except to the French, maybe, and they ain't much better than devils themselves."

"I'm not entirely sure this happened for real or not, but I wanted to thank you for helping me make the Dive," Tracey said. "I'm glad you were out of there when the bomb went off."

"Me, too," he said, suddenly serious. "I usually stay in the coral only for the winter, then come back to work the park in the summer. This year I was going to stick around for longer. I'm retired now, you know. But something told me to get the proverbial hell out of Dodge, and I'm old enough to listen to whatever that something is."

"Even if that something is a flying pickle."

"Flying pickle . . . as fine an example of the *Credo Quia Absurdum* as one will ever find," he whispered. "Of course, one could argue that coming back here and getting shot by a bunch of stripes is an example of jumping out of a frying pan and into the fire."

"Thanks for helping, Mr. Bell," Ron said. "They were out to kill me, you know. Is there anything I can do to help you out?"

"You can get me a prettier nurse, for starters. I may be a retired old man, but I'm not above enjoying a good sponge bath."

"What did you do before you retired, Mr. Bell?"

"I was a minister."

"Figures," Tracey said. "First a whole congregation at once, now you just work one-on-one as a Dive guide."

*****

Ron watched as Seattle flew by beneath them, looking very

different without the concrete streets and roads. He was amazed at how much room streets and roads had taken up, now that they'd been replaced, not just with more houses, but with green parks, fountains, market places, and occasional landing pads and parking structures for flying cars.

"My house is right there, in Greenwood," he pointed out to the chauffer.

"Ron! You are really exasperating me," Tracey railed.

"Oh . . . right. I guess I don't live there anymore."

Ron was struck by an overwhelming feeling that it was all wrong.

He frowned, took her hand. "Look, Tracey, I feel like I just opened a saved game of 'Dragon Throne' and suddenly the Ancient Dragon is already dead, I've married the princess, the treasure room is already full, and all the quests are already done, without me doing any of it. Without even using cheat codes. In a couple of days we are going to have a meeting. You, me, Jack Strong, and I guess Smithson and the LaGrue twins. We are going to prove that before today, there were two universes, and over the course of the past few months, we brought about events that made them join together like soap bubbles. Or maybe we will fail to prove it to you. We'll see."

"All right, Ron. You do that."

"Where do we live now?"

They were flying over the Puget Sound now, angling north by northwest.

"On your island, of course," she said, wondering if she should start believing him. Even for Ron, this was an elaborate show of oddity.

"My *island*?"

The car was in a graceful, arcing descent over a large, forested island in the San Juans. It had meadows, streams, waterfalls . . . and a house.

"Is that our house?" he mouthed to Tracey.

She nodded, smiled, joining him in his wonder.

They landed on a wide, expanse of green lawn, trimmed with gardens, boulders, and streams.

Ron walked onto the grass, and with a sudden flash,

dropped to one knee and took Tracey's hand. "Will you marry me?"

"Oh, Ron," she said, tears forming in the corners of her eyes. "You sweet moron. We have been married for years. But I'm touched you asked me again."

"Look!" he cried, glancing around at the grass now that he was closer to it.

"What now, Ron?"

"No dog shit! My old house had this lady who would walk her dachshund every morning and it would shit on my lawn."

"Well," she said sagely, "we'll always have dog shit on the lawn. It's only a matter of the scale."

"True," he said taking her hand and walking toward their home, thinking of Eiffelia and Tracey's son and daughter in her power on her home world. He touched the rift generator, still tucked in the waistband of his wrinkled yukata.

"Very true."

Made in the USA
Charleston, SC
28 June 2016